IRRESISTIBLE . . .

Elyssa stared at Hunter across the shadowed room. He was trying to tease her back into good humor, and she was resisting.

She searched his face. "What do you really want from me?" she asked.

"What are you offering?"

"I really hate your answering my question with a question," she grumbled. This wasn't working at all.

"And I hate it when you withdraw from me," he said softly. "What's happening between us has nothing to do with business. What we have here is me wanting you so badly that nothing else matters . . ."

When his lips skimmed over hers, Elyssa realized with a shock that nothing else really did matter—at the moment. And for however long it lasted, she would share this . . . this "what we have here" . . . with Hunter.

"I'd like to have you all to myself," he whispered. "Anytime, anywhere, for the livelong night." His voice was like velvet. "I'd only have to be asked once."

CAROL FINCH

CANYON MOON

ZEBRA BOOKS
KENSINGTON PUBLISHING CORP.

ZEBRA BOOKS are published by

Kensington Publishing Corp.
850 Third Avenue
New York, NY 10022

Second Printing: August, 1995

Printed in the United States of America

This book is dedicated to my husband Ed and to our children—Christie, Jill, and Kurt—with much love . . .

And to our new son-in-law Jon Nelson.
I wish you love, laughter, and happiness.

One

Elyssa Rawlins Cutler slumped against the seat of her fire-engine red Corvette. Lord, Oklahoma City was a sight for sore eyes! She'd just about had it with business flights to Washington, D.C. Playing political games and kissing up to departmental frogs was turning her into a certified cynic. Of course, one more of those televised congressional hearings like the Thomas-Hill fiasco that made *Saturday Night Live* look tame would send the whole bureaucratic system crashing down. And Elyssa would be there to do her part to make it crash! Capitol Hill was no Camelot. Her ideals had been shattered after shuttling to Washington the past four years.

In her estimation, what good old Uncle Sam needed was a garbage disposal to remove the waste that cluttered government offices. She had spoken with figureheads who were afraid to make any kind of decision on Cutler Corporation projects until they had conferred with a half-dozen other government bigwigs who were equally hesitant about making a decision for fear of losing their plush jobs.

Washington was full of overpaid do-nothings in gridlock. The capital's buildings were filled with human parasites who were sucking the life out of taxpayers and accomplishing nothing. It made Elyssa want to throw up.

If her stepfather ran his corporation with the same loops in the chain of command, with such extravagance and inefficiency, he'd have a debt equivalent to the national deficit. Unfortunately for Uncle Sam, once he'd established an agency to study a major problem facing the country, he was stuck with it. Bureaucracy had become a sinking ship laden with free-loaders who dreamed up projects to evaluate, filling out forms in triplicate to justify their existence. No wonder Uncle Sam now had so many layers of fat hanging off him that he couldn't function!

Elyssa backed out of her parking space at Will Rogers Airport just as another jet soared off into the great blue yonder. She couldn't wait to get back to the office and forget about those three frustrating days in Uncle Sam's fantasyland. These jaunts always made her appreciate the organizational efficiency of her stepfather.

Cutler Corporation designed and manufactured all those clever little gadgets the Defense and Communication Department purchased to ensure that the military, the CIA, and the FBI were well equipped. Luckily, Daniel Cutler was not only an acknowledged genius in the world of hi-tech electronics, he was also a savvy businessman who had streamlined his company until it ran like a well-oiled machine. His one flaw was signing contracts to do business with Uncle Sam. His patriotism was now being lost in the shuffle of paperwork and red tape.

Elyssa tried to unwind and relax as she drove down the interstate, reminding herself that she would soon be enjoying her well-deserved two-week vacation. She planned to become a couch potato for a couple of days. No diplomacy, no smiling when she felt like screaming in frustration, no kissing up to bureaucrats. She and her fiancé would kick back and take life easy . . .

Elyssa groaned. She had wedding arrangements to make, and she was already behind schedule. Flying to the East and West coasts every week to check on cooperative projects with other companies or to nudge a reluctant government agency into approving and funding projects it had wanted completed yesterday was taking a toll on Elyssa's private life.

Elyssa stared at the high-rise on the north side of the city that housed Cutler Corporation. She would brief her stepfather on her trip, present him with the stack of triplicate forms, and then she would be out of here for two glorious weeks of R and R. She imagined her stepfather and mother were feeling that same anticipation themselves. They were booked for a Caribbean cruise—a week of sailing a tropical sea and eating themselves into oblivion.

Since her stepfather had surrounded himself with a dependable, devoted staff, he could enjoy an occasional vacation without fearing the corporation would fall apart at the seams during his absence. Too bad Uncle Sam couldn't enjoy that luxury.

Stop being such a cynic, Elyssa told herself as she headed toward the elevator, limping, a dull ache knotting in the region of her left hip, as it always did when she was excessively tired. The throb was a constant reminder of the accident that had required two surgeries and lengthy physical therapy to correct. Elyssa had tried to forget the incident for twelve years, but couldn't because of the nagging pain. The ordeal, like an ever-present nightmare, continued to haunt her.

My, aren't we getting philosophical, she chided silently.

Three days in Loony-Tune Land with Uncle Sam's cardboard characters had put Elyssa into a mighty dark frame of mind, but her sour mood sweetened considerably when she saw Valerie Mitchell at a desk surrounded by state-of-the-art computer equipment. Her roommate of three years, warmhearted and energetic, was dressed in her usual attire, the latest in Western wear that Sheplers had to offer. Valerie also wore a smile as radiant as sunshine.

Although the twenty-eight-year-old divorcée was city born and bred, she had fallen head over heels for Garth Brooks, George Strait, and Vince Gill. She had taken to country music and Western style like a duck to water. Her calf-length denim skirt, cowboy boots, and turquoise jewelry were the talk of the corporate staff. The executives playfully teased Val about her fashion statements, though they had the utmost respect for her intellect. There wasn't a computer program Val couldn't master or adapt to the company's needs. She just happened to be a whiz in silver conchos, leather, and denim.

"God, I'm glad you're back." Silver bracelets jangled when Valerie scooped up the phone messages from the corner of her desk. "Your father has been ringing continually. Your secretary has camped out in the ladies' room, hoping you return before he calls again."

Elyssa set her briefcase aside and accepted the stack of messages. "What did Dad want?"

"He didn't say. He told your secretary to have you call him the second you returned from D.C." Valerie sank back in her chair to stare ponderously at the monitor. "It's my night to cook. What do you want for supper?"

"A bottle of Scotch." Elyssa grabbed her briefcase and headed to her office.

"D.C. was *that* bad?"

"Don't ever marry a government man, Val. He couldn't make a decision if his life depended on it."

"I wasn't planning to." Valerie tapped the keyboard with perfectly manicured nails. "My ex-husband cured me for life. I'm holding out for a cowboy with Garth Brook's voice and George Strait's laid-back country charm. One desk jockey was enough for me. I want a man who's the salt of the earth, with old-fashioned values, a *real* man who hankers for the love of a good woman."

"Then you'd better place your order early," Elyssa tossed over her shoulder. "Santa Claus is going to have a helluva time filling that boot."

She closed her office door and picked up the receiver to call her father. The phone didn't even complete its first ring before Ely Rawlins's booming voice came down the line.

"Hello!"

Elyssa smiled and plopped down onto her chair. Her father never failed to amuse her when he answered the phone. He seemed to think he had to yell to be heard all the way from the ranch in Blaine County to the high-rise in the City.

"Hi, Dad. I'm home."

"About time," Ely Rawlins grumbled. "Does that stepfather of yours keep you on jets all the damned time? Hell, you're in the air so much it's a wonder you haven't sprouted wings. Honey, it's time for you to change your lifestyle. You need to get back to your roots and you can't grow roots on airplanes."

Salt of the earth. That was what her father was. If Ely Rawlins wasn't sixty-five years old, Valerie Mitchell would latch onto him in one second flat.

"Elyssa, I need to talk to you about the ranch," Ely insisted. "I'm coming over tomorrow morning to spend the day with you."

She began making mental cancellations in order to accommodate her father. She would have to notify her fiancé that they wouldn't be spending the afternoon making out their wedding-guest list.

"Will my coming to the City put a wrench in your plans?" Ely questioned.

"No, Robert and I can reschedule our activities—"

"Damn it, girl, are you still going to marry that flake?"

Robert fell into the yuppie-nerd category, if he fell anywhere at all. He wasn't a flake; he simply wasn't Ely's type. And sure, Elyssa knew what she felt for Robert Grayson wasn't the kind of affection that shook the earth and caused bells to chime. Theirs was a practical, sensible relationship that would mutually benefit both parties. Robert was gentlemanly, courteous, attractive, intelligent, and . . . adequate.

Besides, Elyssa was twenty-seven years old and had never been married, thanks to a jet-hopping career that made it difficult to form any kind of relationship other than the comfortable one she'd established with Robert. The timing was right. After she and Robert spent a year adjusting to married life, they would begin a family. Everything would fall neatly into place. A woman should have her children early so she could enjoy them, it was said.

A click interrupted the silence on the line.

"Dad? Are you still there?"

"Hell yes, but it sounds like somebody was listening. Damned extension phones anyway. That's why I'm coming to the City to talk privately with you."

"About what?"

"We'll discuss it tomorrow, honey."

"Dad, is everything all right? You sound a little impatient . . . frustrated."

"Things will be fine after I talk to you and get a few matters squared away here."

Resentment took hold of Elyssa's tongue. "I'm surprised I can be of help. I thought Hunter waved his arms and magically resolved every problem that arose on the ranch."

"Hunter is a damned sight more man than Robert the flake," Ely said with absolute certainty. "I don't trust that guy."

"You don't trust anyone who doesn't wear cowboy boots and a Stetson," Elyssa said.

"If I had my druthers, you'd drop your membership in the jet setters and come back to the ranch—once and for all. You can see and understand the world a helluva lot better when you're on the back of a horse, not floating around in the clouds on an airplane. And D.C. sure as hell isn't reality, nor is Robert the man for you—"

"Now, Dad—"

"Don't *'Now, Dad'* me. I've seen you and Robbie the flake together. Nothing's happening. Nothing ever will happen. Take the advice of a man who didn't marry well himself. When it's wrong, it's wrong, and nothing is going to make it right."

To say that crusty, down-to-earth Ely Rawlins disapproved of Robert Grayson was the understatement of the decade. The two times Ely had consented to let Robert join him and his daughter for dinner, he had been deliberately rude and noticeably hostile.

True, Robert and Ely had nothing in common. And on both occasions, all Ely talked about was how wonderfully competent Hunter was. Ely constantly threw Hunter in Elyssa's face, sing-

ing the man's praises to high heaven. Her father spoke of
Hunter as if he were God's brother, and Elyssa sorely resented
the fact that Ely spent more time with that man than he ever
had with her. But then, nobody had promised that life would
be fair.

"I'll pick you up before noon and we'll talk over lunch,"
Ely announced. "I have a few things to wrap up around here,
and I need to check on some grass before dark."

"Grass?" Elyssa echoed.

"We'll talk tomorrow, honey."

"Dad?" Elyssa eased back in her chair, staring affectionately
at the photo of her father that sat on her desk.

"What?"

"Love you . . ." she murmured.

"Me, too. See ya tomorrow. And don't bring that flake. This
is strictly between you and me."

The line went dead. Frowning, Elyssa replaced the receiver.
Ely had seemed impatient, his tone clipped and agitated. She
sensed that whatever frustration he was experiencing wasn't
directed at her. But good ole Hunter The Magnificent would
calm Ely down, she mused.

For years, Elyssa had listened to Ely boast that Hunter had
done *this* and Hunter had said *that*. She had once thought of
Hunter as Ely's protégé. Lately, it seemed their roles had become reversed. Hunter had somehow become Ely's mentor.

Elyssa thought Hunter was taking advantage of a lonely old
man who had always wanted a son to follow in his footsteps.
As fate would have it, Ely only had a daughter, and she had
been removed from his life at the age of seven, then allowed
very little contact with him. There were times when Elyssa
had wondered if her mother had suggested to Daniel Cutler
that she play hopscotch from one side of the continent to the
other, representing the corporation. That way she had had little
time to see her father and very little time to herself.

Rising, Elyssa smoothed the wrinkles from her red linen
suit, ran a hand through her dark hair, and strode off. Another

hour and she would be on vacation. No work. No worries. Just relaxation and a long-awaited visit from her father.

She paused at the open door of her stepfather's office. Daniel Cutler's salt and pepper head was bent over an open file, which he was studying with profound concentration. Elyssa considered herself lucky to have been blessed with a caring father and a generous stepfather. Daniel Cutler had always treated her as if she were blood kin. He'd provided for her, adopted her, and seen to it that she had had every opportunity life could offer.

Of course, Ely Rawlins had cursed and growled about the legal adoption, but he had complied with his ex-wife's demands. Elyssa had always wondered what threat Jessica Rawlins Cutler held over Ely, but she had been too young at the time to demand information about the divorce and adoption.

"Come in," Daniel invited when he glanced up to see Elyssa hovering by the door. "This can wait." He set the file aside and smiled in greeting. "How was your trip to D.C.?"

Her shrug belied her distaste for dealing with indecisive muckamucks, but Daniel knew what those infuriating conferences were like. He'd been a party plenty himself when the company was first established.

"As usual, the Defense Department will need time to consider the funding of the projects they requested and to evaluate the suggestions you made."

Daniel leaned back and smiled as Elyssa sank gracefully into a chair. He listened to her brief, concise report, silently admiring her poise, intelligence, and professional capability. He knew she was tired of leapfrogging all over the country, but she was damned efficient. Brains and beauty made a combination that was tough to top. Daniel had been grooming one of his assistants to replace her as the corporation's contact with Uncle Sam, but the man simply didn't have her panache. Furthermore, Elyssa's replacement had yet to receive the security clearance necessary because of some of their projects.

As a wedding gift, Daniel would reassign Elyssa to overseeing design and production, so she wouldn't have to play aerial hopscotch. He would also grant Robert Grayson the promotion the man pushed for at least once a month.

When Elyssa concluded her report, she sighed. "Since the project has been put on hold you and Mother can fully enjoy your cruise."

"I'm sure we will. Jessica has been anticipating it for weeks, and I won't feel I have to check in with the office every day. You can enjoy your well-earned time off, too. Any plans?"

"Sleep, for one. Staying in one place for more than three days at a time sounds like heaven."

Daniel nodded in sympathetic understanding. "Why don't you call it a day?"

He didn't have to offer twice. She was ready to kick off her shoes, soak her aching leg in a warm bath, and forget there was a world outside her apartment. With a wave of farewell, she limped off to inform Robert Grayson of the change in plans.

"He's out for the afternoon," Valerie called out when she saw Elyssa veer toward Robert's office. "After lunch, he took his secretary with him to check on Peterson's microchip project."

Elyssa detoured into her office to leave a message on Robert's answering machine, only to find he hadn't bothered to turn the damned thing on. Deciding to stop by his apartment to leave a note on her way home, she headed for the door, smiling in anticipation. She could almost feel the relaxing effects of the Jacuzzi. She wouldn't wade out of the tub until she was a soggy noodle, either. Nothing was going to spoil her evening of lounging. Hallelujah, she was vacation bound!

Fifteen minutes later, Elyssa pulled into the lot by Robert's apartment complex. She used her key and took two steps into the living room before pulling up short. Articles of clothing, like Hansel and Gretel's bread crumbs, formed a path down the hall. If Robert hadn't taken to wearing slinky female lingerie, he had a helluva lot of explaining to do!

Outraged at betrayal coiled in the pit of Elyssa's stomach as she limped down the hall, to be serenaded by heavy breathing and muffled moans. She wasn't prepared for the scene that unfolded before her. Though she had told herself to expect the worst, *thinking* and actually *seeing* were different matters entirely.

For what seemed a full minute, she stood frozen, feeling as if she were watching an X-rated movie; only this was worse because she knew these lovers all too well. Or maybe she didn't.

"You bastard!" Elyssa hissed before spinning away from the disgusting scene. She pelted down the hall and reached for the doorknob, only to hear the swish of a sheet and bare feet padding toward her.

"Wait a minute, Elyssa."

She fought the urge to grab the closest object and smash it onto Robert's skull. "Why should *I*? *You* obviously couldn't." The wedding is off. You and Bambi can romp through fantasy forest for all I care."

Robert grabbed her arm before she could storm off. "I can explain."

"What makes you think so? Is it because I've been so gullible all these months? You've never been loyal, never faithful, have you, Robert? And you weren't planning to be after we married, were you?"

A bare arm slammed the door shut before Elyssa could stalk out. "I hardly think I should have to shoulder all the blame for this," he snapped, furious that he'd been caught in the act.

Elyssa glared over her shoulder at him. His blond hair was tousled, compliments of Bambi's accomplished bedroom gymnastics. And despite his striking good looks and muscular physique, in his makeshift toga, he suddenly reminded Elyssa of a worm enshrouded in a cocoon.

"Surely you don't expect me to believe Bambi dragged you up to your apartment and forced her attentions on you," Elyssa scoffed.

"No, you have yourself to thank for this," Robert responded.

Incredulous, Elyssa wheeled around, her eyes flashing like polished obsidian. "What?"

She couldn't believe he'd said that! If *she* had betrayed *him,* she would be down on her knees begging forgiveness for destroying his trust and forsaking his affection. Robert, however, was trying to pass the buck. It was infuriating that he had so little respect for *her* feelings. She was the injured party here, and he was behaving as if he expected *her* to apologize for driving him into another woman's arms and then interrupting his tryst.

"You and your Puritan ethics are to blame," Robert growled. "Your little Miss Goodie-Two-Shoes attitude and your outdated ideals have brought me to this."

How Robert's twisted male mind had arrived at that ridiculous conclusion, Elyssa couldn't fathom. But she would be damned if she was going to take the blame for his hopping in the sack with that blond bimbo he called a secretary!

Robert leaned closer, pinning her against the door. As she automatically leaned away, he smirked down at her. "That's the reaction I always get when I try to breach that invisible wall you've built around yourself. What is it with you? If I could get what I need from you, I wouldn't be screwing around with—"

Flesh connected with flesh, leaving Elyssa's handprint on his clean-shaven cheek. "It's not my responsibility to provide you with recreational sex," she said. "You never really made a commitment to me if you could do something like this!"

"I am supposed to commit myself to an iceberg? You probably won't thaw out until after the wedding—if ever!"

When Elyssa lurched around to leave, Robert braced his arms to block her escape, but she had watched enough NBA games on TV to know how to throw an elbow and employ a body block. When her elbow connected with Robert's belly, he instinctively doubled over and gasped for breath. Her shoulder then rammed against his ribs, and he stumbled over the trailing hem of the sheet he was wearing. He was still sucking air when the door slammed shut behind his former fiancée.

Struggling to hold himself upright, Robert pivoted to see Bambi Carlson hovering uncertainly at his bedroom door, clutching the bedspread around her.

"Oh, God! We'll lose our jobs over this!" she wailed.

"No, we won't. I'll talk to Elyssa tomorrow—after she's had a chance to calm down." Robert stalked over to retrieve his discarded clothes. "I'll take you back to the office to pick up your car, and we'll just pretend this didn't happen."

Bambi nodded mutely, trying to assure herself everything would be all right but only half believing it.

TWO

Elyssa couldn't remember driving back to her apartment. Her red Corvette must have been on automatic pilot. She was still fuming when she sailed through the front door with a suitcase in one hand and a briefcase in the other.

"Bastard." She slung the briefcase across the room, wishing it were her unfaithful ex-fiancé. She then used every dirty word, every oath, she knew on Robert before turning curses on herself.

Despite the outrage and frustration that consumed her, she had known from the beginning that there was no spark between her and Robert. She had never once experienced with him that tingle, that intuitive sense she relied on. According to her great-grandmother, that feeling was part of her Cheyenne heritage—a deep sense of knowing that needed no explanation, only a simple acceptance of its existence.

Elyssa kicked off her red pumps and flounced onto the sofa. Robert Grayson was a Casanova without integrity or conscience, and she was every kind of fool for talking herself into a relationship because of timing and practicality. She had trusted him, harboring no suspicious thoughts about the fact that he had been hauling Bambi around with him to conferences and meetings, as if the Carlson woman were his invaluable assistant. Elyssa had been naive and now she was paying for her blind trust. Well, no one would be granted her unquestioning faith again!

In the back of her mind, she had always known that a part

of what drew Robert to her was the fact that Daniel Cutler was her stepfather. Robert was aggressively seeking promotion, and she was the rung on the ladder of success that could get him where he wanted to go—to the top of Cutler Corporation. And, Elyssa thought bitterly, her connection to the Cutler fortune was an additional incentive for Robert. The man had mercenary tendencies she had blithely ignored. If she was to be faulted for something, it was for that. But it certainly was no fault of hers that Robert Grayson played around. Damn him!

She raked her fingers through her windblown auburn hair and expelled a few more curses. As much as she despised what Robert had done, she supposed she couldn't really blame him for *her* hangups or her idealistic expectations.

He wanted position, power, and prestige. She had wanted a family, had wanted to marry a man who wouldn't expect too much from her physically. Robert had been courteous and respectful throughout their six-month courtship, though he had invited her to bed with him on three occasions, each time being politely refused, he had never tried to take more than she was prepared to offer, had never badgered her about her standoffish position toward sex. She had hoped her reluctance toward intimacy would dissolve with time and a deepening of affection. She had dated Robert longer than any other man, after all, and she'd had every intention of making the marriage work, somehow or other.

So much for good intentions and a seemingly rational, calculated approach to marriage.

Levering herself off the sofa, Elyssa hobbled toward the kitchen to pour herself a Scotch and then propelled herself toward the Jacuzzi. It was time to accept reality. The accident that had left her with unsightly scars on her left elbow and hip still loomed like an unconquerable obstacle in her relationships with men. Perhaps if she hadn't been so terrified and ashamed, she could have discussed what really happened that dreadful day, could have dealt with the emotional scars that refused to heal.

Certainly, Robert wasn't the first to notice that she instinctively withdrew when a man ventured too close. She usually terminated relationships when her male acquaintances began to expect more physical satisfaction than she was able to offer. Backing away had been the defense that held old ghosts at bay and allowed her to avoid situations similar to the one that had left her scarred, emotionally as well as physically.

Elyssa had been fifteen when disaster struck, too immature and inexperienced to understand what she had done to deserve the furious accusations that had rained down on her. Yet the incident had changed the entire course of her life, making her self-conscious and insecure when it came to dealing with men in anything except platonic or professional relationships. She told herself the sooner she accepted the fact that the life she now led was as good as it ever would get, the better off she'd be.

Elyssa stripped off her clothes and sank into the tub, letting the pulsating jets sooth the tautness from her muscles and the tension from her nerves. She wondered if she would ever be able to disrobe in front of a man without feeling physically inferior and embarrassingly self-conscious. She knew the inevitable questions would come, and she wasn't sure she could bring herself to explain without reliving the nightmare all over again.

Valerie Mitchell was the one person with whom Elyssa felt remotely comfortable wearing a short-sleeve T-shirt. With Valerie she didn't dread prying questions about the scars. Elyssa and Val had made a pact soon after they'd leased the apartment. Elyssa had vowed never to question the failings of Val's marriage and Val had promised not to pry about the crisscross scars on Elyssa's left arm. As for the unsightly flesh on Elyssa's hip, Val didn't know that existed. Only Elyssa's physician had viewed it.

Elyssa sipped freely at her drink, not caring if she became

so intoxicated she couldn't think, see, or feel. She simply wanted to forget she was a freak with a helluva good-paying job, the love life of a nun, and an ex-fiancé with the scruples of an alley cat.

While Bambi and Thumper were bounding around the bedroom, Elyssa had been limping around on an idealistic crutch, trying to convince herself that sex didn't have to be a vital part of a solid marriage. Lord, with her scars and hangups, how did she ever think she could escape the inevitable? Hadn't she known Robert would search elsewhere to get what he couldn't find with her? Luckily, she was dealing with his premarital affair. An extramarital one would have been even more humiliating.

The creak of the front door jolted Elyssa from her troubled musings. She tensed, wondering if Robert had used his key to invite himself into her apartment as she had done earlier at his. She breathed a relieved sigh when she heard the CD player burst into one of Garth Brooks's greatest hits. While Garth crooned about being too young to feel this damned old, Elyssa grabbed a towel and hurriedly dried off. Only after she'd been swallowed up by a bright purple sweatsuit that made her look like an oversize grape did she emerge from the bathroom to greet her roommate.

"Damn, I'm about to starve to death," Valerie said as she made a beeline for the kitchen. "Does spaghetti suit you, Ellie? I need nourishment fast . . ."

Valerie pulled up short when Elyssa's flushed face appeared above the neck of the grape-colored sweatsuit and a shaky hand, with a death grip on a tumbler of Scotch, protruded from the baggy sleeve. "What the hell happened to you? Are you all right?"

Elyssa definitely wasn't. Discovering that her fiancé was thumping Bambi, and probably had been for months, could take the starch out of anybody's shorts.

"You wanna talk about it?" Valerie questioned, concerned now.

She marched over to the refrigerator to grab more ice cubes and dropped them into Elyssa's glass. "Spit it out, Ellie," she ordered. "You always keep everything to yourself. Me, I blow like a volcano spewing hot lava and get it over with. But you look like an eruption wouldn't hurt you."

After shepherding Elyssa to the stool at the kitchen counter, Valerie grabbed a pot to boil the water for the spaghetti. "Give it to me straight. Did Daniel decide to fire me because I refused to wear anything in the office except Western clothes? Did he leave it to you to give me the ax?"

Valerie's attempt at humor was mildly effective. Elyssa managed a faint smile. "No, your job is secure for the next hundred years, as long as you don't join a nudist colony and insist on wearing your birthday suit to work."

"What's the problem?" Valerie grabbed a jar of Ragú spaghetti sauce and headed for the microwave oven.

"The problem . . ." Elyssa paused to take another drink, thankful that the whiskey was beginning to have the desired effect—the numbing of her pride, which had taken a beating. "The problem is I caught Robert in bed with a woman when I stopped by his apartment to leave him a message."

"Holy shit!" Valerie's green eyes were as wide as salad plates. Her arm dangled in midair as she swiveled her blond head toward Elyssa. "Robert turned out to be as big a jerk as my ex?" She muttered something Elyssa didn't ask her to repeat. "I never said much about that asshole I married, but maybe you need to know there are plenty of Robert Graysons in the world. You're lucky you found out about Robert's Don Juan tendencies before you married him. I wasn't so fortunate. Not only did that freeloading creep I married cheat on me, he also cleaned out my bank account and charged so much against my credit cards it took me three years to pay off the debts!"

Valerie set the jar in the microwave oven and heaved a sigh. "Sorry, I guess I've needed to get that off *my* chest for a long time. So . . . who was Robert shacking up with?"

Elyssa stared at the contents of her glass. "I'd rather not say. But I will tell you he blamed me for his infidelity."

"Figures." Valerie strode over to pluck a bag of broccoli from the freezer and dumped it into a saucepan. "But I gotta tell ya, Ellie, I never did think Robert was the right man for you. Those corporate types can be bad news, especially when you're the boss's relative. If you're a successful business-woman, you never know if you're wanted for yourself or for your income contribution. That's why I've set my sights on—"

"Salt of the earth," Elyssa finished for her and then guzzled more Scotch.

"Right. That's my present philosophy, and I'm sticking with it."

"So you've convinced yourself that cowboys won't fool around on you? God, you're turning out to be as naively ide-alistic as I was." Elyssa laughed humorlessly. "I don't want to burst your countrified bubble, Val, but men are men. I don't think you can trust any of them farther than you can shot-put them."

Valerie braced her hands on the formica counter and stared somberly at Elyssa. "And I think you know as well as I do that you *decided* Robert was right for you, because of what you considered perfect timing. You're an objective, insightful, and reflective kind of person who has an uncanny knack of pegging people for what they are in an extraordinarily short period of time. I've seen you do it a dozen times at the office.

"Take your secretary for instance. You call Brenda Landon 'Patty Perfect' because she has a fetish for insignificant detail and goes bonkers when things are out of place. You refer to the night security guard who patrols the office as Barney Fife because he's an amusing klutz who's more likely to shoot him-self in the foot than apprehend a burglar. You pegged Robert as a yuppie nerd the day after he came to work for Cutler Corporation, but you decided you could live with that because it was *time* for you to settle down and Robert was as good a candidate for a safe, uncomplicated marriage as anybody."

"Thank you for agreeing with Robert that this is all my fault," Elyssa grumbled. "That's just what I need right now, accusations rather that compassion."

"I'm not agreeing with that ass!" Valerie loudly objected. "I'm saying you *settled* for Robert because you thought he was decent marriage material and you two had enough in common to make the relationship work. You've never been more than lukewarm about the man, and we both know it."

A lot Val knew! Elyssa had never been more than lukewarm about any man since her twelve-year curse had begun.

"Val, I think there's something you ought to know about me." Elyssa took another drink of liquid courage. "I—"

"You've never slept with a man." When Elyssa blinked owlishly, Valerie grinned. "I already figured that out. You've never once asked me to make myself scarce around here while you're entertaining. You don't come home looking the least bit disheveled. I, on the other hand, have requested that you take your time coming home on Saturday nights a few times over the years."

Elyssa stared at the spaghetti that was boiling on the stove. "Do you think I'm too old-fashioned for my own good, Val? Do you think my reluctance to become . . . intimately involved drove Robert to another woman?"

Valerie poured herself a drink and lifted it in a toast. "I think you know your own mind better than most people do. I also think you possess upstanding values that most folks ridicule because they don't have the gumption or willpower to resist men who have a line for every reluctant woman they want to get into bed. Some women take the big step out of simple curiosity and later wish they had waited until they were absolutely certain they'd slept with the right man the first time.

"If I'd had your self-control, I wouldn't have a divorce to my credit. Marrying that deadbeat who charmed the panties off me was the worst mistake I ever made. My guilty conscience hounded me until I decided I must have loved him if

I chose to go to bed with him, but the truth was, I didn't know how to say no when he made me feel foolish for resisting.

"Agreeing to marry Robert when you knew you weren't completely in love with him was the worst mistake you made, Ellie. Just think what a tangle you would've been in if you'd been married and your stepfather started doling out privileges to him. Robert would've been screwing around like he is now, and you would've been reluctant to demand a divorce because he'd brown-nosed his way into Daniel Cutler's close circle of trusted associates. Robert would've gotten a foothold in the company, and you might never have been able to pry him loose. He might have taken the company to the cleaners if you tried to divorce him."

Elyssa leaned heavily on the counter. "How'd you get so damned smart in only twenty-eight years?"

"By learning one too many lessons the hard way." Val took a drink and stirred the spaghetti. "As for you, you'll know when the right man comes along and when the timing is right. In the meantime, don't consider yourself a freak because you have enough respect for yourself not to screw around just for the hell of it. Anybody who does that is just asking for trouble."

"So it's okay for me to be an iceberg?" Elyssa asked.

"That's from Robert, I'm sure." Valerie chuckled and shook her head. "Ah, men. God love the bastards. Somebody has to. In this day and age, you can't be too careful, you know. That has certainly made me think more than once—or twice—when some good-looking hunk of a cowboy invites me to bed. I want more than sex from a relationship. Nowadays I want respect and companionship, not notches on my bedpost."

As she spun about abruptly, Valerie's attractive face brightened. "Why don't we go down to the Two-Step Tavern and mingle with the country set this evening? It'll take your mind off What's-his-name."

"I'm not in the mood," Elyssa replied between sips of Scotch.

"You'd rather mope around here feeling sorry for yourself so you can make an early night of it and wake up at the crack of dawn to feel sorry for yourself some more?" Val sniffed in disapproval. "Take it from somebody who knows, men aren't worth the waste of emotion, especially not the Robert Graysons of the world. After a night of listening to a country western band and dancing the Cotton-Eyed Joe all over Robert's back, you'll be on your way to recovery."

"Oh, what the hell," Elyssa decided impulsively. "My dad said I needed to get back in touch with my roots. Maybe he's right."

"That's the spirit!" Valerie enthused. "You were born country. It's about time you dragged out your jeans and boots and shed those sophisticated business suits."

"I don't own any boots these days." Her droopy gaze slid over Valerie's Western attire. "And I don't have the fashionable garb to go prancing into a honky-tonk, come to think of it."

"I'll loan you what you need."

Elyssa managed a smile. "You've got a deal."

While Valerie buzzed around the kitchen preparing supper, Elyssa retrieved the silverware and plates. Between the jet lag and the whiskey, she was feeling no pain. She would show Robert Grayson that even his betrayal couldn't get her down. She didn't need him or any other man. She could continue fighting the bureaucracy in D.C. and high-jumping cross-country.

If this was as good as her life was going to get, why fight it? Some people never fell in love, and she was obviously one of them. It was time she faced reality and quit chasing rainbows. The chemistry had never been right with Robert or anyone else. If she was doomed to be an iceberg who retreated instinctively when men crowded her space, then that was just the way it was.

Robert Grayson could have his voluptuous young secretary as many times as he wanted her, but he wasn't getting a promotion in Cutler Corporation because he wasn't marrying the boss's stepdaughter. That door would remain closed forever.

Elyssa Rawlins Cutler wasn't going to succumb to the pressure of any man ever again. And she would never again be *used!* That was a vow she was never going to break!

"I'll drink to that."

"You'll drink to what?" Valerie questioned when Elyssa blurted out her proclamation.

"Nothing. Eat your spaghetti, Val."

Valerie didn't pry into Elyssa's private thoughts. She simply ate her meal while Elyssa wrestled with the frustration Robert—the unfaithful jerk—had caused her.

Three

The last rays of sunshine splashed crimson and gold on the horizon. Nathan Hunter reined the blood-red gelding along the rim of the rock canyons that tumbled down to the pasture that lay along the flood plain of the river. Cattle dotted the rugged terrain, and the occasional bellow of a cow calling to her calf was the only sound that broke the peaceful silence of the spring evening.

Nathan had returned to Rawlins Ranch two hours earlier, hoping to finish his conference with Ely. He had been called away earlier that morning when they'd talked, to pick up a truck-load of newly purchased rodeo stock from western Oklahoma. When Ely hadn't returned from whatever errand had sent him out on horseback, and after the housekeeper had expressed concern, Nathan had gone looking for him.

This had been one hectic day. Ely had been fit to be roped and tied since his argument that morning with his brother. In between unsuccessful attempts to get in touch with his jet-setting daughter, Ely had spewed curses that would have burned the ears off a priest. Nathan didn't know if he'd had ever gotten hold of his disrespectful daughter, but Ely's lengthy disappearance was setting Nathan's nerves on edge.

Althea Gilbert, the housekeeper, had said Ely had stalked out to the barn around four o'clock and hadn't been seen since. He should have been back by now. Nathan had ordered every available ranch hand to saddle up and begin searching the rugged acreage where pickups couldn't go.

The section of the ranch on which Nathan rode was criss-crossed by creeks, dense timber, and labyrinthine canyons. The land looked exactly as it had in the pioneer days. Civilization hadn't quite caught up to this part of the country, and that suited Nathan just fine. He didn't like humanity crowding his space. The less populated an area was, the better he liked it.

The nicker of an unseen horse caught his attention. "Ely?"

Nathan's voice echoed in the canyon that was choked with underbrush and trees. Nudging his mount, he followed the narrow cattle trail that circled the rim and meandered off toward the antiquated stock pens and the dilapidated homestead the Rawlins family had established in the 1890s. The home Peter Rawlins had built when he'd taken his Cheyenne bride was barely more than a shadow in the distance. And Ely Rawlins was nowhere to be seen.

The gelding pricked his ears and whinnied when another muffled nicker pierced the silence. Nathan glanced down the steep slope to see clumps of uprooted grass and hoofprints in the loose dirt. A jack rabbit bounded up from the weeds in front of him, causing the gelding to bolt sideways. Nathan jerked hard on the reins before the horse skidded down the slope . . .

As he glanced down the canyon, he saw more freshly turned earth that suggested a horse and rider had recently tumbled into that vast expanse of timber and brush.

Nathan grabbed the walkie-talkie that was holstered on his belt. If Ely's horse had been spooked and had stumbled over the edge, Nathan knew he wasn't going to like what he saw after he picked his way down the wild tumble of rocks.

"Twig, I think I've located Ely. Call the other men and send them over to the canyons on the river section."

"Is Ely all right?" Ray Twigger was concerned.

"I don't know yet." Nathan replaced the walkie-talkie and swung from the saddle.

After tethering his mount, Nathan sidestepped down the steep incline, seeing more evidence of an animal scrambling to regain its balance. He pulled up short and cursed foully when he peered over the cascade of jutting rocks to see a body tangled in the timber below. Ely Rawlins's favorite mount, a piebald gelding he had raised and trained to work cattle, lay on its side a few yards farther down the slope. The gelding struggled to regain its feet, failed, and whinnied again.

Ely Rawlins didn't move a muscle . . .

Spurred by a sickening urgency, Nathan zigzagged around the boulders, trying to find footholds in the crumbling sandstone. By the time he reached Ely a sense of doom had settled over him like a black cloud.

Nathan sank down on his haunches to ease Ely onto his back. The look on Rawlins's weather-beaten face told the grim tale. Dark brown eyes gazed sightlessly at the spectacular sunset.

One Ely would have appreciated. He had always enjoyed the simple things life had to offer, carrying on the ranching traditions of his father and of his father's father. They had been men of vision, and industrious; a vanishing breed who took pride in the accomplishments of their pioneer ancestors.

Ely had sometimes fought with Mother Nature and cursed her for refusing to yield, but he'd been too damned stubborn to knuckle to droughts, floods, or destructive storms. Rawlins had had great respect for the land he'd claimed, for the livestock and crops he'd raised, for his way of life.

Nathan squeezed his eyes shut and cursed soundly. Ely Rawlins didn't deserve a death like this. Neither did he deserve to be ignored by his one and only daughter who hadn't even bothered to come to the ranch to see her father. Oh no, Elyssa Rawlins la-de-da Cutler was too sophisticated to waste her time out here in the sticks with her father. Hell, she'd spent more time with her stepfather than with Ely. Nathan wondered if the news of Ely's death would have the slightest affect on that snooty little career woman who camped out in the City.

Well, she might not care about what had happened to Ely, but Nathan sure as hell did. Grief knotted his belly.

Ely had been a tough, crusty son of a bitch, but he had become a father to Nathan, who had lost his own years earlier. If it were not for Ely's generosity, Nathan would still be scratching and clawing to make a place for himself in this world. Now, knowing he had lost his mentor, Nathan suddenly felt he had nothing, no one.

"Nate? Where the devil are you?" Mo-Joe Denson blared over the walkie-talkie.

Nathan heard the drone of voices in the background. Before he could reply, trickles of rock and dirt slid down the slope, pelting his shoulders. He glanced up to see Ray Twigger, Les Fykes, Mo-Joe Denson, and Skeeter Jeffries poised on the ledge above him.

"I need a rope and a rifle," Nathan said gravely.

More pebbles dribbled down the canyon wall as Twig jogged along the rim to retrieve a rope and rifle from his saddle. In a few minutes, a lariat dangled over the ledge. Nathan fashioned a harness for Ely and gave the signal to hoist him up.

With grim determination, he then clasped the rifle that had been tossed down to him. He stood over the piebald gelding that nickered in excruciating pain.

Steading the weapon against his shoulder, he peered bleakly down the sight. As big brown eyes stared back at him, Nathan's gut clenched. He loved this cow pony as much as Ely did.

But Ely wouldn't have wanted his favorite horse to suffer. Nathan squeezed the trigger; the explosion echoed around the chasm.

He wondered how much Ely had suffered . . .

Gil Rawlins dropped the receiver in its cradle. "Elyssa isn't answering the damned phone."

Nathan was sprawled in the leather chair in the study, staring at the lifelike portrait of Ely Rawlins that hung above the mantel. For several minutes he looked at Ely's dark hair and bronzed features, so different from the coloring of his younger brother Gil. It was Ely who carried the traits of the family's Indian heritage, the proud nobility of Cheyenne chiefs that had been handed down from his grandmother. Gil Rawlins had the coloring of his father and grandfather—red hair, pale blue eyes, and freckled skin.

The two brothers had inherited this sprawling eight-thousand acre ranch in Blaine County, and their partnership had spanned three decades. Nathan knew what was to become of this partnership as well as Gil did, but he had his own speculations about what Gil planned to tell his citified niece.

No doubt, Elyssa was out on the town, flaunting that shapely figure of hers and squandering money as fast as she made it.

"I can't make the arrangements without Elyssa," Gil grumbled. "I guess I should send Virgil over to the City to track her down. Late phone calls aren't good for much except sleepless nights anyway."

Speaking of Virgil Rawlins, Nathan wondered where Gil's high-rolling son was. He sure as hell hadn't been around when the grim procession returned to the ranch house. Ely and his nephew Virgil had never been what one could call close, but family ties had bound them, and those ties should have obliged Virgil to haul his ass out to the ranch to console Gil, who had just lost his only brother. Knowing Virgil, Nathan figured he was probably putting on the dog to impress buyers interested in his registered quarter horses, horses that weren't worth half as much as Virgil expected to be paid for them.

But why Gil was concerned about his niece receiving the bad news at this late hour, when she obviously didn't give a damn about her father, was beyond Nathan. Elyssa Rawlins Cutler hadn't set foot on the ranch during the nine years Nathan had been employed. The thankless bitch spent her time in Cutler's high-rise office, frittering away her stepfather's fortune. Whenever Ely wanted to visit his only daughter, he had to call to make an appointment and drive to the City. Hell, it was a wonder the corporation queen could work Ely into her busy social schedule. She had all the gratitude of a rattlesnake.

"Damn, there's still no answer at Virgil's house in town," Gil muttered, slamming down the phone.

Nathan unfolded himself from the chair, his gaze still focused on the portrait of Ely Rawlins. "I'll go track Elyssa down. Do you have her address?"

Gil jotted down the information and reluctantly handed it to Nathan. "Just tell her what she needs to know. I'll handle the rest."

Thick black brows flattened over narrowed blue eyes. "Meaning?"

The challenge in that deep voice put a curl on Gil's lips. "I'm only sending you to fetch Elyssa because none of the family is around to do it. Just back off, Nate. I'm in charge around here now."

If the command and declaration were supposed to intimidate Hunter, they were a waste of breath. He was too busy cursing life's injustices and the loss of a man who'd been not only an employer and business partner but also a close friend and more of a father than Sid Hunter had ever thought about being. Just as Nathan had been more of a son to Ely than prissy Elyssa Rawlins Cutler had been a daughter.

She had walked away from her father without looking back. Hell, she probably hadn't been able to shake the dust off her heels quick enough to hit the fast lanes of Oklahoma City. But that little prima donna was going to take charge of her father's final arrangements if Nathan had to nudge her with a cattle prod. Elyssa may have ignored Ely in life, but she wasn't going to shrug off his death!

"You may as well go on home, Gil," Nathan suggested, ignoring the earlier ultimatum as if it had never been spoken. "I don't know how long it will take me to round Elyssa up."

Gil pushed away from the desk and stalked toward the door. "Just remember what I said. Elyssa has arrangements to make. Nothing else. I want you to stay out of this. Ely's gone now."

"I wonder if you consider that a relief," Nathan replied sardonically.

Gil lurched around to glower at the swarthy cowboy who towered over him. Then years of bottled-up resentment came pouring out. "You're an outsider, Nate. You always were and you always will be. I won't have you influencing Elyssa for your own benefit. You may have pulled the wool over my brother's eyes, but you damned well aren't going to pull it over mine."

This seemed to be the night for speaking one's mind. "And I don't intend to let you influence Elyssa, either," Nate said. "I know exactly what you and Ely discussed this morning, and why Ely wanted to do what he was planning on doing."

Gil snarled and wagged a finger at the looming giant who stood before him. "I'm warning you, Nate. All you're going to do is bring Elyssa back to the ranch. Anything else will be considered grounds for battle. You're not getting by on my brother's generosity any longer. I'm the one you have to contend with now, and you'd better not forget it."

Heaving a sigh, Nate half turned to stare up at the portrait that thoroughly dominated the room.

"Your call, old man," Nathan murmured.

The room hung heavy with silence. Nathan waited a long moment before he walked away, reflecting on his last conversation with Ely. He knew what he had to do. He also knew he wasn't going to make any friends around here when he did it. More than likely, he was going to create several powerful enemies . . .

Elyssa tugged at the skin-tight blouse she had borrowed from Valerie. Although the Rocky Mountain jeans were a comfortable fit, she couldn't say the same for the flashy, pumpkin-colored top that strained across her breasts and displayed more flesh than suited her modest tastes.

While Valerie was two-stepping around the dance floor to one of Vince Gill's latest hits, Elyssa was nursing another drink and studying the cowboys who lined the bar. Suburban cowboys, most of them, she decided as she propped her chin on her hand. She wagered that half the males in the honky-tonk had never sat a horse. Their roughest rides entailed taking speed bumps at thirty miles an hour in a Subaru. Valerie was kidding herself if she thought this brand of cowboy was her answer to Mister Right.

As for Elyssa, she had decided to swear off men one hour and two drinks ago. She was fed up with the lines tossed at her like baited hooks. One Western-dressed pickup artist borrowed George Strait's Excuse-Me-I-Think-You've-Got-My-Chair line. Another hot shot in tight-fitting jeans tried out his Don't-I-Know-You-From-Somewhere routine on her. Then there was the lanky cowboy whose Stetson was pulled down so low over his eyes it was a wonder he hadn't bumped into the wall when he'd moseyed over to greet her with Clint Eastwood's "Make my day." God, didn't anyone around here have any originality?

Elyssa had finally gotten fed up and had written NO on her napkin, flashing it at the one-night-stand crowd to save them the trouble of hitting on her. Elyssa had only one purpose in remaining at the club—hanging in until Valerie's feet gave out and they could go home.

Checking her watch, she wondered how many more minutes of this "fun" she would have to tolerate before Valerie had had her fill of dancing. If Val ran true to form, the club would have to close down before she left.

Since Elyssa's internal time clock was still marking Eastern Standard Time, she was ready to call it a day—and not one of her best, either. The combination of jet lag, too many drinks, and Robert's afternoon fling had taken their toll.

When Valerie finally returned to the corner table, Elyssa levered herself out of her chair. "Let's go home," she said.

"Come on, Ellie, the night is young."

"The night may be," Elyssa mumbled, "but I feel as old as Methuselah."

Valerie gave her one of those pleading looks before glancing over her shoulder at a stockily built man in form-fitting denim. Elyssa wasn't so far gone that she couldn't interpret Valerie's reluctance to leave a promising prospect.

"I'll take a cab. I don't want to spoil your fun," she insisted.

"Are you sure you'll be okay?"

"I'll be fine." Elyssa wobbled toward the bar to call a cab.

Vaguely, she remembered rattling off her address to the cabbie before exhaustion overtook her. Twenty minutes later, a hand clasped her elbow, jarring her awake. Elyssa climbed out of the vehicle and limped toward her apartment, wishing she had never left it in the first place.

When a shadow materialized in front of her, she shrieked in panic and stumbled back to ward off what she expected to be a mauling.

"Calm down, Cutler," came the gruff voice. "It's just me."

Elyssa tilted her head back to peer up into the vaguely familiar face that was enshrouded in shadows. It took a minute for a name to attach itself to the massive body. Before her stood six feet, four inches and two-hundred-twenty pounds of compact brawn and muscle, a potential force waiting to explode into action.

Nathan Hunter. Her father's right-hand man, the son Ely always wanted. Salt of the earth.

Valerie would love this guy. Elyssa, however, resented him. Hunter didn't look as if he had much use for her, either.

He scowled at the inebriated city slicker who was trying to pass herself off as a cowgirl in the bright orange blouse that clung to her full breasts like a second skin. She looked about as country as a New York bagel.

Nathan snatched the key from Elyssa's well-manicured hand and steered her up the steps. "We need to talk, Cutler."

"I'd rather just go to bed, if it's all the same to you," she mumbled drowsily.

The key stalled a good twelve inches from the door lock. When she propped herself against the wall, Nathan shot her a glance, reappraising the curvy figure silhouetted by the porch light. Was she propositioning him? That was undoubtedly her style. What a tease this female was. And here she was supposedly engaged to some executive Ely had labeled a flake.

Nathan muttered under his breath and unlocked the door, wondering whether to break the bad news to this playgirl while she was sauced or to wait until she sobered up. Then he asked himself what difference it could possibly make to her. Why should he concern himself with sparing her feelings or trying to lessen a nonexistent emotional blow?

When the door swung open, Elyssa hobbled into the apartment, willing her eyelids not to slam shut. She didn't have the foggiest notion what Nathan Hunter was doing in the City, unless he'd come by after a hot date to rub her nose in the fact that he was sucking up her father's affection like a sponge while she had been deprived of it for years. She didn't want to hear what Hunter had to say, not when she was in desperate need of sleep. It would take one of Rip Van Winkle's century-long naps to replace the energy she had depleted during her tiring stay in Washington's wonderland and at Robert's den of ill repute. God, she was dead on her feet.

Elyssa left Nathan Hunter lurking in her doorway. Without a word or another glance in his direction, she aimed herself toward her bedroom. She was simply too tired to think or to care about anything beyond climbing into bed. Her brain had short-circuited somewhere between the night club and Meridian Avenue. Nathan Hunter could stand there all evening holding up the wall for all she cared. She just wanted a pillow to cradle her head and a night of uninterrupted sleep.

Moaning in relief, she flounced into bed. When the mattress sagged unexpectedly, she felt herself roll toward the heavy weight beside her. Her head collided with Hunter's thigh and a baritone curse echoed in her ears.

"Cutler, pay attention. I've got something to tell you." Nathan gave her a few shakes when she half collapsed against him. "Are you listening to me?"

"Go 'way," she mumbled tiredly.

Damn it, he didn't have the time or the inclination to play nursemaid to an intoxicated playgirl. He glanced around the elegantly furnished room to see the suitcase propped against the dresser and made his decision.

After scooping Elyssa up in one arm, he swooped down to retrieve her luggage and carted her into the hall. Locking the door behind him, he half carried her to his pickup and deposited her, none too gently, on the seat.

"What's going on?"

Nathan climbed into the cab of the truck and pulled Elyssa across the seat, letting her use his thigh for her pillow. "Just lie down and go to sleep, Cutler."

She didn't have to be told twice.

Four

An hour and twenty minutes later Nathan veered down the I-40 off ramp, headed for the outback of Blaine County. Elyssa was still curled up on the seat of the pickup. A tumble of silky auburn hair cascaded over his lap and two feminine hands were clasped around his thigh, as if his leg were her pillow.

When Elyssa stirred in her sleep, Nathan decided he'd waited long enough to deliver the news to her. She had slept over an hour and he had to tell her what had happened before they reached the ranch.

"Cutler, wake up," he demanded gruffly.

Nothing.

Nathan shook her shoulder, and she moaned groggily.

"Cutler!"

Elyssa heard someone calling to her through a foggy tunnel—the airport terminal, no doubt. She was about to miss her flight and she would be stuck in the weird wonderland of Washington, D.C., for the rest of her life! She would be spending eternity in hell!

"Hey, watch it!" Nathan sucked in his breath when the heel of Elyssa's hand lanced off the zipper of his jeans as she pushed herself upright on the seat.

She shot upward, her heart hammering ninety miles a minute, her dark eyes frozen in a stunned look. It took a moment to orient herself, to take in the unlighted gravel road and the looming hulk of a man beside her. Elyssa inhaled a steadying breath and slumped against the door, positioning herself as far away from Hunter as she could get.

"What's going on?" she croaked.

"I'm taking you to the ranch."

"I don't want to go back there."

"That's tough, lady. You've got no choice," he said brusquely.

She raked the tangle of thick hair from her face. "Where's Dad?"

Nathan set his mouth in a grim line. "That's what we have to talk about."

His bleak tone caused alarm sirens to clang in Elyssa's pickled brain. "What happened to him?" she demanded.

"Near as we can tell, his horse spooked when a rabbit jumped up in front of him. Ely was following the cattle trail around the red rock canyons—"

"Is he going to be okay?"

"No," Nathan said very deliberately and quietly. "He's gone."

Elyssa sat in stunned disbelief. This was a bad dream, she assured herself. Ely was perfectly fine. Any minute she would wake up in her own bed and find herself staring at the ceiling . . .

"Did you hear what I said?" Nathan asked after a moment.

The rich baritone voice filled the cab of the pickup, shattering Elyssa's composure, forcing her to face bitter reality. "No! It's not fair!" she burst out.

It had never been fair, and now it was too late. Elyssa had been deprived of seeing her father as often as she pleased all these years. Nathan Hunter, on the other hand, had enjoyed Ely's affection and attention, his companionship—the lost yesterdays that should have been Elyssa's! All she had were a few days a year—stolen moments—and vague memories of childhood times with her father toting her around with him, filling her head with philosophies handed down through generations of hardworking pioneers.

Tears welled up in Elyssa's eyes, but she couldn't afford the luxury of crying, as she had when her mother had packed her up and hauled her away from the ranch twenty years ago. She had arrangements to make, and she didn't even know where or how to begin the grim process. What was she supposed to do first?

Nathan stared straight ahead, his hands clasped around the steering wheel, swearing under his breath. In his opinion, Elyssa was taking Ely's death too damned well. But then, why shouldn't she? She and Ely were practically strangers. She was closer to her stepfather. Why should she miss a phone call here and there, a few hours of conversation once a month over lunch?

She hadn't cared enough to visit the ranch Ely had toiled and sweated over all his life. She didn't appreciate wide-open spaces, the satisfying sight of cattle herds grazing on thousands of acres of fertile Oklahoma pastures, the ripening wheat fields rippling in the wind. She preferred city lights and bustling freeways, a weekend of carousing at night clubs, and jaunts across the continent at the speed of sound.

While Nathan sat there resenting Elyssa's lack of interest in her natural father, she cast him a bitter glance. Here was the man who'd shared the good times as well as the bad with her father.

Without a family of his own to occupy his time, Ely had taken up attending rodeos for weekend amusement. Elyssa knew her father had always wanted to try his hand at rodeo competition in his younger days, but he had never mastered the exceptional skills that came so naturally to Sid and Nathan Hunter. Ely had admired, and had even sponsored, the father-son team on occasion.

When age and hard times caught up with Sid—the All-Around Cowboy, three years running—Ely had proposed a business arrangement. Elyssa had never been told the entire story of that venture mixing friendship and business, but she had picked up bits and pieces from conversations with her father. What she did know was that Ely had taken Nathan in after Sid had been killed in a traffic accident. Ely, who hadn't gotten custody of his own child, had adopted a full-grown man of twenty-three. Nathan Hunter had reaped all the benefits of Ely's generosity and had become the son he'd never had.

Now, at thirty-two, Hunter probably considered himself one of the family. No doubt he was going to try to manipulate her the way Robert Grayson had. Before long, Hunter would be kissing up to her to maintain his foothold in the business built by someone else's efficiency and hard work. Well, Elyssa wasn't going to fall for deceitful tactics again . . .

When she turned her attention on Hunter, a jolt of unwanted awareness shot through her.

In her early years, when Ely and Jessica Rawlins were having marital problems, Elyssa had been left in the old woman's care. She had been fascinated by the stories and legends her great-grandmother told, intrigued by that "deep sense of knowing" that Maishi—or Mae, as Great-grandmother Rawlins had come to be called by her family—had mentioned.

In the rat race of city life, those feelings were usually suppressed. Occasionally, however, Elyssa had felt them burgeon inside her, causing goose bumps to rise on the back of her neck. The sensations had been much stronger during the years when she had been allowed to return to the ranch for brief visits in the summer. It was as if she replenished that sixth sense while in close contact with nature.

Elyssa absently massaged away the lingering sensations that caused the hair to prickle on her neck and stared at her companion. Nathan Hunter was handsome in a rugged, half-civilized sort of way. She recalled classifying him—genus: cowboy; species: hard-ass—the first time her father introduced them.

This ex-rodeo star, who had followed in Sid's footsteps, had physically tested himself to the limits against unruly beasts in arenas. Steer wrestling and team roping were his specialties, and these certainly weren't contests for pansies. The man had shoulders like a bull and thighs like solid stone columns. His very size and stature were intimidating.

With those piercing blue eyes and leonine features, Hunter looked ominous when he wasn't smiling. And she didn't recall him cracking too many smiles on the six or seven times they had met. Ordinarily, he remained distant and aloof, while she accepted his presence with stiff politeness.

Elyssa didn't really know Hunter at all, except through the glowing accolades her father heaped on him. Those didn't count in her book. She suspected her father had directed the affection that rightfully belonged to *her* toward Hard-As-Nails Hunter. The scenario fit perfectly—orphan child adopted by lonely old man. Come to think of it, Hunter probably resented *her* existence as much as she resented *his*. To him, she was the outsider. To her, Hunter should have been the outsider.

While Elyssa sat there staring at him without saying anything, Nathan's frustration festered like a boil. He needed to talk about Ely, to reflect on the passing of a life that had directly and dramatically affected his. Of course, Elyssa Rawlins Cutler probably couldn't understand that. She probably didn't feel much of anything. He wanted to lash out at her, to draw some kind of emotion from this dispassionate little iceberg with eyes as dark and intriguing as her father's.

The similarities in appearance between father and daughter were enough to torment Nathan to the extreme. Why couldn't Elyssa act more like her father? Why couldn't she care about and appreciate the same things Ely did? If she did, then he could share these torturous feelings that were bottled up inside him.

"Don't you have one damned thing to say?" he burst out as he turned off the country road and followed the half-mile driveway to the secluded ranch house set among a grove of cedars and cottonwoods.

Elyssa jerked upright at the gruff sound of his voice. The change in his tone triggered the resentment that had been in her mind. "I have plenty to say to you, Hunter. I just don't think now's the time."

"If you ask me, there was plenty you should have said to your father all these years while you were ignoring him. And if you put on a teary display at his funeral after refusing to give him the time of day while he was alive, you can bet your sweet ass you're going to hear a raft of curses from me that your sophisticated fiancé wouldn't dare utter in your regal presence."

"You don't know what you're talking about, Hunter," Elyssa flung back at him. "For your information, Robert is my *ex*-fiancé. I returned from D.C. this afternoon to catch him fooling around with his secretary. I'm sure all I was to him was a means to gain a foothold in my stepfather's company."

Her eyes narrowed accusingly on Nathan. "Of course, I hardly think you could fault Robert for that; you employed the same deceptive tactics to work your way up to managing my father's interest in the ranch. Well, you and Robert are through kissing up," she flung at him. "As far as I'm concerned, you can both kiss off! You have deluded yourself into thinking you knew everything about my relationship with my father, but obviously he didn't take you into his confidence completely. Thank God!"

"What secret was he supposedly keeping from me?" Nathan hurled out nastily. "The fact that you were flirting with the ranch hands when you came home for your visits all those years ago? Was it better for everyone involved if Ely came to see *you* instead of your prancing around here and getting the hired help hot and bothered and then fired?"

Damn, the man had a vampire's instinct for drawing blood! His rude remark made her positively furious!

Nathan's face was the second one Elyssa had slapped in the course of this rotten day. She had set a record. She couldn't remember having to slap a man in years because she rarely let one close enough enough to do or say anything disrespectful.

Hunter took her retaliation better than Robert had, she noticed. He didn't even flinch.

"I want you off this ranch by morning, Hunter," Elyssa declared, teeth bared. "I'm the one in charge of my father's estate."

"What makes you think that?" He smirked.

"So help me, if you convinced my father to change his will, I'll have it contested so fast it will make your head spin. I've had it with the human leeches of this world!"

"Lady, you're stuck with me and I'm stuck with you, like it or not, which I certainly don't," Nathan muttered. "In case you've forgotten, your father and mine established a side business eleven years ago. And until we decide what to do, you and I are partners in that prosperous endeavor, if nothing else."

Elyssa cursed under her breath. Damn, she didn't need to be roped into the running of the company her father had created outside his ranching partnership with Uncle Gil. Ely's fascination with rodeos had evolved into a business that supplied bucking broncs, bulls, and steers for some of the best-known rodeos in the country. With Sid Hunter's connections and Ely's financial backing, contracts for providing and transporting livestock had been offered and readily accepted.

Elyssa found herself wondering if Nathan had been swindling money from Ely over the years, taking advantage of her father's generosity. If there was the slightest indication of fraud in the rodeo-stock company, Elyssa would . . .

Her spiteful thoughts came to a halt when the Ford pickup skidded across gravel and its headlights beamed on the two-story ranch house that was surrounded by an upper-level balcony that granted a view of rolling pastures and wheat fields spreading out in all directions.

Memories flew at Elyssa like phantoms, making her instantly and vividly aware of why she hadn't set foot on the ranch since her fifteenth birthday. Those unpleasant recollections, coming at her on the worst day of her life, hit her like a rock slide. It was as if the whole world had come tumbling down. She felt like an outsider on her father's ranch, enclosed in the pickup cab with a man who didn't have a sympathetic bone in his massive body. Hunter couldn't possibly understand all the ways she was hurting.

"I'll take you into town in the morning to make the final arrangements."

From the sound of his voice Elyssa surmised that he wasn't graciously volunteering his assistance. He was announcing a plan, and she was supposed to accept it.

"No thanks, I don't want your help." She climbed down from the truck, trying to concentrate on her irritation and her dislike of him rather than the haunting memories of the last time she had been at the ranch.

Nathan followed her onto the porch. "Nonetheless, I'm going with you," he assured her before reaching around her hip to open the door. "Since I was close to your father the last few years, I'm in a better position to know what he wanted."

Elyssa gnashed her teeth at the goading remark. Hunter had successfully managed to make her feel like an outcast, as her mother had when she'd remarried and broken all ties with Rawlins Ranch. Jessica Rawlins Cutler and Nathan Hunter would probably get along famously in their efforts to place obstacles between father and daughter, obstacles that death had now made unnecessary.

Damn, Elyssa almost hated this hulking mass of a man who strode through the hall beside her, more at home in her own house than she was. The sooner she could remove Nathan Hunter from this place—and her life—the more satisfied she would be!

Five

Gil Rawlins stared out the window of his house on the edge of the rural community that had been named after his grandfather. Rawlins was a sleepy little town in Blaine County, inhabited by farmers and ranchers who preferred to drive out to their old homesteads rather than actually live on them. Gil had moved into town after his wife had died ten years earlier.

Ely had had no interest in leaving the ranch house their father had constructed in the late thirties. He'd preferred to modernize the spacious old house, retaining the original architecture. Gil, on the other hand, had built a brick house in Rawlins, two blocks from his son's home and a half-mile from his daughter's ultramodern place. If Gil had known Ely was going to move Nathan Hunter into the ranch house—as if he were family!—he wouldn't have left the place.

He was certain Nate had sabotaged Ely's thinking the last few years, instigating the resentment that had been building during the past month and had finally erupted the previous day. All hell had broken loose, and Gil held Nathan accountable for coming between him and his brother.

Now, with Ely gone, the partnership was on shaky ground. Rawlins Ranch could fall apart unless Gil received Elyssa's full cooperation. He was counting on the fact that she had been out of touch with the cattle and farming operation and didn't know diddlysquat about the agriculture industry. He needed her to become a silent partner who would leave the decision making to him.

The contents of Ely's will had Gil worried. He knew his brother had made changes recently, probably because of Nathan's influence. If Nathan inherited, that was going to generate problems. Gil hadn't even given a thought to the trouble Nathan could cause until this morning when he'd finally calmed down enough to think straight. He wished he had considered that possibility before Ely died!

Ely was probably enjoying watching this little scene unfold while he sat on his piebald gelding, staring down at all of them from the far side of the horizon. Gil had the inescapable notion that his brother was out there somewhere, wearing that ornery smile of his, waiting for the man he had groomed in his own image to take up the reins. Well, it wasn't going to happen, Gil vowed. He had his own son and daughter—and his grandchildren—to protect. Elyssa would inherit a fortune from that businessman Jessica married. She didn't need or deserve the Rawlins fortune. She was barely even considered family these days.

When Virgil's pickup pulled into the driveway, Gil lurched toward the door. "Where the hell were you last night?" he demanded the second his son appeared on the front lawn.

Virgil lifted a shoulder in a noncommittal shrug. "I was tending to unfinished business."

Gil muttered under his breath and stood aside to allow his son to enter the house. "I had to let Nate track Elyssa down. I didn't want him to have the chance to influence her—you should have been the one to fetch her home."

"Calm down, Dad. You'll have a stroke over this." Virgil flicked a speck of lint from one leg of his trousers and settled himself in a chair. "Nate's an outsider. Why should Elyssa give a damn what he says or thinks?"

"She's an outsider herself, and I intend to keep it that way."

"How much trouble do you think Nate is going to cause us?" Virgil asked as he watched Gil wear a path on the carpet.

"Plenty, I expect. He stands to lose as much as we do. But if we can talk some sense into Elyssa, we can come out of this without financial difficulty. I asked her to come over to the house this afternoon, and I want you here with me, Virgil. Between the two of us, maybe we can convince her to side with us."

"I'm not sure anything I have to say will have an effect on Elyssa."

"What's that supposed to mean?"

Virgil shrugged evasively. "It just means that we were never close enough for my opinion to matter to her."

Virgil reflected on that day twelve years ago, as well as on some of the other times when Elyssa had paid her summer visits to the ranch. He knew she definitely didn't remember him fondly. But then, he hadn't thought much of his wide-eyed little cousin who was enjoying all the luxuries and the glamor of city life while he was down on the farm, busting his ass, breaking his back, and smelling like a sweat factory from dawn until dusk. When the prodigal cousin made her regal return, Virgil became just another lowly farm hand Uncle Ely expected to cater to his precious daughter.

To Virgil's way of thinking, Elyssa still had it all—a golden opportunity and two fortunes at her disposal. Virgil was still struggling to build a name for himself in the horse industry. He needed time and the financial security to become established. At thirty-three, he was gaining ground with the members of the American Quarter Horse Association and with the racing commission, but he was miles away from where he wanted to be. It was frustrating to know that Cousin Elyssa could make or break him, depending on the extent of the grudge she held against him for what he'd done in the past.

Gil's right, thought Virgil. *The family needs to sit down and persuade our citified cousin to side with us.*

What happened years ago was muddy water under the bridge. Virgil had been a resentful teenager at the time; now he was a resentful adult who had damned well better conceal his feelings and practice diplomacy if he expected to have any influence over Elyssa. God, he hoped her childhood memories weren't too vivid and bitter. If they were, it might take more charm than he possessed to convince her to follow Gil's suggestions.

Virgil had learned to play the game when dealing with associates in the horse business. He just hoped Elyssa hadn't gotten too good at mind games while she was wheeling and dealing in Washington. He couldn't afford to find himself outsmarted when his business of raising quarter horses and cutting horses, as well as his financial interest in Rawlins Ranch, was on the line.

Reminding himself that he was going to have to make an attempt to be civil if he wanted to obtain Elyssa's cooperation, Nathan eased open her bedroom door and walked inside, his faithful dog Ricky trotting at his heels. In less than a heartbeat, his simmering irritation with her was transformed into something more along the line of unwanted desire.

The revealing blouse, with its diving neckline, displayed the creamy swells of her breasts. The top button of the garment had come unfastened, leaving the lacy fabric of her bra exposed to his appreciative gaze. Elyssa lay on her side, clinging to her pillow in much the same way she had clutched his thigh during the drive to the ranch. The curvy terrain of denim-clad hips and her tantalizing cleavage sent Nathan's testosterone count to dangerous levels.

Elyssa had inherited enough characteristics from her Cheyenne ancestors to give her features an exotic air that captivated and aroused. No doubt about it. She was one gorgeous woman, even at her worst.

Despite his resentment of her, Nathan had never denied that he found her physically appealing. But he wasn't about to provide a sturdy shoulder for her to lean on, though the man in him wouldn't have minded the physical contact.

As for his disapproval of Elyssa's do-si-doing around the honky-tonks and drinking a little too heavily, he supposed she had a legitimate excuse. It hadn't been so long ago that Nathan couldn't remember returning from the Mesquite Rodeo to find his wife shacked up with one of his rodeo competitors who had been disqualified and had gone home early. Little had he known Wheat Stevens was consoling himself by practicing his bronc-riding skills in bed—Nathan's bed. Nathan had gotten rip-roaring drunk that night.

The barrel-racing queen Nathan had wed—when he was too young to know better—had tied the matrimonial knot with Wheat Stevens as soon as the ink dried on her divorce papers. Nathan wondered if Robert the flake and his secretary also planned to tie the knot. Whatever the case, he couldn't fault Elyssa for drinking until she couldn't think. For her, yesterday must have been one helluva bad day.

Nathan strode across the carpet to set the breakfast tray on the night stand. When he sank down on the edge of the bed to nudge Elyssa awake, she groaned.

"Cutler, you've got to get up. It's nine o'clock and we have to be in town by eleven. I brought you some breakfast."

"Go away."

Bongo drums pounded against Elyssa's skull and her stomach pitched like a ship in a hurricane. Her body complained when she tried to roll over, so she stayed where she was.

"Have a piece of toast, Cutler," Nathan insisted.

She shoved away the food he stuffed under her nose. She didn't want to be awake, much less eat.

"Forget the toast and hand me the phone," she demanded in a voice she barely recognized as her own. She sounded like a frog with laryngitis croaking to the beat of the bongo drums that surely must have been plugged into an amplifier the size of a Mack truck. No wonder she usually limited herself to one or two drinks at a sitting. She would make a lousy alcoholic. No iron-lined stomach, no padding in her skull, and not enough suicidal tendencies to tolerate self-imposed torture.

"Give me the number and I'll dial," Nathan volunteered,

reaching for the phone. "I'm not sure you can see straight yet, Cutler."

Elyssa rattled off her home number and pushed up against the headboard, oblivious to the gaping Western blouse and the second button that had worked loose.

"God, this better be an emergency or whoever I'm talking to is going to be tailed by a hit man," Valerie finally muttered into the phone.

"Val, it's Elyssa." She raked unruly auburn strands away from her face.

"You're calling me from your bedroom?" Valerie hooted. "Jeezus, I didn't think you had *that* bad of a time last night!"

Nathan overheard the comment and smiled to himself. From the sound of things, Valerie had dragged Elyssa out to paint the town red, hoping to exorcise the memory of her unfaithful fiancé.

"I'm at my dad's ranch, Val."

Moisture gathered in Elyssa's dark eyes, and she turned away from Hunter's probing gaze. "My dad died in an accident yesterday. I just wanted to let you know where I was. I'll be back in touch when I have more details."

"Oh God! I'm so sorry," Val said. "If there's anything you want me to do, anything at all, just tell me. I'll see it's done."

"I'm afraid it will be up to you to give Mother and Daniel the news when they call. They flew to Atlanta early this morning to make the connection for their cruise."

"Anything else?"

"No, I'll come back to the apartment to pick up what I need when I have time."

Nathan sipped his coffee and retrieved the receiver when Elyssa thrust it at him. "I'm sorry, too," he reluctantly apologized. "I came down hard on you last night. Despite what you think, I was very fond of your dad and losing him was a blow. I guess I took it out on you."

Elyssa blinked back the tears without glancing in Hunter's direction. She had been prepared to dislike her father's right-hand man as much this morning as she had last night. Her emotions were in enough turmoil without his changing personalities on her. Of course, she'd expected him to change his tune eventually. It was hard to kiss up and be an ass at the same time.

"Yeah. Well, lucky for me your opinion counts for nothing," Elyssa muttered. "You don't like me, and I don't like you. Let's leave it at that without confusing the issues, shall we?"

It was then that she glanced down to see her breasts practically spilling out of the confines of white lace and pumpkin-colored poplin. Her watery eyes shot upward to catch Hunter staring at her over the rim of his coffee cup. She thought she detected a rakish grin behind the mug. The jerk.

She snapped her blouse together and glared at him good and hard. "Get out, Hunter. I'd like to eat breakfast without a vulture circling."

"I'm here to make peace."

"Go make it somewhere else, or were you planning to follow me to the shower in your effort to kiss up? What do I get out of this? The benefit of your expertise in seduction *if* I consent to do whatever it is I suspect you want in order to ensure you get a cut of the Rawlins's pie?"

Nathan hid another smile and sipped his coffee. He rather liked Elyssa's spunk, even if he didn't like her. She reminded him of Ely when she got her dander up. She was definitely her father's daughter.

"Last night you invited me to bed," he mockingly reminded her. "Now you're inviting me to your shower? Maybe some other time—"

"I most certainly am not!" Elyssa jerked upright, forgetting her gaping blouse. The instant she saw where those twinkling blue eyes, surrounded by thick curly lashes, had strayed, she snatched the garment around her and glowered. "You're getting on my nerves, Hunter."

"That's the whiskey," he diagnosed. "Hangovers are notorious for giving you the jitters."

"Out!" Her right arm shot toward the door. When she spied the speckled dog that lay beside Hunter's size-twelve boots, she recoiled in disgust. "And take that fleabag with you when you go."

"Ricky doesn't have fleas," Nathan insisted, rising to his feet.

"Maybe not, but he's probably plagued with some sort of disease, considering the company he keeps." When Nathan and Ricky ambled toward the door, Elyssa exhaled an agitated breath. "I need the keys to Dad's truck to get to town."

"They're in my pocket."

Nathan pivoted slightly, presenting an utterly masculine profile that Valerie Mitchell would have killed to get her hands on.

Salt of the earth. A man's man.

Elyssa gnashed her teeth when that unaccountable sensation tightened the back of her neck. Nathan Hunter oozed sex appeal. He stood poised by the door in form-fitting faded denim, looking infuriatingly appealing. She didn't want to notice, didn't care to be attracted. But the magnetism was there, just like that feeling at the base of her neck. It was something that defied all the knowledge she'd acquired through years of education and experience.

She muttered when he patted his pocket, daring her to come get what she wanted. "You're a Grade-A ass, Hunter."

"And since you're a sassy bitch, we ought to get along just fine, just as soon as we establish our separate territories."

"You don't have any territory left, Hunter."

He definitely looked predatory when he wheeled to stalk back to her. His jaw was set in a grim line, and his blue eyes pierced like lasers.

"I'm going to tell you this just once more, Cutler," he growled, his teeth clenched in visible restraint. "No matter what you and the rest of your family think of me—and I really don't give a damn what any of you think—I'm not butting out until I ensure that Ely's wishes are formalized. After we get through the unpleasant ordeal this morning, and you have unloaded that block of wood that's resting on your shoulder, we're going to have a little talk. And before your dear Uncle Gil plies you with his version of the argument that took place between him and your father yesterday morning, you need to know that I'm the only one around here you can trust to offer you Ely's side of the story. While you're listening to Gil pitch his song and dance, ask yourself what he might have to gain—"

"As opposed to what *you* have to gain, Hunter?" she challenged, even while he loomed over her like the towering red rock cliffs that cut a slash through the western sections of Rawlins Ranch.

Nathan had the wildest urge to take Elyssa's lush lips beneath his and kiss the breath out of her. She would label the gesture as kissing up, even if it truly was nothing more than the man in him instinctively responding to the lure of a desirable woman.

When Elyssa automatically shrank back into her own space, Nathan's eyes narrowed curiously. For a woman who usually projected an air of savvy and self-assurance, she retreated pretty damned quick. He suspected her reaction stemmed from her dislike of him.

Gaining Elyssa's confidence and trust wasn't going to be easy, he predicted. Of course, he hadn't exactly gone out of his way to charm her. But he was going to put a better foot forward in the future. Still, she was prepared to believe the worst about him, and Gil Rawlins's side of the family would be on hand to encourage her in that. To them, Nathan would always be an unwelcome outsider.

Without Ely to serve as a buffer, Nathan expected his ears would be burning when the Rawlins tribe had their little pow-wows to maneuver for power and position. Elyssa didn't have a clue as to what she faced. She had been away too long. Gil probably considered her as much of an outcast as Nathan, even if the man wasn't stupid enough to say it to her face.

"Your father always claimed you had good instincts, Cutler.

I don't know you well enough to say for certain. I guess I'm going to have to trust *you* to do the right thing."

When he turned and walked away, his obedient dog trotting at his heels, Elyssa stared after him. She knew enough about psychological warfare from her battles with government agencies and corporate business to make her leery. But she didn't know what to make of Nathan Hunter and his remarks. It could very well be that his declaration of placing faith in *her* was a cunning ploy to convince her to place trust in *him*. He probably wanted her to side with him in the conflicts he predicted she would encounter with Uncle Gil and Cousin Virgil.

Elyssa plopped back on her pillow and groaned. She wasn't up to this, not yet anyway. She felt as if she'd been put through a wringer. Her skull was vibrating like a tuning fork, and she was queasy enough to have the shakes. On top of all else, she had to cope with what had happened to her father and with a deceitful ex-fiancé, not to mention dealing with the infuriating Nathan Hunter!

Rolling off the bed, Elyssa wobbled to the shower. The dam threatened to shatter now that she was alone and could let her guard down. She'd be damned if she'd let Hunter see her cry. He would love that, wouldn't he? Then he'd really bully her around and try to intimidate her.

Elyssa hurriedly peeled off her clothes and stepped into the shower. And not a second too soon, either. Her composure cracked wide open. She cried for all those times in years past she had shouldered the haunting and humiliating secret of what really had happened that day she'd cartwheeled over the side of the cliff.

She cried to release her pent-up frustration over a fiancé who had used her as a step on his stairway to success. She grieved for her father and all the years Hunter had been his confidant and friend instead of her. And she cursed herself for being unable to confront the twelve-year-old nightmare that dictated her behavior to this very day and prevented her from fully enjoying all the lost yesterdays that she and her father might have spent together.

Now it was too late. Ely would never know how precious her childhood memories of him were, how she envied what he and Hunter shared.

Nathan laid his head back against the door that joined his bedroom to the bathroom. Even the hum of the shower couldn't drown out Elyssa's wailing sobs. For all her bluster and hauteur, Elyssa Rawlins Cutler mourned the loss of her father. It was comforting to know she wasn't quite as hardhearted as he'd thought she was.

These next few days were sure to take their toll on her, no matter how strong and independent she pretended to be. Nathan made a pact with himself to be there for her, even when she tried to push him away, suspicious of his ulterior motives. The bottom line was that he needed her cooperation. In this upcoming ordeal, Elyssa might perceive him as her enemy, but he was her best friend because he knew exactly how Ely Rawlins wanted things to be . . . even if she was going to have one helluva time believing it.

When Ricky pricked his ears and stood up, Nathan knew an intruder was about to arrive upon the scene. Sure enough, Claudia Gilbert sashayed into his room.

Claudia was the housekeeper's twenty-two-year-old daughter. Her mother cooked and cleaned the ranch house and bunkhouse to support herself, her recently divorced daughter, and her two-year-old grandson. Althea was a diamond in the rough with a heart as big as the whole outdoors. Her daughter was a pain in the ass.

Claudia could have learned a lot from her hardworking mother if she had paid attention, Nathan reflected as he surveyed Claudia who was garbed in blue jeans that fit like tights and a fuchsia tank top that clung. Her bosom was showcased by a plunging neckline.

It wasn't that Claudia wasn't reasonably attractive and fairly personable. It was that she was always doing the chasing that got on Nathan's nerves. Besides that, she was ten years younger than he was. She liked hard rock concerts, and Nathan was strictly a country music man. He and Claudia had few common interests, which prevented him from leaping the generation gap for the sexual satisfaction she was eager to provide.

"Hi, Nate," Claudia murmured, the batting of her eyelashes sending a draft across the room. "I just wanted to convey my sympathy. I know how close you and Ely were."

He wasn't surprised that she pretended compassion to lure him, just in case the revealing cut of her clothes hadn't gotten his attention. Claudia didn't have any finesse or good taste. A great body, yes. But she came on to a man like a freight train.

When she sidled close to toy with the buttons on his denim shirt, Nathan monitored the movement of those hot pink acrylic fingernails with cool distaste. He would rather see Claudia dedicating herself to little Timmy's potty training.

"Sometimes distraction heals the hurt, you know, Nate."

She batted her hazel eyes a couple more times for effect and tried to look properly remorseful and sympathetic. The ploy fell short of the mark. Her perfume was strong enough to choke a bull; her tank top was too revealing, and her mouth was too glossy from a fresh coat of passion pink lipstick. It was another cheap pass at a man old enough and worldly enough not to fall into such a trap. Little Timmy needed a daddy, but it wasn't going to be Nathan.

Nathan removed Claudia's hand from his shirt and ambled away from the bathroom door. Elyssa was down to sobbing gasps by then. All emotion had been wrung out of her after twenty minutes of wailing. Nathan hoped she felt better. The sounds of her grief had gone through him as if it were his own. It was. He just hadn't let himself succumb to it yet. He knew what Ely would have wanted him to do, and he couldn't let his guard down until he had put Ely's plans into motion.

"I was wondering if I could ask a favor of you, Claudia," Nathan murmured.

She brightened immediately. "Sure. Anything. You know that."

"I'd appreciate it if you would give your mother a helping hand around here and in the bunkhouse. She's worked for Ely for years. I think she'd like to have some time to do her own grieving. You could give her that time by assisting with her chores."

Claudia's face fell beneath the thick coat of makeup. "Whatever you say, Nate. But if there's anything else, you know my door is always open for you. I think you know how I feel."

No kidding! Claudia might as well have tattooed AVAILABLE on her chest and had herself delivered by express mail.

"Thanks. Now if you'll excuse me, I need to change so I can drive Elyssa into town."

Claudia glanced at the closed door and then refocused on Nathan. She studied him consideringly. "Virgil says Ely's daughter wouldn't fit in around here very well. Too citified for the likes of us. What do you think, Nate?"

"I think I need to shower and change," he repeated, refusing to be baited.

Claudia looked as if she intended to comment and then changed her mind at the last second. She must have decided to stick to her kissing up routine—as Elyssa would probably say.

Even after Claudia sauntered out and closed the door, Nathan could smell her cheap perfume. She had probably bathed in that stuff so often it had saturated her pores and had solidified in her copper blond hair. Elyssa, on the other hand, had a classy, subtle scent that didn't meet a man halfway across the room and clog his nostrils. Her aroma lured a man ever closer, tempting him to savor her fragrance and lose himself in those obsidian eyes . . .

God, twenty-four hours ago Nathan wouldn't have given a plug nickel for Elyssa Rawlins Cutler. Now he was lusting after her. Maybe Virgil was right, Nathan mused. Those who were at home on the ranch weren't in the same league with the sophisticated Cutlers of urban society.

He stood under the shower and pondered that thought. Then he scrubbed himself until he shone, until the shower massage had relaxed the tension triggered by thoughts of his unwanted attraction to Elyssa, of the inevitable arrangements that had to be made, and of Elyssa's upcoming encounter with Gil and Virgil Rawlins—over which Nathan was going to have no control.

Damn, it was going to be a long day . . .

Six

Elyssa kept her emotions reasonably in check while she was put through the paces of making the final arrangements. To Hunter's credit, he remained by her side, offering moral support without imposing his ideas on her. When she fumbled, he offered suggestions, but he left the decisions to her.

It wasn't until she and Hunter slid into a booth at the local sandwich shop to grab a hamburger that Elyssa allowed herself to slump against the seat in relief. She hadn't realized how much she had relied on Hunter's dynamic presence, how tense she had been until she finally let down.

Was it any wonder that Ely had taken Hunter under his wing to groom him as a son? The man had a commanding self-confidence that was both impressive and reassuring. Hunter seemed more like Ely than Ely's niece and nephew. From what Elyssa remembered of Virgil and Patricia, they weren't likely to have much in common with her father.

"You appear to be deeply immersed in thought, Cutler," Nathan observed as he scooped up the greasy hamburger that had been dropped unceremoniously on a pile of French fries. "You okay?"

"I've never had to do what I just did," she confessed on a sigh. "It's hard to pretend to be objective and unemotional when everything inside me rebels against doing what I must, as if *not* doing it would bring Dad back." She waved her hand in a helpless gesture. "I don't suppose that makes much sense."

"Oh, it does," he assured her. "I know what you're feeling. When I lost my father in an accident, Ely was there to walk me through the paces, the same way I tried to get you through your ordeal. He left all decisions to me, offering suggestions only when I faltered."

Nathan took another bite of his burger and stared deliberately at Elyssa. "Dad was hauling a load of livestock to a rodeo in Las Vegas. The rig jackknifed on an icy stretch of road in Colorado. Ely was supposed to have made that trip. I think that was the weekend he had the chance to meet you in the City before you flew back East from Christmas break during your first year of college."

Elyssa vividly remembered that week. She hadn't wanted to go back to school after a long, lonely, miserable semester. She had called her father, in tears, and he had come running to cheer her up, boost her morale, and send her bravely on her way.

"Ely thought my dad had taken that one-way trip in his place and that he had escaped fate. I think that's why he took me in. He felt guilty about what happened," Nathan explained.

Elyssa nodded mutely. She could understand how her father would have been affected by losing his friend and business partner in such a way.

"Reckless Sid Hunter never had a dime to his name," Nathan confided. "When I was a kid, he dragged me around on the rodeo circuit and left me with his girlfriend of the week. He rode bulls by day and squandered his winnings by night. But high-rolling and hard living isn't much of an investment in the future. My dad had already sold a run-down house and a few hundred acres of land in west Texas that raised more cactus than cattle to put up his share of the money for the Hunter-Rawlins rodeo-stock company." He smiled bitterly as he stabbed a fork into the pile of French fries. "My ex-wife had already gotten my share of the cattle, and Dad and I got the cactus."

Another layer of resentment fell away while Elyssa sat

across the booth, watching Hunter consume two hamburgers and enough French fries to last her a month. Now she understood why her father had bent over backward to give Hunter financial opportunity and a home. Sid Hunter had left his son down on his luck, while Ely could thank his lucky stars he hadn't been in that truck on a treacherous stretch of icy Colorado road. Unfortunately, fate had eventually caught up with Ely . . .

A knot coiled in the pit of Elyssa's stomach. She fought back the wave of grief that washed over her. She was going to get through this ordeal with class, dignity, and style, just as her father would have expected her to do—somehow.

"Hunter?"

"Yeah, Cutler?"

He didn't glance up at her. He had seen the haunted look in her eyes, so he purposely stared at his silverware. Elyssa didn't like anyone knowing she was hurting and vulnerable. He allowed her the luxury of thinking he didn't notice that her emotions were getting to her.

"I'm . . . sorry." Elyssa stared wide-eyed at the far wall, afraid to blink for fear of squeezing out the tears that swam in her eyes.

"Sorry for what? For picking at your lunch without eating it?" Nathan sprawled out in the booth and tried to look oblivious to what had upset her. "That's okay. You probably aren't used to high cholesterol meals. But I wasn't in the mood for lunch at Ma's Diner today. I've eaten there four times this week already. Ma's chicken fried steak and gravy sticks to your ribs. If you've seen Ma lately, then you know how her cooking affected her. She could play center for Oklahoma State University's football team and the opposition couldn't touch the Cowboy quarterback. Ma's got fifty years of cream gravy stuck to *her* ribs. Before long it'll be stuck to mine."

Elyssa managed a watery smile. Nathan Hunter could pour on the distracting charm when he felt like it. Oh sure, he was probably preying on her vulnerability even now, but it wouldn't hurt to let him *if* she was aware of what he was doing and why. As long as she kept reminding herself that Hunter was after the same things Robert Grayson had been after, she could handle him.

"Want another cup of coffee, Cutler?"

"No thanks, I'm already swimming in it."

"Would you rather take a swim then?" he asked with a dazzling smile and an endearing twinkle in his blue eyes.

Her expression sobered immediately, despite his attempt to tease her into good humor. "I don't swim."

Nathan frowned at her tense expression and the odd catch in her voice. He couldn't help but wonder why she had no interest in sports that required skimpy attire. He didn't pry; he simply made note of her overly sensitive reaction to his teasing question.

"I'll drop you off at Gil's house for the family powwow. Call me at the grain elevator when you're ready to go home. I need to order cattle cubes. Your father had planned to do it this morning before he drove to the City to meet you . . ."

His voice dried up when he noticed the mist of tears floating in her eyes. Nathan reached down to assist Elyssa to her feet. Heightened awareness tingled through him during those few seconds when her supple body brushed against his. But she moved away as quickly as she had shrunk back into her own space that morning when he'd leaned over her. Damn it, what was with her anyway? Just when he thought they had managed a truce, she shied away from him again.

"Take it easy. I wasn't going to take a bite out of you," he assured her. "I've been well fed."

Elyssa cursed her lack of emotional control. It wasn't that she wanted to retreat from Hunter's supporting touch. That was a reaction which had hounded her for years.

Although Elyssa would never forgive Robert for what he had done, she supposed she couldn't really blame the man for turning to another woman for satisfaction. As he had said, she wasn't worth a damn at physical affection and probably never would be. It had become second nature to back away when a man ventured too close. Old habits were difficult to break.

Before Elyssa had time to collect her composure, she stepped outside to encounter the one man she definitely hadn't wanted to see again as long as she lived. But there he stood, all spruced up in his brown police uniform, looking like the blond Adonis she remembered from her teenage years. Gavin Spencer had been Rawlins High School's golden boy, the superstar athlete and heartthrob. But he had also been a bully, as Elyssa had discovered too late. And she had paid dearly for that.

When the nightmare from her past leaped at her, she reflexively stepped back, finding herself plastered against Hunter's solid, muscular form. She couldn't move, not even when Hunter slid a supporting arm around her waist, and she didn't bother fooling herself into thinking Hunter was unaware of the tremors that rippled through her. His chest was pressed against her back, and her reaction would have been impossible to miss.

"I heard you were in town," Gavin said as he pulled off his mirrored sunglasses and flashed her that roguish smile he had been famous for. "I was sorry to hear about your dad."

"Thank you for your concern," Elyssa said in a brittle voice. She veered across the grass, giving Gavin all the space he needed on the sidewalk and then some.

While Nathan chatted with Gavin, Elyssa piled into the pickup and cursed the man who had caused her untold anguish a lifetime ago. It didn't say much for Rawlins Police Department if Gavin Spencer was in command. As for Elyssa, she wouldn't have put Gavin in charge of picking up litter off the streets!

Returning to the ranch had stirred up too many discomforting memories for her. She was being bled emotionally, stripped down to raw nerves. Hour by hour, her determination to endure was eroding away. Disturbing memories converged on her at the speed of light.

She had to get away! And she would, just as soon as her conference with Uncle Gil and her cousins adjourned. She would make her escape, if only for the night, if only to give herself time to regather her poise and self-control!

Nathan noticed the way she clutched the hem of her navy blue jacket, the way the muscles of her jaw tensed before she forced herself to relax. Even when he slid onto the seat beside her, Elyssa didn't acknowledge his presence.

Nathan wondered where Gavin Spencer fit into Elyssa's past. For sure, they had met before. Nathan had felt her flinch when she'd backed into him on the sidewalk. He had heard the tremor in her voice, the underlying tone of hostility.

"You want to explain what that was all about?" he questioned as he started the engine.

Elyssa stared straight ahead. "No."

"Our illustrious chief of police just returned from the county courthouse," Nathan said. "He wrapped up his second divorce. He now lays claim to two ex-wives and three children. His alimony and child support will probably keep him doling out speeding tickets to anyone who dares to drive three miles over the limit."

"Is that so?"

"Yeah, that's so." Nathan stifled a grin and tossed Elyssa a discreet glance. A slab of marble could not have been more rigid and unyielding. She was really uptight! "Still don't want to talk about it?"

"Back off, Hunter. I just want to get through this day without falling to pieces. If you keep badgering me, your country cop will be hauling me off in a paddy wagon. Then you'll have to fight your way through court and have yourself declared guardian for a crazy woman to get my money."

"Who said I was after your money?"

Her head swiveled on her stiff shoulders, sending a fan of auburn hair gliding around her face. "Isn't that what Uncle Gil is going to tell me during our powwow? That you're after my money?"

"More than likely he will." Nathan veered off Main Street and drove toward Gil's brick home. "And later, I'm going to refute everything he tells you this afternoon and assure you that your father had other plans for the ranch, *not* the ones Gil mentioned. Then you aren't going to know who the hell to believe and you'll hightail it back to the City to see if you can puzzle it all out over a bottle of vodka."

"Scotch."

"Over a bottle of Scotch," he corrected and then casually continued. "Then you'll awake in the same condition you did this morning, only I won't be around for you to bite my head off."

"Why not?" Elyssa felt the tension drain out of her, marveling at Hunter's knack of putting her at ease when she probably should have been anything but. After all, he was playing mind games with her and she knew it. How safe and relaxing was that?

Nathan pulled into the driveway and turned to confront Elyssa face-to-face. "I won't be there because if I was there in the morning, I would also have been there to tuck you in at night. And I wouldn't have left it at that. I would have wanted to spend the night with you—I would have said so. *You* would be wondering if I wanted to sleep with you because *I* thought it would eventually get me what *you* think I want."

Elyssa actually managed to laugh for the first time all day. It felt good. It eased the unbearable tension. "My, I'm an incredibly perceptive woman if I can delve into all that analytic reasoning while intoxicated, not to mention skillfully seduced."

He grinned in response to the pleasurable sound of her laughter. "According to Ely, you are the smartest thing in skirts."

"Would I have turned down your offer, do you think?" she questioned, her onyx eyes sparkling with amusement.

"Absolutely," he said with firm conviction.

A curious frown knitted her brow. "And why would I have done that?"

"Because for one thing you have recently decided to swear off men. For another, you know that you and I have business dealings to conduct. You haven't quite decided how to manipulate *me* to *your* best advantage."

"You lost me, Hunter. I must not be as shrewd as you let me think I am. Either that or you're trying to let me outsmart myself." She smiled wryly at him. "Or maybe *you* wouldn't want to complicate matters by having to accept half the responsibility for the consequences of the night we almost spent together. And if I had been unable to formulate the word *no* until it was too late, I would be clambering for an advantageous position after winding up on my back and wondering how to turn the situation around so I would be the one on top—so to speak . . . Hunter? Did *I* lose *you?*"

Nathan jerked himself to attention. He had gotten sidetracked by visions of Elyssa lying on her back beneath him.

Instinctively, his hand lifted from the back of the seat, hovering an inch from her flawless cheek. He watched her watch him with the wariness of a wild creature trying to decide whether to accept a human's touch. He waited, letting Elyssa adjust to the idea of his caress before his fingertips brushed her creamy flesh. And then he retreated, slowly, deliberately.

Just one infinitely gentle caress, the slightest physical contact. No threat, no demand, just a breath of a touch that sent heightened awareness rippling through Elyssa's body, causing her pulse to throb.

Elyssa had that funny feeling at the base of her neck again. Her gaze locked with those fathomless blue eyes that could spew fire or pour down like warm sunshine from a morning sky. Intrigued, she reached out to trail her forefinger over the square line of his jaw and the sensuous curve of his lips. She was drawn to this man for reasons she couldn't begin to comprehend. She didn't trust his motives, but she was attracted to him nonetheless.

Of course, Great-grandmother Rawlins claimed you didn't have to attach labels or explanations to those intrinsic and in-nate reactions. They were simply there, a gift granted by ancestors who had been in touch with the powerful inner self and the natural world around them.

When the front door of the house swung open, the spell shattered. Elyssa snatched her hand away, feeling awkward and self-conscious. "I'd better go. Uncle Gil looks as if he's chomping at the bit."

"Call me when you need me, Cutler," he murmured in a voice as soft as velvet.

Elyssa strode toward the house, reflecting on her unsettling encounter with him and the sensations he had triggered with his tender touch and hushed words. If she wasn't careful, that man could really get to her . . .

Now she was about to face Uncle Gil and her cousins. She was curious to see what approach they planned to take to influence her thinking. Thanks to Hunter's clever strategy, she was suspicious of her family before she ever set foot in the house!

Seven

Elyssa found herself bustled into a chair at Uncle Gil's dining-room table, where a steaming cup of coffee awaited her. Uncle Gil sank down into the chair at the head of the table, as if he were taking his inherited position as patriarch of the Rawlins family. Elyssa ignored the impact the symbolic gesture was supposed to have on her.

Cousin Virgil parked himself beside her and smiled charmingly. She decided she could be as full of pretense as he, so she returned his shallow smile.

Virgil looked like a younger version of his sixty-two-year-old, red-haired, freckle-faced father. Both men stood six feet tall, most of their height noticeably displayed in their long, storklike legs. They were short waisted, but their broad shoulders testified to years of physical labor. The only difference between the two men was that Uncle Gil's thick chest had sunk to his belly, while Virgil maintained a reasonable physique, considering he was built like a clothesline pole. It was his personality and questionable character that had always offended Elyssa.

She had always sensed that Virgil didn't like her. His childhood teasing had been too vicious to be considered playful. He'd insisted on playing cowboys and Indians in the early years when she'd come for visits, always assigning her the role of the evil Indian. Since he was six years her senior, he considered himself the one to make all the decisions.

Elyssa couldn't begin to count the times she had been left

tied up in the old barn on the original family homestead or staked out in the sun and left to bake while Virgil rode off to swim in the river. She had a scar on the underside of her chin, a souvenir of an encounter in which Virgil had played a little too rough while he'd tormented the Indian he'd captured. Elyssa suspected Virgil still liked to play rough, even though he was twelve years older and was smiling cordially at her.

She shifted her attention to Patricia, Gil's thirty-year-old daughter. Patricia took excellent care of herself, but she still resembled the prissy, pampered child Elyssa remembered playing fashion consultant for her Barbie dolls. While Elyssa had thrived on the great outdoors and had tolerated Virgil's pranks, Patricia had been ensconced in her bedroom with its pink canopy bed and frilly lace curtains. The girl had primped and preened so she had made Elyssa nauseous.

To this day, Patricia probably cringed at the thought of having a mahogany-colored strand of hair out of place or a chip in her elegantly manicured nails. Her makeup was perfect, her gestures refined. She also had the personality of a limp dishrag. Patricia reminded Elyssa of a Barbie doll that had been propped in a chair, wearing a painted-on smile. She wondered if the woman still played with her dolls or if she dressed her two young daughters up instead.

Dennis Humphrey, Patricia's husband, was also in attendance. Although Elyssa couldn't call him handsome, he had earthy, virile qualities that were mildly appealing to the feminine eye. His broad forehead was lighter in color than the rest of his face, suggesting he was in the habit of wearing a ball cap to shield his eyes from the sun when he worked on the ranch alongside his father- and brother-in-law, doing whatever he was told to do, Elyssa suspected. Dennis didn't seem to be a free thinker with a good brain. After all, he *had* married Patricia.

Gil Rawlins's side of the family was well represented. Elyssa felt like an outsider intruding in a place where she didn't belong. She wondered if that was how she was supposed to feel since the other outsider—Nathan Hunter—hadn't been invited to the conference.

"I know this is a difficult time for you, Elyssa. It is for all of us," Uncle Gil began, staring at the contents of his coffee cup. "Ely was not only my brother but my partner. It is customary for a partnership to dissolve when one of the partners passes on, but seeing how this is also a family ranch that has survived for generations, I want to maintain the longstanding tradition—"

"How did my father feel about that?" Elyssa questioned.

"He had strong feelings about the continuation of tradition," Uncle Gil readily assured her. "I haven't seen Ely's will yet, but I imagine he left his half of the partnership and joint holdings to you."

"And what about Nathan Hunter? Don't you think Dad left him something?"

Gil ground his false teeth. He was accustomed to dealing with his daughter Patricia who simply did what she was told when it came to the workings of the ranch. Elyssa was a bird of an entirely different feather. Nothing got by her.

"I'm sure Uncle Ely generously bequeathed his half of Hunter-Rawlins Rodeo Stock Company to Nate," Cousin Virgil spoke up, flashing Elyssa another smile that she suspected was coated with NutraSweet rather than real sugar. "Your dad was fond of Nate, of course. But Nate isn't *family*."

Elyssa stared pointedly at Dennis Humphrey. "Neither is Dennis. If he was invited here today, why not Hunter?"

"Dennis is married to Patricia. That makes him family," Gil declared emphatically. He then eased back in his chair to inhale a calming breath. Hell's bells, Elyssa was as difficult as Nate! The man had probably sabotaged her thinking. He would pay for that, Gil vowed.

"The point of this meeting," Virgil stated diplomatically, "is to ensure that the ranch continues to operate smoothly under the terms of the partnership. What we propose, Elyssa, is to give you Ely's share of the yearly profit as your part of the ranch. You will still own your father's share of the undivided property and will hold the title of financial advisor so you can collect the yearly payment your father was allowed in the government wheat-subsidy program."

Gil took up where his son left off. "We're trying to make the transition as simple and efficient as possible in hopes of keeping the partnership going. Each member of the family is entitled to the fifty-thousand-dollar subsidy, provided he makes a significant contribution to the ranch operation. Dennis, of course, collects his subsidy payment because he not only shares in the obligations of farming but he also manages the feeder steer operation."

"And Cousin Patricia?" Elyssa inquired with an uplifted brow.

"She also collects her salary and subsidy payment because she signs the payroll checks and distributes them," Gil answered.

Elyssa wondered if that was stretching "significant contribution" in the eyes of the law. But having dealt with Uncle Sam's agencies, she suspected the squandering bureaucracy was too busy feasting on taxpayers to notice gray areas.

"Am I to understand that all farm hands, family included, draw salaries from the profits of cattle, wheat, and alfalfa and that government subsidy payments are deposited in the partnership's account?" Elyssa questioned.

"Exactly," Gil assured her. "The total income from USDA subsidy, actual wheat sales, and cattle sales—minus operating expenses and machinery purchases—provides an equally distributed profit that will now be divided between you and me."

Somewhere in this watered-down explanation Elyssa expected to find several loopholes. Nathan Hunter's comments had prompted her to read between the lines, and they had also piqued her curiosity. She wondered how Hunter was going to come at her after Uncle Gil finished with her.

Still wearing one of his artificial-sweetener smiles, Cousin

Virgil produced a contract as if he were a magician pulling a rabbit out of his hat.

"All you have to do is sign on the dotted line and you will receive your half of the ranch profits. You won't be obligated to put on work gloves and stack alfalfa bales or feed cattle cubes to the stock. You will have to sign the tax forms, but essentially you'll reap the dividends because you are Uncle Ely's daughter."

In other words, Elyssa could trot back to Oklahoma City and get paid for keeping her nose out of ranch business. She stared consideringly at Uncle Gil, Cousin Virgil, Patricia, and cousin-in-law Dennis. All three men were poised on the edges of their chairs, waiting for her to agree. Patricia simply sat there like a Barbie doll.

Before Elyssa had a chance to study the document, see her father's will, or hear Hunter's sales pitch, Gil extended the pen with which she was to sign the partnership contract.

Casually as you please, Elyssa picked up her cup, leaving all three men waiting with bated breath. And then the damnedest thing happened. The coffee dribbled out the corner of her mouth and slopped right smack dab on the contract.

Elyssa flicked coffee off her jacket. Some of it also splattered on the contract. "I'm sorry." She offered her most apologetic smile. "Making the final arrangements this morning really got to me. I'm still a little shaky."

All three men collapsed in their chairs like deflated balloons. Patricia simply glanced down to make sure no coffee had gotten on her pale pink ensemble.

Elyssa stood and ran a hand through her hair. "I need to go home and get some rest. Hopefully, in a few days, I'll be able to cope and will be in a better frame of mind to deal with business decisions." She glanced at Gil. "May I use your phone?"

His expression hardened. "A word of warning about Nathan Hunter. I know he is trying to influence you. Don't listen to him, Elyssa. He is after your money, and he doesn't have your best interest at heart the way we do. We're family, and family sticks together through thick and thin."

"I'll keep that in mind. Now, may I use your phone?"

Gil absently gestured toward the hall. Elyssa walked off in the direction he indicated and paused outside the door to watch the men put their heads together for a hushed discussion. She had the feeling she had been rushed through the proceedings like a cow prodded up a ramp to be hauled to the slaughter.

By soiling the contract, she had bought herself precious time to assess the situation. The problem was, she couldn't figure out why her father wouldn't want to keep business running as usual. The longstanding partnership had been passed down from his grandfather, from Oklahoma Territorial days. The ranch was a landmark.

Perhaps the real culprit here was Nathan Hunter who was greedily scrambling for position by using Elyssa as his tool. The way Elyssa saw it, Gil's side of the family was in conflict with Nathan Hunter. Why should she trust a stranger over her own kin?

This mental tug of war had given her a headache on top of the skull-thumping hangover that aspirins couldn't touch. All Elyssa wanted to do was pile into bed, pull the pillow over her head, and sleep the next few days away. Instead, she dialed the number of the local grain elevator and asked for Hunter.

"Did you survive all the vultures, Cutler?" he asked.

"No, I haven't dealt with you yet." She let out her breath in a rush. "Come get me, Hunter, and *you* can do *your* worst."

A husky chuckle came down the line. "Still don't trust my motives, do you, Cutler?"

"Nope."

"At least you're honest. I appreciate that."

"I appreciate honesty, too. I just don't know where to find it."

Elyssa hung up and strode outside to await Hunter's arrival. She grimaced when the patrol car cruised down the street and halted beside the curb. Debating turning on her heel and dashing back into the house, she reminded herself that she was a big girl now, she could deal with Gavin Spencer. Although the symbol of law and order in this part of the country was a first-class jerk who deserved to be treated as such, Elyssa made an attempt to be civil.

"That wasn't much of a greeting I got earlier," Gavin said after he had rolled down the window.

"What were you expecting?"

"I was hoping to let bygones be bygones." Gavin smiled charmingly. "We were both just kids back then, Elyssa. I'd like the chance to make peace and start all over."

Elyssa asked herself if she was the kind of person who held longstanding grudges, and she decided she was—at least in this case. She didn't owe Gavin Spencer one damned thing, especially not forgiveness for his unspeakable cruelty. He hadn't said he was sorry about what had happened. But then, he had never seemed the type to shoulder blame for much of anything.

She was positively certain that, to hear Gavin tell it, both his ex-wives were at fault in the failed marriages. This blond Viking god couldn't have been the problem, now could he? Yeah, right, thought Elyssa.

When she saw Hunter turning the corner, she gave Gavin the cold shoulder and turned away. "Excuse me, I have to go."

"I'll be around, sugar," he called after her.

Elyssa didn't miss Gavin's sharklike smile, the husky tone of his voice, or the way his silver-blue eyes slid over her body in masculine speculation. The creep. Ten to one, this Casanova cop had been screwing around on both of his wives and they'd found out about it. Gavin was free again and definitely on the make, but he was crazy if he thought Elyssa wanted anything to do with him. As far as she was concerned, he could go straight to hell and she would be glad to tell him what he could to himself when he got there!

* * *

Nathan noted the clenching of Elyssa's jaw and her rigid carriage as she marched toward the pickup. He had detected the same degree of hostility when she had confronted Gavin Spencer outside Hollister's Cafe. There was definitely a conflict here; he just didn't have a clue as to what it was.

Nathan had made a point of posing a few questions at the grain elevator. There had been a cluster of farmers and ranchers in the office, sipping the free coffee Harvest Grain Company doled out. From what Nathan could ascertain, Gavin Spencer had worked on Rawlins Ranch in the summers while in high school. That would have put him there at the same time Elyssa was making her yearly visits to her father.

Had there been a budding romance, at least on Elyssa's part? Maybe she harbored resentment because Lover Boy Spencer had jilted her. Gavin's love-'em-and-leave-'em philosophy had to have originated somewhere.

The pickup shuddered when Elyssa slammed the door and flounced onto the seat. She stared straight ahead, steaming mad. Nathan broke into a smile. Beneath that sophisticated poise and elegant beauty was a feisty temper—another testimonial to the fact that she was her father's daughter.

"Still don't want to talk about it?" he asked.

"No, and it doesn't say much for the community of Rawlins if they hired that butthead as their chief of police!"

"I have the same reaction when I cross paths with my ex-wife."

Nathan cruised past the patrol car and waved cordially to the chief of police. Elyssa's seething glance indicated she considered Nathan a traitor for acknowledging Gavin's presence, though she didn't come right out and say so.

She twisted around to note that the pickup bed was stacked with feed sacks. Nathan's faithful dog Ricky sat atop the pile like a king on his throne. Elyssa reflected on those days—a lifetime ago—when her father used to load her up in his truck and drive into town to purchase feed for the cows he planned to breed. She and Ely had had long discussions on every topic imaginable during those trips. Those were pleasurable moments. She mourned the fact that there hadn't been more of them.

Although Jessica Rawlins Cutler had tried to make Elyssa forget her country background by uprooting her and replanting her in the City, Elyssa remembered the contentment of ranch life. As a teenager, she had lived for those three-week visits . . . until her accident.

Conflicting sensations warred inside her. Serenity clashed with remembered terror. Coming home after all these years, under such bleak circumstances, was tearing her to pieces. She wanted to recapture that sense of peace she had discovered here. And yet, she needed to seek refuge in her apartment, surrounding herself with distractions that kept the disconcerting memories at bay.

Nathan cast Elyssa a thoughtful glance as they drove toward the ranch. He could sense her anxiety. It was as palpable as the wind. Something was eating her up inside. He just didn't know what that something was. The lady was obviously accustomed to keeping her own counsel. Nathan followed the same practice, so who was he to complain? Ely Rawlins was the only man he had ever confided in. Now he had lost a friend and business partner, and a substitute father . . .

The thought made Nathan all the more determined to see Ely's wishes enforced. He couldn't just throw up his hands and walk away. He owed Ely favors that could never be repaid. He was going to have to try his hand at influencing Elyssa.

"Before you head back to the City, there is something I would like to show you at the ranch," he said.

Her head whipped around, her dark hair catching fire in the sunlight. "How did you know I wanted to go back to my apartment?"

His broad shoulder lifted in a shrug. "It stands to reason. I hauled you out here on short notice to perform duties neither of us wanted to face. You haven't been around for years. Why would you want to stay here?"

"Why indeed?" she muttered.

Nathan fell silent as he sped toward the ranch. Elyssa needed time to compose herself after an emotionally taxing morning and a frustrating afternoon. She also needed time to recover from the shocking jolt of running into a man she obviously didn't remember with fond affection—Gavin Spencer.

And Nathan had to decide how to handle Elyssa.

There were things she needed to know, but Nathan hesitated about telling her before she calmed down. For certain, he wasn't going to shepherd her into a room and overwhelm her the way Gil and Company probably had. He wasn't going to patronize her, either. Elyssa was too intelligent not to see through that ploy.

No, he would come up with a subtle strategy to gain her cooperation. He had fifteen miles to figure out what the hell that strategy was going to be.

Valerie Mitchell cursed whoever was beating on her front door. After her earlier conversation with Elyssa, she had lain back in bed and indulged herself in more sleep. She had stayed out until the honky-tonk had shut down for the night, sipping a little too freely on drinks that had left her head feeling like an overly ripe cantaloupe. She had come home alone, despite the invitation from a man who turned out to be less of an authentic cowboy than he had led her to believe. All he had to his credit was the fact that he had attended a Garth Brooks concert at the Myriad and two rodeos at the fair grounds!

Elyssa was right. There were a lot of urban cowboys milling about in the City streets. Valerie's ongoing search for a *real* man was as frustrating as Prince Charming's quest for the matching glass slipper.

The incessant hammering at the door provoked Valerie's mumbled curse. Levering up, she grabbed her robe and mopped the tangle of blond hair away from her face. When she opened the door, she scowled at the unwanted guest.

"What do you want?"

Robert Grayson toyed with his stylish necktie and switched on his hundred-watt smile, Valerie squeezed her eyes shut against the glare.

"I want to talk to Elyssa," he requested.

Valerie had never been a Robert Grayson fan. Less now than ever. She had never been more than distantly polite to the man, and she had good reason to be even less sociable now.

"In case you haven't figured it out, Robert, you're at the top of Elyssa's shit list. And for excellent reasons. She doesn't want to see you. *I* don't want to see you, either, and *I* wasn't even engaged to you!"

Robert invited himself inside, much to Valerie's dismay. "I have to talk to Elyssa. I have to apologize for something I deeply regret."

"Like screwing around on the side?" Valerie asked.

"It was all a mistake—"

"Yeah, and you made it. Party's over. Take your eternally sorry routine somewhere else. Elyssa isn't buying it."

"I think," Robert said, struggling to control his temper, "this is between Elyssa and me."

"Obviously not." Valerie smirked. "You already invited in a third party. Anybody I know?"

Robert was relieved to hear Elyssa hadn't gone into detail. "It just happened. It didn't mean a thing."

"That's supposed to make Elyssa feel better?" She scoffed at his feeble explanation. "Let's face it, Robert, you fouled up big-time. I always thought Elyssa could have done a lot better. You proved it to her yesterday. Besides that, she's got other things on her mind right now. Her father died in an accident—"

"David Cutler's dead?" Robert choked out.

"No, Elyssa's real father. She is going to be busy, and she doesn't need your disruptive presence right now. So why don't you trot back to your bimbo and leave her alone."

Robert glanced toward the bedroom door. "I want to see her."

"She isn't here, and I don't know when she'll be back."

"Is she at the ranch?" Robert persisted. "What's the address?"

Valerie rolled her eyes. "Ranches don't have addresses. They have directions."

"Then give me directions. I need to be there for Elyssa."

"Just like you were yesterday when she caught you with your pants down?" Valerie glared at him through bloodshot eyes. "Give it up. You're history."

Robert spun toward the door. Somebody around here knew how to get in touch with Elyssa . . . Her secretary! Robert recalled hearing Brenda Landon grumble about all the calls she'd received from Elyssa's father. At least he could get the phone number of the ranch. That was a start.

When Robert strode off, Valerie closed the door with a "Good riddance" and aimed herself toward the shower, thankful she had been able to head him off at the pass. The last thing Elyssa needed right now was to deal with that ass.

Virgil Rawlins stood on his father's front porch, reflecting on the conference with Elyssa. Things were in a bigger tangle than he had expected after Ely died. He had presumed the situation would resolve itself without much fuss, but that hadn't happened. Elyssa was going to be difficult. Nathan Hunter had gotten to her first and had planted suspicions in her mind. Virgil wondered how much Nathan knew—and to what extremes he intended to go to ensure he wasn't cut out without a cent.

There had to be a way to sway Elyssa, to make certain she didn't fall into Nathan's trap. The man could be very persuasive when he wanted to be. Hadn't he won Ely over?

Too bad Virgil wasn't in a position to seduce Elyssa into cooperation. He figured that was the technique Nathan planned to employ. Perhaps that tactic could work to Virgil's advantage if he warned Elyssa of what to expect.

Virgil ambled toward his truck, an idea beginning to hatch in his mind. He knew a way to throw a wrench in Nathan's strategy and convince Elyssa to side with her blood kin. Things would work out just fine. Virgil had a few other tricks up his sleeve, too. When he got through with Hunter, Elyssa wouldn't put stock in anything that pesky cowboy said or did.

Eight

Elyssa stumbled to a halt when Nathan ushered her into her father's office. The tactic might be a little cruel, but it was unmistakably effective, Nathan realized. The instant Elyssa spied the portrait of Ely hanging over the mantel, she gasped for breath and stared, entranced, at the lifelike painting.

"Damn you, Hunter," she said. "I don't need this!"

Nathan steered her toward the chair, directly across the room from where Ely Rawlins stared down with those dark, penetrating eyes. "I think you do," he contradicted. "You need to be reminded of what your father stood for *and* against."

"Meaning?" Elyssa felt that niggling tingle at the base of her neck as she peered at the portrait. She was too vulnerable, too aware, too entangled in a maelstrom of conflicting memories. Nathan Hunter was shrewd, she'd give him that. He was a master at emotional sorcery. He struck *where* she was most vulnerable, *when* she was most vulnerable.

Nathan stood behind Elyssa, captivated by the portrait. "The bottom line is that you are now part owner of Rawlins Ranch, no matter what caused your lack of contact with the place these past years. You're still Ely's daughter. You're still the extension of his will, and so am I."

"Why? Because you were so fond of him or because you want part of what he had?"

Nathan didn't respond to the pointed question. He simply ambled around in front of her, blocking the overwhelming effect of the portrait. "I want you to take a ride around the ranch with me before you leave," he requested.

"Why?"

He smiled down into her haunted features. "I think you'll know the answer to that by the time we get back. I won't have to tell you. I'll let the ride speak for itself. Then we'll talk."

"Hunter, did anybody ever tell you you are an exasperating man?" Elyssa grumbled, massaging her neck where that unnerving sensation pebbled the skin.

"Do you have appropriate clothes for horseback riding?"

Elyssa was beginning to realize that Hunter usually answered a question with a question. Was she playing out of her league? He was nothing like the men she was used to, and she could never quite decide how to handle him.

Salt of the earth, Valerie would say. And there was nothing shallow about Nathan Hunter, despite Elyssa's skepticism about his motives. Indeed he might be every woman's fantasy come true, with his powerful physique and rugged good looks, but he could become Elyssa's worst nightmare if she didn't watch out.

Before she could deny his request—avoid being alone on the wide-open range with a man Valerie Mitchell would kill to get her hands on—Nathan moved away, letting the impact of Ely's portrait take hold of Elyssa again. The unexplained feeling that had assailed her earlier struck hard and deep, searing her very core like a laser beam. It was the damnedest thing she had ever experienced. The intensity of her father's probing gaze had been accurately captured on canvas. It was as if he were staring down at her, trying to tell her something, silently calling out to her from beyond.

"If you don't have riding clothes, I might be able to borrow something from Althea or Claudia," Nathan was saying when Elyssa touched down to earth.

She didn't take her eyes off the portrait. "Round me up a suitable outfit, cowboy. If nothing else, I'm curious to know what it is you really want from me. Obviously you have decided not to use Uncle Gil's whirlwind approach of thrusting a contract under my nose and cramming a pen in my hand so I might sign on the dotted line."

"I'll see what I can do about riding wear," he offered before he left Elyssa alone with the silence and the unsettling effect of her father's portrait.

Tears pooled in her eyes as she peered at Ely's image. His arms were crossed over his wide chest, and his head was tilted at a familiar angle, as if he were on the verge of making a comment. Elyssa would have given anything to know what her father had wanted to discuss with her before the accident.

According to Uncle Gil, he'd intended to ask her to accept the title of financial advisor to ensure that the ranch received another government subsidy. According to Hunter, Ely had had other things on his mind, too. Hunter was being suspiciously patient in making his move, setting her up with far more finesse than Uncle Gil had employed. But that didn't mean the outcome wouldn't be the same, Elyssa reminded herself.

"Elyssa?"

She glanced up to see Althea Gilbert hovering at the door. The housekeeper had aged considerably, and presented a contrast to the image Elyssa had carried in her memories. Althea hailed from sturdy country stock. Her features were plain, but when she smiled her whole face lit up and her indigo eyes sparkled with youthful spirit. Elyssa remembered this woman had rarely minced words and had held her own with the hired hands who'd playfully teased her.

Althea had been a permanent fixture at the ranch, raising her daughter without a father, for he had refused to marry Althea when she'd become pregnant. Ely had taken Althea on despite Jessica's objections and distaste, and the housekeeper had always been kind to Elyssa.

"I'm really sorry about your dad," Althea now murmured. "I . . ." She swallowed hard before walking over to lay the clean but faded clothes on Elyssa's lap. "If there is anything I can do, just say the word, hon." She reached out to place a comforting hand on Elyssa's shoulder and gave it a gentle squeeze before adding, "Nate went down to the barn to saddle the horses. He said to come down when you're ready."

Althea lingered by Elyssa's side for a long moment. She peered at the portrait and then glanced down to see the mist in Elyssa's dark eyes. "Are you going to be okay out there, honey? You haven't ridden since the—"

Elyssa shot out of her chair and clutched the faded clothes to her chest. "I'd better change." She cast Althea a teary smile. "Thanks."

When Elyssa stepped into the hall she found Claudia lurking within earshot. What a contrast between the stout, unadorned Althea and Claudia, mother and daughter. Althea had never been one to plaster on makeup or dress in a manner that called excessive attention to her feminine assets. Claudia, on the other hand, was wearing skin-tight jeans and a blouse that clung to her full breasts like syrup to pancakes. And when it came to facepaint, Tammy Faye Bakker had nothing on Claudia. It was a wonder the younger woman could keep her eyes open with all that black mascara caked to her lashes.

Elyssa sensed she was being sized up during those few seconds of silence. When Claudia finally pushed away from the wall, there was a hint of unexplained hostility in her expression, though Elyssa suspected the younger woman was trying not to show it.

"Sorry, Elyssa," Claudia mumbled awkwardly.

"Thank you." Elyssa strode toward the stairs, revising her impression of Claudia as she went. The little girl in pigtails who had tagged along behind the hired hands had changed drastically. Now Claudia was all grown up. Elyssa imagined she was still chasing after men, though. She wondered how many Claudia had caught, and whether Hunter was one of them.

* * *

Ray Twigger swung down from his horse as Nathan emerged from the barn with two saddled mounts.

"What's up?" he asked.

"I'm taking Elyssa riding."

Nathan checked the leather straps to make certain the tack was in good working order. The last thing he wanted was for Elyssa to take a spill because of faulty equipment.

Les Fykes hopped off his horse and shot a glance toward the house. "I'll volunteer to give the little lady a grand tour. I got a look at her when she left this morning. Man, is she stacked! And did you notice the size of those bumpers—?"

"Les!" Nathan snapped. "A little inappropriate, don't you think, considering what happened recently?"

Les glanced every which way except at Nathan. "Yeah, I suppose so. But she's gorgeous."

"I'm sure she'll be pleased to know you think so," Nathan said.

He focused his attention on Ray Twigger, who had been a friend since their childhood days in Texas. When Ray had been hired to transport the livestock to rodeos, Ely had become fond of Twig—Ray's nickname—and had offered him a job on the sprawling ranch, in between runs to rodeos.

"I picked up the cattle cubes while I was in town this morning," Nathan informed Twig. "Why don't you and Mo-Joe string out the feed in the north pasture after I introduce you to your new boss."

"Sure thing, Nate . . ."

Twig's voice trailed off as he swiveled his head around to see what had drawn the other ranch hands' attention. "Good Lord, I don't know if I'll be able to regard her as a boss, either, Nate," Twig confided. "That's one well-constructed woman."

Nathan chafed at the spectacle of four ranch hands devouring Elyssa with hungry eyes. Nobody deserved to look *that* good in faded jeans and a flannel shirt. The soft fabric hugged her curvaceous figure, making the graceful sway of her hips poetry in motion. Even the hint of a limp didn't detract from her naturally provocative gait.

The sunlight danced in her auburn hair and sparkled in those black diamond eyes that reminded him so much of Ely's. There were no two ways about it; Elyssa Rawlins Cutler had the kind of class and style that defied the cut of any clothes. She would look terrific in anything . . . and even better in nothing at all . . .

Nathan felt he was betraying Ely's memory by thinking things that would offend the father of this beautiful woman, and he was amazed that Elyssa was unaware of the rapt attention and lusty speculation she had drawn. Damn, was the lady always this oblivious of her effect on men?

If it had been Claudia Gilbert standing there, she would have been soaking up the attention. Elyssa, however, appeared to be engaged in surveying the area for changes that had taken place over the years.

Nathan shook himself out of his pensive trance and gestured toward Twig and the other farm hands. "Elyssa . . . Ray Twigger, Les Fykes, Mo-Joe Denson, and Skeeter Jeffries."

Elyssa offered each man a cordial smile, thinking Valerie would consider herself in heaven if she were here. Salt of the earth, Elyssa mused. These were men who considered ranching a way of life, not just a job. They were challenged mentally and physically on a daily basis, and they defied the worst Mother Nature could fling at them. These men preferred to straddle a horse and commune with nature rather than push papers about on a desk while buttoned into a three-piece suit.

"Glad to meet ya, ma'am." Ray Twigger swept the hat from his head, revealing sandy brown hair, wiped his hand on his shirt, and extended the hand to Elyssa.

She was certain Valerie would have been drooling if she'd gotten an eyeful of Ray. His face was deeply tanned, his features distinct. With those golden brown eyes, those dimples, that lopsided smile, and his Texas drawl, he could turn a lady's head—and fast.

Mo-Joe Denson was a few inches shorter than Ray Twigger and not quite as muscularly built. He wasn't, Elyssa noted, quite as handsome, either. He certainly was no match in size and stature for Hunter, but he had an engaging smile and silver-gray eyes that were fanned with thick, black lashes.

Elyssa gave herself a mental shake for making those comparisons, then turned her attention to Les Fykes. His assessing gaze was still sweeping from the top of her head to the toes of her scuffed boots, and when she met his dark eyes with a challenging lift to her brows, he ducked his head and kicked at the clump of grass beneath his foot. Clearly he felt awkward about being caught gawking. That gave Elyssa the chance to scrutinize this lanky, rawboned cowboy with wavy brown hair.

Finally turning her attention to Skeeter Jeffries, she smiled at the awe-struck expression on the younger man's face. His boyish features gave him an endearing quality that made her want to reach out and ruffle that tuft of sun-bleached brown hair. Skeeter was adorable in a rugged sort of way.

"Are you ready, Cutler?" Nathan questioned, breaking the silence.

Elyssa found herself led toward a roan gelding and deposited in the saddle. It had been years since she had been on a horse. She would probably wind up with bowlegs and saddle sores by the time Hunter finished dragging her all over creation. She still hadn't figured out what strategy he planned to use to persuade her to his way of thinking—whatever the hell that was.

When the pair rode off, Les Fykes whistled wolfishly. "Damn, that's one female who can make a man's nuts ache at first glance."

"Don't be crude, Fykes," Twig admonished, his gaze still glued to Elyssa's departing back and the aureole of sunlight that glowed around her dark head.

"As if you aren't thinking the same thing," Les said with a chuckle. "You can't take your eyes off her, either."

"Maybe not," Mo-Joe spoke up, "but at least Twig has the

good manners not to blurt out his thoughts. Your problem is you don't get enough female attention to keep your hormones in check."

"There aren't a lot of women moving in my circles," Les grumbled. "Especially ones that look like *her.*"

"That's hardly Elyssa's fault," Skeeter interjected. "I think we should show her respect. She just lost her dad, and she doesn't need to be hit on by the likes of us."

Les stared at the two riders who had maneuvered through the gate and now trotted across the pasture. "I hope Nate can remember that. He was looking her over himself."

"Get to work, Fykes," Twig ordered. "We have cows to feed and calves to check."

"I hate to say it, Twig, but Fykes is right," Mo-Joe piped up. "Even Cool Hand Nate is going to have trouble remembering Elyssa is going through rough times right now. It'd be hard as hell to offer a little compassion and leave it at that." He frowned as another thought skipped through his mind. "I wonder what she plans to do with her half of the ranch?"

Twig stuffed his hands in his gloves and smiled wryly. "I imagine Nate intends to find out . . ."

"I reckon so. I just wonder how susceptible he is to distraction?" Mo-Joe mused aloud.

Twig was wondering the same thing himself about his long-time friend. Nate had his work cut out for him if he thought he could keep his interest strictly on business. Not one man hadn't taken his Texas time in giving Elyssa the once-over.

Nate definitely wasn't immune, Twig mused. Only time would tell how much willpower he had when it came to the new boss on Rawlins Ranch . . .

Nathan halted his horse on the knoll that overlooked the grassy slopes where purebred Beefmaster cows grazed alongside their young calves. To the north was a pasture stocked with Simmental cows. Purebred Limousins grazed in the pas-

ture to the south. Nathan had convinced Ely to crossbreed the
various herds to develop the best beef cattle on the market.
Their experimentation had been successful, and Nathan was
proud of his contribution to the success of this ranch and to
the cattle industry. His degree in agronomy and agricultural
economics—Ely had insisted he acquire it—had paid off for
Rawlins Ranch.

Nathan set aside his memories of the work he and Ely had
done together and stared into the distance. The panoramic view
of Oklahoma prairie was spectacular. He didn't know how such
a magnificent scene could help but have a soothing effect on
Elyssa. It damned sure did wonders for his own disposition.
His grief and frustration flitted off in the breeze as he stared
across the rolling countryside.

God's country. Nathan could commune with nature here. He
could get back in touch with himself, shrug off troubling
thoughts, and let his soul soar.

"Ely used to say he would rather have these eight thousand
acres of fertile Oklahoma soil—"

". . . than a hundred thousand acres of sagebrush and
sparse grass in west Texas, New Mexico, or Arizona," Elyssa
finished for him. "We can raise one cow to three acres on
these plush pastures while those damnfool ranchers to the west
can stock only one cow to twenty-five acres."

Nathan glanced over to see the rueful smile on Elyssa's lips,
the sparkle of tears in her obsidian eyes. Impulsively, he
reached out to reroute the betraying droplet that cascaded down
her cheek, but she automatically jerked away from his touch.

"Sorry, Cutler. No harm intended. I didn't mean to depress
or startle you."

Elyssa blinked back the tears and straightened in the saddle.
"Didn't you? Isn't that what this little jaunt is all about? Now
that I'm vulnerable, sitting here on the verge of tears, you plan
to tell me what my father *supposedly* wanted when he called
yesterday."

"No. I brought you out here to remind you of what Ely

worked for all his life." Nathan nudged his blood red gelding along the cattle trail. Elyssa's mount followed obediently behind. "Your father loved this ranch. It was his heritage and now it's yours. It behooves you to remember what this place meant to Ely before you decide what you want to do with it, or rather what *he* would have wanted you to do with it."

Elyssa stared at Nathan's broad back. To hear him talk, one would think he was promoting the continuation of the pioneer tradition. If so, why the conflict between Uncle Gil's clan and Nathan? Was she supposed to be overwhelmed by a ranch where you could sit atop a horse on a high rise of ground and not see the boundaries of the property, even with binoculars? Was she to then dump her heritage in Nathan's lap and let him carry on as he claimed her father would have wanted her to do? Damn it, what was this man's angle? What was it he really wanted from her?

They rode in silence for a half-hour before Elyssa spotted the plunging red rock canyons that were not only part of her own nightmare but also of her father's last living contact with this ranch. Flashbacks from her past shot through in her mind.

Willfully, she battled the painful images and strove to maintain control of her emotions. She had come this far, she reminded herself. She had returned to this ranch after a twelve-year absence. If she could exorcise those ghosts, maybe the wounds of adolescence would finally begin to heal.

As Elyssa nudged her horse along the path that circled the western rim of the yawning canyon, Nathan watched her curiously. He had wondered if she would insist on avoiding this area after he'd told her what happened to her father. Obviously not. There was a determined set to her spine as she followed the trail.

He rode in her wake, feeling strangely drawn to her, wanting to peek beneath that reserved shell of hers, dying to know why she had abandoned this place and her own father.

Elyssa paused near the crumbling ledge. She didn't know if she had come here in the hopes of revisiting the scene of her own accident and of making peace with herself . . . or to fuel old resentments.

The last time she was here, she had tumbled down these canyon walls. Her gaze dropped to the jagged boulders, remembering them cutting into her flesh as she'd plummeted over the slope to land in a mangled heap. The fall had changed the course of her life, leaving her with physical and emotional wounds, scars she refused to let the rest of the world see.

After she had cartwheeled down this slope, it had been six months before she'd been able to attempt to walk again. Her mother and stepfather had hired the best surgeons in the state to piece her back together, the way the King's men had tried to patch up Humpty Dumpty, all because . . .

The tormenting memories Elyssa kept locked deep inside came boiling to the surface. All these years she had been too ashamed and guilt ridden to confide in another living soul. As a result the haunting visions she experienced flung her into a turmoil. She wanted to face the terrifying incident, but it was still too painful, too poignant . . .

Nudging her horse, she trotted off, hearing the echo of tormenting voices, remembering her anguish and the years of suffering.

Nathan watched, bemused, as Elyssa thundered off, looking as if she were chased by demons. Damn, maybe this hadn't been one of his brighter ideas. He had wanted her to find that same inner peace he enjoyed. For him, this was part of the healing process—accepting the loss of a friend, a father figure, and a mentor. For Elyssa, it must have been a visit to hell, though he couldn't understand why she'd reacted as she had while she sat staring over the western edge of the canyon.

When Nathan's mount sidestepped beneath him, he pulled on the reins, letting Elyssa ride off her frustration alone. She flew across the pasture as if she had spent years in the saddle—she probably had, if Ely had had anything to do with it.

To Nathan's stunned amazement, Elyssa reined to a halt not twenty yards from the crumbling edge where Ely had been found. He watched her swing down to walk along the cliff. She stood there, the wind lifting her hair like an unseen hand, and stared down the rock-cluttered slope that ended in a jungle of trees and underbrush.

Nathan held his breath when Elyssa sidestepped down the steep incline he had followed to where Ely lay in a broken heap. She was gutsier than he was at this moment. He wasn't sure he was ready to face that particular spot again. Ely's horse hadn't been removed from the base of the canyon. If Elyssa didn't know for certain what site she had stumbled upon, she would very soon.

A wail that resembled the cry of the damned echoed off the chasm's walls. The sound went through Nathan, making his nerves taut as harp strings. Christ, he had probably outsmarted himself by bringing her out here. Now she would probably sign any document Gil shoved at her and would then hightail it away from this ranch. Ely wasn't going to be pleased with the way Nathan had handled things. From the anguish in Elyssa's voice, he had screwed up royally.

Nine

Elyssa collapsed on a chair-size boulder before her knees gave out on her. The indescribable feeling that had assaulted her the instant she'd torn off across the pasture was now so overwhelming it stole her breath away. It was as if she had been instinctively drawn to this site, lured down the ragged tumble of rocks . . .

The sound of her own tormented shriek reached her ears before she realized she was howling like a dying coyote. The carcass of the piebald horse had told the tale. Elyssa trembled, broke into a cold sweat. She cursed the wasted years, a father's love come and gone, a broken marriage that deprived a young daughter of the father she had worshipped. Her bottled-up resentment came pouring out, and she realized she had never forgiven her mother for stealing precious times from her.

Still it was her own foolishness, her ignorance, that had contributed to severing the last bond she'd had with her father. That and Cousin Virgil's cruel prank, she reminded herself between shuddering sobs.

Nobody had asked her what she'd wanted in all those troubled years. Nobody had considered how she'd been hurting inside, how guilty she'd felt when she'd been torn between her natural father and the kind, generous man who had adopted her. To Elyssa, Jessica Rawlins Cutler didn't deserve the love of two good men. She believed her mother would have been just as happy without a daughter, except that Elyssa was the perfect tool to ensure that Jessica got everything she wanted, when she wanted it.

To all the world, Elyssa was a pampered debutante, an heiress to two fortunes. Elyssa Rawlins Cutler had it made. How many times had she heard that? Too damned many to count. The statement had been whispered behind her back when no one thought she could hear. But she had heard. And what did she really have? The best clothes and education money could buy? Perhaps, but she also had physical and emotional scars that went bone deep, soul deep.

She sobbed, drawing in air in huge gulps. For a moment, she wondered if a person could drown in her own tears.

Nathan Hunter probably thought she was having a nervous breakdown. Well, maybe she was. God, she didn't know she had so much water in her! Her eyes were flowing like twin rivers. Elyssa put her face in her hands and cried some more. She didn't even hear Nathan's approach until he wrapped a comforting arm around her.

Immediately she pulled back into her own space, out of force of habit. She was all set to take her frustration out on anyone within shouting distance until she tilted her head to see the pinched expression on Hunter's bronzed face . . . and the glistening mist in his eyes.

Either Hunter was one helluva an actor or he was hurting, same as she was—if not for the same reasons. No matter what Uncle Gil and Cousin Virgil said about this man's true purpose, he must have cared about Ely.

"You shouldn't be down here," Nathan rasped. *"I* shouldn't be down here, either. Yesterday was bad enough. I never intended for you to—"

To Elyssa's surprise, and to Nathan's, she flung her arms around his neck and hung on to him as if he were her lifeline. It was uncharacteristic for Elyssa to let anyone this close. According to Robert Grayson, icebergs froze solid and never thawed. Well, wouldn't that two-timer be shocked if he could see his ex-fiancée wrapped around a man—one who was practically a stranger.

Nathan was shocked when Elyssa grabbed him and held on for dear life, but he wasn't complaining about having the stuffing squeezed out of him. He drew her closer while she soaked the front of his shirt with tears. His chin rested on the silky strands of hair on the crown of her head, and his arms contracted when shudders undulated through her, vibrating through him like echoes of his own remorse.

He wanted to console her, wanted to magically wave his arms and make everything right again; but he couldn't, not for either of them. So he simply held her while she cried, and he wept silently inside.

After what seemed an eternity, Elyssa's composure began to return. She had done her grieving this morning and again this afternoon. She had to accept what had happened, had to learn to cope. She must get through the next few days. Eventually time would heal the open wounds.

She tipped her head back to apologize for throwing herself at Hunter in mournful desperation. When her gaze locked with glistening pools of blue, however, the words she'd intended to voice evaporated on her lips. His full, sensuous mouth was a hairbreadth away from hers. The musky scent of his cologne filled her senses. She was aware of the whipcord muscles of his back beneath her suddenly sensitive fingertips, of the hardness of the chest meshed against her. Every ragged breath he inhaled reverberated through her, intensifying her keen response to him.

That strange sensation tickled the base of her neck again. Something more intense and powerful than common sense, something beyond the normal realm of understanding was luring her closer to him, was calling to her. Although she would ordinarily want to withdraw when a man was this close, Elyssa didn't experience any such desire when Hunter's dark head dipped down and his moist lips took gentle possession of hers.

Funny, it was like the Prince kissing Snow White back to

life after she had munched on the witch's poisoned apple. Corny, Elyssa thought as she melted beneath a kiss that gave more than it demanded in return . . .

To her own amazement, she didn't even protest when Hunter's hands glided over her hips, pulling her even closer. Now it was difficult to tell where his powerful body ended and hers began.

Elyssa could feel the changes that overcame Hunter when he kissed her, and she was starkly aware of her own heated response. A coil of hot desire burgeoned inside her when his hands scaled her ribs to brush the swells of her breasts. His darting tongue fanned the flames that spread through her with the speed of a crown fire.

Then, suddenly, Elyssa recoiled in embarrassment and shame. Dear Lord, her father hadn't even been laid to rest and she was— Damn it, she didn't know *what* she was doing!

But she did, now that she had put enough space between her and this sensual wild man to think straight. She was playing right into Hunter's hands. Cousin Virgil couldn't utilize this tactic, but Hunter could. And he possessed all the skills necessary for seduction, didn't he? He had been on this ranch long enough to consider it home. He wanted to stay; that was obvious. Was this what the touching little soliloquy on the hilltop was all about, not to mention this steamy kiss in the canyon.

Hunter had brought her out here to tear down her defenses and expose her vulnerabilities. He probably knew about her accident twelve years ago.

Nathan knew immediately that suspicion had begun to cloud Elyssa's mind. She had wrapped her arms around herself and stepped away, staring at him with mistrust. Damn, he hadn't meant for things to go quite that far because he'd known exactly how she would interpret it.

"I know you think—"

"Spare me, please," she muttered, presenting her back.

He admired her resilience. The lady had true grit. Ely would have been damned proud. As for Nathan he was frustrated as hell because he knew he would have been as suspicious as she was if their roles were reversed.

"Okay, Hunter, I concede this round to you," Elyssa said begrudgingly. "And granted, you have a lot more panache than the Rawlins clan. But don't you have a pen and a document stashed in your jeans—something you want me to sign right about now?"

"There is nothing in my pockets that your passionate response didn't put there, Cutler."

Elyssa lurched around to pick her way up the jutting rocks, but not before hurling a glare that didn't invite translation. That look was worth a thousand words, none of them flattering.

He shrugged off Elyssa's glower. "I let myself get carried away. So did you, even if you're too hardheaded to admit it. What just happened wasn't about contracts or expected favors."

"No? A simple attack of lust then?" she challenged as she grabbed hold of a seedling to hoist herself upward.

"Is that what it was to you, Cutler?" he queried as he followed after her.

She wondered if he kept responding to her questions with questions to throw her off balance. Probably. "No, what just happened was nothing more than grief and frustration reaching out for compassion," she maintained.

"Are you sure I wasn't the warm body you used to punish your ex-fiancé for what he did?"

That did it! Elyssa impulsively scooped up a rock and cocked her arm. Before she could launch her improvised missile a deep chuckle reverberated in his chest.

"Before you start throwing things, ask yourself *who* was using *whom*. Or maybe the truth is, *you* got to me to the same degree I got to you. Just plain old mutual attraction at work, Cutler. Is that such a hard thing for you to admit? Or are you still too knee deep in your I've-sworn-off-men-forever rituals to admit— Hey!"

Nathan leaped sideways when the rock sailed down at him. The toe of his boot caught in the tangle of vines and he stum-

bled, off balance. Gravity got hold of him, and he went down
with all the grace of a falling giraffe.

Despite her irritation, Elyssa broke into a grin. This predatory cowboy didn't look quite so intimidating when he was
sprawled on the ground chewing on a mouthful of dirt.

"You were saying, Hunter?" she sassed him.

Nathan propped himself up on an elbow, wiped his mouth
on his sleeve. His arm stalled when he noticed the playful
smile that lit Elyssa's stunning face. Desire struck, hot and
heavy, and he wanted to be the reason for that enchanting
smile, not the brunt of her retaliation. *He wanted her.* If he
knew nothing else, he definitely knew that for a fact. His body
didn't lie.

"As I was saying . . . or trying to say . . ." He didn't release her from his probing gaze as he sat up cross-legged to
untangle vines from his boot. "All I really want is to go to
bed with you, for no other reason than we would both enjoy
it. At least I know I would . . ."

Elyssa nearly fell off the boulder she was perched on. She
and Hunter would never be intimate, no matter how startling
and intense her reaction to him was. It wouldn't be because
she wouldn't let it, not even if she wanted to. She was sure
she would confront the same insurmountable obstacles that had
always spoiled her relationships with men. It was better not to
tamper with something that could end in disaster.

"Only in your dreams, Hunter," she muttered before she
twisted around to scale the red rock cliff.

Nathan picked himself up and dusted himself off, marveling
at the speed with which she changed her disposition. One minute
she was grieving, the next she was passionate, in the blink of
an eye she was suspicious and aloof. And then he had opened
his big mouth . . . and stuck his size-twelve boot in it.

Damn it to hell, hadn't he come down hard on Les Fykes
for remarks made at inappropriate moments? Yet he wasn't a
damned bit better. He had alienated Elyssa with that bold dec-

laration. But she had gotten to him in ways he hadn't anticipated.

What really rankled was he knew she had been as deeply involved in that kiss as he had been. The only difference was, he openly admitted what he wanted. Elyssa didn't want to face the fact that there was a powerful chemistry between them. She was bound and determined to deny what had just happened.

Nathan glanced up at the ridge where Elyssa sat her horse, staring at some distant point. He really couldn't blame her for being wary of him. Thanks to Robert the flake, she anticipated being used and betrayed.

When Nathan scrambled up the slope, she was waiting for him, rubbing that spot on her neck that seemed to bother her constantly. She was also regarding him, an odd, trancelike expression on her face.

"Was he coming or going, Hunter?" she asked, strangely preoccupied.

Nathan did a double take. "What?"

"My father." She stared at the conglomeration of hoofprints trampled on the grass. "Do you think Dad was going out or coming home when the accident occurred?"

Nathan pulled himself onto the ledge and strode toward his horse. When he had swung into the saddle, he stared down at the prints left by the rescue party. "It's impossible to say one way or another. Something bothering you, Cutler?"

Something was, but Elyssa couldn't satisfactorily explain the niggling feeling channeling through her. It wasn't a premonition because she didn't consider herself psychic. It was . . .

She dropped her hand to the pommel of the saddle, letting the sensation run its full course without trying to massage it away. Great-grandmother Mae's words came back to her in a whisper. She could almost see the old woman sitting on the porch of the cottage Althea and Claudia now occupied, telling the stories passed down to her, stories about the People, as the Cheyenne called themselves. The Cheyenne claimed to possess a deep sense of understanding that manifested itself in their close communication with the spirits.

Elyssa squirmed in the saddle, unaccustomed to riding and unaccustomed to this . . . whatever it was that hammered at her so relentlessly when she reclaimed her roots, her childhood.

"Cutler, what the hell's wrong?" Nathan demanded to know.

Elyssa tossed him a distracted glance. "You'll probably think I'm crazy if I tell you."

That certainly got his attention. He didn't have the slightest idea where this conversation was going. "Try me."

She looked at him then, squarely in the eye. "How serious was the argument my father had with Uncle Gil?"

His blue eyes narrowed in questioning uncertainty. "What are you driving at?"

"Was it serious enough that Uncle Gil could have felt threatened by whatever Dad intended to tell me? Could someone have been desperate enough to make certain Dad wasn't around to keep our appointment?"

Nathan felt as if an invisible fist had landed in his midsection. His brows shot up and he couldn't breathe normally for a few seconds. "Jesus Christ, Cutler! Do you know what you're suggesting?"

Elyssa backed her horse away when she heard the thundering of hoofs, another rider approaching. "I do." She studied his shocked expression for a moment, wondering if it was a pretense or a sincere reaction. "Who found my father, Hunter?"

"I did."

"And how did you know where to look?"

"You think I shoved Ely off the cliff?"

"According to Uncle Gil, Dad planned to ask me to accept the title of financial advisor to acquire a government subsidy from the wheat program. How do I know for certain that Dad and Uncle Gil didn't argue about you? How can I be sure Uncle Gil didn't dig up some dirt and Dad confronted you with it? Uncle Gil has certainly made a point of warning me away from you, without coming right out and telling me why he sees you as a threat."

Elyssa backed her mount a little farther away. "All I know is I'm accosted by these strange feelings when I'm around you, Hunter. I sense something, but I can't interpret it. I can't quite trust you . . . or these unsettling sensations. But thanks to you, I can't put blind faith in my family, either . . ."

"Ms. Cutler!" Mo-Joe Denson galloped toward her, waving his hat over his head.

Damnation, if this messenger was bringing more bad news, Elyssa was going to adopt the ancient tactic of disposing of the courier. She was having enough trouble trying to ascertain who she should believe, if anyone. She didn't know which side of this simmering feud to take. She didn't need to have to deal with another emotional blow.

Mo-Joe skidded to a halt and stuffed the hat back on his head. "There's some guy at the house who insists he needs to see you immediately."

"Who is it?" Elyssa questioned.

"He didn't say. He just marched up and wanted to know where you were and started yammering about how he wasn't leaving until he saw you."

Elyssa didn't have the vaguest notion who awaited her, but she was thankful for the interruption. Those feelings were coming at her like bolts out of the blue, disrupting her sense of peace, provoking unnerving questions that refused to attach themselves to logical answers.

Nathan cursed foully after Elyssa cantered off with Mo-Joe Denson. He cringed at the thought of someone purposely disposing of Ely. Losing Ely was hell in itself. The prospect of someone having given him a fatal shove was unthinkable. Still, if Elyssa's weird feelings were correct, she could be in danger. Someone around here might want financial control of Rawlins Ranch.

Nathan trotted his mount back to the house. Elyssa's suspicions put him in one helluva position. If he kept his vow to fulfill Ely's wishes and did manage to convince her to side with him, he could be placing her life in jeopardy. Yet if he trusted her intuition and backed off, he might later discover she was simply suffering the stress of repetitive emotional blows. Then it might be too late to effect Ely's intentions.

And just who the hell was demanding Elyssa's presence at the house? Nathan wondered. Some hotshot lawyer Gil had called in to speak on his behalf? Odd, wasn't it, how the world could flip upside down in the time it took to draw a breath—or to take one's last breath?

Nathan glanced toward the horizon, watching clouds pile up like fluffy cotton balls. He swore he could see a ghost rider appearing and disappearing in those vaporous masses that were waiting to swallow the sun.

Ely Rawlins was out there somewhere.

Nathan was experiencing a few eerie feelings himself, and he, like Elyssa, didn't know what to make of them. Shrugging off his overactive imagination, he nudged his gelding into a canter. He needed to see what complications were awaiting him at the house . . .

"Elyssa? What the devil have you been doing?" Robert Grayson stared aghast at her faded clothes and scuffed boots, and at the wild tangles of hair that swirled around her puffy face. "My God, you look like a victim of Chernobyl!"

Elyssa halted in midstep when she spied her immaculately dressed ex-fiancé standing in the middle of the living room and looking ridiculously out of place.

"What are you doing here?" she asked.

"I came to offer my condolences, of course." Having recovered from the shock of seeing Elyssa looking like a tawdry orphan, Robert scurried forward to wrap a consoling arm around her. When she shrugged him off, his arms dropped limply to his side. "I feel like a royal ass," he confessed.

"How nice." She smiled spitefully. "Because I think you

are one. Now go away, Robert. I have nothing more to say to you."

"You don't know all the trouble I went to, just to find you."

"You don't know how little I care."

"I went to your apartment to apologize, and Valerie told me what happened."

Val had never been a member of Grayson's fan club. He had probably caught an earful from her, Elyssa guessed.

"I had to call your secretary at home and get her to come down to the office with me to locate the phone number. It took a half-hour to clear our entrance with security, then another hour to find the number because the janitor had burned the messages in the trash cans. Brenda Landon thought she might be able to remember the number since she'd jotted it down so many times. But by the time we finished calling the numbers she *thought* were right, I had talked to people from one side of the state to the other. When I finally got the right connection, I received directions from some screwball woman who used landmarks. It took me over two hours to drive out here."

Robert must have gotten Claudia on the phone, Elyssa decided. Althea would have been more precise.

"Well, don't you have anything to say, Elyssa?"

"Yes, if it takes you two hours to get home and you want to be there before dark, you'd better hit the road. I'd hate to have you keep Bambi waiting."

"For God's sake, do you think she means anything to me?"

Elyssa picked up an apple from the fruit bowl on the coffee table and took a bite. It had been a long time since lunch—a meal she hadn't bothered to eat. "Apparently she does," she said between nibbles.

Strange, she felt nothing except annoyance that Robert—yuppie nerd of the Cutler Corporation—was wasting her time and disrupting her thoughts. She must have wrung out every emotion while she was bawling her head off at the base of the canyon. There was simply nothing left but a residue of regret, a wish that she had never settled for engagement to a man like Robert. She must have been desperate to start a family.

"Elyssa, you've got to believe me." Looking properly repentant, Robert strode forward to gather her in his arms.

She automatically retreated a step. "You know how we cold fish are, Robert. Don't waste your time—or mine."

"We're engaged to be married," he insisted.

Elyssa erupted in laughter, nearly strangling on her bite of apple. "Who? You and Bambi? Congratulations."

"No, damn it, you and I. What's the matter with you? You're acting strange. You're not yourself."

Elyssa swallowed, cleared her throat, and regarded Robert curiously. "Then who am I?" she asked straight-faced.

"I think you're in shock," he diagnosed. "I'd better take you home. You look like you could use a decent night's sleep."

When Robert's hand snaked out to grab Elyssa's arm, a brusque voice came at him. "Leave her the hell alone."

Elyssa flinched, unaware that Hunter had come through the back door and had been standing in the hall, eavesdropping on the conversation. Whether she could trust him or not, it was extremely gratifying to watch Robert shrink away from the ominous figure that filled the doorway. Male power rumbled through Hunter's massive body, ominous as a storm cloud. Like him or not, the man could be extremely intimidating.

"Who is *that?*" Robert questioned, staring at Hunter with wary trepidation. "Your bodyguard?"

"I'm her business partner and ranch manager," Nathan snapped. "Got a problem with that?"

Robert thrust out his chin, annoyed that he had to look up to match the swarthy cowboy glare for glare. "No, but I would like to know why someone around here didn't have the sense to call a physician to prescribe medication. My fiancée is obviously undergoing stress. Just look at her!"

Hunter took his own sweet time appraising Elyssa's windblown appearance. "She looks good to me. If I had been engaged to her, I sure as hell wouldn't have been *penciling* in appointments with my secretary—"

Elyssa choked on a bite and then turned as red as the apple she was eating. "Hunter!"

"Sorry, darlin'," he drawled without taking his piercing gaze off Robert. "You want me to show Romeo to the door or do you think he can find it all by himself?"

"Well, Robert?" Elyssa inquired, stifling a grin. "Are you leaving or do you want Hunter to escort you off the premises? I can't swear he isn't capable of violence. Your Armani might suffer irreparable damage if he gets hold of you, and I know how fussy you are about your expensive suits."

Robert wheeled toward the door. "I'm leaving, but I'll be back."

"I'll be waiting," Nathan promised.

When the front door slammed shut, Elyssa breezed past Nathan, depositing her apple core in his hand before propelling herself toward the stairs.

"I thought guard dogs were treated to steaks," he said, staring at the remains of Elyssa's snack.

She didn't reply. She marched up the steps to collect her luggage. As she snapped her suitcase shut, she turned to find Hunter blocking her exit as effectively as a boulder.

"I'll drive you home," he volunteered.

"No thanks. I'll take Dad's truck."

"When are you coming back?"

"When I have to." Elyssa held her suitcase in front of her like a shield. "Move it, Hunter. I'm on a short fuse."

Nathan studied Elyssa's peaked face. Robert was right. She looked like death warmed over. She was running on sheer adrenaline, and she had been all day. When she finally let down, it was going to be one helluva crash landing.

"I don't think you should be alone."

"Valerie will be at the apartment." Elyssa raised her suitcase like a weapon sighted on the most vulnerable part of his anatomy. "Are you going to step aside or am *I* going to have to resort to violence?"

Nathan reluctantly retreated and watched her zoom off, looking like a time bomb set to detonate. He wondered if Robert would hound her the minute he learned she was returning to the City. He also wondered if Gil and Virgil would be calling every hour on the hour to persuade her to sign the partnership agreement. Damn it, the little lady could use a break. Unfortunately, Nathan couldn't afford to give her one.

As for Gil Rawlins, Nathan wondered where the man had been when Ely had met with calamity. He pivoted around to hunt down Ray, hoping Twig could shed some light on the subject. Nathan hadn't taken two steps before Claudia materialized from one of the upstairs bedrooms.

Not now, he thought irritably. Every time he turned around, she was making a pass at him. If it were not for Althea, he would long ago have told Claudia to take a hike. Maybe he ought to sic Claudia on Robert Grayson, he thought spitefully. Robert obviously had a penchant for sexual variety. Still, weasel though he was, he must have been reasonably competent in bed or Elyssa wouldn't have . . .

Nathan scowled at the vision that leaped to mind. Robert didn't deserve Elyssa.

When Claudia sashayed toward him to make another blatant offer, he muttered to himself. He was beginning to want the woman who distrusted him. Going to bed with Elyssa would be both heaven and hell. No matter how good it might be between them, she would be suspicious of his motives.

Nathan hated himself for wanting what he knew he shouldn't have. He was driving himself crazy wondering what it might be like to finish what he and Elyssa had started at the bottom of the canyon . . .

Ten

Nathan had not been able to find out where Gil or Virgil had been on the afternoon Ely died. Impatient, he stalked through the back door of the ranch house, the speckled dog following.

Althea Gilbert smiled at him. "Come sit down and I'll fix you something to eat," she offered. "You missed supper with the hired hands, and there wasn't so much as a scrap left."

She set a cup of coffee on the table. "How is Elyssa taking the loss of her dad?" she asked.

Nathan shrugged and fiddled with the salt shaker.

"She was always close to her father as a kid," the housekeeper went on. "And, of course, Ely thought the sun rose and set on her." Althea reached for four slices of bread and dropped them into the toaster. "He used to haul his little angel all over creation, despite her mother's objections. Jessica wanted Elyssa to be a prim and proper lady, not a farm hand. The smartest thing Ely ever did was divorce that woman. Too bad he lost his daughter in the deal."

Nathan stretched his long legs out in front of him and stared at Althea's broad back. Her comment reminded him of something Elyssa had said about his not knowing the full story of her past. At the time, he couldn't imagine that hearing about Elyssa's misspent youth was going to make a damn bit of difference to his opinion of her. He hadn't really wanted to like this uppity socialite who had treated Ely more like a casual acquaintance than a father. Now, though, he was curious about her, unwillingly intrigued by those onyx eyes.

He straightened in his chair. "What do you mean Ely *lost* his daughter?"

"You mean Ely never told you?" Althea spared the handsome cowboy a quick glance before retrieving the ingredients for an omelette from the refrigerator.

Nathan shook his head.

"I spent plenty of time eavesdropping on conversations in those days," Althea said with a wry smile. "Jessica was always whining about being stuck out here in Nowhere, Oklahoma. She wanted to travel and see the world, but Ely had obligations in his partnership with Gil. While Jessica was on one of her sight-seeing trips, she met that Cutler character, and they must have hit it off big-time. When she demanded a divorce a few months later, Ely said it was fine by him, only he wanted custody of Elyssa."

"I suppose Elyssa wanted to be with her mother." Nathan reached down to pet Ricky before sipping his coffee.

"As I recall, nobody even asked her what she wanted, but I can tell you she would have preferred to stay here. Jessica cut a deal with Ely to ensure she got her way. She knew how devoted he was to this ranch that's been handed down for generations, so she promised not to ask for child support or alimony or to sue for her legal portion of this place and its profits if Ely wouldn't object to Daniel Cutler adopting Elyssa."

Nathan's cup hung in the air, halfway between his mouth and the table. "Sweet lady."

"A real bitch, if you ask me," Althea muttered. "To her, social status was everything. It was no longer enough to be married to the biggest rancher in eight counties. She craved the city life and lights. Daniel Cutler could provide all that. Jessica had always attracted men, and she used her power over them to get what she wanted. She planned to raise Elyssa in her image. It nearly killed Ely to give up his daughter, but Gil assured him that Jessica would break up the ranch and ruin the partnership if Ely made waves."

Althea frowned. "You know, I never could figure out why Gil sided with Jessica on that issue. Must have been greed on his part." She shrugged off the thought and continued. "At any rate, he convinced Ely not to fight the adoption for the sake of the ranch and the family tradition."

Nathan sipped his coffee, digesting the information. "So Elyssa was banished from visiting the ranch after the divorce?"

"No, the Queen Bitch decreed, with a great deal of reservation, that her little princess could visit for three weeks each summer, so long as Ely promised to keep a constant vigil on her. That was Jessica's only concession. But when Elyssa was injured while riding on her fifteen birthday, Jessica went berserk. She secured a restraining order that prohibited Ely from going near Elyssa, even while she was recovering from the accident. That accident was similar to the one Ely . . ." Althea swallowed the rest of the comment and shuddered.

Nathan set down his cup and peered at the housekeeper. He had the sickening feeling he knew what Althea had intended to say. He had seen Ely's body and was vividly aware of the condition it had been in. If plunging over jagged rocks and bristly brush hadn't broken Ely's neck, he would have required hours of surgery to stitch him back together.

Suddenly, Nathan wasn't nearly as hungry as he'd thought. It made him physically ill to think of anyone plummeting into the canyon, of the terror that would accompany such a painful fall.

He had come down on Elyssa like a ton of bricks, unaware that she had suffered an experience similar to the one that had taken Ely's life. He should have gotten the facts straight before he'd judged her.

"Don't tell me Elyssa took a fall in the same place Ely did," Nathan choked out.

"Same quarter section of land, but on the west side of those red canyons," Althea clarified.

Nathan remembered how Elyssa had halted her horse on the western rim and then had thundered off as if the hounds of hell were nipping at her heels. Christ! He had taken her to the last place she wanted to be!

"Elyssa didn't fall with her horse rolling down on top of her, but the jagged rocks cut open her arm and hip, as if she'd landed on spikes. There's no telling how much money the Cutlers spent on reconstructive surgery and physical therapy before she could walk without crutches. She was in and out of hospitals all through high school, and finally the doctors told Jessica nothing more could be done."

Nathan recalled the slight limp that had hampered Elyssa's all-too-seductive gait when she'd strolled toward her apartment the previous night. He had chalked it up to too much whiskey. Obviously he had leaped to a few ill-founded assumptions.

"After the accident Jessica refused to allow Elyssa to set foot on the ranch again, claiming Ely wasn't fit to watch over her," Althea confided. "Ely was so beside himself he didn't put up a fuss. He simply made arrangements to drive to the City to see Elyssa whenever Jessica allowed it. Of course, Jessica sent Elyssa to the most expensive private girls' school in town, and she notified the headmistress that Ely would only be allowed to see his daughter with Jessica's permission."

Nathan was beginning to feel like a first-class ass. His snide remarks had alienated the one person who could help him see Ely's wishes carried out. It didn't help that Elyssa now viewed him in the same light as her recently discarded fiancé, either. Damn, getting into her good graces was going to be as difficult as extinguishing the fires of hell with a cup of water.

When he went up against Gil Rawlins, Virgil, and Dennis Humphrey, Nathan was going to have a battle royal on his hands. He needed Elyssa's trust and cooperation, but he had treated her like dirt. He wished he had kept his mouth shut the night he'd brought her back to the ranch. But he had been hurting and had just lashed out.

"I still don't understand why Elyssa never came back to the ranch after she grew up," he mused aloud.

"Who knows what tactic Jessica used to keep her away from her father. It wasn't as if Ely didn't apologize over and over for what happened to her. She'd been in so much pain and in such a state of hysterics when he found her and brought her back to the house that day she could barely explain what had happened. Maybe neither of them wanted to rehash the awful memories. Ely never spoke of the accident after the ordeal was over. He just wanted to forget it."

"Why haven't you told me all this before?" Nathan asked. "It would have explained a lot."

"Ely was so burdened with guilt he didn't want to discuss what had happened, nor did he want it mentioned by anyone else."

Althea scooped the omelette onto the plate and then frowned when Nathan got up and walked off. "Where are you going? Aren't you hungry?"

Nathan did not hear her. He was beside himself. He had dragged Elyssa out to the site where she had met with disaster twelve years earlier, and there she had found the spot where her father died. Then, to make matters worse, he had treated her with a lack of respect and consideration from the moment he'd arrived at her apartment. How could he even begin to apologize for his behavior? He had to see her.

"Nate? Where are you going?" Althea called after him.

"I'll be back later," he said before he charged up the steps to shower and change.

Althea glanced down at Ricky who sat with his tail wagging, staring at the omelette and licking his chops. Muttering at Nathan's odd behavior, she set the plate on the floor and let the speckled dog have at it.

The minute Elyssa reached her apartment, she expelled the breath she felt she'd been holding since she'd left the ranch more than an hour earlier. Here in the City, she wasn't as susceptible to the riptide of emotions that bombarded her back there. She didn't have to cope with unpleasant memories of her accident or her father's death, and she was miles away from the potent spell cast by Nathan Hunter . . .

What was it about the man that really got to her? If she was going to delve into that question, she was going to have to be completely honest with herself. The first basic truth she had to accept was her physical attraction to that swarthy cowboy. Despite her wariness regarding his hidden motives, she felt a bond because of his close association with her father. If Ely had trusted Hunter, why shouldn't she? Or had Ely's trust in Hunter led to his downfall? Why should she question Uncle Gil's motives if he had been Ely's partner all these years?

Elyssa dropped the suitcase by the door and massaged her temples. It had been one incredibly hectic day, and she had a megaheadache to prove it. She would like nothing better than to soak in the Jacuzzi and then hibernate for a month.

"Ellie! You're back!" Valerie emerged from the bathroom, a towel wrapped around her head, her shapeless caftan doing nothing for her trim figure. She pulled up short when she noticed Elyssa's unusual attire, faded denims and flannel shirt. "What the devil have you been doing?"

"Horseback riding, and I can cite the exact location of every aching muscle in my hips and legs." Elyssa collapsed on the couch, head thrown back, gaze focused on the ceiling. "It's no wonder *real* cowboys have thighs like rock and buns of steel. Have you ever been riding, Val?"

"Yeah, on the carousel at Frontier City's amusement park," she replied as she towel-dried her hair. "Nobody ever invited me to a ranch to hone my skills in the saddle."

"The invitation is open," Elyssa assured her.

"The invitation is accepted." Valerie's smile faded abruptly. "Robert came by today."

Elyssa nodded tiredly. "I know. He showed up at the ranch."

"You didn't take that sneak back, did you?"

"Nope, but I doubt he's going to give up easily, not when he was expecting a promotion at Cutler Corporation."

Valerie was silent for a moment. "Your mother called a couple of hours ago."

Resentment stung like a wasp. For years Elyssa had repressed her feelings about her mother's refusal to let her see Ely. Now she realized how turbulent were the emotions she'd buried deep and kept concealed for years.

"Your mother isn't cutting her vacation short," Valerie went on. "She said they had their reservations made for weeks and they couldn't just drop them."

"Of course not," Elyssa said bitterly. "Why should she pay her respects to a man who was merely the first step on her path to sophistication and influence."

The phone rang, and Elyssa lifted the receiver to offer the caller a weary "Hello."

"Elyssa? This is Virgil."

Elyssa rolled her eyes and sighed. "Yes?"

"I've been worried about you since I saw you this afternoon. I just wanted to make sure you got home all right."

Didn't he just. Cousin Virgil was all a-quiver with sympathetic concern. Quite a change from the brat of a teenager who'd played spiteful pranks on his younger cousin when she'd come to visit.

"I thought I'd let you know I had another partnership agreement drawn up and it's ready for you to sign."

"You work fast, Virgil."

"With the ranch operation hanging in limbo, Dad and I felt we should move quickly. Life goes on, you know."

"Thanks for calling." Elyssa started to drop the receiver onto its cradle, but Virgil's insistent voice gave her pause.

"One more thing, Cousin, watch your step with Nathan Hunter. I heard the two of you were out riding together this afternoon. Don't let him pull the wool over your eyes or come on to you for his own greedy purposes."

Elyssa frowned, wondering who had provided Virgil with that information and why.

"Be careful you don't fall for his lies and manipulation. He wants whatever he can get from the estate. Ely was just beginning to discover that for himself before he . . ." Virgil didn't finish his sentence. He didn't have to. "Just don't let Nate force you into a decision you'll regret. Don't forget *we*'re family, and family sticks together. Blood is thicker than water, Cousin. Remember that."

"Sure thing, Virgil." Elyssa smiled humorlessly. "And let me take this opportunity to thank you for being so kind and caring years ago when I used to come for summer visits. We both know what happened on my fifteen birthday, and we know *why,* don't we? I wonder if Uncle Gil knows how that all came about. Maybe I ought to tell him."

"Elyssa, I—"

"Thanks for calling, Cuz." She dropped the receiver and gave Virgil the sound cursing he deserved. Too bad she had been polite enough not to share it with him.

"What was that all about?" Valerie inquired.

"My—"

The phone blared again. This time it was Robert.

"Elyssa? I'm glad you're back. I called the ranch to see if you were still there. Are you feeling better?"

"I was—until you called."

"I'm coming to see you."

"I have nothing more to say."

"We can work this out. We can't just throw something this good away!"

"This good?" Elyssa burst out laughing. "You must have me mixed up with Bambi."

"You're kidding!" Valerie squawked when Elyssa accidentally blurted out the name she had previously withheld. "Bambi? All boobs and no brains? *That* Bambi? Gawd, good ole Robert really has lousy taste when he's out screwing around, doesn't he?"

"Elyssa. I am *not* giving up!" Robert blared over the phone.

"Robert, I am *not* giving in!" Elyssa blared right back and then hung up.

Valerie's green eyes twinkled with amusement. "Ellie, I think you've spent too much time around me. You're becoming a smartass."

"Sorry, roomie, you can't take all the credit. Losing Dad brought the walls down. There were too many things I should have said and done all these years, too many times I bit my tongue and played the diplomat. Losing Dad drove home the point that life is too short and unpredictable to keep your feelings bottled up. Who knows? I might even decide to have a few affairs just for the hell of it. Why shouldn't I give it a try? One never knows if one will still be around tomorrow."

"Don't get carried away," Valerie warned. "That what-the-hell attitude is fine when tempered with sensible restraint."

"Ah yes," Elyssa mused. "Live every day as if it were your last, but plan as if you're going to be around forever. Be happy but not at anyone else's expense. That was also my father's philosophy."

Valerie breathed a relieved sigh. "I'm glad to see you intend to use common sense instead of turning wild and reckless because you're hurting on the inside." She patted Elyssa on the shoulder. "What do you say to a harmless, enjoyable night on the town?"

"I already had one, thank you. I'll have to recuperate from all that excitement—"

The door rattled in response to a firm insistent knock.

"Good Lord, what now?" Elyssa muttered. "If that's Robert, pull your six-gun and get rid of him—permanently."

"My pleasure." Valerie heaved herself off the couch and marched to the door, ready to blast the two-timing son of a bitch who had done Elyssa wrong. The barrage of words died on her lips when she confronted a mountain of muscle wrapped in Wrangler jeans and a Mo'Betta shirt.

"And you said Santa Claus had trouble filling tall orders?" Valerie said, as she glanced over her shoulder at her roommate.

Elyssa stared at Nathan Hunter. "What do you want?"

Valerie recovered enough to extend her hand. "I'm Valerie Mitchell. And you are . . . ?"

"Nathan Hunter."

Valerie offered her best smile. "Give me ten minutes and I'll be ready to saddle up and ride away with you, cowboy."

Nathan broke into a broad grin, and his eyes sparkled like sapphires as he stared at Valerie. But his attention was focused on Elyssa who was draped on the couch. "Some other time maybe. I need to talk to Elyssa."

"You and everybody else," Valerie grumbled. "This place is worse than Grand Central Station."

Elyssa made no attempt to assume a more ladylike posture in the presence of her guest. The what-the-hell syndrome had a hold on her. She was tired and frustrated and confused, and she didn't give a damn about much of anything.

"Go away, Hunter. I'm having a bad life."

Ignoring the remark, Nathan strolled forward to loom over her. "I wanted to give you time to recuperate, Cutler. But you've got to know what's going on before Gil and Virgil try to get to you—again."

"Virgil already called," Elyssa reported. "He warned me away from you—again."

"Understandable. He's desperate."

"And you aren't?"

"I'm getting desperate," Nathan said. "But as far as I'm concerned, the only *hot* property around here is you, not the ranch."

He made no attempt whatsoever to conceal the naked hunger in his eyes. He, like Elyssa, had reached that phase of grieving in which nothing mattered quite so much as finding distraction, a much-needed sense of peace and contentment—temporary or otherwise.

A jolt of awareness sizzled through Elyssa before that maddening little tingle started at the base of her neck. Damn it, she had just begun to relax and unwind, when Hunter, looking as predatory as a panther, knocked her legs out from under her with his shocking comments and smoldering glances.

Valerie stood listening to the quiet exchange, knowing she might as well have been a stick of furniture for all the notice she was receiving. Not once in the three years they had lived together had she seen Elyssa so attuned to a man's presence. The aloofness was gone, and Elyssa was staring at Nathan in a way she had *never* stared at a man, not even Robert.

About time, Valerie thought. And with a salt-of-the-earth kind of man, too. Valerie couldn't have been more delighted, unless this sinewy hunk of male had aimed himself in *her* direction.

"Well, I can see you two have things to discuss. I'll be out of here in fifteen minutes."

When Valerie scampered to her bedroom and closed the door, Elyssa levered herself upright on the sofa. "Now that you've managed to convince Valerie we are about to start up a steamy affair—which cannot happen, of course—what is it you really want?"

He grinned scampishly. "The tactic worked, didn't it? She volunteered to leave us alone. And we definitely need to be." His smile faded, his expression became somber. "I've come with the facts, Cutler. Go take a bath and change while I rustle up something for us to eat. Then we're going to get down to business."

"Now hold on," she protested. "This is *my* apartment. I don't appreciate your bulldozing your way in here and taking command!"

He stood there, the faintest hint of a smile twitching his lips. "You don't want a warm, relaxing bath to soothe the aches and pains of horseback riding when you're unaccustomed to it? You don't want food when all you've consumed all day is a measly apple?"

"Well, yes . . ."

"Then what's the problem, Cutler?"

"You're the problem," she snapped irritably. "I don't like being bossed around."

As Nathan shrugged those unbelievably broad shoulders and swaggered toward the kitchen to rummage through the refrigerator, Elyssa threw up her hands in defeat. It seemed she was destined to get no more rest this evening than a relaxing bath could provide. She might as well get used to it. Hunter had that determined look about him. He was ready to make his sales pitch, and only an act of God could stop him.

Elyssa ambled off, resigned to doing what she had been told to do, even if she didn't appreciate being bade to do it.

"Nathan?"

He glanced over his shoulder while searching for a loaf of bread to make sandwiches. Valerie stood poised in the doorway, decked out in her Western finery. The petite blonde looked tremendously appealing in her tailored clothes and fashionable hairstyle, her thin coat of makeup enhancing pixielike features. If Nathan's tastes hadn't leaned heavily toward auburn hair and obsidian eyes that harbored untold secrets, he might have taken Valerie up on her previous offer.

"You look nice, Val," he said. "I like you better without that turban."

"Thank you. For a while there, I didn't think you even noticed I was alive."

"I've been distracted since Ely died. Elyssa seems to think she's the only one who cared about the man, and she refuses to trust me."

"I know this isn't any of my business, and I don't poke my nose in where it doesn't belong—not usually. But go easy on Ellie, will you? She's had a stressful week, and it isn't over yet. She just broke off with a two-timing fiancé she should never have agreed to marry in the first place. She got hung up on all that nonsense about starting a family early, and she's been hurt. Besides, there are other things you don't know about her that would knock you out of your boots."

Nathan regarded the shapely blonde curiously. "What things?"

Valerie smiled enigmatically. "That's for her to say, not me."

"You're a lot of help," he grumbled. His shoulders slumped and he stared unseeingly into the kitchen cabinets. "I don't want to hurt her. I only want to help her through the rough times that lie ahead, but she's leery of my motives so it's been an uphill battle. I'm trying to be patient and understanding, but there have been times I'd like to shake every cynical thought out of her."

Valerie laughed softly. "Well, can you blame her for being wary? She returned from the hassle of dealing with government officials in D.C. to find her fiancé doing the horizontal tango with his dim-witted secretary. And while she was still reeling from that humiliating blow, I talked her into hitting the honky-tonks to drink her troubles away. My methods were totally ineffective. She wouldn't even get up on the dance floor, much less let herself fall for any of the come-ons men tossed at her. To top off a bad day, Elyssa came home to news about her dad's accident. Now she's caught up in a whirlwind of obligations regarding her father's estate. What Ellie needs right now are friends who are truly concerned about her, not more headaches."

"I get the message, Val." Nathan pivoted, leaning leisurely against the counter, arms crossed over his chest. "I don't want to be a headache. I'd rather be a cure."

Valerie nearly swooned. Salt of the earth, thought she. Damn, the man had a natural charm that wouldn't quit. He looked like a throwback from the Old West in modern clothes—tough, resilient, tested, and capable.

"You got any friends who like blondes who love Garth Brooks and Vince Gill?" she asked all of a sudden.

Nathan chuckled. He liked Elyssa's saucy roommate. "A couple."

She smiled impishly. "Good, when can I meet them?"

"As soon as you tell me what I need to know about Elyssa."

Valerie sashayed over to retrieve the bread from behind the sack of sugar and handed it to Nathan. "My advice is to take it slow and easy, cowboy. If you rush Ellie, you're history. And then you'll have one helluva time with her as your business partner. She may be gorgeous, but she's also a little skeptical and a lot smart."

With that, Valerie walked off, her silver and turquoise bracelets jingle-jangling, leaving Nathan to stare ponderously after her.

Eleven

Elyssa slid down into the tub with a sigh. This was almost heaven. She hadn't realized how much she relied on her Jacuzzi. Maybe she would just spend the night right here and face Hunter another day . . .

"Are you ever coming out, or do you want supper served in the tub?"

Elyssa nearly leaped straight out of her bubbling bath when the deep voice boomed on the other side of the door. "Don't rush me, Hunter."

He smiled to himself. That was what Valerie had told him. "Are you coming out tonight or not?"

"Not," Elyssa muttered.

"Then I'm coming in."

"Don't you dare, damn it!"

"Five more minutes, Cutler. That's it. We've got a lot to discuss."

Elyssa scowled and reached for the towel. How was she supposed to enjoy paradise with the devil beating on the door? Grumbling, she snatched up her robe, but not before she'd encountered her reflection in the mirror. The ugly, discolored scars glared back at her, reminding her of how self-conscious she had become of her own imperfections. Her hip and elbow looked like a patchwork of skin stitched together with a dull needle. She told herself it didn't matter, but who was she kidding? It mattered to her. It always had. Whenever she looked at herself, she remembered that day twelve years ago as if it were yesterday. She couldn't bring herself to discuss the incident, though. She knew the inevitable questions would come if she allowed a man to get too close, to see her too clearly. Then she would freeze up and feel so damned awkward and blemished it would spoil the moment.

So she had made sure that disquieting moment had never come. She had concealed the scars and avoided the prying questions. She wasn't the iceberg Robert accused her of being. It wasn't that she couldn't feel; it was only that she dreaded allowing any man to discover what she had hidden, even from those closest to her.

Elyssa began to mentally prepare herself to deal with Hunter. She opened the door to find a shadowed silhouette lurking in front of her. She automatically shrank back, clutching the robe tightly around her.

But Nathan latched onto her arm and herded her down the hall. "I'm starving to death, Cutler."

"You didn't have to wait for me."

She tried to wriggle loose, but Nathan was as strong as a bull. She found herself deposited on a chair before a ham sandwich that only an alligator could have gotten its mouth around. Two of these huge sandwiches were on Hunter's plate. Keeping this man in food could be expensive.

Although Elyssa was self-conscious sitting there in her robe, nothing beneath it except skin, Nathan had the decency not to call attention to her lack of clothing. He merely attacked his meal like a shark. She had to give the man credit. He was playing it cool. No sizzling glances like the ones he'd leveled on her when he'd barged in. No sexual innuendos. He was all business, thank goodness. That gave Elyssa time to get herself in hand.

"When we're finished eating, you'll need a pen and paper to jot down the information I'm going to give you," Nathan said as he reached for the glass of Coke and purposely stared at its contents.

Hell's fire, he was going to have to stitch his eyelids shut to keep from staring at the diving V of that robe. He wondered if Elyssa would be wise to him if he knocked his knife to the floor and got down on his knees on the pretense of retrieving it so he could gawk at those long, shapely legs of hers.

In truth, Nathan was far from immune to what lay beneath that terrycloth robe. He didn't want to sneak a peek; he wanted to memorize every lush curve and scintillating swell, to assure Elyssa that what she had gotten from Robert could be improved upon—if she gave him the chance to show her.

On the trip to the City Nathan had told himself he needed to keep his distance, otherwise he would only complicate the situation and would risk losing what little trust Elyssa had in him. But he had also remembered the delicious taste of her kiss, the feel of her supple body in his arms. He had had just about enough temptation to whet his appetite and leave a hungry craving gnawing at him. If nothing else, he knew making love with Elyssa would be the best mistake he had ever made.

The rap at the door jostled Nathan from his erotic musings. "Damn, this *is* Grand Central Station," he grumbled. When Elyssa started to rise, he held up his hand. "I'll get it. You eat. You need to keep up your strength."

"Don't be so damn bossy, Hunter," she muttered.

When Nathan opened the door, Robert Grayson stood before him, holding a bouquet of flowers and a box of candy. "Thanks, but I'm not into that sort of thing," Nathan snorted.

Robert's suave smile suddenly turned down. "What are you doing here?"

"Having sex and supper with your ex-fiancée," Nathan replied. In the background he heard Elyssa choking on her ham sandwich.

"You miserable bastard—"

"Actually my parents were married. I just came along prematurely." Nathan smiled nastily. "And speaking of marriage, I've proposed to Elyssa and she's accepted. I guess you're out of luck, Bobby boy."

Robert's face turned the color of raw hamburger. Before he

could unglue his tongue from the roof of his mouth, Elyssa appeared at the kitchen door in her robe. Robert's eyes bulged from their sockets, and he emitted a strangled curse of outrage.

Although Hunter's remarks were outlandish, Elyssa appreciated the spirit in which they were spoken. He had given Robert a dose of the bitter medicine she had had to swallow when she'd found Bambi in her fiancé's bed. If Robert thought she had rebounded into Hunter's bed, that was fine by her. The sooner Robert abandoned his futile attempt to return to her good graces, the better. She had neither the time nor the inclination to deal with him while her father's estate must be settled.

Robert veered around Hunter's hulking form to face Elyssa. "I am *not* calling off our wedding!" he all but shouted when his vocal apparatus began to function properly. "You and I are two of a kind. We belong together."

"Watch it, Bobby," Nathan growled from behind him. "I don't appreciate your referring to *my* fiancée as an asshole."

Robert didn't dare face him. He was operating under the theory that Nathan was gentleman enough not to hit him from behind. "Tell him to leave, Elyssa. We can work this out."

She smiled, thoroughly enjoying herself for the first time in weeks, years maybe. If nothing else, Nathan Hunter provided a spark that put fire in her life. "You want me to drop the man who provided the best loving I ever had?" she asked, taking wicked delight in watching Robert swallow his Adam's apple. "Sorry, Hunter and I have something good going. You know, kind of like what you were having with Bambi when I interrupted."

With impish glee, she watched Robert's face fall. He was clutching his bouquet so tightly he seemed to be strangling it.

"Besides, I've decided I don't want my stepfather to give you that promotion you so often mentioned. I'm going to recommend a shift in your position. I think you would be terrific as the new government-relations director. You can make the jaunts to D.C. since you're getting so good at kissing up."

"Daniel Cutler isn't going to refuse my promotion on your recommendation," Robert seethed.

"You're right," she agreed. "He'll refuse because he never did think you were worth your salt. He only made the offer to please me." Her arm shot toward the door. "Now get out of my apartment. You're old news. No, make that *bad* news."

While Robert stood there, steamed, Nathan clamped a hand on his shoulder and turned him around. "You had your chance and you blew it, desk jockey. You can walk out of here under your own power, or I can throw you out. But decide real quick. You're wearing my patience thin."

Robert tossed the flowers and candy on the sofa and stalked out, taking the first option Nathan had offered.

"Good God, Cutler, what in the hell did you ever see in that man anyway?" Nathan asked when the door slammed shut.

"Nothing much," she replied honestly. "He was safe."

One thick brow arched in teasing curiosity. "And I'm not?"

"No, you are extremely dangerous, but I found I like living on the edge better than I'd thought." Elyssa lifted dark eyes to meet sparkling pools of blue. "Thanks, Hunter. I think you managed to convince Robert that I'm no longer his meal ticket at Cutler Corporation. I owe you one."

He smiled rakishly as he swaggered past her to finish his supper.

Elyssa studied Nathan's striking physique from the rear and smiled ruefully, wondering if the affair they hadn't actually had would have been as gratifying as getting her revenge on that two-timing weasel Robert.

Too bad she would never find out, not when she couldn't overcome the hurdle of considering herself scarred merchandise with limited experience. And the worst of it, Elyssa realized with a start, was that she didn't want to disappoint Hunter. He was probably accustomed to experienced women. She wouldn't even know how to begin to please a man. A bungling romantic encounter would spoil their budding friendship—or at least the charade of friendship Hunter projected for her benefit. She had yet to hear those facts he claimed would convince her to side with him in his feud with Uncle Gil and Cousin Virgil.

"Are you ready for this, Cutler?" Nathan asked as he settled himself on the sofa beside her. "I'm going to be quoting facts and figures fast and furiously. If you need an explanation, stop me."

"Fire away."

Elyssa had changed into a pale blue, long-sleeved cotton-knit sweater and gray slacks after polishing off her sandwich. With her legs curled beneath her, a clipboard on her lap, and a pen in hand, she waited for Nathan to update her on the operation of Rawlins Ranch.

"The Rawlins partnership owns fifty-two quarter sections of pasture and cultivated land. Of those eight thousand three hundred and twenty acres there are forty-four hundred acres of improved grasses."

Elyssa glanced up questioningly. "Improved grass?"

"Five years ago, I talked Ely into overseeding the native pastures with Midland bermuda, Plains bluestem, and fescue so we could graze more cattle to the acre with supplemental cubes and hay during dormant seasons. The operation has thirty-six hundred and twenty acres of wheat and three hundred acres of alfalfa. The assessed average worth of the land is seven-hundred-fifty dollars per acre, which makes the ranch property worth about six million," Nathan explained while Elyssa took notes.

"If we have adequate spring rains, we usually get five cuttings of alfalfa. The second cutting is usually the highest quality with plenty of leafy vegetation. It sells at top price to horse breeders—"

"Such as Cousin Virgil?" Elyssa inquired.

Nathan nodded. "Except Cousin Virgil has developed the annoying habit of loading bales to feed his registered horses without paying the partnership for them. Your father looked the other way and let it happen in the past because Virgil was his nephew and a few bales were no staggering cut to profits. But over the past two years, your dear cousin has decided to take all the bales he needs without asking permission or paying for his purchases."

"And that is one of the 'lies' Uncle Gil doesn't want me to believe, I expect."

"One of several," Nathan assured her. "But if you doubt my accusation, check with Twig, Denson, Fykes, or Jeffries. They've all seen Virgil stopping by after dark to load alfalfa and haul it to his breeding barns."

"What is this business about government subsidies and fifty-thousand-dollar payments?" Elyssa wanted to know.

Nathan propped his feet on the coffee table and sighed tiredly. She wasn't the only one who'd had a long, trying day. He would have preferred to be doing something more stimulating and satisfying than having this conversation, but she was never going to be able to deal with Gil and Virgil without knowing the necessary facts. He had to pay attention to business and put his unruly desires on hold.

"According to the government agricultural program, each quarter section of cultivated land has to be registered and certified with its own average wheat yield. Most of Rawlins Ranch cropland yields between forty and forty-five bushels to the acre, barring bad years of flood, drought, and storm damage," Nathan explained.

"The USDA sets its target price at four dollars per bushel for wheat, knowing that's what it costs to put in the yearly crop and harvest it. Since Uncle Sam tried to help farmers by sticking his nose in a market that was functioning fine without him, grain prices have dropped to all-time lows. Most farmers are lucky to get three dollars a bushel for their wheat. To compensate, the government pays a subsidy of one dollar for each bushel. That number is multiplied by the average crop yield per acre. That deficiency payment compensates for what the price of wheat *should* be—if the damned government hadn't messed with the market in the first place."

"Whoa!" Elyssa erupted. "You're going too fast, Hunter. Are we talking welfare payments to farmers here?"

"Hardly," Nathan grumbled. "We're talking yearly payments on wheat to cover the cost of investment in land, machinery, and crops. Too many farmers and ranchers have gone under because the middle man reaps the benefits of the high prices consumers pay for agricultural products. The farmers have been getting the shaft for decades. In fact, the market price of wheat is the same as it was fifty years ago while expenses have shot through the roof. Compare subsidy payments to minimum wage, if you wish. There has to be some sort of protection, or the farmers who grow all the food we consume will be out of business and—forget world hunger—we'll have more starving Americans than Uncle Sam will know what to do with."

"And without efficient farm management, more and more farmers are knuckling under because expenses override profit," Elyssa paraphrased.

"That's about the size of it," Nathan agreed. "The government, however, has set a limit on how much of a subsidy can be paid, which is ridiculous because aggressive farmers with large landholdings are forced to tighten their belts instead of receiving equal payment for each acre of land."

"So if Rawlins Ranch's average wheat yield is forty bushels per acre for thirty-six hundred and twenty acres of cropland, we should receive . . ." Elyssa punched numbers into the calculator. "Almost one hundred and fifty thousand dollars as a subsidy, plus about a half million dollars we'd get when the crop sells at three dollars a bushel at market."

"That's what you *should* receive," Nathan amended. "But you don't because of the USDA limits on subsidy. That's why Gil wants you to become the financial advisor so you can collect your fifty thousand dollars and deposit it in the partnership account. Each member of the family who makes a significant contribution to the operation is entitled to a payment, determined by average yields on cultivated acres."

"And if I married you, would you also receive a subsidy which would be collected and included in the gross profit?" she inquired.

"Yes." His gaze locked with hers momentarily before he glanced the other way. "You and I would be doing the ranch a favor by adding more income to the profit."

Elyssa sank back on the couch and stared musingly at the poster of Garth Brooks she had purchased for Valerie's birthday. "Is that what Dad wanted to discuss with me? A marriage to benefit the ranch? Was that why he objected to my engagement to Robert?" She was fairly certain of what the answer would be . . . or so she thought.

"No," he said simply.

"Well, thank God for that." She let out her breath in an audible sigh. "I would have been bitterly disappointed if my father planned to *use* me, too."

"I didn't say the idea hadn't occurred to him," Nathan clarified. "He certainly sang your praises to me often enough over the past few years, suggesting I accompany him to the City for visits. I had a hunch he considered playing matchmaker, so I only agreed to accompany him a half-dozen times at well-spaced intervals."

Elyssa fiddled with her ballpoint pen. "But you didn't find me appealing enough to ask me out, even for the fortune you could inherit." She smiled bitterly. "It's a shame you didn't take lessons from Robert. He learned to overlook my flaws in his quest to become the grand Pooh-Bah of Cutler Corporation."

Nathan half turned, resting his arm on the back of the couch. His gaze focused on the enchanting face framed with silky auburn hair, in which the darkest, most expressive eyes he'd ever stared into were embedded. "I didn't say I didn't find you appealing, Cutler. I thought you were out of my league. Still do, but that doesn't stop me from wanting you."

A blush worked its way up from the base off Elyssa's neck to the roots of her hair. Heat pooled in the lower regions of her body, and that strange sensation trickled down her spine for the zillionth time! Speculation dogged her, imagining what it would be like to be loved by a man who was way out of *her* league. Hunter would devour her, she predicted. He would expect her to be experienced and passionately uninhibited. Most men did.

Clearing her throat, she tried for a normal tone of voice. "Then what did my father want to see me about—according to *you,* that is?"

Nathan dreaded what would come next, knowing Elyssa wasn't going to believe him. He didn't want to see that flicker of suspicion in those intriguing onyx eyes. He hesitated, reluctant to break the companionable truce they had shared for most of the evening.

"Hunter?" Elyssa prompted when he simply sat there staring at her.

He took a deep breath and forced out the words. "Ely wanted to retire, to dissolve the partnership, divide the land holdings, and make me beneficiary of half his holdings."

Elyssa couldn't have been more shocked if Hunter had dropped a grenade in her lap. "Split Rawlins Ranch in half?" she croaked in astonishment. "You think I'm going to believe that?"

The phone blared and Elyssa stared dazedly at it, as if a miniature UFO had touched down on her end table. Finally she picked up the receiver.

"Hello?" she said stupidly.

"Elyssa? This is Uncle Gil. I just called to see how you were holding up."

Not well at all. Hunter's announcement had knocked the props out from under her. "I'm fine," she lied, her voice wobbly.

"Good. Glad to hear it. Have you seen Nate? I haven't been able to get in touch with him at the ranch."

Elyssa darted Hunter a glance. He was staring intently at

her, having recognized the voice that boomed over the line. He also heard the question Gil posed. He waited, watchful, poised in an almost predatory way while Elyssa struggled with her suspicions.

"Well?" Gil persisted.

Nathan's hand curled around her kneecap, firm and insistent. "Give me just one night, Cutler," he whispered. "Give me one chance to explain without letting your uncle know so he can plan his countertactics. You claimed you owed me one. Here's your chance to even the score. One night . . ."

Elyssa teetered mentally while that unnerving sensation tripped down her spine like nimble fingers flying over a keyboard. Hunter's touch, simple though it was, aroused warm sensations and confounded her thoughts. She was as unsure of him as she had ever been, especially after he'd declared that Ely wanted to dissolve a partnership and break a tradition that dated back to territorial days.

She knew she was allowing emotion to overrule logic. She also knew her perspectives had altered after losing her father. And deep down in her soul, she admitted that she had never wanted to take such a risk on a man as she wanted to take on Nathan Hunter.

Salt of the earth. A man's man . . .

Damn you, Valerie, for planting those thoughts in my head!

Her eyes locked with his, and words passed through her lips, as if drawn forth by his will. "No, I haven't seen Hunter," she told Gil.

"Well, damn. I don't know what that rascal is up to," Gil muttered. "But be on your guard, Elyssa. He's hellbent on making trouble for our family. He's gotten greedy over the years. We have to band together to stop him."

"I'll remember that, Uncle Gil."

"Good night, Elyssa."

She put down the phone and peered at Hunter in consternation. "You realize you're asking me to disregard everything I thought my father stood for and believed in, don't you?"

He leaned forward, his hand curling beneath her chin, forcing her to meet his piercing gaze. "It's even more serious than you think," he said quietly. His attention focused on the lush contours of her mouth. "If you suspect someone killed your father, you'll be placing yourself in jeopardy by believing me and dissolving the partnership as Ely wanted."

A shudder undulated through Elyssa, unfamiliar desire mingling with fear. She well remembered the unexplained sensation that had assailed her while she'd lingered at the edge of the red rock cliff where her father had tumbled to his death. She recalled the whisper in the wind and how she had faltered in indecision, wondering if she should trust her instincts while her emotions were riding so high.

Now, Hunter had her wondering if what she'd believed to be true wasn't necessarily so. And if she did side with him to break this longstanding partnership, she could endanger her own life. If Ely had died before he could revoke the agreement, she could be next in line for a date with disaster.

"Cutler," Nathan said gravely. "If you want to walk away from all this, I'll understand. But I owe your father for giving me a chance to make something of myself. Ely had very definite reasons for wanting to split the ranch. Not only has Virgil been stealing thousands of dollars worth of hay from the partnership to support his expensive horse-breeding business, but he and Gil have accumulated staggering debts by expanding their horse industry and trying to build a name for themselves with their race horses at Remington Park Race Track in the City. You can imagine how expensive it is to breed, train, and promote race horses. It's costing Gil and Virgil like you wouldn't believe! It could eventually cost you the ranch."

When Elyssa frowned, bemused, Nathan heaved a sigh and tried to explain. "In a partnership, both partners are legally bound to absorb all debts. Your cousin persuaded Gil to co-sign for a quarter of a million loan. Virgil can't make his interest payments, much less pay on the principal. When that loan comes due, the bank Virgil borrowed from intends to foreclose.

It will assume control of the horse-breeding business Virgil has established if he doesn't pay off part of the debt. Should the partnership still be intact, you will be taken to the cleaners. Your dear uncle wants you to pay half Virgil's debt to save his son from bankruptcy and humiliation."

Elyssa sat there like a marble statue, grappling with the overwhelming thought of brother betraying brother . . . and perhaps even resorting to murder to save the conniving Virgil. Or was this a clever pack of lies, meant to shock her into siding with Nathan to ensure that *he* got what he wanted?

"I want you to give me power of attorney," Nathan insisted. His forefinger lifted to close her sagging jaw before gliding across the satiny curve of her cheekbone. "Let Gil and Virgil deal with me, not you. If anyone is going to be at risk I want it to be me. Those two have always resented me. You're family. Let them hate the outsider."

His head moved deliberately toward hers, eclipsing the lamplight and filling Elyssa's world with the powerful male aura that surrounded him. She closed her eyes at the first touch of sensuous lips whispering over hers in the slightest breath of a kiss. She told herself she was in danger of being seduced into believing what Hunter wanted her to believe. It would take days for her to verify his accusations. But she didn't have that much time, not with Gil and Virgil breathing down her neck and Hunter pressing her for a decision.

And he was making it impossible for her to think straight by kissing her with such persuasive tenderness she found herself offering as much as he wanted to take. She longed to see just how far she could go before instinct made her freeze up in his arms the way she usually did when things got too intimate and she faced the prospect of exposing her unsightly scars and answering tormenting questions.

"I'd gladly take on your family if spending the night with you was my reward," Nathan told her huskily. "I want you. I think I have since the first time I saw you. I just wouldn't let myself admit how much."

When his hand dipped beneath the hem of her sweater to swirl over her belly, fire leaped through Elyssa's nerve endings to scorch flesh and bone. That feeling of knowing Great-grandmother Mae had harped about kept tapping in on Elyssa's faltering thoughts. What had always seemed all wrong with the men who had come and gone from her life finally seemed natural and right. She could lose herself in Hunter's brawny arms, if only he wouldn't have to see . . .

She sighed as his thumb brushed the beaded peak of her breast. She was unbelievably sensitive to his touch, so vividly aware of his every move, his alluring scent, his addictive taste. She could feel herself letting go, inch by inch, savoring each newly discovered sensation and eager to learn where they would lead.

Nathan groaned at the feel of silky skin beneath his exploring fingertips. His hands fairly shook as they swirled over the generous swells of her breasts, feeling their soft crowns grow hard in response. He wanted to pull her beneath him and ease the pulsating throb that hammered inside him. But Valerie's words of advice echoed in his mind.

Take it slow and easy . . .

God! That was proving damned near impossible. Slow and easy the second or third time—maybe. But the first? Nathan didn't know if he had it in him to proceed at a snail's pace when his male body was rebelling against the commands sent down by his brain.

Elyssa swore she'd come uncoiled when his hands slid beneath the band of her slacks to investigate the quivering flesh of her abdomen. His fingertips splayed out as they glided ever lower, and she found herself gasping for breath while her pulse rate pounded in triple time. When she realized he had eased her slacks down her hips, she reflexively froze.

"No!" she panted, her hand clamping tightly over his. "I can't!"

Twelve

Nathan fought for control. "Why? Because you think I'm using sex as a device to get what I want from your father's estate?"

"Yes and no."

He muttered sourly. "Damn it, Elyssa, this isn't about anything except you and me."

"You don't understand."

"I'm not getting much help in doing it." Nathan reined in his frustration and tried to think logically. "Is it because of the scars? If it is, I already know about them." His gaze fastened on her quivering lips, aching to devour them all over again.

She flinched, wondering if she had been correct in thinking he had taken her to the red rock canyon to peel away another layer of her defenses and to leave her more vulnerable to his ploys. He had used her, she thought shakily. He was using her now, and she was too attracted to him, too emotionally devastated, *not* to let him get away with it.

"Althea told me how you came by the scars. I'm sorry about what you had to endure. But they don't matter to me," he told her slowly and deliberately. "Do you understand? They don't matter."

Elyssa squirmed, attempting to cover herself. "They matter to me. And I . . . I don't think I can." She averted her gaze from his. "I can't face the humiliation of your . . . disappointment!" she blurted out.

Nathan frowned, confused. How could she think she would disappoint him? Her fervent responses had made him feel very manly, and had brought an incredible satisfaction.

"Lady," he said with a roguish grin, "you're doing everything except disappointing me. Mostly you're driving me crazy with wanting you. Why would you even think I would give a damn about the scars when other men have seen—?"

"That's just it."

The time of reckoning had come. Always before, she had terminated a relationship before it reached this point. But she couldn't walk away from Hunter. Their lives were too closely entwined and would be for weeks to come. She was going to have to face the embarrassment of telling him the truth, even when she knew she had absolutely no reason to be ashamed of her lack of experience. Chastity and discretion were virtues; they always would be. Even so, she felt awkward about broaching this unprecedented discussion.

"What's just it?" Nathan persisted.

"Damn it, Hunter. Are you deliberately being dense, just to embarrass me? Nobody else has seen the scars."

Those intense blue eyes shot into her like nails projected from a gun. "Nobody?"

"Nobody."

"You mean you always do it in the dark?"

Elyssa swatted him on the shoulder. He was making this harder than she imagined. "No, you dimwitted cowboy, I don't *do* it at all."

Nathan felt like an ass for pressing her, but Elyssa tugged her clothes back into place and then rose off the sofa. She stared at the the poster of Garth Brooks that hung above the CD player. "I would appreciate it if you would stop staring at me like I'm an endangered species or an accomplished liar and you can't figure out which. And I hope you're satisfied, damn you. I just told you what no other man knows, and I wouldn't have if we didn't have business to conduct in the future. Since we have to work together, you need to know my limitations so you won't try to seduce me into giving you what you want from the ranch."

Nathan felt as if an unseen fist had rammed him in the belly. He was still stuck on her claim of being a virgin, still trying to make himself believe it. "You've never—?"

She flashed him an annoyed glare. "I thought I just said that."

"But Robert—"

"—was getting it from somebody else because he *wasn't* getting it from me." Embarrassment gave way to frustration and then to anger. "Maybe you'd better leave, Hunter. I expect you're accustomed to things I've only read about and seen on movie screens. And if you dare ridicule me, I'll grab a skillet and pound you over the head. Now, kindly get out of here!"

This, Nathan decided, was the thing he didn't know about Elyssa that Valerie had hinted at. No wonder she withdrew when she found herself in uncharted territory. But if she thought he'd been put off because she hadn't fallen into bed a few times to test the waters and determine what all the fuss over sex was about, she was sorely mistaken. The thought of being Elyssa's first lover drove him wild with anticipation . . . and apprehension.

"Cutler?" Nathan found himself staring across the room at Elyssa.

"What, Hunter?"

"What if we do make love and *I* disappoint *you?*"

She glanced back at him, studying his ruggedly striking profile. "Is that supposed to be a joke? If it is, I don't think it's very amusing."

"I've got news for you, darlin'," he said with an awkward smile. "I'm a little out of practice. There aren't all that many women running around down on the farm. And few females hang out at the John Deere Implement dealership and local grain elevator. You may be expecting a helluva lot more than I can deliver. Just how high have you set your expectations?"

Elyssa burst out laughing. If nothing else, it released the

tension. For years, she had imagined what it might be like to experiment with intimacy, if she ever overcame her feelings of inadequacy and self-consciousness. Her hesitation and cautious restraint went even deeper than the scars, deeper than Hunter could comprehend.

He grabbed her hand and tugged her down on his lap.

"What is so damned funny, Cutler?" he demanded.

"You are." She fought to smother her giggles. "The one time I have come remotely close to letting go, you imply that the moment I imagined as unique and special will be a disappointment. You've shattered my illusions."

"You were expecting fireworks and clanging bells, I take it?" He finally managed a grin.

"Sure, why not? If I'm going to fly, why not travel first class?"

Nathan set her down beside him on the sofa, then stood up and reached over to switch off the lamp. She peered curiously up at the shadowy figure that towered over her.

"Shall we see what we can do about setting fuses to fireworks and about ringing bells?"

He extended his hand, waiting for her to decide whether to reach out to him, whether or not she actually trusted him enough to extend the boundaries of their relationship. He knew it had to be her choice. If she thought he was pressuring her, things would end up exactly as they had before—with him aching and her scared stiff.

Elyssa stared at his proffered hand. She had never wanted to take a chance with a man as much as she wanted to now. Still, she hesitated, afraid she would freeze up again and knowing how unfair it would be to Hunter if she did.

"Elyssa?" His voice was as soft as velvet, as gentle as a caress. "It's your call. All I'm asking is for you to make up your mind. You know what I want. I don't think there are any recorded cases of men actually dying of sexual frustration. I might not like being turned down, but I'll live."

Despite his attempt to amuse her, she swallowed nervously,

still staring at his hand. "I'm afraid you're going to wish you had walked away."

"I seriously doubt that."

Her hand lifted to his, and warm fingers enfolded hers, steady and reassuring. As he slowly drew her to her feet, anticipation mingled with nervousness inside her. "Are we going to start with a quickie in the bathtub?" she questioned, hoping to break the tension that was escalating furiously.

"I think we'd better stick to basics for starters," he advised with a chuckle.

"Gee whiz, Hunter. I didn't know I had so much to learn. Should I be taking notes?"

He smiled in the darkness and turned toward the hall. "No, we'll just keep practicing until we get it right. Better than right, actually," he amended. "Until it gets as good as it can get . . ."

Elyssa trembled when he paused by her bed and reached for her . . . slow and easy. She wanted this—wanted it with him. She wanted to let go of every inhibition, every hangup; wanted to explore a world of sensations she had only read and heard about. And she wanted to entrust him with her first voyage into passion.

Just this once, Elyssa promised herself, she wasn't going to withdraw as she usually did when a man ventured too close. She was going to shut her eyes, to forget past and future, forget everything except the feel of Hunter's body.

She nearly knocked the pins out from under Nathan when she yielded so sweetly to his first touch. He was starkly aware of the uncertainty she was battling to overcome. And he had the feeling there was more behind her avoidance of intimacy than self-consciousness about her scars. How bad could they be, after all? Perhaps when he and Elyssa were as close as two people can get, she would trust him enough to confide in him.

Even as Elyssa surrendered to his kiss, Nathan knew she was holding something back, reserving judgment, waiting to see if he would eventually betray her, and half expecting that he would. She had decided to trust him with her body, but she wasn't taking chances with her heart. But he was determined to demolish each and every emotional hurdle he encountered; and he was going to see that Elyssa savored and enjoyed each new sensation before experiencing the next. He wasn't going to rush her from one phase of passion to another, even if that drove him mad with impatience.

Elyssa blinked, bewildered, when Nathan withdrew from what had been an incredibly passionate kiss. She stared up into his shadowed face outlined by the glowing night light in the hall. "Did I do something wrong already, Hunter?"

"No, honey. I want you to undress me. We're going to do this at whatever pace you decide to set. However much you want, however you want it. Show me the way you want to be loved."

Tentatively, she reached up to unfasten the buttons of his shirt, feeling the thudding of his heart beneath her fumbling fingertips. Her hand slid across the muscled plane of his chest, marveling at the contours of hair-roughened flesh. She learned him by touch and scent, enthralled with the privilege of setting her own inquisitive pace.

When her exploring hand skimmed over his belly to trace the band of his jeans, Elyssa heard his ragged breath catch, felt him flinch.

"Did I hurt you?" she questioned, hands stalling.

"Yes . . ." When she started to retreat, Nathan caught her hand, folding it against him. "But you're inflicting the kind of pain I gladly welcome, the kind that burns from inside out," he told her hoarsely.

God! He hadn't realized how conditioned and monotonous sex had become until proceeding slowly and gently, fully experiencing and anticipating each caress. Her touch went through him like an explosion of intense heat. Every inch of skin she touched was scorched and smoldering before her hand drifted away in timid exploration.

He battled for control when her fingers limned the masculine rounding of his biceps and then skittered over his ribs. Her fingers splayed over the clenched muscles of his stomach, and by the time her hand brushed against the denim that covered his swollen manhood and he heard the rasp of the zipper on his jeans, he was very nearly insane!

"Am I . . . ?" Elyssa hesitated when she heard his muffled groan. "Am I being too bold and curious? You said—"

"I meant what I said," he assured her in a strangled voice. "Whatever you want, however you want it." *Unless this sweet torture kills me first!*

"Then would it be all right if I . . . touched you?"

"Where?" he whispered huskily.

"There?" Her dark eyes focused below his belt buckle. She was thankful for the darkness that concealed her blush.

"Only if you're sure that's what you want," he managed to say without choking.

"No one ever asked me what I wanted before," she confided as she tested the velvety hardness of him.

Nathan was certain now that his willpower was nowhere near as strong as he had hoped it would be, as a laugh bubbled in Elyssa's throat and her hand folded around the throbbing length of him in awkward and yet wickedly tantalizing exploration.

"First rule of sex," Nathan croaked as he took her hand and held it in his own. "You never laugh at the size of a man's basic appliances."

Elyssa chortled at the very idea that she found him anything except wonderfully, gloriously, and largely male. "It's not that," she assured him, her eyes sparkling as she wormed her hand loose to caress him. "I was just thinking that refraining from experimentation all these years wasn't really to my advantage. If the truth be known, I don't know what the hell I'm doing. I kind of wanted this to be a little bit special for you, too. And Hunter?"

"Yes?" He sucked in his breath when the pad of her forefinger glided over the moist tip of his manhood in a maddeningly slow caress, and then retreated, leaving him arching toward her like a love-starved cat eagerly responding to a stroking hand.

"How are we supposed to plug a two-hundred-twenty-volt appliance into a one-ten socket?"

Nathan did burst out laughing then. His arms encircled her and he lifted her off the bed to nuzzle his forehead against hers. "I think we'd better come at this from a different direction before you take me so far over the edge I can't hold back. I'll lead and you follow. If I startle you or change tempo too fast, you'll let me know, won't you? The last thing I want to do is frighten you off."

Elyssa watched in rapt fascination as Hunter pulled off his shirt and jeans. There was just enough illumination in the room to accentuate the male contours of his powerful body. She stared at him in feminine appreciation, certain the male models who posed for calendars and book covers couldn't compare to this brawny mass of honed flesh.

The mattress shifted as he settled his weight upon the bed, and Elyssa found herself rolling toward a living column of hard, warm strength. Her entire body clenched as he levered up to remove her sweater and trace the edge of her lacy bra.

"Relax, honey. We're a long way from where we're going. I want you to enjoy every moment of getting there. I won't rush you. I want to explore you as thoroughly as you explored me."

"But I wasn't finished with you," she protested.

His thumb grazed the ultrasensitive tips of her breasts, then swept leisurely over her supple flesh. "That comes later, in Chapter Two of *Hunter's Love Manual.*"

"How many chapters are there?" she whispered, his languid caresses leaving her body radiating with pleasure.

"I don't know yet. I'm still doing extensive research . . ."

His moist lips feathered over her throat and glided lower to capture the taut peak of a breast. Elyssa melted in the fire that flamed in her in deliciously sensual degrees. His hands whispered over her skin while he suckled first one beaded nipple and then the other, and she arched helplessly toward him, responding with mindless abandon, marveling at the force of the need that rippled through every fiber of her being.

Sweeping hands and sensuous lips discovered her, tantalized her until a soft moan escaped her lips. Elyssa swore she had sunk into the mattress, as if it were a puffy cloud. Sensation after scintillating sensation hummed through her, each one more profound and mystifying than the one that came before.

She wanted more, needed something she couldn't explain and no longer even questioned. She felt certain Hunter had dissolved her every inhibition . . . until his inquiring hand slid inside her slacks to brush over the slick scars and uneven skin on her left hip. And suddenly those self-conscious feelings came thundering back, followed by the nightmare of what had caused her to plunge over the cliff that fateful day.

Nathan felt her become rigid when he dared to touch what she couldn't bring herself to let him see in full light. Her hand settled over the scars to discourage him from touching her there, but he pushed it away to brush his lips over her hip. Her skin was tightly drawn in between bunches of lacerated muscles that had been severed and stitched back together. Beneath his lips, he could feel the artificial joint that had been constructed to replace damaged bone and cartilage.

If Elyssa thought for one minute that discovering her scars and imagining the agony she had endured offended him, she was wrong. Her healed wounds didn't make her less than perfect. She was still the essence of femininity, a delightful treat to his starved senses.

Nothing could have stunned Elyssa more than his display of tenderness, his acceptance of her imperfection. He had silently and unequivocally assured her that what had happened to her didn't matter to him. And he was slowly but surely silencing that cruel, taunting voice out of past—the one that had always shattered her self-confidence when it had come to intimacy with men . . . until now, until Hunter. His soft whispers drowned out the raging voice and looming face that had made her freeze each time she'd wandered too near the boundaries of restraint.

All she could hear now was Hunter calling her name like an incantation. The husky chant was hypnotic, arousing. *He* made her feel wanted and desirable, no longer a prisoner of a nightmare from her past. She would always love him for that, for unchaining her and setting her free at last.

"God, Elyssa, I want you more than I want breath," he groaned, in torment.

His seeking hands tunneled beneath the silk panties that clung to her skin, pushing away the hindering garment that concealed the sultry petals of her womanly secrets. He nudged her legs apart with his elbow to sketch the satiny texture of her inner thighs, and felt her tremble at the disturbing newness of a man's touch. Then he caressed passion's tender bud, savored the feel of her soft, quivering flesh beneath his fingertips. And when he slid his finger inside the heated folds of femininity to stroke her, he heard her gasp and felt her burning around him in the most innocent and incredible kind of pleasure. Her shivering response drew a wild answering heat from him, and Nathan fought with every nerve and muscle clenched to restrain his need.

Maybe it was old-fashioned to harbor the satisfaction of knowing he was the first man to discover Elyssa's sweetest secrets, but he treasured the experience nonetheless. When he sought the moist softness of her untried body and felt warm rain melting on his fingertip, he shuddered with the overwhelming desire to feel himself surrounded by her silken heat, to become a part of that shimmering flame that seared like liquid fire.

This was more than just a swift tumble to appease his male needs. Whatever the reason Elyssa had waited for passion, he wanted her to cherish these moments. For her this was to be a time of reverent discovery tempered by a tender patience Nathan hadn't even realized he possessed until he'd wanted to ensure that Elyssa confronted no fears or disappointments in his arms. He wanted her first time to be the best time either of them had ever had . . .

Elyssa's composure shattered like crystal with the gliding penetrations of his fingertip, which stroked, receded, and then gently caressed her all over again. A crescendo built deep inside her and then fanned out like ripples on a pond, triggering wild, ardent sensations that left no part of her untouched by their intensity.

A coil of searing heat unfurled inside her, fanning flames that robbed her of breath and rational thought. When his lips skimmed over her thigh she swore she would go mad with unbearable wanting. He had lured her to the edge, then left her dangling in mindless oblivion. She wasn't sure she could endure much more of this sensual torture without bursting into shameless pleas that he appease the burning ache that consumed her.

Nathan felt the first tremors of excitement vibrate through Elyssa as he inserted two fingers into the moist heat he had summoned from her. He slowly spread his fingertips, preparing her for masculine invasion. She was so tight, yet so overwhelmingly generous in her response to his touch.

Much as he wanted to bury himself deep within her, he waited until the moment when she convulsed around his fingertips, then he braced himself on one arm, watching her eyes widen in the dim light that illuminated the room.

"Good God, Hunter!" Elyssa gasped when the most incredible sensations assailed her. Exquisite pleasure more shocking than pain riveted her, devoured her with its intensity. "Hunter . . . ?"

"I'm right here, honey," he whispered with a smile.

He came to her then, at the exact moment when she shivered in wild climax, her lush body instinctively waiting to accept him. Nathan squeezed his eyes shut and slowly sheathed himself in the satin warmth of her. He felt her tense at the unfamiliarity of masculine possession, knew that claws of pain raked through her, even while she bravely tried to conceal that from him. He wondered if she felt he was tearing her in two, and wished he could spare her discomfort, granting her only the quintessence of pleasure.

When she melted around him, whispering his name and clinging trustingly to him, Nathan lost what little control he had left. She was like a shimmering fire and he was burning alive in her arms. Tenderness buckled beneath hungry needs that he'd held too long at bay, and he clutched her to him, surrendering to a passion that exploded with killing force. As he drove into her, Elyssa didn't resist; she met each urgent thrust with such selfless generosity that Nathan was humbled by the precious gift she offered him.

And when the last tumultuous waves of ecstasy crested over him, he clutched her so tightly to him that he could no longer tell where her soft, feminine body ended and his own masculine form began. They were closer than close. They had become a living breathing entity, flesh melded to flesh. They were no more than what they had become to each other, two complementary halves, now whole, transcending all dimensions of time . . .

Nathan didn't want to come down from this phenomenal emotional high. He would have preferred to drift aimlessly until the last remnants of indescribable splendor ebbed. Elyssa, however, seemed to be of another opinion.

"Hunter?" Her voice was thick with the aftereffects of newly discovered passion.

He lifted his head from the curve of her neck to see luminous eyes peering up at him. "Don't ask me for a repeat performance too soon. Once with you damned near killed me," he rasped.

The contented smile faded from her lips. "That bad?"

He chuckled softly and dropped a kiss onto her petal-soft mouth. "No, honey, it was that *good.*"

"Thanks, Hunter. You're doing wonders for my confidence, but—"

"I'm being honest."

"So am I." Elyssa glided her fingertips over the massive width of his shoulders. "But I'm disappointed that I couldn't give you the same thing you gave me, except in reverse."

He frowned, puzzled. "You wanna explain that? I'm afraid I'm not following your drift."

Elyssa was not surprised. She wasn't expressing herself very clearly. She collected her thoughts. Hunter's warm strength pressed down upon her, but it was a satisfying weight she didn't really want removed. She enjoyed having his swarthy body forged to hers, the exceptional closeness they shared.

"You made tonight a cherished memory for me, but I know you've experienced the feelings I just realized existed before. I couldn't give you what other women could because I haven't learned how. Now I wish I *had* experimented, so I didn't have to fumble around trying to figure out what you might like."

Nathan laughed softly. "Honey, what I like is loving you, *exactly* the way I did and *exactly* the way you responded. No pretense, just pure instinct. I'm anything but disappointed . . . And you?"

"Hardly." Elyssa smiled impishly, gloriously content and bubbling with elation. "I'm ready to try out the Jacuzzi."

"What if Valerie comes back?" Nathan questioned as he eased down beside her and propped his ruffled raven head on his hand to stare down at her shadowy profile.

"She'll have to get her own man," Elyssa declared. "I'm too conventional for kinky stuff."

"I wasn't planning on inviting her into the tub. I just don't want any unexpected bystanders lurking around."

What Nathan really wanted was to spend the entire night with Elyssa, to wake with her by his side. He couldn't do that with Valerie in the same apartment, not without making Elyssa uncomfortable.

And he wanted to be with Elyssa when she started analyzing what happened between them and why. He had the uneasy feeling her mistrust would begin to hound her when he wasn't around to reassure her that their night of lovemaking had nothing to do with the problems on the ranch. He knew she took nothing at face value, not after her unpleasant experience with Robert Grayson and the warnings of Gil and Virgil.

Elyssa had a natural tendency to get to the bottom of everything, to establish possible motives. Although she was capable of unbelievable passion, she was also amazingly objective about the people she liked or admired. Blind trust was something she simply couldn't give. She would have to be constantly wooed and won, and it would take time to earn her trust.

Nathan was just going to have to hope this night of pure heaven didn't become his own private hell. He didn't want to sacrifice something this rare and sublime, not even to see Ely Rawlins's last wishes carried out.

"If Val holds true to form, she won't be back for hours." Elyssa traced the full curve of his mouth with her index finger. "You, on the other hand, may not come back at all . . ."

"I wouldn't bet on it," he said, as he agilely came to his feet with Elyssa cradled possessively in his arms. "I want this to be the beginning, not the end of a wild, sweet dream."

Elyssa wondered if, come morning, she was going to regret casting caution to the wind and going along with those unexplained feelings that bombarded her when Nathan Hunter was around. But when he turned on the faucets in the darkened bathroom and drew her down into the tub with him, she decided that she would follow Scarlett O'Hara's policy of worrying about that tomorrow.

Shortly thereafter, the touch of his skillful hands and the warm, searing demand of his kiss made her forget there was such a thing as tomorrow . . .

Thirteen

Valerie Mitchell was the best roommate anybody could have, Elyssa decided. She hadn't tried to wheedle information about Nathan Hunter's evening visit, which was a good thing because that would have been awkward to discuss. Elyssa felt guilty about letting her vulnerability lead her into an unprecedented situation with a man—a man she still wasn't sure she could trust.

She was not about to allow newly experienced passion to turn her into a foolish romantic. She wouldn't let herself trust what she felt, or to blindly accept what Hunter had told her as absolute truth. She had to display caution when dealing with a man who proved to have a devastating effect on her.

All she had was Hunter's word against her uncle's when it came to the conversation that had taken place between Ely and Gil that fateful day. Gil and Hunter presented contradicting stories, and, quite honestly, Elyssa didn't know who to believe. It was maddening to wonder if she had fallen prey to Hunter's persuasive charm and that he would eventually betray her. Furthermore, it was frustrating to think that her own uncle might have lied to her.

Throughout the days that followed, Elyssa wrestled with indecision and forced herself to handle bleak obligations. Valerie's moral support was a godsend. She had insisted on taking a personal business leave to join Elyssa at the ranch, and was serving as a distraction and a confidante while Elyssa recovered from her loss.

Uncle Gil was none too happy when Elyssa informed him that she was still pondering the partnership contract and intended to delay her decision for several days. Nor was he thrilled with the announcement that she had placed Hunter in complete charge of her half of the ranch until further notice—which meant Gil had to discuss his farming practices with an outsider.

With the ranch gearing up to swath and bale the first cutting of alfalfa, Nathan and the hands were busy checking equipment and machinery. And that, Elyssa had noted with amused interest, was a shame because Valerie had found herself intrigued by Ray Twigger, whose Texas drawl had sparked her attention at first meeting. She had been in cowboy heaven when Ray asked her to go horseback riding with him when he got off work.

The only one around the ranch who didn't appreciate Valerie's and Elyssa's presence was Claudia Gilbert. Elyssa had the feeling the younger woman considered them rivals who were stealing her limelight. At any rate, Claudia was as unsociable as a disturbed rattlesnake. Every day that passed found her trying to call more attention to herself. Her skin-tight clothes were shocking. Even Althea was taken aback by some of her daughter's provocative getups.

As for Elyssa, she didn't quite know how to deal with her one-night fling with Hunter. It seemed the moment had come and gone. He had left her to herself the past few days, as if nothing significant had happened. She didn't know whether to be relieved or insulted by his polite but distant attention. Obviously, once the deed had been done, he'd been ready to settle back into his normal routine, and he didn't plan to come trotting to her door until lust overcame him.

Without so much as one private word between them, Hunter deposited Ely's will in her hands on the way out the door after lunch. Elyssa had procrastinated for two hours before forcing herself to venture into Ely's office to face his lifelike portrait and read his last will and testament. But once she settled into

Ely's well-worn chair at the desk, she sensed a comforting presence and felt Ely was looking over her shoulder, watching her from the beyond.

She wasn't surprised to learn that Hunter had been appointed executor of the estate. And because of what he had told her earlier in the week, she was not shocked to see that Ely had willed his undivided property to both her and Hunter.

If what Hunter had told her was true, Ely wanted the partnership terminated before Gil's and Virgil's debts could cripple the ranch. She could understand why Uncle Gil would want to let the partnership share his debts. It was a matter of self-preservation, *if* Hunter's accusations were correct.

Elyssa had just picked up the phone, intending to leave a message requesting Cousin Virgil to contact her, when he came barging through the door, wearing an angry scowl.

"Tell me it isn't true," Virgil muttered without bothering to offer a civil greeting.

"It's true," Elyssa replied. "And you didn't bother to knock. Your manners haven't improved over the years, Cuz."

"I'm talking about the will, damn it!" he exploded. "Your father *did* leave half your property to that greedy bastard, didn't he?"

How, Elyssa wondered, had Virgil known that? Had the Rawlins family lawyer imparted that information or had Hunter rubbed it in Virgil's freckled face?

"Are you going to stand for that, Elyssa? If I were you, I'd contest it long and loudly. Nate has no right whatsoever to Rawlins property. He's a freeloader!"

"I have no intention of going against what my father obviously wanted," Elyssa informed her irate cousin.

"Oh, for crissake, Elyssa, just how naive are you? Don't you know how many people there are out there who attach themselves to wealthy senior citizens in the hope of being included in a will? Uncle Ely was a prime target with you out of the picture for so many years, and Nate took advantage of every opportunity to play up to him. He constantly reminded your father that Sid Hunter died while making a run with a truckload of stock Ely was supposed to have driven to the rodeo. Everybody around here knew how bad Ely felt about that. But every time Nate wanted something, he'd mention losing his father and Ely would crumble."

Elyssa wondered just how many ways that incident could be twisted and used. Two, so far—Hunter's version and Virgil's. Still, when it came to deciding who was more likely to be honest with her, Elyssa found herself leaning toward Hunter. Virgil had been a red-haired weasel in years gone by, and he probably was just as much of one now.

"Sorry, Cuz. My father depended on Hunter and practically adopted him. Therefore, I will bend to his wishes."

"God, you're turning out to be as blind as Ely! For years I've listened to Nate boast about how he'd pulled the wool over your father's eyes and how he was going to have the whole damned ranch. And now you're letting him get away with it," Virgil muttered sourly. "You're going to stand aside and let him gain a stronger foothold. Before long he'll have absolute control!"

"I'd rather have Hunter for a partner than a bank," Elyssa shot back.

Virgil stepped back as if she had slapped him. "What?"

"You heard me."

Virgil's face puckered and he swore under his breath. "I was afraid Nate was going to try any tactic to turn you against your own family. He has. That's nothing but a pack of lies! I didn't go into debt."

"No? Then give me the name of the bank so I can double check."

"I most certainly will not!"

"Why?" One perfectly arched brow lifted challengingly. "Afraid I'll discover Hunter is the one who speaks the truth?"

"Of course not." Virgil slapped both hands on the desk and leaned forward to confront Elyssa face-to-face. "It's because I don't want rumors of a scandal tarnishing Rawlins Ranch.

And may I remind you, such gossip would effect you, too, Elyssa.

"Well then, may I remind *you*," Elyssa countered, rising to match his intimidating stance, "Cutler Corporation retains a criminal investigator who would do me the favor of checking you out. In two or three days, I'll have an axe poised over your neck if you're lying to me."

"Damn it, woman. Who the hell do you think you are?"

"The cousin you set up in a malicious prank," Elyssa hissed, giving way to the need to vent years of pent-up resentment. "I suspect Uncle Gil would be appalled to learn what really happened that day twelve years ago. He might even react the same way Dad did when he felt responsible for Sid Hunter's death. In fact, Uncle Gil might be persuaded to side with whatever decision *I* make in regard to this ranch and the leeches infesting it."

Virgil's face turned bright red. "Don't mess with me, Elyssa. You're out of your league. Always were. You keep screwing around with Nate and see where it gets you. And I don't doubt you've been sleeping with that cocksman. You and everybody else," he added with a derisive snort. "Just ask Claudia what rules Nate plays by. Knowing him, he's probably got you thinking he cares about you. But, too late, you're going to discover you've been had in more ways than one and you're going to learn that all he cares about is himself. If he cons you into thinking he wants what's best for you, I promise you'll regret it."

Elyssa valiantly fought to conceal her reaction to those damning comments. She would have preferred not to hear Claudia's name linked with Hunter's. It was more than obvious that young woman was attracted to him. Now that she thought about it, Elyssa wondered if Claudia did see her as a rival. Finding herself in the same category with Claudia was a slap in the face.

Virgil smiled nastily. "You think I'm lying about Nate and Claudia? Think again. You were probably seduced into taking Nate's side. The man works fast, doesn't he? All I can say is you're goddamn lucky to have a stepfather with a fortune of his own; otherwise, you'd find yourself penniless. Sure as hell, Nate is going to *screw* you out of this one. Keeping this partnership going is the only chance you've got. It's too bad it wasn't Nate who had that nasty accident."

When Virgil whirled around and stalked off, Elyssa wilted into her chair, feeling as if she had gone fifteen rounds in a boxing match. She tucked the will away and called John Preston at Cutler Corporation. If Virgil was lying about his debts, she would fry him alive. And if he was telling the truth about Hunter and Claudia, she would . . .

You'd what, Cutler? she asked herself. Play the role of the woman scorned—again? Damn it, she could not afford to mix business with emotion. She knew better. Just because she and Hunter had made love didn't give her an exclusive right to him.

When Valerie poked her head around the office door, Elyssa mustered a smile. She wished Val's enthusiasm were contagious. She could use some of that vitality right now.

"I'm off to my riding lesson, Ellie." Valerie beamed. "I might miss supper so don't wait for me."

Elyssa glanced past the petite blonde to see Twig lingering behind her, all spruced up and smiling in anticipation. At least some people around here were enjoying themselves.

After the beaming couple strode off, Elyssa ambled outside to see Claudia lounging in the swing on the cottage's porch while two-year-old Timmy toddled across the lawn, chasing a kitten. Elyssa sallied forth. She wasn't sure what approach to take with Claudia. She'd just fly by the seat of her pants, she decided.

Claudia glanced up and frowned when Elyssa stepped onto the porch, decked out in bright red Roper jeans and a colorful Western blouse. "You must be bored to tears if you're looking me up for companionship."

Charming little thing, wasn't she? Elyssa didn't figure little Timmy would have much of a chance in life unless his grandmother took him under her wing. With Claudia's influence, the poor kid would turn out as sour as curdled milk.

"You've been pretty standoffish since I came back," Elyssa said for starters. "Any reason why? If I've offended you somehow, I'm sorry."

Claudia filed her hot-pink fingernails and buffed them on her "painted-on" blouse. "Let's just cut all the crap and get down to brass tacks, shall we? How do you expect me to behave around you when I think Nate has been buttering you up for what he can get?"

"You think that's what he's doing?" God, Cutler, you sound like a damned shrink! Elyssa told herself.

Claudia scoffed, her thick makeup wrinkling like a mask. "I *know* that's what he's doing. All of a sudden, I've become invisible. Nate treats you like visiting royalty and me like the doormat he walks over to get to you." She stared pensively at Elyssa. "Have the two of you . . . ? Never mind. I don't want to know. I already know Nate has been avoiding me lately. For a man who knows his way around a woman's anatomy like he does, one who has the sexual appetite of a bull, I call that suspicious."

Elyssa suddenly felt sick. From all indications, jealousy was eating Claudia alive. The woman hadn't come right out and said she'd been sleeping with Hunter every chance she got, but she certainly had given that impression. It was all Elyssa could do not to storm off in a huff, but that would reveal her own foolish involvement. Determinedly, she held her ground.

"Hunter and I are business partners now. We have to maintain a working relationship," she said.

"Yeah, well, just make sure that's all it is. If you know what's good for you, you won't play into his hands like I did. I thought we had something good going until recently. Now I think I'm the place he comes to when he wants physical satisfaction."

"Claudia!" Althea emerged from the back door of the ranch house, hands on her hips. "I thought you were going to help me get supper on the table for the haying crew. Nate called on the CB and said the rest of the men will be in to eat in a few minutes."

"Coming." Claudia unfolded herself from the porch swing and sauntered over to scoop Timmy up in her arms before sparing Elyssa a bitter glance. "I guess I can't really blame you. Nate's all man, and I've got no hold on him. Just don't expect more than he intends to give . . ."

Elyssa unclenched her knotted fists and decided to walk off her frustration. She hadn't gone fifty yards before the patrol car crunched across the gravel and halted beside her. She immediately stiffened when Gavin Spencer slipped his athletic frame from beneath the steering wheel and swaggered toward her. A rooster couldn't have strutted better than Gavin.

"*Killing* time, Officer Spencer?" she inquired sarcastically.

"No, making up for lost time," he replied with a suave smile, flaunting the shallow charm and unwarranted arrogance he had cultivated in high school.

"Come on, sugar, give me a chance to make amends. Don't you think I've punished myself for what happened way back when?"

"No, you're hardly the type." Elyssa spun about and strode toward the barn. She preferred to stare at a real horse's ass than to share Gavin's company.

Big mistake. Gavin followed her into the barn.

"I don't think you realize what benefits you could receive by showing me a little respect." He snagged her arm, turning her to face him. "I'm the local law enforcement around Rawlins."

"And I'd like to have you arrested. Now let me go!" Elyssa jerked loose, only to find herself pinned against the nearby stall, her body mashed by Gavin's, his arousal evident. Damn. The man had a problem. His hormones obviously clicked in at the mere sight of a woman.

"Like I said, sugar. I'm the law—"

"God help us all," Elyssa spat out. "Now back off, Gavin, before I—"

The sound of footsteps forced Gavin to retreat. He glanced sideways to see Nathan striding inside with the ever faithful Ricky at his heels. "Hi, Nate. How's the swathing going?"

Nathan took one look at Elyssa's pinched expression and knew there was more going on between her and Gavin than renewing old acquaintances. She looked like a pressure cooker bleeding off steam through its safety valve.

"One of the swathers broke down," Nathan reported. "Les Fykes is overhauling it. Other than that, we're on schedule."

"I hope we don't get any rain while the alfalfa is down. Your first cutting would be ruined if it hasn't been baled and stored." Gavin cast Elyssa a wry smile before sauntering off. "Just thought I'd stop by while I was making my rounds. Talk to you later, Nate."

When Gavin climbed into his car, Nathan pivoted toward Elyssa. "Don't you think it's time you told me what the hell's going on with you and our local cop?"

"And don't you think it's time you told me what the hell's going on with you and the resident call girl?"

Nathan blinked at the abrupt change in subject. "What?"

"You know what." Elyssa battled for control and lost. "Claudia all but told me the two of you have been making your own hay after the sun sets. And you tried to feed me that line about being out of practice! To think I almost believed you!"

"Claudia told you we were lovers?" Nathan stared at her as if she had sprouted antlers. "That's a damned lie."

"Not according to Cousin Virgil *and* Claudia," she countered.

"You're all too ready to believe the worst about me, aren't you, Cutler? Did you stop to think you might be playing into Virgil's hands?"

"Like I played into yours?"

Nathan took a step forward and Elyssa took two steps back. He halted, studying her somberly. "Don't spoil what we had. I've kept my distance to protect your reputation, but mine is the one that's getting tarnished by a lazy divorcée and your spiteful cousin who is probably desperate to get your cooperation."

"Well, we'll see if he's as desperate as you say. I questioned him about his debt and—"

"You did what!" Nathan growled. Then he cursed under his breath.

"I asked him if he had outstanding loans," Elyssa informed him.

"Damn it, Cutler, that was a stupid thing to do! Now you've given Virgil time to cover his tracks. It'll be my word against his. Your father and I hadn't planned to let him know we were wise to his debts until after the partnership had been revoked." Nathan jerked off his straw hat and slapped it against his thigh. "You're going to have to announce that the partnership won't be reinstated, and you're going to have to do it fast. And when you do, you're placing yourself in jeopardy. You could wind up conveniently dead. Then your loving family will inherit your share, unless you have a will. Do you?"

"No."

"Hell's fire, woman. Use your head once in a while." Nathan loomed over her—something he did exceeding well, in Elyssa's opinion. "I want you to sign over power of attorney to me, first thing in the morning. We'll hold an auction to divide up the land and we'll inventory the machinery. And in the meantime, you're going back to the City."

"I'm not going anywhere, and I am certainly not going to give you power of attorney. How stupid do you think I am?"

"Stupid enough to let Virgil know you have something on him. You've got him running scared. He's desperate. What if Ely's death *wasn't* an accident, as you seem to suspect? How do you plan to protect yourself?"

"I'll go to the police and—" Elyssa shuddered at the thought. Gavin was already trying to lord it over her, and she could guess what he'd expect in the way of gratitude for opening an investigation.

Nathan watched Elyssa freeze. He was in no mood for more of her evasive answers when it came to Gavin Spencer. He wasn't backing off this time, either, no matter what he had to say to break her vow of silence.

"What's the local cop got to do with you? And don't feed me any bullshit, Cutler. I'm not blind. You look like hostility personified every time Gavin sniffs around you. Old boyfriend? Is that it?"

"It's none of your damned business, and I don't want to talk about it." She made a beeline for the barn door, but Nathan clamped a hand on her arm before she could whiz by. "Let go!"

"Not until you tell me why the man torments you."

Elyssa launched herself away, only to be slammed back against unyielding muscle. She struggled; he restrained her. She lashed out at him, and he caught her wrist before her palm connected with his cheek.

"Quit fighting me. That's the last thing we need right now. Just tell me how Gavin fits in."

"No."

"Yes," he ordered gruffly. "I want to know *now*. I'm not letting you go until you tell me why you react the way you do every time he comes within ten feet of you."

"Just leave me alone, damn it!"

"No way, baby," he growled at her. "We're going to be here long past the day hell freezes over, waiting for you to explain."

Elyssa was so frustrated she was ready to explode. "He pushed me off the cliff," she blurted out before she could swallow the tormenting confession.

Nathan went perfectly still, but he didn't release his grasp on her. She was quivering like a tuning fork. "Why?" he asked softly.

Elyssa drew away, only to be drawn back against him. "Because Virgil told Gavin I had the hots for him. Gavin wanted to find out."

"Did you?"

"I had a crush on him, yes. I was fifteen and starry eyed. He was eighteen and eager for another conquest. When he stuck his hand up my blouse, I resisted and that made him furious. He said he knew I wanted a good . . ." Elyssa focused her tormented gaze on the shaft of sunlight that splintered into the window of the barn. "That I wanted him," she paraphrased. "Virgil had told him I was ready and willing, and Gavin expected me to . . ."

"Go on," Nathan demanded, silently cursing the men in the tale Elyssa had told. He watched her tremble from repressed rage, but he refused to release her until he'd heard all of it. "What did Gavin do when you resisted him?"

A coil of anger knotted in Elyssa's belly as the scene unfolded in her mind as it had so often in her dreams. "He grabbed the front of my jeans and jerked me to him. He was too strong to fight, and I was terrified by what was happening. In that moment, all my idealistic dreams were shattered. Gavin started groping me, and I reacted out of sheer desperation by raising a knee. It only made him furious. He shoved me backward in a fit of temper and I tripped."

Elyssa drew in a shuddering breath and squeezed back the memory of falling pell-mell over the jagged tumble of rocks. "As I lay there screaming and in pain Gavin threatened to do even worse to me if I breathed a word about what had happened. He swore he wouldn't send for help until I promised to keep his name out of it. When I refused, he started ridiculing me about not being woman enough to satisfy him or anyone else. He said the only thing I had going for me was family money."

Tears glistened in her eyes, but Elyssa blinked them back and plowed on, "All he cared about was keeping his job at the ranch. He said he really hadn't wanted to have anything to do with me in the first place, that he'd only planned to give me the birthday present I wanted because I was the boss's daughter. He made it clear he thought I'd be a lousy lay. I finally gave in to him when I couldn't bear the pain and humiliation any longer. To this day, I wonder if he would have left me there if I hadn't agreed to his demands."

"That miserable son of a bitch," Nathan muttered savagely.

"He's just a man." Elyssa's voice quivered with resentment. "Mistreating and using women seem to be characteristic of the gender."

She battled for composure. "Satisfied now, Hunter? Seems like I've spent my whole life getting used one way or the other, always the pawn to be played to somebody's advantage. It never seems to end."

Laughter and the murmur of voices prompted Elyssa to turn away to hide her tears. When Valerie and Twig swung from their saddles, Nathan blocked the other couple's view of her while she got herself in hand. But it didn't matter, Nathan realized a moment later. He and Elyssa could have been a couple of stabled horses for all Valerie and Twig noticed them. The pair had paused just inside the door where the shadows concealed them.

Nathan stood there feeling awkward and highly amused while his longtime friend dipped his sandy blond head to compensate for the differences of height, and Valerie's arms glided up and over Twig's shoulders, her lips parting.

From where Nathan stood, it seemed the mutual venture was becoming more intense by the second, if heavy breathing counted for anything. It did in Nathan's book. He wished he and Elyssa hadn't been placed at odds by Claudia's spiteful prank. To Elyssa, her lies were damning testimony. He'd thought he had begun to earn Elyssa's trust, and wham! The delicate bond between them had been severed. Nathan was going to have to read the riot act to the troublesome Claudia.

When Twig's hands glided over Valerie's hips and drew her full-length against him, Nathan shifted uncomfortably from one foot to the other. He could feel Elyssa's breath stirring against his arm, indicating that she was peeking around his shoulder to monitor the budding romance between her roommate and Nathan's best friend.

Since the couple were too involved to notice they had an audience, Nathan decided to make his presence known before he was treated to a firsthand account of Twig's seductive maneuvers.

"So that's what kissing is all about." Nathan stifled a chuckle when Val and Twig shot apart.

Even the shadows couldn't disguise the blush that flooded Twig's cheeks. "Damn it, Nate, you should've said something."

"I just did."

Twig flung his friend a disgruntled glare. "I meant *sooner*," he grumbled before he pivoted around and walked out.

Valerie chuckled good-naturedly when she saw Elyssa's dark head hovering behind Nathan's broad shoulder. "Salt of the earth. Sure fire winner every time," she declared before following in Twig's wake.

The supper bell that hung on the back porch clanged in the evening air.

Nathan automatically moved forward a few steps before he realized Elyssa hadn't budged. "Come on, Cutler. It doesn't pay to be late to a meal, not with this pack of starving wolves. There won't be anything left."

"I'd rather take a ride before dark," Elyssa declared.

Nathan half turned to stare at the determined set of her chin. Damn, there were times when he saw so much of the father in the daughter that it nearly knocked him to his knees. Ely was in those black diamond eyes, that stubborn stance. Jessica Rawlins Cutler had dragged her daughter off the ranch, but not before Ely had left a lasting mark on Elyssa. He would have been pleased to know his daughter had inherited some of his mannerisms.

"Would you like some company?" Nathan questioned.

"No, thank you." Elyssa surged forward to retrieve the mare Valerie had been riding. "I'd rather be alone right now. And I'm sure Claudia wants to have you for supper—or rather, for dessert."

"Christ, Cutler, I told you there's nothing going on between Claudia and me."

Elyssa halted, her back as stiff as a corner post. She didn't even grant Hunter the courtesy of looking at him when she spoke. "Oh really? Then maybe you should tell her. She thinks otherwise."

When she mounted up and trotted off, Nathan scowled. He needed her cooperation now more than ever, and he wasn't getting it. He was getting suspicious glances and stiff-necked belligerence.

He strode off to wash up for supper, making a mental note to set aside a plate of food for Elyssa. If he didn't, she and Ricky would have to fight over the scraps.

Fourteen

Elyssa brought the sleek black mare to a halt on the rim of the red rock canyon. She hadn't been aware of where she'd needed to go until she got there. It was as if an inner compass had led her to the cliff and had left her lurking on the edge, grappling with her troubled thoughts.

The mare snorted and sidestepped uneasily, ears pricked, nostrils flared. Elyssa swore the horse shared that same sense of awareness, a disturbing feeling that . . .

Elyssa tried to clear her cluttered mind. Just what did she feel besides those indecipherable sensations that ricocheted down her spine? God, she wished she understood what she felt! What she *did* understand was the more she learned about the circumstances surrounding Ely's death, the more she doubted her father's fall had been accidental.

There was Ely's supposed disagreement with Uncle Gil to consider. If what Hunter said was true, Virgil and Gil could have panicked at the thought of the termination of the partnership. They would then have had to absorb the entire debt Virgil had amassed in his attempt to build a reputation in horse-breeding circles and at the race track. That could mean disaster for half the Rawlins clan, not to mention the dissolution of a family business and century-old tradition.

Absently, Elyssa massaged the goose flesh at the base of her neck. Her pensive gaze circled the pasture, searching for some sign, some clue that foul play might have been involved in Ely's death.

Although four-wheel-drive pickups could manage the rugged landscape during dry weather, this rough terrain was more accessible by horse. Elyssa imagined this section of the ranch looked much as it had in pioneer days, with native grasses waving over its rolling hills and sprouting in its plunging stone canyons. The constant migration of cattle herds had created the trail along the precipice that tumbled into the rock and timber ravine where coyotes gathered to howl at the moon and other wild creatures sought the protection of the boulders and the nourishment of the spring-fed stream that meandered through the labyrinthine canyons.

Elyssa nudged the mare along the cattle path, halting abruptly when she heard a cow bellow in the distance. She scanned the canopy of trees that formed a natural cover for the mouth of the canyon, where a primitive road had been dug out to form a section line—and at no small expense, Elyssa wagered. The country road, a mile away, looked like bedrock.

She followed the trail down the incline, serenaded by the bawling cow and the faint response of its calf. Fifteen minutes later, she reached the fence line that skirted the primitive road which disappeared around a towering cliff. She glanced eastward, noting the sagging section of fence. Climbing down, she left the mare tethered to a tree and walked toward the spot where barbed wire swayed in the breeze. The long stretch of fence was in good condition, except for one portion that looked as if it had been hastily patched together.

Elyssa stared north at the looming walls of the canyons she had circled. It was entirely possible that during the heavy rains that surged through the ravines, debris had weakened the fence beside the road. Sections of fence were constantly being washed away by rushing water. If the fence wasn't repaired, cattle would eventually find the openings and would scatter along the road. Ely always claimed cattle weren't particularly intelligent creatures. If they had not been a source of meat, milk, and hides, the whole species probably would have become extinct.

Cattle characteristically wandered through downed fences and went in search of fresh, tender grass, but they weren't smart enough to remember where they had gotten out so they could get back in.

Elyssa smiled as she thought of all the tidbits of information Ely had offered each time she had come for yearly visits. He had related stories about his growing up on a ranch without the conveniences she took for granted, of herding horses, cattle, and mules from one side of the sprawling ranch to the other when his grandfather wanted livestock moved to better grazing areas. And he'd spoken of the customs his Cheyenne grandmother insisted on handing down through the generations so their heritage wouldn't be forgotten . . .

Elyssa had almost forgotten how much she had enjoyed those visits, the drawing of strength from her country roots. It had been like returning to a spiritual retreat to communicate with oneself. Too bad Jessica Rawlins Cutler had never appreciated communing with nature and nurturing the inner spirit. If she had perhaps Elyssa wouldn't have been deprived of the pleasures she was experiencing now.

Elyssa glanced down to see hoofprints that had dried in the dirt beside the sagging portion of fence. She'd expected cattle tracks rather than horseshoe prints. But then, she supposed one of the hired men had been checking the fence after a rain and had clomped through the mud. Still, the man hadn't adequately done his job. The fence was still sagging and any discontented cow could stick its head through the wires and mosey down the road.

Elyssa pulled the patched ends of barbed wire apart and tugged with both hands to put more tension on the strands before twisting them back together. She repeated the process four more times until the five-wire fence looked taut enough to discourage cattle from stepping through it. She could have done with a pair of work gloves and fencing tools, but without the appropriate equipment she could do no more than tighten the weak patch. And as Ely had always said: "A pasture fence is only as good as its worst section."

Elyssa had certainly collected a lot of information in those days when her father had toted her around in his pickup or had set her atop a horse to trail after him. Too bad all that practical knowledge of ranching hadn't been put to use. Elyssa had her mother to thank for that. Jessica had always cringed at the thought of her daughter working alongside farm hands.

The bawling cow again drew Elyssa's attention as she swung into the saddle. She was beginning to wonder if the noise was a cry for help. She went to investigate, thinking maybe she would give up her corporate career and turn to range riding. She would rather deal with stupid, contrary cattle than their well-dressed counterparts in D.C.

A thrashing in the underbrush of the canyon caught Elyssa's attention. The mare sidestepped beneath her and jerked up its head, prancing a little too near the rim for Elyssa's comfort. Flashbacks from the past assaulted her, and she remembered the terror she had experienced when she'd plummeted over rocks that had cut into her like serrated knives. That odd tingling trickled down her spine, and she knew her father had endured that same overwhelming feeling of helplessness, the stabbing pain . . .

She pulled on the mare's reins before they stumbled over the crumbling edge. Wouldn't Cousin Virgil breathe a huge sigh of relief if she wound up cartwheeling into the canyon right about now?

Before Elyssa could follow that thought, she again heard the rustling in the underbrush. Dismounting, she went to investigate, hoping her insatiable curiosity wouldn't lead her into disaster, though the way things were going on this ranch, that was a clear-cut possibility.

Nathan paced back and forth across the lawn, pausing at regular intervals to stare into the distance. He checked his watch and cursed for the umpteenth time. Where the hell was Elyssa? It had been two hours since she'd ridden off. He didn't like the nagging uneasiness that made him edgy. It hadn't been that long since he had gone in search of Ely and had found him and his favorite horse mangled at the bottom of the canyon. But surely Elyssa had enough sense to ride on open range rather than skirting that labyrinth of ravines alone . . . didn't she?

"Nathan?"

He glanced around to see Valerie poised on the back porch.

"Is Ellie back yet?" she asked.

"No," he muttered.

"Well, I can't wait around much longer to say good-bye. I have to be at work in the morning. Tell her I'll call tomorrow."

When Valerie went inside the house, Nathan resumed his pacing. He had only been at it another ten minutes when Twig appeared from the bunkhouse, his blond hair combed neatly, his garb a new pair of Wrangler jeans, polished Justin Roper boots, and a brightly colored Western shirt.

Nathan smiled despite his concern for Elyssa. "Going somewhere, Twig?"

Ray Twigger flung him a withering glance. "You've certainly gotten interested in my off-duty activities all of a sudden. What are you doing? Applying for a position as my mother?"

"Is there a farmer-stockman meeting in Rawlins tonight that I forgot to pencil onto my calendar?" Nathan questioned wryly.

"Nope."

"Then where are you going, all decked out in your country best?"

"Knock it off, Nate. It's none of your damned business." Twig scowled. "I haven't asked you why you're pacing around out here like an expectant father, have I? And did I ask what you and Elyssa were doing out there alone in the barn before supper?"

"Nope."

"Well then, there you go. I knew it wasn't any of my business."

When Twig stalked toward his pickup, Nathan grinned scampishly. "Tell Valerie hello for me, will you, Twig? And make sure you're back by seven in the morning. We have a lot of alfalfa to swath and bale."

Twig jerked open the pickup door before lurching around to glower at his ornery friend. "Good night, *Mother*," he grumbled before he drove off in a cloud of dust.

Nathan glanced at his watch again and decided that since his motherly instincts had been activated, he might as well saddle up and hunt Elyssa down. Better that than wearing a path in the grass, wondering if she had met with calamity. And it would be a damned sight easier to locate her while there was still light.

Deciding to look for trouble first, Nathan headed toward the red rock canyons instead of the rolling hills to the east. Once he had relieved his fear that Elyssa had met with an accident in the same area her father had, he would have time to get good and mad before he caught up with her. He didn't plan to make a habit of fretting over that independent female because he was going to put his foot down and insist that she didn't ride alone again. He wondered how well that ultimatum was going to go over.

But that thought deserted him when he caught sight of the black mare wandering along the western rim of the canyon without its rider. His heart seemed to stop beating, and the only sound to reach his ears was the bawling of a cow that dropped its head to graze momentarily before bellowing again.

Nathan rammed his heels into the gelding's flanks and took off like a rocket. He circled the red stone chasms and thundered down the slope, vowing that if Elyssa hadn't killed herself already he was going to volunteer to do it for her. Hell and damnation! That woman was going to give him a nervous breakdown!

"Cutler, damn it, where are you?" Nathan yelled as he bounded out of the saddle.

"Down here."

He got himself under control before staring down the cliff, prepared for the worst. He couldn't determine how bad that would be because he couldn't see much due to the shadows cast by the cliff and the dense underbrush.

"Are you all right?"

"I'm fine."

"Then what the devil are you doing? It's almost dark."

"I can see that, Hunter."

A rustle of underbrush produced a dark head that was hunkered over a— Nathan didn't know what! Muttering, he picked his way down the eroded slope, steadying himself against the boulders as he went. He skidded to a halt when he realized Elyssa was half dragging, half carrying a newborn calf up the incline. The creature protested feebly and tried to struggle to its feet, but to no avail.

"Here, let me have him." Nathan sidestepped down to move Elyssa out of his way.

"I heard him thrashing around when I was riding back to the house," she explained, her breath sawing in and out from the exertion of hauling the hundred-pound calf.

Nathan scooped up the wriggling animal and propelled himself up the slope, pausing every few yards to catch his breath. It was a large calf and a steep incline. He wondered where Elyssa had found the strength to bring the animal as far up the canyon as she had without collapsing in exhaustion.

"Who's supposed to be checking cattle and fences in this section?" Elyssa questioned as she positioned herself behind Nathan to be sure he kept moving forward. She had discovered how easy it was to topple off balance with the squirming calf. She had landed on her backside twice.

"Les Fykes usually checks these eight sections," Nathan informed her. "Most of the cows have already calved, but some of them bred late last summer because the Simmental bull in a bordering pasture knocked down the fence to claim this herd of cows and wound up in a battle royal with the Limousin bull. They nearly killed each other before we got them separated. Both bulls were so beat-up, they even lost interest in mating for several weeks. And that is saying a lot because bulls would rather mate than eat."

Elyssa smiled at the comment, wondering if men suffered from the same obsession.

Nathan halted before tackling the steep incline ahead of him. "This little rascal hasn't been too long in the world. He must have tumbled off the rim while he was trying to get his wobbly legs under him."

"And if he doesn't nurse soon, we could lose him. Those first feedings of colostrum are vital." Elyssa blinked, surprised that the comment had popped out of her mouth.

Nathan chuckled and eased another step higher on the slope. "God, Cutler, there for a second I'd've sworn your dad was standing behind me. He did a job on you, too, didn't he? If I jotted down all the cowboy knowhow Ely pumped into me, I'd have enough information to fill a book."

When Nathan finally set his feet on level ground, the mother cow came trotting over to sniff her calf. She was none too happy to have had human hands on her offspring, and when she lowered her head to charge, Nathan grabbed Elyssa's hand and hauled her out of the way.

In silence, they watched the cow fuss over her recovered calf. Despite the new mother's tireless ministrations, the weak calf couldn't get its noodly legs beneath it. Nathan could understand how the little critter might have tumbled off the ledge when it couldn't even balance on level ground.

"We'd better take him and his mother back to the corral and milk her," Nathan decided, watching the sun sink into the splash of crimson and gold on the far horizon. "If the calf goes twenty-four hours without nourishment, he'll be too weak to survive."

Elyssa walked over to retrieve her horse while Nathan

chased down his gelding, which was showing signs of contrariness. Despite the cow's bellowing protests, Elyssa and Nathan levered the calf over his saddle.

"Since I didn't bring Ricky with me, you're going to have to run interference. Keep the cow clear of me," Nathan instructed as he swung onto his horse. "She isn't going to appreciate being separated from her calf after she just located him. And if the cow spooks and circles back to this spot to pick up the scent again, you'll have to herd her to the corral."

"Got it, boss," Elyssa drawled like any self-respecting cowhand.

"Sorry, Cutler, I guess I've gotten used to spouting orders."

"Dad taught you well, didn't he, Hunter?"

"Better than my own father. Sid may have been a world-champion rodeo star, but he didn't waste any time on his own son. Mostly, I was just in his way. Ely made me feel welcome and wanted for the first time in my life."

"What happened to your mother?" Elyssa questioned, curious.

"I didn't have one."

"Come on, Hunter, everybody has a mother."

He stared off into the distance. "I have no idea where mine is. She didn't stick around long enough for me to get to know her."

When Nathan trotted off with the bawling calf, Elyssa frowned pensively. It sounded as if Jessica Rawlins Cutler and Sid Hunter had a lot in common. Their children were considered more of an inconvenience than a blessing. But Nathan's mother must have been a real winner to have taken off the way she had.

If Elyssa ever had children of her own she was going to raise them, not let them grow up like weeds, without nurturing. She wondered how differently she would have turned out if Ely had been the greater influence in her life.

Then she glanced around to see the sun make its final descent, casting glorious colors on the wispy clouds. She could almost feel her father's presence, and she smiled contentedly. Here Jessica couldn't intervene. Elyssa and Ely were kindred spirits once again. When she was on this ranch, he was only a thought away, influencing her, guiding her. It was a comforting thought.

When the mother cow trotted after Nathan, Elyssa veered between them to ward off an attack. Twice the cow broke and ran back to pick up the scent and had to be herded along the trail. It was dark by the time they had corralled the cow and prodded her into the squeeze chute.

"Get the Coleman lantern out of the tack room," Nathan ordered as he yanked down on the lever that locked the cow's head in place so he could milk her. "I'll need a bucket and a bottle for the calf."

Elyssa scurried off, returning a few minutes later to watch the furor in the squeeze chute. The cow wasn't the least bit cooperative. Each time Nathan reached between the metal bars to milk her, she kicked out at him and bellowed in outrage. Scowling, he stood up and stalked off to the barn. He returned with a lariat and proceeded to lash the cow's back legs to the bars. Within a few minutes, despite her bellowing protests, he had milked the colostrum for the calf.

Together Nathan and Elyssa managed to steady the calf on its legs and to provide it with the vital meal it had missed while it was floundering in the canyon.

"Why don't you move the breeding stock to another pasture while they're calving?" Elyssa questioned while she bottle-fed the calf. "I'm surprised we haven't lost more newborns in this fashion."

"The cows were on another section of grass during the winter, but the pasture gave out last month and we had to put them on better grass. Ely thought it was better to take our chances with the last few cows that hadn't calved rather than risk having the whole herd break down fences to get to plush pasture. We don't usually use that canyon section for breeders. It's just a reserve pasture. As soon as the other pastures have had their spring growth, we'll move the cows again. Right now we're too busy putting down alfalfa, spraying, and fertilizing to keep a close eye on the cows."

"Then I'll check on them," Elyssa volunteered.

"It will be a long drive from the City, Cutler."

"I'm not going back to the City just yet."

Nathan took the empty bottle from her hand and released the calf. "Yes, you are."

Her chin went airborne. "Look, Hunter, this happens to be *my* ranch, too. Just because Dad left you part of the property doesn't mean you get to run my life!"

"Somebody sure as hells needs to," he grumbled before he walked over to free the cow from the squeeze chute.

"Be that as it may, I'm not leaving until I'm damned good and ready. You're beginning to sound like Uncle Gil and Virgil. They can't wait to get me out from underfoot. They consider me as much of an outsider as you are, even though they try to feed me that line about being family and family needing to stick together. And I *have* decided to terminate the partnership, in case you're wondering."

Nathan stared at the shapely silhouette of the woman propped against the corral rail. "You realize, of course, that the shit's going to hit the fan when you announce your decision. I want power of attorney, Cutler."

"I want a lot of things I'm not getting, Hunter," she flung back at him. "I guess we'll both just have to tough it out."

He strolled over to where she was standing and rested a brawny arm on the rail behind her head. "I'm not kidding about this power of attorney business. If somebody has to play the heavy around here, it may as well be me. Your uncle and cousin already have a lot of practice resenting me. I've always been their whipping boy. Each time Ely objected to their shady wheeling and dealing, they threw me in your father's face. There's no reason for you to get in the cross fire of this on-going feud."

Her chin tilted higher, meeting his steady gaze. "Isn't there?

I have a vested interest here, and you aren't going to catch hell for me, Hunter."

"Damn, but you're bullheaded," Nathan muttered.

"You want me to slink back to my apartment tonight and let you fight my battles for me, do you? That's not the way modern women do things. I'm independent—and I can take care of myself, thank you very much!"

Nathan grinned at this defiant feminist. "I didn't mean I wanted you to hightail it out of here tonight. You'd be in the way since Valerie headed home and Twig decided to follow her, just to make sure she got there safely, of course. You know how we old-fashioned men are, overprotective and all that."

Elyssa's bubbling laughter was sweet music to Nathan's ears. He hadn't heard much of it since the night he and she had . . . A coil of longing knotted in the pit of his belly. He'd like nothing better than to make a late-night visit to Elyssa's room, to determine if the heady pleasure they had shared was as phenomenal as he remembered.

He had spent days trying to keep his distance, avoiding the kind of gossip that would spread like wildfire and provide more fuel for Gil and Virgil's arguments. With Elyssa's wealth, he would never be considered more than her hired man, a gold digger. That complicated the situation, made it more than a man following his instinct to possess the woman who captivated him. And Elyssa was too leery of his motives to take his interest in her seriously. Nathan knew that. But how many cold showers was a man expected to take? One night with Elyssa wasn't going to be enough to satisfy him. It had only whetted his appetite. And the craving was getting stronger, not weaker.

"Cutler?" Nathan pivoted to face her.

"What, Hunter?"

Elyssa stared up at the sinewy figure that all but enveloped her. She could feel her body calling out to his, feel the potent and compelling need she had recently discovered. She really had let this man get to her, hadn't she? She had become so aware of him that it took little to trigger the sizzling sensations that coursed through her. She remembered the touch of his hands, the whisper of his lips on her skin, and she went hot all over. Those sensations were too new, too intense, too difficult to control . . . And she couldn't begin to control them when his lips slanted over hers . . .

The world shrank to fill a space no larger than Hunter occupied when he leaned into her, molding his aroused body into her yielding contours. Her arms glided up his chest to anchor on his shoulders, and before she knew it she was squeezing the stuffing out of him. He responded accordingly. His darting tongue inflamed her, imitating more intimate gestures that reminded her of their most intimate moments. Remembered passion burst through Elyssa like a kaleidoscope of colorful sensations.

With considerable effort, Nathan withdrew. The last thing he needed was for someone to see him and Elyssa climbing all over each other in the corral. It did, however, come as a relief to know she still found him desirable, despite the stumbling blocks between them.

"I'd better mosey down to the bunkhouse and make sure the men know our schedule for tomorrow," he said, his voice rustling with unappeased passion. "Thanks for rescuing the calf."

"My pleasure, Hunter," Elyssa got out. She was shocked to realize that her throat had gone dry. Probably that first kiss. The man had an immediate and pronounced effect on her.

"And my pleasure would be having you all to myself—anytime, anywhere—for the whole livelong night," he murmured, his voice like velvet. "I'd only have to be asked once."

The impact of his words shot through Elyssa like an electrical shock, bringing her every fiber to heightened awareness. Did she dare take the risk a second time, dare to become more deeply involved?

"Do I have an invitation?" he asked simply and directly.

Elyssa licked her lips, and Nathan nearly groaned aloud.

He'd kill to have her silky tongue gliding over his flesh and to taste every delicious inch of her in return.

"I . . ." Elyssa swallowed and tried to draw air into her lungs. It was damned near impossible when his lips grazed hers in a feathery kiss.

"Tell you what, Cutler. I'll make it easier for you. The door to my room is never locked." His voice dropped to a soft, husky pitch as he continued, "You'll know where to find me if you want me. You already know what I want . . ."

Nathan had closed the gate behind him and walked off long before Elyssa collected what was left of her wits and convinced her paralyzed body to move. Maybe Valerie had decided "salt of the earth" was the only way to go, but Elyssa wasn't sure she could survive an out-and-out affair with a man she couldn't handle. If she caved in and went to Hunter, he would know she was genuinely intrigued because he knew she didn't have affairs. And if she turned him loose with that weapon to use against her . . .

You do too damned much thinking, you know that, Cutler? Elyssa told herself. *You need an attitude adjustment. Treat yourself to a reckless fling and call it what it is. Keep things purely physical and you've got nothing to lose.*

She shook her head in disbelief. A woman could talk herself into just about anything when she wanted to, couldn't she? If the conversation she was having with herself was any indication, she needn't wonder where she would be spending the night.

Fifteen

Nathan returned from the bunkhouse with Ricky at his heels and veered into the office to contact the chairman of the National Finals Rodeo. He hadn't even made it across the room before the impact of Ely Rawlins's portrait hit him. In silence, Nathan stared at the image of the man who had had a significant influence on his life, and still did. He could almost hear Ely spouting philosophy, training him to follow in his footsteps. And sometimes he saw so much of Ely in Elyssa that it was uncanny.

Take this evening's incident with the calf, for instance. It wouldn't have mattered to Ely that he was an aging rancher who had no business skidding down the canyon to hoist up the lost calf, even if he risked a heart attack from overexertion. Ely had always operated on the theory that a man did what he had to do when he had to do it. Elyssa followed the same policy. Rather than ride back to the house for assistance, she had scrambled down to rescue the calf, even when she only outweighed the damned thing by twenty-five pounds—tops.

Nathan smiled to himself. He had certainly gotten the wrong impression of Elyssa when they'd met in the City on occasion. He'd had her pegged as a spoiled, pampered bitch who hadn't given her father the attention he'd thought Ely deserved. But in a less than two weeks, Nathan had made startling discoveries about Elyssa, about the torments that had shaped her into the woman she was.

And he was nurturing a strong dislike for Jessica's spiteful tactic of keeping father and daughter apart, and for Gavin Spencer. Nathan wasn't sure he could face that bastard again without giving in to the urge to knock his teeth down his throat. The man had all but destroyed Elyssa's self-confidence and her faith in men.

Nathan didn't want Gavin sniffing around Elyssa, triggering nightmarish memories. But to a cocksman like Gavin, she was the one who got away and he still saw her as a potential conquest. The very thought aroused Nathan's protective instincts. Elyssa had been hurt enough, but he had the unpleasant feeling that her anguish wasn't over yet. She was confused by all the propaganda being launched by both sides in conflict over terminating the partnership.

Sighing tiredly, Nathan picked up the phone to make arrangements to haul rodeo stock to the next competitive event on the circuit. Twig wasn't going to be anxious to transport the livestock now that he had taken an interest in Valerie Mitchell. Those two had hit it off from the word go, and had been going great guns ever since. They were probably doing a little target practice in Valerie's apartment at this very moment.

If only he and Elyssa could walk away from this emotional tangle and shut out the world the way they had that night. He wished Ely were still here to assume responsibility so he and Elyssa could take some time for themselves . . .

The damnedest sensation imaginable swirled through Nathan as he sank down in Ely's chair. He could feel Ely's dominant presence, as if the man's spirit had taken up residence in the corner of the room. Nathan told himself he was being ridiculous until Ricky pricked up his ears and whined.

"We must both be going crazy," Nathan said to the dog.

Before he ended his phone conversation, headlights flashed in the window and the sound of an idling engine penetrated the room. Nathan jotted down the information about the rodeo and rang off. He was at the front door before the visitor could announce himself.

A very irate Gil Rawlins loomed on the porch, looking like

a grenade ready to explode. So much for a quiet evening at home, thought Nathan.

"You son of a bitch," Gil seethed, stalking inside without an invitation. "You've been sabotaging Elyssa's thinking again, haven't you? Now you've got her believing that Virgil—"

"Don't try to unload that bullshit on me, Gil." Nathan interrupted what he knew to be a well-rehearsed tirade of lies. "Ely had it from a reputable source that Rancher's Mutual was calling in Virgil's loan and that you had co-signed it. Ely spent years looking the other way while you and Virgil took more than your share from the farming operation."

"Goddamn it, you have no proof of any of this, and you're twisting Elyssa's thinking for your own benefit." Gil sneered. "Now where the hell is she? I'm going to set her straight, and when I finish telling her the way it is, she'll kick your cocky ass out of here and you won't have a roof over your head!"

"And just how is it, *exactly,* Uncle Gil?"

Both men whirled to see Elyssa poised halfway down the stairs, propped against the wall, her arms crossed over her chest. Her stance and the tilt of her head so reminded Nathan of Ely that he almost staggered backward. Gil must have been struck by the resemblance, too, because he stepped back a pace and blinked like a man who had seen a ghost.

Eyes the color of ebony glittered in the light as Elyssa descended the steps with a hint of a limp. She looked as pure and fresh as a spring blossom, dressed in deep purple Rober jeans and a matching blouse. Her silky hair, gleaming with shiny highlights, swirled around her flawless face like a cloud. She was wearing one of Ely's wry smiles. It kicked up the left corner of her mouth. The lady was a knockout, and when she took on that dominant air her father had always possessed, the effect was unsettling.

"Elyssa, I'm . . . sorry you had to overhear that kind of language," Gil stammered.

She shrugged him off and strolled past both men to step

into the office. "Why don't you come sit down, Uncle Gil, and tell me 'how it is'?" she invited.

Gil stalked inside and plunked himself down on a leather chair. "You get *him* out of here and we'll talk—family to family."

Elyssa glanced over to where Nathan stood. His brow arched in silent question. She had the feeling he very much wanted to stay, to defend himself against Gil's accusations; but he was doing her the courtesy of letting her make her own decision. That pleased Elyssa. As forceful and commanding as Hunter could be at times, he was showing her respect. He must have been paying attention earlier that evening when she'd launched into her spiel about being independently assertive. She wondered if he knew how much it pleased her that he hadn't tried to commandeer this encounter. Probably. Hunter seemed to know her very well.

When she smiled faintly, he nodded. "I'll be in the den making some more phone calls if you need me."

"She won't," Gil snapped. "You may as well start packing. You can stop by the post office in the morning to change your mailing address."

Nathan didn't retaliate, though he looked as if he would have liked to. He simply called to the dog and ambled away. This was one time when he was going to have to stand aside and let Elyssa deal with her uncle. Hopefully, she had inherited Ely's strength of character. She was going to need it to deal with the fuming Gil.

Valerie Mitchell was in country heaven. During the years since her divorce, she had been in search of a man with whom she could form a relationship based not only on physical attraction but also on common interests and values, on mutual respect. The Texas-born and -bred Ray Twigger fit all qualifications in Valerie's book. In fact, he had almost been too much the gentleman. She had finally invited him to bed. That was a first!

Now, she lay beside Ray in absolute contentment, remembering the pleasure they had shared moments earlier—long, fervent moments when she'd liked to die from exquisite torture. This cowboy was all brawn and muscle, but he had a lover's tender touch.

"I'm really sorry, Val," Ray apologized as he slid a bare arm around her and hugged her close.

"Sorry?" she parroted.

"Yeah, sorry. I planned to play straight with you."

All her recently formulated dreams shattered like eggshells. Apparently, she had been living in a world of delusions. She'd thought she and Ray had something good going. So much for optimistic thinking. This sounded like the first paragraph of a Dear Jane letter. He had gotten what he wanted—a one-night stand—before waving farewell.

She eased away, presenting her back. "Just spit it out, cowboy. I'm not good at long good-byes."

"What do you mean good-bye?" He levered up on an elbow to stare down at the tousled blond hair that concealed her pixielike face. "That's not what I meant. Is that what you want?"

Val rolled onto her back to peer into his rugged, suntanned features. "No. What did you mean?"

"I wanted to go slow with you instead of diving in," he explained as he traced her cupid's bow lips. "So much for good intentions. And sure enough, you were all braced for a quick tumble and an even quicker retreat. I don't want you thinking I'm only in this for the sex."

That was one of the things Val adored about this hunk of a cowboy. He was open and honest—straightforward. "You don't want sex?" she teased, her self-confidence and good disposition restored.

Ray tossed back his head and barked a laugh. *That* was one of the things he liked about Valerie. She had a delightful sense of humor. "I want all the sex you want to give me. I just didn't intend to wind up here tonight, for fear you would think I make a habit of this sort of thing."

"Do you?"

"No."

"Neither do I."

"Val, I really want this to mean something."

"As in . . . I get to hold the reins to your horse?" she questioned playfully.

"Yes, as in." His disarming smile melted Valerie. "You can hold my horse's reins any time you please. I want this to be the beginning of a commitment in which I can trust you while I'm off hauling rodeo stock and you can depend on me not to take advantage of the good deal I've got."

Val looped her arms over his muscled shoulders, her lips parting in invitation. "Cowboy, you've got yourself a deal."

While Garth Brooks and Chris LeDoux harmonized on the CD player about what a woman was supposed to do with a cowboy when he didn't saddle up and ride away, Valerie surrendered to the scintillating feel of Ray's masculine body gliding over hers.

Her fantasy come true ended with the blaring of the phone. She planned to ignore it, but the damned thing rang ten times. Whoever was at the end of the line was persistent.

Grumbling, Ray leaned out to retrieve the receiver and hand it to her.

"Hell—o," Valerie muttered.

"It's Nathan Hunter. Is Twig there?"

Ray grabbed the receiver. "Now what, Mother?"

"I'm not interrupting, I hope."

Nathan didn't sound the least bit apologetic, Ray noted.

"Are you going to make a habit of this?"

"No, but I needed to talk to you," Nathan explained, amusement evident in his baritone voice.

"Can't it wait?" Ray looked down into expressive blue eyes, and his body clenched with need. Nate's timing was absolutely horrible!

"If it could, I wouldn't be calling you now. I need to know whether you can transport stock to Kansas City for the International Pro Rodeo Association tomorrow. They're putting on a charity benefit for the children's homes in the area. I promised to provide the livestock for the evening performance." He paused momentarily. "I also wondered if you wanted to buy my half of the company."

Ray nearly dropped the receiver. "Buy the . . . ?"

"Company," Nathan supplied. "Do you want to?"

"I'm not sure I can afford it."

"I think you'll like the price. The livestock will provide the collateral for your loan. I just wondered if you'd be interested."

"Well sure, but—"

The door bell chimed and Valerie grumbled at this second interruption. She scooted away, grabbing her discarded clothes and running a hand through her disheveled hair before scurrying off. Ray tucked the receiver against his shoulder and stabbed a bare leg into his jeans, dressing while he talked.

"What's going on, Nate? Why this sudden decision to sell?"

"What do you want now!" Valerie demanded from the other room.

Ray peered around the corner to see a man surging inside as if he owned the place. "Nate, can I get back to you? There's some guy at the door, and Valerie doesn't seem too happy to see him."

"What does he look like?" Nathan questioned.

Ray took a closer look while he zipped his Jeans. "Blond hair, six foot tall, wearing a business suit that looks like it cost a fortune."

"Must be Robert Grayson, Elyssa's ex-fiancé."

"He's acting like a real jerk," Ray noted.

"That would be Robert. Give him my regards. I kicked him out of there last week. I'm sure he remembers me fondly."

"My pleasure, Nate. Oh, and I'll take the company and the run to Kansas City. I wonder how this Robert character would like to ride in the back of the semi with broncs and bulls, all the way there."

Nathan chuckled wickedly. "I can't think of a better place for that prick."

"Speak to you later. Now I've got to go kick some ass," Ray replied before tossing the receiver onto its cradle.

Robert glanced over Valerie's head to see a haphazardly dressed cowboy swaggering down the hall. "My, my, this place has turned into a regular whorehouse, hasn't it?"

Valerie ignored the remark. "I asked you what you wanted, Robert."

He flicked a condescending glance at Ray before focusing on Valerie. "I just stopped by to inform Elyssa that I spoke with her stepfather and her mother this evening. They just returned from the Caribbean."

"I'm sure your visit made their day." Valerie smirked.

"They were upset to learn that Elyssa jilted me and that she's been screwing around with that clown of a cowboy who manages her father's ranch."

Valerie's eyes rounded in disbelief. "You told Ellie's parents that?"

Robert smiled. "I warned her that she was asking for trouble. Daniel Cutler considers me an asset to the firm—"

"An *ass* at it is more like it," Valerie amended. "God, Robert, I can't believe your gall. Do you actually believe Ellie's family will take your word over hers?"

"Indeed I do," Robert said with great conviction. "Jessica is still in favor of our marriage, and she promised to speak with Elyssa as soon as possible. She is none too happy to hear her daughter has been at the Rawlins Ranch."

Valerie was livid with anger. She had never liked Robert's superior air or the charade he played for Elyssa's benefit.

"Just wait until I get to work in the morning, buster," she fumed. "Everybody in the building is going to know about you and your secretary."

"And they'll hear about your activities," Robert threatened.

"Corporate call girls like you have a different man in your pants every—"

Robert was slammed against the wall so fast his eyes blurred. Two hundred pounds of taut muscle rammed into him, and an elbow connected with his solar plexus. Robert sucked in air like a landed fish.

"This *lady* happens to be *my* lady," Ray roared in Robert's flushed face. "And that clown of a cowboy you mentioned is my best friend."

Robert's eyes widened and very nearly popped out of his head when Ray raised a knee to his crotch.

"Apologize to the lady," Ray gritted out. "Unless you want to leave here with your head stuck up your ass."

"I'm sorry," Robert said quickly.

"You've got that right." Val beamed in delight while Ray grabbed Robert by the hair of his head and ejected him from the apartment.

Locking the door behind him, Ray pivoted to face Valerie, only to find himself the recipient of a zealous hug and a steamy kiss. He smiled rakishly and scooped her up in his arms.

"Now, where were we?" he murmured as he made his way to the bedroom.

Valerie grinned, her blue eyes sparkling. *"I* was about as close to heaven as anybody can get without actually dying."

"You, too, huh?" he said before he stopped thinking altogether and made up for lost time.

Elyssa walked over to the desk and sat down in her father's chair for psychological effect. Uncle Gil couldn't look at her without seeing the portrait of Ely behind her. Although Gil had tried to even the odds by refusing to let Hunter sit in on the conference, Elyssa utilized the lifelike painting of her father to give her the edge. Now that she had made her decision, she wanted it executed immediately.

Gil leaned forward, trying not to notice the portrait behind

Elyssa. It was like trying to ignore Mount Rushmore. "No more of this nonsense," he said sternly. "I brought along the contract to reinstate the partnership. I want you to sign it and to stop trying to assume responsibilities you aren't prepared to handle."

That was the wrong thing to say. Elyssa's back stiffened. She didn't appreciate the implication that she was incompetent.

"You've let Nate convince you that Virgil is having financial problems. Nothing could be further from the truth. His horse-breeding operation is sound and is rapidly growing in reputation. Clients from all over the nation call him about breeding mares to his studs. Virgil already has three champions running the track at Remington Park."

And life is just a bowl of cherries, Elyssa mused sardonically.

"My division of the ranch operation is not only stable but profitable. For years we have put the weaning-age steers from Ely's cow-calf operation on wheat pasture for quick weight gain, and we've sold them to feed lots when they reach eight hundred pounds. All the money we have made is deposited in the account. I don't know what Nate has told you, but this partnership was working superbly—and it still can."

Gil reminded Elyssa of an incumbent president praising his accomplishments during a campaign. The world was a rosy place and the policies in practice were incomparable—according to Gil. The fact that Virgil had refused to disclose the name of the bank that held his loans had aroused Elyssa's suspicions. Gil's late visit had clouded her mind with more doubt. She had the feeling he and Virgil were in constant contact, each keeping the other abreast of his success in manipulating her.

"We'll assume for the moment that what you say is true."

"It *is* true," Gil hastily assured her.

Elyssa smiled dryly. He was in a flaming rush to second his proclamation, wasn't he? "The facts and figures from the tax form will bear that out, I'm sure. Now, as for the salaries being paid to the family and hired help . . ."

Elyssa watched Gil ease back in his chair. His green eyes narrowed warily. "I already told you that all farm hands and family members who made significant contributions to this ranch operation were on payroll."

"Yes," Elyssa agreed. "But I have been here for almost two weeks and I haven't seen Virgil make the slightest contribution. He wasn't with the swathing crew, and he doesn't seem to be riding fences and checking the herds, either. Therefore, I must assume that the pickup that has been provided for him through the partnership, and the fuel that powers it, are being written off as expenses against this ranch. Not only is Virgil abusing the tax laws, grazing and stabling his horses on partnership property without paying rent, but he is also receiving a salary as well as a government subsidy for doing little or nothing around here."

"Bullshit!" Gil erupted, forgetting himself. "Virgil checks the steers every day!"

"You mean from the window of the ranch-owned pickup while he is on his way to meet a client who is interested in contracting stud services?"

"No, I mean he works alongside the men."

"Not according to the hired help I've questioned," Elyssa challenged. "Just what is Virgil's present salary?"

"Fifty thousand a year," Gil reported.

"The same as the government subsidy received from the USDA wheat program?" Elyssa scoffed. "Forgive me for being blunt, but Cousin Virgil is highly overpaid and he's well imbursed for a job he isn't doing. That in itself constitutes two counts of fraud. I doubt my father was pleased, and I know Uncle Sam frowns on that sort of thing. I suspect an audit would turn up some shocking discoveries that would keep the IRS looming over Cousin Virgil like a buzzard for several years to come."

"Are you threatening me?" Gil growled, his eyes menacing. "Because if you are, I assure you you'll regret it."

"Just as my father did?" Elyssa studied her uncle ponderously, noting the flicker of hostility in his gaze. "Just how desperate were you to hold this partnership together so your side of the family could take full advantage of my father? Desperate enough to act when he called a halt to something I consider nothing short of embezzlement?"

"What are you suggesting?" Gil demanded sharply.

"I'm not so sure my father's death was an accident."

Gil bounded out of his chair, his face red with rage. "You're accusing me of killing my own brother because he wouldn't—"

"Wouldn't what?" Elyssa prodded.

Gil didn't respond. He was off on another tangent. "I will *not* tolerate you and Nate flinging accusations and spreading outrageous rumors. You can't threaten me, young lady. I'm your uncle!"

"And I'm still trying to decide whether that is a blessing or a curse. In my father's case, it may have been a curse."

Gil pounced forward, looming over the desk to breathe down on Elyssa. "You can revoke the partnership and sic the IRS on my son, but I promise you'll suffer the consequences of messing with something that never was any of your damned business." He sneered. "You've got your stepfather's money and that bitch of a mother to watch over you. As far as I'm concerned you never were family. Now you've gotten greedy and decided you'd rather have two fortunes at your disposal, as well as a lover who is willing to let you do whatever you want if it keeps him rolling in the clover. You wanna talk curses, little girl? Mark my words, Nate Hunter will be yours. When he finishes destroying the empire that has been in operation for generations, he'll destroy you, too. Ely never wanted any of this to happen!"

"No, but I doubt he wanted you and Virgil to betray him, either," Elyssa contended, rising to look down her nose at her raging uncle. "If you fight the revocation of the partnership,

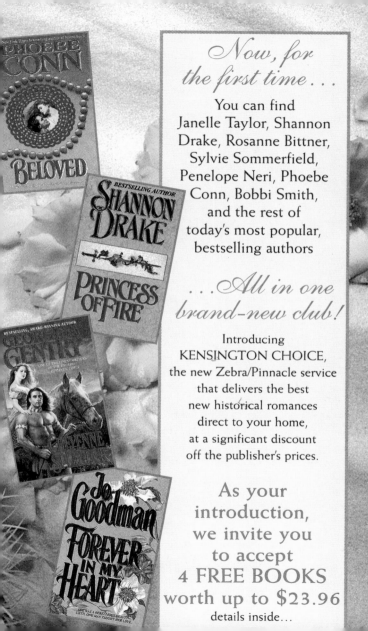

We've got your authors!

If you seek out the latest historical romances by today's bestselling authors, our new reader's service, KENSINGTON CHOICE, is the club for you.

KENSINGTON CHOICE is the only club where you can find authors like Janelle Taylor, Shannon Drake, Rosanne Bittner, Sylvie Sommerfield, Penelope Neri and Phoebe Conn all in one place...

...and the only service that will deliver their romances direct to your home as soon as they are published—even before they reach the bookstores.

KENSINGTON CHOICE is also the only service that will give you a substantial guaranteed discount off the publisher's prices on every one of those romances.

That's right: Every month, the Editors at Zebra and Pinnacle select four of the newest novels by our bestselling authors and rush them straight to you, usually *before they reach the bookstores*. The publisher's prices for these romances range from $4.99 to $5.99—but they are always yours for the guaranteed low price of just *$4.20!*

That means you'll always save over 20% off the publisher's prices on every shipment you get from KENSINGTON CHOICE!

All books are sent on a 10-day free examination basis, and there is no minimum number of books to buy. (A postage and handling charge of $1.50 is added to each shipment.)

As your introduction to the convenience and value of this new service, we invite you to accept

4 BOOKS FREE

The 4 books, worth up to $23.96, are our welcoming gift. You pay only $1 to help cover postage and handling.

To start your subscription to KENSINGTON CHOICE and receive your introductory package of 4 FREE romances, detach and mail the card at right *today*.

I'll have an auditor on your doorstep within a week. Then you can explain how Cousin Virgil and Patricia can draw salaries and government subsidies when they perform no tasks beneficial to this ranch. Having your daughter do nothing more than sign checks is hardly considered a time-consuming contribution. The closest Patricia ever came to a cow was staring at the slab of beef on her plate. Her husband Dennis is the one who earns his keep, and the word is you treat him like a lowly farm hand who is supposed to be at your beck and call. I wonder what task you expected him to perform when it came to my father's supposed accident?"

"You really are a bitch, just like your mother," Gil snarled.

"And this little bitch expects you and Virgil to be in attendance at the private auction to be held on Monday to divide property that is jointly owned by the partnership. I hereby declare this partnership dissolved. I will be in contact with my stepfather's lawyer first thing in the morning to draw up a legal document revoking the partnership and absolving my father's estate from any debts incurred by your side of the family. And since my father's will deeded this house over to me because you were given funds from joint profits to build a home in town—"

"How do you know that?" Gil muttered sourly.

"Because I've spent the last two hours scanning the files in my father's room," Elyssa informed him. "Now I think you had better leave *my* house before I'm forced to call the police to have you removed and restrained."

"Planning on using Officer Spencer against me, are you?" Gil smiled nastily. "Think again, little girl."

Elyssa forced herself not to react to the threat. She matched her uncle glare for glare, refusing to back down. "Good night, Uncle Gil. I'll see you at the auction."

When he lurched around and stormed out, she wilted back in her chair. She had burned a monumental bridge, and it was still on fire. She wondered if Gil had reacted the same way the day he'd argued with Ely. The man was mad enough to take a bite out of her. Luckily, he'd already had supper.

Gil slammed the pickup door and expelled a torrent of foul language. He should have known Jessica would find a way to haunt him, even after all these years. That woman had been trouble since the moment he'd laid eyes on her. She had played him for a fool, like she'd done with Ely. Elyssa was even worse because she had brains and she had Nate Hunter as an advisor and bodyguard. Gil had no doubt Elyssa was supplying fringe benefits to Nate and he believed that little bitch was playing right into Hunter's hands. If Gil could turn back the clock he sure as hell would have changed the course of events that had led to this infuriating situation. He had been young and reckless, ignoring consequences to get what he thought he wanted. He wondered if Ely had suspected the truth, wondered if Jessica had . . .

The passenger door opened and Virgil slid inside to peer expectantly at his father.

"Where have you been?" Gil thundered.

"Making a few arrangements," was all Virgil said.

"Well, you'd better make a few more and you'd better make them fast. Elyssa just dissolved the partnership and called for a private auction to distribute property."

"What!" Virgil howled.

"And she's threatening to call in an auditor if we object. She's got to be stopped. You'd better get on the phone when you get home and make sure all bases are covered. And worse," he muttered as he cranked the engine, "she is questioning the circumstances of Ely's death."

"Oh, shit," Virgil said. "That's all we need right now."

Gil put the truck in gear and sped off, cursing his association with Jessica and her daughter. Sure as hell, the past was coming back to haunt him.

Sixteen

Elyssa watched the headlights of Gil's pickup fade into the darkness before venturing upstairs. She was still on an adrenaline high after her confrontation with her uncle, her body tightly drawn as a bow, her nerves humming. Would Great-grandfather Rawlins forgive her for destroying the sprawling ranch he had wanted to endure for centuries? Elyssa had broken tradition and had turned her back on her family, leaving them to the wolves—if what Hunter said was true.

"Having second thoughts, Cutler?"

Elyssa started as the deep voice that rolled down the shadowy hall. She glanced up to see a masculine form leaning negligently against the door jamb of her room.

"Did you eavesdrop on the conversation, Hunter?"

"Didn't have to. I heard Gil slam the door so hard the house rattled. That was indication enough that you had cut off the funds to cover Virgil's debts."

Elyssa paused beside him. "I feel as if I've betrayed my ancestors and their visionary dreams," she confided.

Nathan's callused hand cupped her chin, lifting her downcast gaze to his. "Don't hold yourself accountable for what Gil and Virgil did to destroy the ranch's stability. They are the ones who risked tradition because of greed and a craving for notoriety. Having this ranch wasn't enough for them, and Virgil is going to have to pay for his arrogance and his desire to become too big too fast. I've seen it happen before with upstart sons who want to outdo their fathers. Most of them end up breaking their family and destroying what their fathers spent a lifetime creating. Besides, Ely was going to make the break. You only carried out his wishes."

"I still don't like feeling like a traitor to my family. It seems—"

"Ruthless?" Nathan sketched the lush curve of her mouth with his thumb. "No, honey. It's called survival. You salvaged half of this ranch. It will remain a landmark, tied to tradition, but times change and we have to change with them. You did the right thing."

"And you aren't planning to sell me out?" Elyssa asked.

"Well, actually, I plan to sell out," he admitted.

Elyssa jerked away from his caressing touch, and he noted her immediate hostility toward him. He still didn't have her complete trust. He wondered if he ever would.

"Fact is, I just made arrangements to sell my half of the rodeo stock company to Twig. Since your father assigned me more duties on the ranch the past few years so he could semi-retire, I left most of the transportation and the connections to Twig. I just signed contracts and organized scheduling. Ely and I had discussed the move earlier. Of course, I didn't speak on your behalf and you're welcome to do what you wish with your half of the stock company. I'm sure you and Twig will be compatible business partners since you have so much in common."

"Like what?" Elyssa wanted to know.

"You are both exceedingly fond of Valerie. I'm afraid I interrupted them when I called to talk to Twig. Then your dear friend Robert arrived on the scene."

"What did *he* want?" she grumbled.

"To make more trouble, I expect. Twig was on his way to show Robert the door when I hung up. I don't think that sneaky little creep plans to give up on you."

"He has a lot to lose," Elyssa said bitterly. "Meal tickets are hard to come by these days. Greed doesn't run only in the Rawlins family, you know."

"No, there are several strains of it in the Hunter family as well," Nathan murmured as his hands framed Elyssa's face, tilting it to his kiss. "You have something I am very greedy for . . ."

Shock waves of awareness and need rippled through Elyssa when moist lips descended on hers. She couldn't have resisted, even if she'd wanted to. When his arms went around her, her hands glided over the sinewy expanse of his chest and she heard him groan in response.

"God, I've been starving for the sweet taste of you."

She knew the feeling well. She had battled the delicious memories each night when darkness stole softly into her room, wishing Hunter had been among the shadows. He had become her addiction, a fire she couldn't put out. Despite the turmoil in her life, she couldn't withstand the compelling attraction he aroused in her.

That very first time, he had become her salvation, her port in the storm. She had been reaching out for comfort and distraction, taking her first risk with passion and marveling at the satisfaction she discovered in his arms. Hunter had reestablished the confidence in her femininity that Gavin Spencer had ruined years ago, had made her feel whole and alive again. She cherished the feelings he'd awakened in her, and always would, no matter what the future might bring.

Tonight, Elyssa wanted to give Hunter treasured moments like those he'd offered her when he had loved her so thoroughly and tenderly. She wanted to discover every powerful inch of him, to memorize him, to taste him until, when she closed her eyes in days to come, she could recall each curve and crevice of his body, each sensation of loving him.

Elyssa withdrew from Hunter's arms and clasped his hand, leading him into the dark room, barely able to breathe over the furious pounding of her pulse.

When she halted by the bed and stepped in front of him to work the buttons of his shirt, Nathan glanced down to monitor the movement of her hands as they hovered on his chest. As she pushed the garment off his shoulders and pressed dewy lips to his skin, his breath caught in his throat.

"Tonight I'm going to try *my* hand at seduction," she whispered. "Do you mind, Hunter?"

Did he . . . ? He could think of nothing he wanted more! Except for having her luscious body beneath his, surrounding him, absorbing him. "No, I don't," he said shakily. "Wanting you the way I do, I just don't know how much I can stand."

"Standing? That sounds interesting . . ." She smiled against the clenched muscles of his belly, her kisses descending as her fingertips eased open the snap of his jeans.

"Elyssa . . ." Nathan groaned, in torment when her hands tunneled inside his jeans and briefs, pushing them down until they pooled at his feet. His ragged breath sawed in and out of his chest as she knelt in front of him, her lips skimming his throbbing shaft. His mind reeled as desire pounded through him and hammered at his nerve endings. Then she took him into her mouth and flicked her tongue across the velvet tip of his manhood.

"Don't!" Nathan hissed when his body arched into her intimate kiss.

She retreated, her breath stirring against his aching flesh. "I didn't mean to hurt you. I only wanted to pleasure you as much as you pleasured me."

He dragged in a shuddering breath and closed his eyes against the tormenting need that played havoc with his control. "I'm afraid my response might repulse you," he admitted. "You're hell on my willpower."

Elyssa smiled against his pulsating length, stroking him with gentle fingertips. "Good, that makes us even."

When she cupped him in her hand and tasted his helpless response, Nathan decided somebody might as well draw a pistol and shoot him to put him out of this delicious misery. He wasn't going to survive. Elyssa was killing him by agonizingly sweet degrees. Her caresses swirled over his thighs and circled his knee caps before making a maddening ascent to stroke him, enfold him. Over and over again her hands migrated and her lips whispered over ultrasensitive flesh until he was staggering, almost unable to hold himself upright.

"That's all I can stand. I . . ." Nathan groaned when she laughed softly against his throbbing flesh.

"Then you won't mind taking it lying down, will you, Hunter? Being new at this, I can use all the practice I can get. You do understand that, don't you? We late bloomers have to make up for lost time."

"All in one night?"

Elyssa eased him back onto the bed and crouched between his legs, watching in impish satisfaction as his shadowed face contorted with unmistakable passion. She reveled in her power over him, thrilled to the knowledge that even her untutored caresses could bring him to the brink and leave him trembling in her hands. She monitored each riveting response, luring him from one rapturous plateau to another before withdrawing, waiting for him to regain his control.

"Damn," Nathan moaned hoarsely. "I think you've had too much practice already. You may have to find yourself another subject for your experimentation."

"I like the one I've got," she whispered as her lips skimmed his satiny tip and glided over the contracted muscles of his belly. By the time she kissed her way up to his sensuous lips, he was breathing heavily. "Challenge yourself, Hunter. Expand your limits."

He laughed softly before nibbling at her lips. "I'm already as expanded as I can get."

She smiled impishly. "I noticed."

Nathan tasted his own desire on her lips, and it was nearly his undoing. Elyssa had discarded all inhibitions to pleasure him: learning how and where he liked to be touched, when to press her advantage, and when to retreat before he lost all semblance of control and flung himself down on top of her in desperate need.

And just when Nathan thought he had replenished his failing willpower, she set her hands and lips upon him again, creating challenges he wasn't sure he could meet. He felt like a lump of clay being sculpted by her hands—and loving it.

When she had him groaning in pleasurable torment again, she eased away to peel off her own clothes. He watched her, devouring her flesh spotlighted by the moon's glow that filtered through the window. Elyssa was careful not to turn sideways and expose her left hip to the light, so Nathan was treated to a shapely vision. She fairly floated back to him, dreamlike, but ready to invent new ways to drive him insane.

Her breasts brushed against his chest, and her thigh brushed his manhood; and he all but passed out. For sure, this dark-eyed goddess had had more than enough practice in driving a man mad with wanting her.

Too bad Robert didn't know what he was missing. He could have had himself one helluva of a bride along with gaining a foothold in Cutler Corporation. The fool.

Gentle hands stroked Nathan again and his willpower strained against its reins. "Come here," he demanded as his arm circled her waist, holding her exactly above him. "You started this. Now finish it before I explode."

Elyssa stared down at his dark face, her body reacting wildly to the gliding fingers that teased her until she was gasping for breath. When he lifted her and eased her down upon him, she knew the wondrous sensation of possessing and being possessed. Velvet flames consumed her as Hunter taught her to move above him, to match him thrust for urgent thrust.

She arched backward, a captive of the hungry needs that seized her and burned within like wildfire. She could feel the pleasure building, burgeoning—until it consumed her. Her body convulsed around him and he pulled her down upon him, burying her head against his shoulder as passion raced through him and rippled through her. Elyssa clung to him for what seemed forever, waiting for the indefinable sensations to ebb.

In the aftermath of their lovemaking, Nathan squeezed his eyes shut and fought to breathe normally. He was numb with pleasure. Good Lord, she was almost too much for him to handle! He was entirely too aware of her, too sensitive to her needs, too responsive to her touch, her scent, the sultry sound of her voice. Was it possible for such sexual pleasure to permanently paralyze a man's body and brain?

He could see himself being wheeled away on a gurney for observation at the nearest medical research center, answering questions about how he'd gotten into this disabled condition. He wondered how the physician would react when Nathan admitted that too much satisfying sex had turned him into a vegetable.

He chuckled at the thought, causing Elyssa to prop herself up, an elbow on his chest, and stare curiously at him.

"What are you snickering about?"

"You wouldn't understand."

"Try me."

"I just did. It damned near did me in, thank you very much."

Elyssa grinned at his playful mood. She adored these moments with him, when they escaped the outside world and reveled in the pleasure they gave each other. It was like living in another dimension of time.

"You know, it's a damned good thing I wasn't paying yearly visits to the ranch when you first came here," Elyssa said candidly. "I probably wouldn't have been able to keep my hands off you then, either."

"Think so?" The thought pleased him immensely.

"Probably not. You have an astonishing effect on me, Hunter. One touch and . . . poof! I lose all the good sense I've spent years collecting. Maybe Gavin's . . ." Elyssa's voice dried up and she eased down beside him, scolding herself for letting that man's painful memory spoil her serenity.

"He was only trying to frighten you into keeping silent because he was a coward, afraid of the consequences." Nathan rolled sideways to curl an arm protectively around her. "You've got to stop letting what happened to you years ago affect you, because if it still does, he ultimately wins. He can only intimidate you if you *let* him."

Elyssa stared across the shadowed room. "Men have always been attracted to me for the wrong reasons. I got used to letting people use me. Even now I'm letting it happen."

"Are you?" Nathan pressed her onto her back, determined to tease her back into good humor. "I thought I was just used—and used exceedingly well. I was the guinea pig for your experimentation, remember?"

Elyssa refused to be amused. She searched his shadowed face. "What do you really want from me, Hunter?"

"What are you offering?"

"I hate how you answer a question with a question," she grumbled resentfully.

"And I hate it when you withdraw from me emotionally and I can't touch you," he whispered before his sensuous lips grazed her mouth. "I told you before; what's between us has nothing to do with business. What we have is me wanting you so badly nothing else matters . . ."

When his hands and lips skimmed over her sensitized flesh, Elyssa realized that was true at the moment. And for however long it lasted, she would share this wild brand of emotion with Hunter. She had learned that life was too short and unpredictable not to enjoy its precious moments to the fullest.

She gave herself up to the disturbing excitement that sizzled through her, returning his passionate caresses eagerly, and they were swept up in a storm, swirling into oblivion, sharing hot, sweet release . . . only to awake again and again in the stillness of the night to feed a hunger that had become an insatiable craving.

Nathan woke at the crack of dawn, determined to have the herd of rodeo stock rounded up and loaded in the semi before the haying crew began cutting for the day. He eased away from Elyssa without disturbing her sleep and stared down at the soft, feminine body from which he derived so much pleasure, satisfaction . . . and contentment. Hesitantly, he reached out to ease the sheet away from her left hip. Although she was always cautious to keep her scars concealed by clothing or darkness when they made wild sweet love, Nathan was curious to know whether they were as bad as she thought.

They were . . .

He gasped at the sight of slick flesh drawn so tightly over bone that there appeared to be nothing more than artificial skin covering the reconstructed hip. Jagged scars crisscrossed each other like markings on a tic-tac-toe board, leaving indentations and elevated patches that reminded him of corrugated tin. Nathan was beginning to realize how devastating those scars and the incident must have been to an impressionable teenager whose mother put such emphasis on appearance.

Gavin Spencer had railed at Elyssa, convincing her that she had never been desirable, except for the lure of her wealth. That ordeal must have convinced her she would never be more than some man's meal ticket. Nathan could understand why she had been afraid of intimacy, too self-conscious to face curious stares and inevitable questions.

He replaced the sheet and swore under his breath. Elyssa had every reason to react fiercely to the sight of Gavin Spencer, even after all these years. And it was no wonder that she had never really become involved with a man. Nathan believed she would never have opened to him, were it not for the emotional blows she had suffered—Robert's betrayal and Ely's death.

Maybe she had only been seeking comfort and consolation that first reckless night, but she had known what to expect on the past one, he assured himself. She was as involved as he was, whether or not she wanted to admit it. She probably didn't, not when she was afraid to trust him completely for fear that he, too, would betray her.

Elyssa might have had her doubts about their relationship, but Nathan had none. Perhaps circumstances had brought him and Elyssa together, but they would also ultimately separate them.

Despite their fierce attraction, Nathan knew, deep down, that this affair would eventually have to be terminated and that he would have to leave the ranch. He couldn't bear to have Elyssa view him as her hired man, and although Ely had been excessively generous, this ranch rightfully belonged to her, not to him.

Having watched his father's stardom wane in the rodeo world, Nathan knew nothing lasted forever. His first marriage had also taught him that forever was a relative concept, no matter how good one's intentions. Times and feelings changed. Eventually, the newness would wear off for both of them, and Elyssa's inheritance would cause problems between them. She could never really separate herself from her wealth, and he could never really forget this ranch was hers. But until he had to make a clean break and walk away from the only place that had ever felt like home, Nathan was going to stand by Elyssa, protect her and assure her that she was very desirable, with or without her wealth.

He padded into the bathroom to shower and dress, still cursing the damage Gavin had caused. That bastard ought to be shot, and Nathan would like to be the one to pull the trigger. He wondered what Gavin hoped to accomplish by hanging around Elyssa after the hell he had put her through.

While Nathan was saddling a horse, Ray Twigger's Ford truck rolled to a stop. "What are you doing back so early?" Nathan asked.

"If I'm going to own part of this stock company, I figured I'd better start acting like an executive and take responsibility," Twig replied before striding to the tack room to fetch a saddle.

"Sorry for the interruption last night." Nathan flipped up the stirrup to fasten the girth beneath the gelding's belly. The horse, of course, was holding his breath, swelling up like a ripe pumpkin. Nathan smiled to himself. They went through this ritual every damned time the gelding heard the jangle of bridles.

"Just don't make a habit of it," Twig replied. He set his saddle in place and peered at Nate over the back of the horse. "Do you think . . . ?" he glanced toward the rising sun. "Never mind."

"Dc I think what?" Nathan questioned, jerking up the cinch the instant the gelding released his breath.

Twig busied himself with equipping his mount. "Is it possible to fall for someone you've only known for a week? I feel like a damned kid when I'm around Valerie—all rioting hormones and hungry impatience. It's kind of a desperate feeling, you know? I'm aware that I'm rushing her, but I'm afraid if I don't I'll lose her to somebody else. She's really something, Nate. I never expected to find anyone else after Cara died. I never felt as if I was betraying my wife's memory before now. This is different."

"I think," Nathan said as he swung into the saddle, "you've got it bad for Valerie and you're trying to talk yourself out of it. You lost Cara. Are you planning on losing the best thing you've had going since your wife died? Would you have expected Cara to remain loyal to your memory forever? Wouldn't you have wanted her to find someone who could make her happy?"

Twig stepped into the stirrup, mounted, and reined toward the gate. "Yeah, I guess I would. But I don't want to overwhelm Valerie, either. You know how I am when I care about someone. I get too possessive. Just like you do. Too intense, too—"

"Is Valerie shying away?" Nathan asked.

Twig grinned, remembering. "No."

"Then there you go. Don't start messing with a good thing. Enjoy it. You deserve it."

"What about you, Nate?"

Nathan flicked Twig a quick glance. "Me?"

"Last night Robert said you and Elyssa were . . . well, you know."

"I was there the night he came slinking back to apologize to Elyssa for fooling around with his secretary," Nathan explained as he nudged the gelding into a trot. "I did imply we were involved, just so Elyssa could have a little revenge."

"Did she?"

"Did she what?" Nathan asked cautiously.

"Have her revenge?"

"I believe she did."

"Well, I hope she enjoyed it because Robert told Elyssa's mother and stepfather you two are involved," Twig reported.

Nathan scowled at the news.

"Somebody is going to have to do more than manhandle that guy," Twig predicted. "He's trying to save his job by making Elyssa look bad."

"I'll take care of him if I have to," Nathan promised.

"If you need any help, let me know. After what he said to Valerie, a knee in the nuts hardly seemed a sufficient response. He's got a hard head that needs a few blows with a two-by-four to knock some sense into it."

Nathan cursed silently. He hadn't meant to cause Elyssa more trouble than she already had. Maybe she would have been better off signing Gil's partnership agreement, not getting involved with the ranch. It wasn't as if she needed the money. But it was the principle of the thing. Nathan would have liked to think he'd had a positive influence on Elyssa, but he wondered if he hadn't brought her more anguish at a time when she was mourning her father and recovering from a broken engagement.

He forced those thoughts aside and got down to business. He needed to load the livestock and head to the hay fields. The first cutting of alfalfa was vitally important. If the crop wasn't swathed and baled before the rains came, the ranch could lose thousands of dollars.

This was going to be one of those days . . .

* * *

Elyssa was jolted awake by the blaring of the phone. One of the nearby ranchers called to say that Rawlins cattle had broken through the fences and had scattered in all directions. Some of the frightened calves had separated from their mothers and had run through other fences to join neighboring herds.

Elyssa had just stepped out of the shower when another call reported stray cattle on another section of the ranch. From what she could determine, only Ely's cows and calves had mysteriously broken out. There had been no news of Gil's steers running wild. That made her highly suspicious, considering the ultimatum she had delivered to her uncle last night. She had the inescapable feeling this outbreak of cattle was a form of retaliation.

Elyssa stuffed her feet in her boots and hurried outside, hoping to catch the hired men before they headed to the hay fields. They had just emerged from the bunkhouse when she reached the barn.

"The neighbors have been calling to say we have cows and calves roaming the roads and ditches," she informed the hands.

"Where's Nate?" Mo-Joe Denson questioned, on his way to the tack room.

"I haven't seen him this morning," she replied.

While the men saddled their horses, Elyssa went to check on the cow and calf penned in the corral. The newborn calf seemed to be in reasonably good condition after its bad first day. He was standing up, nursing, and his tail was wagging like a puppy's. Ely had always said that was a good sign. Mother and calf were doing well. Elyssa hoped she could say the same for the herd that had scattered from here to kingdom come.

Elyssa pulled her mare to a halt on the rise overlooking the gravel road to the north. What she saw changed her worried

frown to an amused smile. Hunter and Twig had corralled the
rodeo stock in one corner of the four-square-mile pasture, leaving the efficient dog Ricky in charge while they rounded up
strays that were strung along the road.

The dog was absolutely amazing! Each time a bronc or bull
decided to wander off to graze, Ricky ran him into the crowded
pack, baring his teeth. The dog was constantly in motion, circling and retracing his steps to hold the herd in position. Now
she understood why Hunter treated Ricky like a family member. Ricky deserved to be on salary rather than dog-food rations. He'd accomplished more in fifteen minutes than Cousin
Virgil and Patricia could manage in the whole damned day.

Elyssa reined back toward the road to gather the cows that
were headed east. Cowboys scattered in all directions, looking
for breaks in the fence. Les Fykes waved his hat in the air
when he located the broken strands of barbed wire. Within
fifteen minutes all riders converged, herding the cattle through
the opening.

Nathan shot Elyssa a meaningful glance as he eased his bay
gelding alongside her. "Helluva coincidence, don't you think?"

"I must have made Gil furious," she murmured confiden-
tially. "Of course, I can't prove he—or Virgil—decided to keep
us preoccupied while they cover up Virgil's dealing with
Rancher's Mutual."

Nathan jerked up his head to glance at Twig. "You and
Ricky take the rodeo stock back and get them loaded in the
truck. The rest of us can track down the missing cattle."

"Don't you think Twig needs more help than a dog?" Elyssa
asked. "Granted, Ricky's skills are impressive, but—"

"Honey, the only reason I'm sending Twig along is to open
and close gates. That's the only thing Ricky can't do by himself," Nathan informed her with a grin.

Elyssa was inclined to agree when Twig gave the command
and Ricky put the rodeo stock into motion, forcing them to
follow the fence to the pasture gate that Twig had circled
around to open. Ricky definitely seemed to have things under

control. He took the herd directly toward the barn visible in the distance, swinging back and forth like a drag rider in a cattle drive. All Twig did was ride at a distance and work the gates. Ricky did the rest.

"Les, you and Mo-Joe repair the fence," Nathan instructed.

"Jim Riley called to say we also have cattle on the west section," Elyssa told him. "Some of the calves got mixed in with his herd."

"Damn," Nathan grumbled. "This could take all morning."

"That's the point, I'm sure." Elyssa reined toward the road. "I'll get a late start contacting the lawyer, and you'll be tied up all day and half the night with cattle and hay crews. Remind me to thank Gil and Virgil for making sure I don't have time to be bored."

"You'd better guard your back," Nathan advised. "I'm sure the Rawlins clan would be beside themselves if you met with an accident. They could get everything but my portion of the ranch back."

Elyssa digested the warning and rode off to locate the rest of the strays. From all indications, Gil and Virgil had decided to make trouble. That lent credence to her feeling that Ely had not met with an accident. She was going to start asking direct questions, first chance she got. But she wasn't prepared to take her accusations to the local law enforcement. The less she dealt with Gavin Spencer, the better.

Damn, the one time she needed a police officer on her side she was stuck with a man who would probably expect illicit favors for his assistance. That was the type Gavin Spencer was.

Nothing like a corrupt cop, she mused bitterly. She would virtually be on her own if she started posing questions. Gavin and Virgil had been good friends in their younger days. No telling what kind of deals Virgil was accustomed to cutting with Gavin.

Seventeen

By the time Elyssa returned to the house her legs felt like rubber bands. She hadn't straddled a horse for so many hours in years. It was little wonder cowboys developed sleek, muscular thighs, she decided. With a great deal of that kind of exercise, she could compete in body-building contests.

She showered and changed for the second time in five hours. She was on her way down the hall when Claudia appeared. The younger woman bore her son on her hip and had a hostile frown on her painted face.

"So you spent the morning with Nate, did you?" she said by way of a greeting.

"Yes I did." Elyssa managed a civil smile and dug into her purse for her keys. "We finally managed to round up all the missing cattle, except for the few calves that Hunter and Ricky are tracking down now. Tell your mother I won't be here for supper. I have errands to run in the City, so I won't be back until late tonight."

While Elyssa drove, she mulled over the information Hunter had conveyed to her. He had not only warned her to expect more trouble from Gil and Virgil, he had related the incident with Robert Grayson at the apartment. The man had unbelievable audacity. He wanted to cause conflict between her and her stepfather out of spite or he was hoping the tactic would bring her back under his thumb.

Some men's thinking was really distorted, Elyssa concluded. Did Robert honestly believe his tactics would get her back?

Probably. He was plagued with a mega ego. Too bad his charm wasn't nearly as effective as he believed it to be. Elyssa had never been overwhelmed by it, not as she had been by Hunter's. And having discovered how electrifying an attraction could be, she wasn't about to settle for less.

Robert was ancient history. But she was going to put a stop to his nonsense. He could hit the streets, hunt for a new job, because Elyssa wasn't feeling the least bit charitable. Robert was beginning to remind her of Gavin and his threats. They were both Class-A jerks who deserved any and all misfortune that came their way.

Valerie broke into a beaming smile when Elyssa sailed into the office, dressed in a stylish yellow ensemble that rivaled the brightness of the sun. "I hope you came armed to the teeth. Good ole Robert has had a heyday spreading rumors about both of us." She gestured her blond head toward the hall that led to the executive office. "He is already with Daniel—tattling. Your mother is here, too."

Great, thought Elyssa. Nothing like fighting battles on all fronts at once. "This is going to be worse than I thought," she said.

"Would you like reinforcements?" Valerie volunteered enthusiastically.

"No, I'll take care of it." Elyssa marched down the hall, firm in her conviction that for the first time in her life she knew what she wanted. Jessica wasn't going to approve, but that was too damned bad.

"Elyssa!" Jessica's exquisite features registered surprise and then disapproval. "It's about time you showed up."

Elyssa nodded a silent greeting to Daniel and then focused on her mother, ignoring Robert. "It has been a hectic week," she began. "I'm sorry I haven't had time to get in touch with you since you returned from your trip."

"From the sound of things, you let your father's death ruin

what would have been the beginning of a good marriage," Jessica said with cool distaste. "Really, Elyssa, I thought I raised you better than to pull a stunt like this."

"Stunt?" Elyssa questioned, determined to let Robert cut his own throat and look the culprit.

"You know perfectly well what I'm referring to," Jessica snapped. "In your grief, you looked for consolation in the first place you could find it. You ruined your engagement to Robert because of a reckless indiscretion. You're lucky Robert has been so understanding, despite his humiliation and disappointment."

Elyssa regarded her mother, trying to recall if even once in her life the woman had taken her side or offered support. She hadn't. So why should it be any different now?

"I don't advise that you spend more time than necessary with that cowboy character," Daniel piped up. "I'm sure you're forced to associate with him in handling your father's estate, but Robert has his pride and you can't expect him to continue being understanding."

Robert had done quite a job on Daniel and Jessica. He was obviously operating on the theory that the first tale told was the one that would be believed. And he'd anticipated that Elyssa would keep her trap shut because she didn't want to lose her own foothold in Cutler Corporation.

Two weeks ago she might have buckled to the pressure. But she was hardly the same woman now. She had simply been going through the paces of living then, performing duties in her stepfather's company—duties she didn't particularly enjoy. She had decided to marry Robert because she had wanted to start her own family. She had been a corporate robot, but she wasn't one now and she would never be one again.

"You have been deceived and misinformed," Elyssa announced, much to Robert's shock and dismay.

His expression clearly indicated he hadn't expected her to contradict him. That wasn't how the game was played. He had expected her to go behind his back, later—a common practice in the business world, where clandestine deals were made in exchange for other favors. Too bad Robert hadn't predicted that Elyssa would play by her own rules.

"The truth is, I returned from D.C. and stopped by Robert's apartment unannounced. He and his secretary were in bed together when they were supposed to be conducting a conference."

Daniel's brown eyes widened and then zeroed in on Robert, who, of course, called Elyssa a liar.

"If you don't believe me, you can verify the story with Valerie. She was at our apartment that evening. I told her what happened. All this took place before I learned of my father's death late that night. I imagine Robert and Bambi have been carrying on for some time, since she has been accompanying him to these so-called conferences for the last few months."

Elyssa paused to glare at Robert, who had turned an interesting shade of purple. It suits him, she thought. "Had you planned to tell me about your affair or just continue it after we married, Robert?"

"Robert, answer the question," Daniel demanded gruffly.

"It's a lie!" he objected fiercely. "And you certainly can't take Valerie's word for anything. She was entertaining one of those cowboy friends of hers last night when I went over to the apartment to try to resolve my differences with Elyssa. And I can guarantee I found Elyssa with that Hunter character last week. He even admitted they were—"

"Of course he did," Elyssa interrupted. "I told him what you had done, and he thought you deserved a taste of your own medicine. The fact is nothing had happened. He only wanted me to enjoy a little revenge."

"You are *not* having an affair with Hunter? Well, thank God," Jessica said with relief.

"I wasn't then," Elyssa clarified. "But I am now. There is no chance whatsoever of a reconciliation with Robert. The wedding plans are off. And if I were president of this corporation, I'd send Robert packing because he can't be trusted.

He proved that with this incident. His moves are dictated by an obsession with prestige and promotion. He's prepared to say whatever is necessary to draw attention to himself. No doubt, he expected you to take pity on him because he said I cheated on *him*, though I most certainly did not!"

"You are twisting everything to your benefit!" Robert sputtered. "This is turning into a conspiracy!"

"Oh, really?" Elyssa said. "What do you call your affair with Bambi—and the rumors you started in the office about Valerie and me?"

"I call it the truth," Robert declared. "Valerie is nothing more than a high-class call girl and always was. Your association with her has corrupted you. You're making me out to be the culprit when I'm innocent."

Daniel glanced back and forth between Elyssa and Robert who stood toe to toe and eye to eye in the middle of the office, each spouting their version of the story, each sounding convincing. There was only one hitch: Daniel had always been especially fond of Elyssa, and he had never been all that impressed with Robert Grayson. Daniel decided, there and then, who it was he preferred to believe.

"Clean out your desk, Grayson, and bring me all the files in your office," he said. "You're fired."

Robert gaped in disbelief. "You've got to be kidding. I thought I could come to you with the truth because you're a fair and just man. But obviously Elyssa pulls more weight, wrong or right, because she is family."

Daniel leaned his elbows on the desk and smiled wryly. "If I hear that version of the story circulating in the office, I'll know for certain that you have concocted a charade. It's the kind of tale a man tells to protect himself from blame. I've known Elyssa a long time, I've only known you for two years. The *truth* is, I haven't been all that pleased with you. You've only lasted this long because of her."

Robert looked as if he had received a blow to the jaw. It

was impossible for his inflated ego to accept Daniel's criticism. He simply rejected it.

Elyssa watched him curse under his breath and wheel toward the door. The man would never admit to himself—or to anyone else—that he was wrong or incompetent. In his false pride, he simply refused to find any fault in himself. That, Elyssa decided, was why Nathan's, Valerie's, Twig's, and her own comments never got through to him. Robert was a classic example of impenetrable arrogance. He would twist incidents in his mind until he'd convinced himself that he had been victimized. Too bad she couldn't muster any pity for this unemployed, no-account executive. Robert Grayson had gotten what he deserved.

When the door slammed shut, Elyssa pivoted to face Daniel. "It means a great deal to know you have faith in me. I made a mistake by agreeing to marry Robert, but I'm thankful I discovered what a deceitful liar he is before it was too late."

"I'm really sorry to hear about your father. I know these are trying times for you. Is there anything your mother and I can do to help?"

"Believe me, Daniel," Jessica cut in, "the last thing you want to do is get involved in Rawlins Ranch." She glanced briefly at her daughter. "Elyssa would be better off if she left everything in Hunter's hands. She walked away from that kind of life years ago, and so did I. This is where we both belong."

"I'm afraid not, Mother."

Jessica jerked up her head, astonished.

"Going back to the ranch was difficult at first, but hard as it is for you to believe, I feel I belong there."

Jessica all but came out of her chair. "My God, Elyssa, you can't be serious!"

"I'm quite serious."

Elyssa glanced at Daniel to see how he was taking the news. He slumped in his chair, fingers interlocked, studying her consideringly. Odd, the kinship she felt for Daniel was stronger than the bond with her own mother. She had been fortunate to have him in her life. His only flaw was being hopelessly in love with and overly indulgent of Jessica. He had spoiled her rotten.

At age fifty, Jessica was still a strikingly attractive woman whose poise and carriage gave her a regal air. She was an efficient hostess for a corporate executive, but she wasn't a caring mother. Elyssa had no doubt that Jessica cared about Daniel. She would have been an idiot not to. But Elyssa and Jessica had never shared the same values or desires, and Jessica had constantly imposed her own on her daughter.

Elyssa rather imagined that her mother, fifteen years younger than Ely, had perceived her first marriage to a wealthy rancher to be an opportunity to escape her lowly roots. After a few years, Jessica grew bored with the life Ely had designed for himself on the fringe of the civilized world. She had wanted glamor and social status. Daniel had been able to provide them, so Jessica had done whatever was necessary to latch onto him and escape the ranch life she had come to detest.

"What is it you want to do, Elyssa?" Daniel asked quietly.

"Don't even ask her," Jessica muttered. "She doesn't know right now. She is still reeling from Ely's death."

Elyssa ignored her mother for the moment and drew herself up in front of Daniel. "I would like you to find someone to replace me. I want to handle Ely's affairs on the ranch."

"Good Lord!" Jessica howled in dismay.

Daniel appraised Elyssa for a long moment. "Perhaps we should begin with a leave of absence," he suggested. "Give yourself time to decide exactly what you want to do without cancelling your options. After you've settled your father's affairs, you may discover you were only driven by what you thought Ely would want you to do. Why don't you make certain that emotion isn't overriding logic, Elyssa. I'll have your position filled with the understanding that you may wish to return. Does that sound acceptable to you?"

Elyssa smiled at her stepfather. "Are you being generous because I'm family? You know Robert will have the story twisted every which way. According to him, I'm probably leaving the firm for a few months of psychological observation and treatment."

"Maybe you should," Jessica insisted. "I think this is a disastrous mistake."

Daniel contradicted his disgruntled wife. "Actually, I think it might be a good idea. Elyssa is undoubtedly going to be involved with finalizing arrangements in the settlement of her father's estate. Trying to keep up with her work in the City will only put unnecessary pressure on her. She's been flying from one side of the continent to the other for years because she's excellent in public relations and well informed about our government projects—"

Daniel nearly choked when Elyssa scampered around the edge of the desk to give him a big hug.

Bless the man! Some daughters didn't have the luxury of even one loving father. Elyssa had had two. "I love you, Daniel. And thank you for being so supportive and cooperative. There are complications to deal with in Ely's estate. And I can use some time to make decisions about my future."

She focused on Daniel. "I would like to ask a favor, though. I need a lawyer's advice on a legal matter, and I would like to use Bernard Gresham. I also have a task for John Preston to perform."

"The criminal investigator?" Daniel frowned in concern. "Is something wrong?"

"That's what I intend to find out."

"Elyssa, I don't like this one bit," Jessica protested. "I demand that you reconsider."

"I have made the commitment and I'm sticking with it," she declared in no uncertain terms.

"Then Gresham and Preston are at your disposal," Daniel confirmed. "Your mother and I will do whatever we can to help."

Daniel, maybe; Elyssa wasn't so sure about Jessica. Her mother had made it clear that she wanted Elyssa to take a wide berth around Rawlins Ranch. Elyssa couldn't help but wonder why. It wasn't as if she had asked Jessica to become involved in the ranch after leaving it twenty years earlier. So what, Elyssa wondered, was the problem?

Despite Jessica's discontented glares, she made her departure. Daniel had accepted Elyssa's decision and had believed her when Robert had twisted the facts. Elyssa couldn't help but wonder if he would catch hell from Jessica for being so understanding and agreeable. Jessica had become accustomed to getting her way in all matters.

Elyssa sank back in her chair to study Valerie after they had finished their meal at Cattleman's. It was one of Valerie's favorite hangouts when she was in the mood to brush shoulders with the country crowd, and she had been glowing all evening, even more exuberant than usual. Elyssa wished she possessed that much enthusiasm, but she was annoyed with herself for jumping the gun and flinging accusations at Virgil and Gil before she had concrete proof.

Just as Hunter had predicted, Virgil had wasted no time setting up smoke screens that made it impossible for Preston to dig up information about the loan from Rancher's Mutual. Preston's sources could provide no more than pat statements that Virgil's dealings could not be disclosed without his permission. Elyssa wondered how much it had cost her cousin to zip a few lips.

She had conferred with Bernard Gresham about legal aspects of setting up a private auction to divide Rawlins property, and he had informed her that she should have a lawyer present to protect her interests. He'd volunteered to act for her at the auction and she had readily accepted his offer. At least she hadn't bungled that, she thought to herself.

The sooner the partnership was legally and emotionally dissolved the better she'd like it. Although she still harbored a sense of guilt about breaking tradition, she kept reminding herself that her father had been prepared to do the same thing to salvage at least half of the ranch, or so Hunter claimed. Everything seemed to hinge on Hunter's claims, and Elyssa hoped he wasn't betraying her. If he was, she was setting herself up for the greatest letdown of her life.

She grinned when Valerie finally got around to mentioning Ray Twigger. He was the reason for her friend's good mood, Elyssa imagined.

"Salt of the earth," Valerie was saying. "I tell you, Ellie, he is the best thing that's happened to me in years."

"You've known him for only a week," Elyssa pointed out.

Valerie waved that off with the flick of a silver and turquoise-encircled wrist. "Since when is time a measure of love?"

"Love?" Elyssa said skeptically. "Good grief, Val, you have gone overboard. What makes you so sure Twig is the right one?"

Her friend munched on a bite of steak and then responded. "Process of elimination. I've spent years determining who *aren't* the right ones. Ray is gentle but strong, considerate, and even protective of me. You should have seen the way he lit into Robert when that fool insulted me. And Ray is honest. In my book, that's worth bonus points."

Elyssa agreed. She wished she could be certain she was getting absolute honesty from Hunter.

"You should have seen the look on Robert's face when Ray pounced on him last night." Valerie smiled in satisfaction. "That scene was as gratifying as the one this morning, when Daniel told Robert to take a hike. Robert slammed around the office, gathering his belongings and flinging mutinous glances at me. I can't believe he ever thought Daniel would swallow his baloney. The man's got incredible gall. I'll bet Robert doesn't ever think he's in the wrong."

"I can't believe I ever was willing to settle for the likes of him," Elyssa said. "Big mistake."

"Luckily, you found out in time. Good Lord, he could have

been the father of your children! Now that's an unnerving thought. I can look at Ray and have pleasant visions of a family, home, and—"

"Slow down." Elyssa chuckled at seeing the disgustingly dreamy expression on her friend's face.

"Slow down and risk losing him?" Valerie hooted, and then slumped in her chair. "Yeah, I suppose you're right. I wouldn't want to scare him off by being too eager." She smiled impishly. "I'll give him a week to adjust to the idea."

Elyssa rolled her eyes. "You're impossible."

"No, I'm in love. You know what Garth Brooks and Chris LeDoux said about a cowboy who camps out on your couch and never leaves? Well, that's fine by me."

"Then maybe it's best if I move a few more of my things to the ranch. I wouldn't want to be in the way."

Valerie's teasing smile faded. "You're thinking of moving out? Are you really going to give ranch life a try after all these years?"

"I really am," Elyssa confirmed as she grabbed her purse. "Until the situation is resolved, I want to be on hand to make sure my cousin and uncle don't turn the place into a shambles out of revenge."

"And what about Nathan Hunter?"

"What about him?"

"Don't give me that, Ellie," Valerie sniffed. "You're living in the same house with the man."

That wasn't all she was doing with him. "We're business partners now."

"Yeah, right. Maybe he hasn't seen the way you look at him, but I have. You never looked at Robert like that."

"Mind your own business, Val."

"After I've spilled my guts to you?" Valerie said with mock indignation. "I thought we'd passed a milestone in our friendship. Why can't you tell me how you feel about Hunter?"

"Because I don't know how I feel or what he feels," Elyssa

admitted as they walked out of the restaurant and headed for her car.

"Well, why don't you ask him?" Valerie suggested.

Elyssa stared at her friend as if Val were a creature from outer space. "Are you nuts? What would that prove? That he can lie and deceive as well as Robert? A man can—and will— say anything to get what he wants. I haven't figured out what Hunter wants yet. Until I do, I can't be sure of him."

"Fine, give him everything you think he might want. If he's still interested in you, then you'll know he's sincere."

Elyssa blinked like a startled owl. "You want me to give him absolute control of the ranch?"

"Is that what you think he wants?"

"Yes."

"Is that all?"

"What else is there?"

"There's *you.*"

Elyssa concentrated on her driving, refusing to meet Valerie's curious stare.

"Ellie . . . there's something you're not telling. You *are* hooked on Hunter, aren't you?"

"Give me a break, Val. I've had a rough two weeks."

"Okay, I'll back off, but not without a few words of advice," Valerie negotiated. "You've always been pretty insightful. If it feels right, then go with it. You already know that logic and all that malarkey about having a family early in life didn't work worth a damn with Robert. He turned out to be a dis-aster—with a loose zipper. If you don't rely on your feelings, you might pass up something really terrific. With Hunter. I happen to like the man. Why don't you give him a chance?"

"You're not qualified to counsel me. You think all's right with the world because you're in love with Twig," Elyssa pro-tested. "I don't know whether I should follow the advice of a woman who's so optimistic she thinks she's the good fairy waving her magic wand."

"Am I that bad?"

"You're nauseating." Elyssa took her eyes off the road long enough to toss Valerie a smile that softened the blow of her words. "You're also the best friend I ever had, and I wish you luck with Twig. I hope he turns out to be your Prince Charming in cowboy boots."

"Thanks. Maybe I'll take your advice and slow down. I may be reading more into what Ray says than he actually means. I haven't exactly pinned him down." Valerie snickered at the thought. "Not yet anyway. I'll save that maneuver for his return from Kansas City."

Elyssa bit back a laugh, reasonably certain that Valerie was speaking literally as well as figuratively.

Eighteen

Nathan stepped out of the shower and heaved a weary sigh. This had been one helluva day. He'd been battling the clock since he got up. The incident that left the cattle strung out along the roads and in neighboring pastures suggested vindictive tampering with fences. By the time he and the men had gathered the stray cattle they were behind schedule in swathing and raking hay.

The meteorologist predicted rain by week's end. If the curing hay wasn't raked, baled, and removed from the fields, it would become too moldy to pass as first-rate alfalfa. It couldn't be sold as a cash crop without the price plummeting.

With fiendish haste, Nathan had driven to the various alfalfa fields to oversee the swathing. The crew was shorthanded while Twig transported stock, and Gil wasn't about to help after Elyssa revoked the partnership. Nathan had kept the crews in the fields until ten o'clock that night. Hay rakes had been running full blast, turning and airing out the downed hay so it could dry as quickly as possible for baling.

It was even later before Nathan returned to the house. While the crew wolfed down the late supper Althea had prepared, he'd driven off to check the fences. Now he was exhausted, hungry enough to lick the pattern off the china, and completely out of sorts. The shower relieved his tension and weariness to some degree, but he didn't imagine that chewing on his fingernails was going to stave off the hunger pains much longer. As for being out of sorts, nothing would relieve that except throwing a few punches at Virgil and Gil for sabotaging the fences.

Nathan padded into his room to pull on a clean pair of jeans. He spun around abruptly when he detected movement in the darkened hall. "Is that you, Cutler?"

No answer.

He veered around the corner to see a dark shape condense in the shadows. A pair of octopus arms engulfed him. The smell of cheap perfume and the molding of a scantily-covered body to his froze him to the spot.

"Claudia, what the hell are you doing in here?"

"Isn't it obvious?" she locked her hands behind Nathan's neck to hold him in place. "You don't seem to respond to subtle invitations. I decided to be more obvious."

A rotten end to a rotten day! "I appreciate the offer—"

"Good, because I enjoy giving it." Claudia pressed closer, brushing her breasts against his bare chest. Her hips ground suggestively into his. "I want you, Nate. I always have—"

The flick of the hall light caused Nathan to jerk back, but Claudia clung to him like English ivy. His gaze soared over her head to Elyssa at the head of the steps. She looked neither surprised nor angry. Hurt was a better description for her expression.

Claudia, still draped against him, swiveled her head and glanced at Elyssa, then took her time about untangling her hands from behind Nathan's neck and pivoting around to rub her shoulder against his bare chest like a loving kitten. Without a word, she then sashayed down the hall. The smile she sent Elyssa was as tacky as her lip gloss.

Elyssa marshaled her composure and stalked toward her bedroom. It was glaringly apparent that Hunter's hormones were running rampant and that he hadn't expected her to be back. It was also obvious that she would be an utter fool to think he wanted anything permanent with her.

"You're dead wrong if you think I invited Claudia up here," Nathan said as he propped himself against the door jamb.

Elyssa debated about launching her suitcase at him. "And you're dead wrong if you think it matters one way or the other to me," she snapped.

"You really don't care?"

She slung the suitcase on the bed and lurched around to glare at him. "Why should I? We are business partners—that's all."

"You think all we've been doing is business? Come on, Cutler. You should know better than that."

"Just get out and leave me alone."

"I'm not going until I've convinced you I had nothing to do with that little scene."

"How long are you planning on living, Hunter? That could take years!"

"I don't suppose Claudia thought you were coming back, since it's so late," he mused aloud. "She probably—"

Elyssa jerked upright, remembering her conversation with Claudia before leaving the ranch that morning. That woman knew perfectly well Elyssa would return late. She could have staged the incident. Then again, the chummy couple might have thought they had time for their tryst before Elyssa did show up.

Damn it, she didn't know what to think. She was hurting inside. She wasn't sure enough of Hunter to know how to handle their relationship. Two nights of lovemaking didn't qualify as an affair, did it? How many tumbles in bed constituted exclusive rights? What she needed was a how-to manual on conducting affairs so she'd have a set of rules to follow.

"Cutler, I told you once and I'll tell you again. I don't want Claudia. I can't control what she wants, and I haven't had time to sit her down and explain that I'm not interested. I just got in twenty minutes ago—I haven't even had supper. No matter what you think, I didn't plan that escapade."

"Fine, you didn't. It was all Claudia's doing. Now go away."

Nathan, already in a bad humor, lost his temper when Elyssa dismissed him with that patronizing tone. He stalked over, grabbed her by the arm, and spun her around to face him. "Look, damn it—"

"The name's Elyssa," she corrected flippantly.

"Look, *Elyssa,*" he said in an unpleasant tone, "it's not my fault you had your confidence shattered at a vulnerable age and never came to realize what a potent effect you have on men—on me in particular. The fact is I haven't wanted anyone but you since our first night together, and I sure as hell don't want Claudia. I'm not sure I want anybody tonight. I'm tired and irritable and sick to death of having you look at me as if I'm a traitor every damned time somebody casts suspicion on me. Now, I'm going downstairs to raid the icebox, just as I'd planned to do before Claudia slunk in here to offer herself as dessert."

When he wheeled around and stormed off, Elyssa stared after him, wanting to believe him but afraid to. He could be putting on a convincing act, for her benefit, or Claudia could have staged that unsettling scene.

She frowned pensively. Which of them did she trust most? Claudia? All the girl had going for her was a mother who was as good as gold. She had known Elyssa planned to return late and could have planned to retaliate against the woman she considered a rival. She might be trying to do no more than stake her claim on the man she wanted. If she had been acting alone, Hunter had reason to be annoyed at Elyssa for thinking the worst of him.

"Oh, the hell with it!" Elyssa exclaimed as she opened her suitcase to put away her belongings. She would give Hunter the benefit of the doubt. He had more character than Claudia, after all. After he cooled off she'd apologize. They didn't need to be at odds in the middle of the feud with Gil and Virgil.

Elyssa's hand stalled in midair. She was ready to drop an armload of clothes in the drawer when she noticed that the accounting voucher she had put on the dresser wasn't where she'd left it. She had mentioned it to her uncle; had he sneaked in to retrieve it while everyone was rounding up cattle?

Elyssa ambled over to the sliding door that opened onto the

balcony. It was unlocked, but she couldn't say for certain whether it had been locked when she'd left the house. She had never even considered security here, knowing Hunter was in the room beside her. She really should have paid more attention to locking doors and windows . . .

Distant lights on the country road to the west drew Elyssa's wary frown. She waited a few seconds, expecting them to disappear when the vehicle crested the distant hill, but they didn't. She lurched around to grab the pickup keys. If somebody was lurking about, cutting fence wire, she had every intention of catching him red-handed.

With plate in hand, Nathan glanced into the hall when he heard the front door open and shut. Elyssa was still irritated, he concluded. So was he. He didn't even know why he continued fighting this uphill battle with her. As she had said, it would be years before she'd be able to trust him. He didn't need this torment. He really ought to finalize the arrangements at the ranch and walk away from it. He could find work elsewhere if he wanted it. He had a degree in agronomy and agricultural economics, and he had been offered jobs on other ranches, even with the rodeo commission. He could buy Elyssa's half of the stock company if he decided to.

Nathan crammed his plate of lasagne in the microwave oven and set the timer. His needs were becoming more simplified by the second. All he wanted was a reheated meal and a soft bed. He was tired of fighting Elyssa's mistrust. Tired!

Cursing, Nathan shook the sting out of his burned hand; he'd absently grabbed the hot plate. He had let himself become distracted, wondering where Elyssa had gone at this time of night and then telling himself he didn't care.

Elyssa stomped on the brake and muttered under her breath when the mysterious vehicle that had stopped on the aban-

doned stretch of road turned out to be Gavin Spencer's patrol
car. She would have preferred to back away, but Gavin sauntered over to pull open her door.

"What are you doing out here, sugar?" he cooed in what
Elyssa presumed to be his most seductive voice.

"I was investigating suspicious traffic," Elyssa told him
stiffly.

Gavin slid his arm around the back of the seat and leaned
closer. Elyssa leaned away.

"I'd like to do a little investigating myself."

She ignored that. "I presume you heard about the stray cattle scattered all over creation. Who told you?"

His shoulder lifted in a nonchalant shrug. "Word gets
around."

"Well, thanks for checking." She reached up to shift the
truck into reverse, but Gavin's hand folded over hers.

"Come on, sugar, how long do you plan to give me the
cold shoulder? I thought I'd made it pretty clear I wanted to
make a fresh start with you."

Fresh was right! Elyssa shrieked when his arm curled
around her shoulder like a snake and his hand fastened around
her breast. When she tried to jerk away, his fingers clenched
and the buttons on her blouse scattered. Her second yelp was
drowned out by his demanding kiss. She gagged in disgust
when his hand slid inside her gaping blouse to fondle her
breast.

Gavin was like a groping bear, shoving her down on the
seat to climb atop her.

Reaching up with her free hand, she gave him a sound
whack upside the head. He recoiled and then scowled while
she sat there hissing like a disturbed cat.

"Stay away from me, Gavin."

"Why? Because you're letting Nate dip his wick?" He
sneered. "I've got news for you, sugar, he's only after titles
and deeds. If your dad was still around, he could tell you what
Nate really wants."

"What do you know about my father's business?" she snapped.

"Plenty. I might even be willing to tell you what I know for a few free rides. If you want some information about what's really going on around here, I'm the man who can deliver it to you. All you have to do is cooperate. I'm in a position to make things happen, for your benefit as well as mine . . ."

His voice trailed off when an unidentified thrashing erupted in the underbrush. Elyssa glanced around, noting they were near the mouth of the canyons she had investigated a few days earlier. The headlights beamed against the same sagging fence she had tried to repair without the proper tools.

Gavin smiled like a shark, seemingly unconcerned about the sounds that had interrupted him. "Think about what I said, sugar. Come by my place Saturday night and I'll tell you a few things you need to know. You could blow this whole thing wide open if the price is right."

Elyssa dodged his intended kiss and slammed the pickup into reverse. She cast one last glance toward the slackened fence and backed away. Gavin Spencer was out of his mind if he thought she would fall for his one-sided bargains. But she did have the nagging suspicion that he knew something she didn't. What? She couldn't imagine. What *whole thing* could be blown wide open? Gil and Virgil's sabotaging of fences? Or was he referring to her father's death? Did he know it wasn't an accident, just as she suspected? And how much, she wondered, was it going to cost her to get Gavin to talk? Who was he protecting until he found someone willing to pay a better price?

She sure didn't need a corrupt cop. Gavin had been baiting her. She wondered if he was simply maneuvering to get her alone so he could satisfy his lusts.

During the drive back to the house, Elyssa mulled over what Gavin had said about Hunter. She didn't want to believe Gavin any more than she wanted to believe Claudia, Uncle Gil, or Virgil. She wanted to believe Hunter was on her side, that what they shared was special. It was too easy for her to remember the passion that exploded in her when she was in his arms, the spark of awareness ignited by the mere sight of him.

Maybe that was why she had been so tormented when she'd found Claudia plastered against Hunter. He had looked utterly irresistible standing there in nothing but his jeans, his hair damp from a shower. *That* was what was bothering her. Perhaps she should adopt the younger woman's seductive tactics. Although she'd had more practice at repelling advances than instigating them, she was going to have to fight for what she wanted.

Good Lord! She was sitting here planning to seduce the man when she wasn't absolutely certain he hadn't invited Claudia to the house or that Gil and Virgil hadn't had legitimate reasons for warning her away from Hunter! Valerie might have been right. She had fallen for Hunter—hook, line, and sinker. If she trusted her feelings and they betrayed her, Greatgrandmother Mae was going to catch hell when Elyssa met up with her in heaven!

Nineteen

For a man who, not thirty minutes earlier, had claimed to be too tired to give a damn about anything, Nathan was pretty alert. He sat on the staircase, watching headlights flare against the open window. As incensed as he had been that Elyssa didn't trust him, he was concerned about her now. It was almost midnight, for God's sake. Where had she gone?

When the front door opened, he slumped in relief, but he jerked up his head in alarm when Elyssa moved into the light and he saw her gaping blouse and tousled hair. He was on his feet, sailing down the steps in a flash.

"What happened?" he demanded.

She hadn't realized how eager she was to be in the protective circle of Hunter's arms until he pulled her to him. She pressed her cheek to the solid wall of his bare chest, and even though she could smell Claudia's cheap perfume clinging to him, she wrapped her arms around his ribs and savored the calming effect his touch had on her.

"Where the hell were you?" Nathan questioned as he cradled her against him, feeling her tension gradually dissipate. "Elyssa?"

She didn't want to talk; she wanted to be held tenderly for a moment, to replace Gavin's groping assault with this sweet experience. Long before she was ready to be released, Nathan withdrew. His penetrating gaze dropped to the buttonless yellow blouse that exposed the lacy bra beneath it.

"Tell me what happened," he commanded.

"I saw headlights on the road while I was standing on the balcony," she explained, tugging her torn blouse together. "I thought maybe Gil or Virgil was lurking around." She paused to draw a steadying breath. "Gavin was patrolling the area."

"That bastard," Nathan snarled. "What did he do to you?"

"The same thing he tried to do twelve years ago, only there wasn't a canyon for me to fall into. Then he tried to bait me by saying he knew what was going on around here. If I gave him what he wanted, he would fork over information."

"About what?"

"I don't know. Like I said, I had the feeling I was being baited and bribed."

Nathan swore under his breath as he ushered Elyssa up the steps. "You go on to bed, and I'll go see if I can track Gavin down."

"No!" Elyssa protested. "I don't want you involved in my feud."

"I'm already involved." Nathan steered her into her bedroom. "I don't want that asshole near you again. Women shouldn't have to tolerate that kind of mauling, especially from a cop. He's a discredit to his profession."

When he turned to leave, Elyssa clutched his hand. "Please don't go, Hunter."

"I don't want that bastard thinking he can get away with something like this," Nathan gritted out. "He's hurt you too much already."

"I don't care about him," Elyssa insisted. "He means nothing to me." Her dark eyes lifted to note the clench of his jaw, the thin stretch of his lips over bared teeth. "You're the one I don't want to be hurt by." She drew in a breath and stepped out on shaky ground. "Because . . . *you* matter, Hunter."

A shudder rippled through Nathan. He stared into those fathomless ebony eyes that reflected the dim light in the hall, and his knees turned to jelly. Suddenly he didn't give a damn about Gavin Spencer, either. He had an overwhelming need to erase the torment of Gavin's touch, to give Elyssa all the gentleness she needed and deserved.

"We're getting in too damned deep," he whispered as he reached out a shaky hand to trace her heart-shaped lips. "Sooner or later everyone around here is going to know there's something going on between us, if they haven't figured it out already. They'll all be wondering if I'm after your money."

They're already saying that, Elyssa thought as the pad of his index finger brushed over her mouth.

"They'll be saying I'm after your body, Hunter," she whispered as her hand splayed across the matting of hair on his chest.

"Are they right, Elyssa?" he questioned before his lips replaced his caressing fingertip.

She drank in the addictive taste of him and the lingering tension drained out of her. "You *do* have an incredibly attractive body."

He chuckled softly as his hands skimmed over her ribs, then pressed her hips familiarly close. "So, now I'm your gigolo? Thanks a lot, honey. You're doing wonders for my ego."

Elyssa tipped back her head and anchored her hands on his shoulders. Funny how quickly she could forget the unnerving incident with Gavin when her body was pressed against Hunter's. All of a sudden everything seemed right and natural, as if she had captured whatever it was that had been missing from her life. She could relax and be herself around him, she could become carefree, playful . . . and wonderfully alive.

"I guess I shouldn't have been surprised to see Claudia clinging to you like a vine," she replied, dark eyes twinkling, her lush lips pursed in a teasing smile. "She may lack class and style, but she knows a real man when she sees one."

Nathan's thick brows jackknifed as he appraised her saucy grin. "Is that a roundabout apology for thinking I invited Claudia in here while you were gone?"

"Kinda sounds like one, doesn't it?" Her forefinger traced

the smile lines that bracketed his sensuous mouth. "I guess I shouldn't fault her for wanting what I can't resist myself."

Nathan's breath caught in his chest when she leaned against him, mimicking Claudia's blatant assault. That tactic, coming from Claudia, had repulsed him. Coming from Elyssa, it drove him wild with anticipation. He could feel her lacy bra skimming his chest, and he remembered all too well how it had felt to have nothing but bare skin between them, to be as close to her as he could get.

"Are you seducing me?" Nathan rasped when her hips gyrated against his aching flesh.

"Sure feels like it, doesn't it, Hunter. Is it working?"

"Remarkably well. But then, all you ever had to do was look at me and I was ready to strip you down to your skin and make love to you. Haven't you figured that out yet?"

The comments pleased her immensely. On this night she let herself believe he meant every word he said. Even if she could never provide more than physical satisfaction for him, at least there was that. For once, a man was after more than her money.

She longed to rediscover every delicious sensation that spilled over her when Hunter sent her plummeting into mindless passion. She wanted to forget all about the fiasco in Daniel's office that morning, the infuriating scene with Claudia, and Gavin's galling attempt to bribe her into bed. She just wanted this blue-eyed cowboy to take her on the ride of her life.

"Make love to me, Hunter. I won't ask for anything else . . ."

Nathan's sensuous lips slanted over hers, stealing her breath. Then his tongue probed into the hidden recesses of her mouth, imitating the more intimate pleasures to come. He already wanted her so badly he was shaking with the need to bury himself within her until he could go no deeper, until passion held them so tightly together it was impossible to tell where his own body met hers, until they were an entity. And he needed to erase all thought of Gavin's abusiveness from her mind. He wanted to cherish her in ways men like Gavin never could—unselfishly, patiently, respectfully, lovingly.

Calling upon his willpower, Nathan lifted his head. Holding Elyssa's luminous gaze, he reached down to remove her blouse. She offered no resistance, only a ragged sigh when his knuckles brushed against the beaded peaks of her breasts.

Slowly, deliberately, he drew the blouse off and let it flutter to the floor. His hand cupped the underside of her breast, his thumb flicking at the taut nipple encased in lace. Fascinated, he heard her quick intake of breath as her body arched toward his caress. His gaze still held hers captive as he took her nipple between thumb and forefinger and teased it until she gasped in helpless response.

His own body caught fire when Elyssa all but melted against him. He wanted to give her so much pleasure that she begged him to end the sweet torment of having him so close and yet so unbearably far away. He wanted to hear his name on her lips, to feel her tremble with uncontrollable need for him. But he wanted to make love with Elyssa one tantalizing step at a time, wanted her to revel in each sensation he could summon from her.

He tucked his thumb inside the lacy undergarment, baring the puckered crest to his devouring gaze. He smiled when he heard her moan in response to his unhurried seduction. When he bent his head to glide his tongue over her erect nipple, her nails dug into his arms.

"God, Hunter . . ."

Nathan was utterly beguiled by her response to this most elemental caress. It made him feel he had invented a seductive technique to pleasure her. When he took the sweet bud into his mouth and suckled, Elyssa quivered with the need he aroused so easily in her. She made loving her so satisfying that he wanted to give her the sun, one beam at a time, until she was burning with infinitesimal need.

"Hunter, please . . ."

Elyssa groaned in torment when his free hand glided up her

belly to swirl around one lace-covered breast, while his teeth and tongue teased the other's throbbing peak, and the knot of her desire unfurled within her, his skillful kisses and caresses making her let go of her inhibitions.

When he eased her down on the edge of the bed and knelt before her, Elyssa cradled his head against her breast and shivered beneath the gentle brushing of lips and fingertips. She forgot to breathe when his hand drifted downward to unfasten her skirt. He lifted her momentarily to remove the hindering garment and peel off her pantyhose, leaving her in nothing but bikini panties and bra.

His lips feathered over her ribs, igniting another round of fiery pleasure, and when his fingertips tracked along the band of her panties, Elyssa swore he meant to tease her until she went mad with wanting. He cupped her, his hand gliding downward to the moist heat he had called from her. Elyssa shuddered uncontrollably as his index finger slid beneath the silky fabric to touch her intimately. Then his warm lips whispered over the sheer silk and wild, desperate sensations pooled deep inside her.

His hand moved slowly over her scented warmth, feeling her feminine body weep in response. Need clenched his body as he brushed his thumb over the nub of passion and felt her quiver against his fingertip. Fire splintered through him as he eased his fingertip inside her and that sweetest kind of heat closed around him.

"I want to taste you," he whispered roughly. "All of you, Elyssa . . ."

She stiffened in shock at the thought of what he meant to do. "No . . ."

He smiled against the silky flesh of her thigh as he eased fabric down until she was wearing nothing but him, until his lips were the slightest whisper on her skin.

"Are you afraid to let me love you completely?" he murmured as his finger glided deeper, calling another uncontrollable response from her.

"It's too . . ." Her words ended in a gasp.

His tongue flicked out to trace the dewy-soft petals that concealed her sweetest secrets, and myriad sensations burst within her as he taught her the most intimate ways a man could caress a woman.

Spasmodic sensations rippled through Elyssa as her every fiber exploded in a burst of indescribable need. His kisses and caresses were like warm rain whispering over her, through her.

She convulsed around him, his body echoing the intense need that riveted hers. His fingertips filled the aching void of ardent longing—spreading, gliding, holding her suspended in climactic ecstasy—as he shifted to take her parted lips beneath his. She could taste her own desire for him on his tongue and that sent her spinning out of control.

Her cry of wild abandon drowned Nathan's throaty groan. He could feel her shivering around his fingertips, burning him with the fire of silky desire. She was his. He knew every sensation that assaulted her, as if it were his own. He could taste her heated essence, could touch her and feel her come to life around his probing fingertips. In their loving, she could withhold nothing, for he breathed her, absorbed her, held her hot and defenseless and shuddering in his hand. He made her want him so completely that she succumbed to his intimate demands and reveled in the pleasure he gave her and himself.

Nathan had never known anything so sweet or satisfying as feeling Elyssa's luscious body melt around him, beneath him. He braced himself up on one arm and stroked her again, marveling at her sultry response.

"Please . . ." she rasped. "Don't . . . I can't . . ."

Her voice trailed off into an astonished gasp when pulse-jarring sensations converged in her again. His fingertips receded and for those few frantic seconds Elyssa swore the empty ache he left burning deep inside her would be the death of her.

"Yes, you can, again and again, Elyssa," he murmured as he eased between her legs and teased her with the pulsating length of his own need. "Love me . . . I've never really been loved, especially not in all the ways I want to be loved by you."

Elyssa's tremors began again as the velvet warmth of him filled her, throbbing in rhythm with her own pulsating need. His words touched her. She could imagine how empty his life must have been, thrust out into the world to fend for himself, having had little in the way of affection or moral support, and then having a wife who betrayed him. She wanted to give him all it was within her power to offer.

Her body arched up to meet his as he hovered above her; then he buried himself in her—deeper and deeper until he became a searing flame. Her lashes swept down to shield her from the probing gaze that bore into her with the same intensity as his masculine body.

"No, Elyssa," Nathan rasped. "Don't close your eyes. Look at me. I want you to see what making love with you does to me."

She peered up into his shadowed face, watching passion shimmer in those sapphire eyes and settle into his rugged features. He held her gaze, drawing it down with his to where they were joined while he moved against her with hungry need and she answered each driving thrust. Her eyes widened at the intimate knowledge they shared and she glanced up at him, seeing the hint of a smile on his lips.

Pure male satisfaction, she decided. That was what consumed him before his powerful body curled over her and her control was swept away as if by a river racing over rapids. He was consuming her, clutching her so tightly to him that she couldn't breathe and felt no need even to try.

The flames fanned in her made her writhe in his arms. She let go with body, heart, and soul, fell through time and space, spun in dizzying circles, until her ecstasy was his and she could know rapture by breathing one word—his name.

Nathan drifted down from the plateaus of rapture slowly, like a hawk gliding on drafts of wind. He couldn't remember being so thoroughly spent and yet so incredibly content. The world around him could come tumbling down and he couldn't have cared less. He was at peace, in a blissful paradise.

Elyssa smiled when she heard Hunter's methodical breathing against her cheek. Lovingly, she reached over to smooth his raven hair away from his forehead. He was exhausted. She was pleased to know she had contributed to his exhaustion. At least he didn't leave her arms wanting, nor she his. All Nathan Hunter had to give was quickly becoming everything Elyssa desired.

She could get used to this, she thought before she followed him into peaceful dreams . . .

Twenty

Althea Gilbert smiled in greeting when Elyssa ambled into the kitchen. "Sit down and I'll bring you coffee, hon. You look like you could use some."

Elyssa plunked herself down and propped her forearms on the table, murmuring gratefully when Althea set a steaming cup of coffee in front of her. She took a sip and then stared at Althea who was gathering the dishes left from the feeding of the hired hands. Elyssa levered herself up to help rinse them and load them in the dishwasher.

"Go sit down," the older woman told her. "I'm paid to do this, you know."

"I'm offering to help for nothing, so move over and don't crowd my space," Elyssa countered with a grin.

"You've gotten mighty independent since you were last here," Althea noted. "No wonder you're giving Gil and Virgil fits."

Elyssa glanced down at the plate she was scraping. "Do you think I should have tried to hold the ranch together, Althea?"

"Just so Gil and Virgil could wade out of debt? Nope. They got themselves into that mess. The way I figure it, they ought to have to get themselves out. Your daddy carried them as long as he could stand it."

"I don't suppose you overheard the conversation Gil and Dad had the day he died."

Althea's lips pursed when she glanced at Elyssa. "Are you asking me if I *overheard* it or eavesdropped on it?"

"I'm not interested in technicalities." Elyssa grinned at the wry expression that came to Althea's plain features. "I just want to know what was said. Gil tells a different story than Hunter."

"And you aren't sure who to believe." Althea went back to stuffing plates in the dishwasher. "Well, from what I overheard Ely wanted to revoke the partnership and Gil was putting up a fuss. He kept yelling about Nate influencing Ely's decisions, and he said Nate was trying to take over the place."

Elyssa could have kicked herself for not coming to Althea immediately. The housekeeper was a wealth of information, but she didn't poke her nose in places without being invited. Elyssa would have to pose direct questions to get answers.

"What do you think Hunter really wants, Althea?"

She chuckled and flicked Elyssa an amused glance. "Now there's a good question. Before you came back, I thought he wanted to see Ely's wishes carried out—and get a little revenge for all the crap he's had to take from Gil and that lazy, high-rolling Virgil."

"You don't like Virgil much, do you?"

"Do you?" Althea asked. "He was always an ornery little brat. He picked on you something terrible. I thought he was jealous of you, even as a kid."

Elyssa blinked in surprise. "Jealous of me? Why?"

"Because your daddy started carrying on a full week before your yearly visits, wanting everything to be just so. Ely was bursting with pride when it came to you. Virgil never got that from Gil. I guess Gil took his son for granted because the boy was underfoot every day. Virgil didn't like having to work like a farm hand, either. He thought you and Patricia were babied and he was mistreated."

"Well, I can't say there was ever any love lost between us," Elyssa admitted. "Virgil made me the brunt of too many jokes."

"And I was here to patch you up after his 'jokes' got a little vicious," Althea grumbled. "Plainly speaking, that boy was no good, and he hasn't changed. I'm glad he doesn't hang around here much these days. I only wish . . ." She clamped her mouth shut and scrubbed the counter vigorously.

"Was Virgil here the day my father died?" Elyssa asked as she sank down to sip her coffee.

"Yep. He was eavesdropping outside the office door. Now me, I was dusting furniture in the living room, right next to the office wall. If you're going to snoop, you might as well look busy while you're doing it, I always say."

Elyssa snickered at the comment. That was Althea through and through. Too efficient to dawdle unproductively, she could do three things at once without breaking stride. Too bad Claudia hadn't picked up that admirable trait.

"I suppose Gil was upset about Dad's plans."

"Mad enough to spit nails," Althea replied before sinking down at the table to enjoy a well-earned break. "He roared out of here like a cyclone and took off down the road, burning rubber. Virgil skedaddled to the machine shop before Gil and Ely knew he was lurking around."

"Do you know why Dad saddled up and rode off that afternoon?"

Althea's sturdy shoulder lifted and then dropped. "He didn't say. All I know is he was trying to get hold of you and grumbling about not being able to trust his own family not to put the screws to him. When you finally called him back, he went out the door in a flaming rush, asking me to tell Nate he'd be back as soon as he could."

"Where was Hunter while all this was going on?"

"He'd driven out to check on some livestock that was being auctioned off by old man Henderson in Western Oklahoma—some bulls and steers that had run wild while Henderson was recovering from his bypass surgery. The animals were prime rodeo material. Nate bought them and hauled them home. By the time he got back, I was getting worried about Ely being gone so long."

"Was anyone else around?"

"Officer Spencer," Althea said before sipping her coffee.

"After they found Dad, you mean?" Elyssa presumed.

"No, he drove in while Ely and Gil were having their shouting match. I wondered if I'd have to round him up to pull those two brothers apart."

"What was Gavin doing here?"

"He always cruises in here and stops to chitchat with the men. I suppose he gets tired of patrolling the area and hankers for companionship. Probably whining about how much alimony and child support he has to pay his ex-wives," Althea added. "I hear they stuck him pretty good. Not that he didn't deserve it."

Elyssa reflected on what Gavin had said the previous night about knowing more than anyone thought he knew. If Gavin did kill time on the ranch, possibly he did have information he could use to his advantage. Although Elyssa cringed at the prospect of encountering Gavin again, she was reasonably certain he could shed some light on the goings-on—if the price was right.

Nathan pulled the straw hat from his head and shook off the dirt that had collected on it. He glanced skyward and scowled at the bank of gray clouds that had piled up on the southwestern horizon. Although the hay crew had been making good time, there were still windrows of alfalfa stretching across the field, waiting to be baled. Nathan had taken a shift on one of the tractors, pulling the implement that raked up the cut hay and tossed it upside down to ensure even drying. Baling damp hay could prove disastrous, and he was taking no chances.

More than one farmer in the area had baled uncured hay, only to have it mold. Or worse, when moisture was trapped inside a tightly compacted bale, spontaneous combustion could set it aflame. No, Nathan couldn't afford to rush haying, nor could he let alfalfa lie in the fields when the rains came. Gil would take advantage of such a costly mistake, would use it to turn Elyssa against him.

When the baler ground to a halt in the middle of a windrow, Nathan climbed into his truck and sped off. Les Fykes was just hopping down from the tractor when Nathan strode up.

"This damned belt is almost gone," Les grumbled. "It's got so much slack it's flapping around inside and causing the baling string to tangle."

Les stuck his arm inside the baler to tug off a web of twine that was knotted with hay. Straw flew around both men like down from a pillow. "Somebody's got to run up to the John Deere dealership to get a replacement belt," Les insisted. "I can fight these clogs until noon, but it'll keep getting worse."

Nathan grumbled under his breath. That *belt* Les referred to cost five hundred dollars. And besides, they couldn't spare a man, not with a storm brewing. "I'll take care of it. Just try to keep the machine running as best you can."

While Les cursed the clogged baler, Nathan strode back to the truck, using the CB to call the house.

"Althea? Is Elyssa still there?"

The housekeeper wiped off her hands and took the incoming call. "She's helping me fix lunch to bring to the hay field. What's the problem?"

"I need a go-fer," Nathan replied.

Elyssa frowned when Althea handed her the phone. "A what?"

"I need you to go for parts," Nathan insisted. "Got a paper and pencil?"

Elyssa grabbed Althea's note pad and jotted down the name, price, and number of the belt Nathan wanted replaced. "And where am I supposed to find this gold-plated belt?" she asked him.

"You'll have to drive to the dealership in Weatherford."

"Weatherford?"

"They don't deliver out here in the sticks, you know. And hurry it up. I needed that part two hours ago. I'm going to be hell to live with until this hay is baled and moved out of the fields."

As the line went dead Elyssa rolled her eyes, annoyed by Hunter's curtness.

"Don't take it personally," Althea advised. "They all get like that when they're fighting the clock. There's a lot of money at stake in that hay field right now."

Elyssa hurried out of the room to retrieve her purse and keys. She desperately wanted to speak with Gavin Spencer, but the questions she wanted to pose would have to wait. Hunter needed that belt—*now.*

Virgil Rawlins paced his father's living room, scowling. The past two weeks had been a nightmare. He'd spent them trying to stay one step ahead of the impending disaster. His life had gone sour the minute Uncle Ely had announced his intention to dissolve the partnership. Since then, Virgil had scrambled to hold his finances together. He had always considered Nate Hunter a pain in the ass, but Cousin Elyssa had proved every bit as troublesome. No matter how he'd tried to handle her, nothing had worked. Not being patronizing, not giving her warnings, not even making threats. Nate had gotten to her—in several ways, he guessed—but every time Virgil had tried a countertactic, it had backfired, especially the most recent one. What the hell was he going to do?

"Will you sit down," Gil grumbled as he watched his son circumnavigate the room for the tenth time. "It's wearing me out just watching you, and you aren't accomplishing a damned thing."

Virgil plunked down on the closest chair and raked his fingers through his fuzzy red hair. "They're going to break us, Dad. I've tried to warn Elyssa away from Nate every way I know how, but nothing works. We've got to change her mind before the auction. We'll have to sell our half of the ranch to them or put it up for sale ourselves to get enough money to pay the debts."

Gil slumped in his chair, looking weary and older than his sixty-two years. Hell, he'd aged a decade these past two weeks. He had more worries than a porcupine had quills.

"There's only one thing to do." Gil stared pointedly at his son.

"Yeah," Virgil muttered. "Get rid of Cousin Elyssa and quickly."

"No. You are going to have to sell your brood mares and studs to cover your debts."

"What?" Virgil gaped at his father in disbelief. "You know how I feel about those horses!"

"And you know how I feel about the ranch and tradition. I'm not letting go of my land. It was your dream of making a name for yourself in the horse circles that got you and me into financial difficulty. You can damn well start putting price tags on those colts and brood mares. Advertise in the *Quarter Horse Journal* and through the Cutting Horse Association. If you can liquidate some of your assets, the bank might give you more time and breathing space."

"It would be a helluva lot simpler just to let the partnership pay the losses," Virgil insisted. "Damn that Elyssa. I swear she's trying to get revenge for all the pranks I played on her when she was a kid."

"What the hell are you babbling about?"

Virgil avoided his father's probing stare. "Nothing important," he said with a dismissive shrug. "Just teenage pranks, teasing her when she came for her yearly visits."

Gil slumped and rested his head on the chairback. "Gawd, for a minute I thought you meant you had something to do with her accident."

Virgil inwardly flinched.

"If you had, I guarantee Ely never would have looked the

other way so many times in the past. That accident nearly killed him. And if Elyssa wanted revenge for that, I'd say she probably deserves it."

"Yes, I suppose she would," Virgil murmured.

He unfolded himself from the chair and headed for the door. He was going to have to pull a few more strings to force Elyssa to back off. He was not going to sell his horses, not after all the pockets he'd had to pad to make a place for himself. He had come too far to walk away now. He just needed more time to make his expensive investment pay off. There had to be a way to block Elyssa, to make her change her mind!

"Where are you going?" Gil wanted to know.

"To make some arrangements," Virgil said before the door closed behind him.

Gil expelled his breath in a foul curse. It amazed him that he could have wished his own brother in hell one week and wanted him back so badly the next. He might have bargained with Ely, once they'd both calmed down. Now he was squared off against his know-nothing niece. She'd come waltzing in after a twelve-year absence and tried to fill her father's boots. If it weren't for Nate Hunter she might have backed off. But the two of them had become a king-size headache!

Gill scooped up his hat and stalked outside. He had steers to feed and he needed to check on grassland that might not be his by the end of the following week. Goddamn it, it wasn't right to have this ranch divided and to have a bank foreclose on some of it. But banks didn't give a shit about tradition or family pride. Money was what motivated them.

Gil exhaled slowly, cursing himself but good. He supposed he'd always known that someday there'd be hell to pay for what he'd done long ago. And he should have expected it would be Jessica's daughter who leveled the humiliating blow.

Gil wasn't so old that he didn't remember the obsessive craving he'd had for Jessica. While his own hypochondriacal wife, obsessed with every sniffle, ache, and pain, turned him away from her bed, Gil had coveted the young beauty Ely had convinced to marry him. He had hit on Jessica several times while his brother was having trouble controlling his restless wife. Then, after she'd given in to him and he'd satisfied his craving, he'd burned with guilt. He should have known she was only using him to gain an advantage, but he had been too crazy over her to think straight.

When Jessica had demanded a divorce from Ely, she had come to Gil, holding his lack of discretion over his head like an ax. She'd insisted that Gil convince Ely to go along with her demands, unless he wanted his brother to know he had slept with her. Gil had to do as she asked or risk Ely's wrath and his own wife's fury.

Twenty years later, he was still cursing himself for that mistake, for lying to his brother time and time again. Hell, maybe he did deserve to lose all he held dear. Breaking the commandments usually got a man into hell, didn't it?

Elyssa eased her foot onto the brake when she topped the hill to see the squad car coming toward her. She didn't have time to grill Gavin at the moment. She was already behind schedule, thanks to a delay at the John Deere dealership. The manager had had to call a nearby dealership to locate the replacement belt. Once one had been found, Elyssa had sped off, defying speed limits.

"I've been looking for you, sugar." Gavin gave her his barracuda smile, then let his gaze drop to her breasts.

"Sorry, I don't have time to chat," Elyssa replied tersely. "I'm running parts."

"I only stopped by to make sure you were coming over to my place this evening so we could talk privately. I'm sure you'll be interested in what I have to say."

"What time, Gavin?" she asked. "And just where is your place?"

"Be there at eight o'clock," he said with a roguish grin

"I'm renting the Fosters' old farmhouse. It's two miles north and three miles west of the ranch. And dress comfortably."

In a coat of armor? "Fine. I'll be there at eight."

"I'll be looking forward to it."

Elyssa rolled up the window and muttered, "I won't be."

Spending time with Gavin wasn't going to be any picnic, she predicted. If she could have dragged Hunter along to run interference she would have, but she doubted Gavin would talk with Hunter underfoot.

She glanced sideways to see the crew working frantically to bale the windrows and haul the hay off the field. One baler was sitting smack-dab in the middle of the field. Elyssa cursed. Evidently, the machine had broken down before she tracked the replacement belt down. It was long past noon and Hunter was undoubtedly standing on his head, wondering where she was.

The minute she turned in the gate and bounced over the rough terrain to reach the stalled baler, Hunter emerged from underneath the implement to glower at her.

"Where the hell have you been?" he snapped. "I told you we were on a tight time schedule. Les and I have been waiting for over an hour to replace the belt. We don't have time for you to chitchat on the road. What the hell did Gavin want?"

Elyssa reminded herself of what Althea had said about racing the clock. Hunter was in a foul mood. That was obvious. He was also covered with leafy alfalfa after crawling around under the baler. She supposed he was entitled to be surly, but he didn't have to bite her head off in front of the others.

"For your information, I had to drive all over creation to replace that belt," she retorted. "The Weatherford dealership was out of them, so I had to go elsewhere. And I didn't ask Gavin to flag me down. Now, do you want to growl at me a little longer or do you want this twenty-four-karat-gold belt?"

Nathan glanced around to see Les Fykes chewing on a stem of alfalfa while Mo-Joe and Skeeter grinned from ear to ear.

"I'm sorry," he mumbled by way of apology. "I'm a little out of sorts."

"Give yourself credit, Hunter. You're a *lot* out of sorts. Be that as it may, I'm willing to help. What do you want me to do?"

He glanced at the John Deere tractor Mo-Joe had climbed off of. "Can you drive?"

"Drive what?"

"A tractor."

"If I have to I suppose I can."

Nathan hitched his thumb toward the stalled baler. "Mo-Joe, you and Les and Skeeter can replace the belt while I show Cutler how to drive this rig. If we can keep both balers running and haul the hay off the field, we might beat the rain."

"Sure thing, boss," Mo-Joe said. "Skeeter and I'll load the hay on the trailers once we get Les going again. Tell Elyssa to watch the clutch on that tractor. It's starting to slip. I think it'll hold until we finish baling if it isn't abused."

Nathan grabbed Elyssa's arm and propelled her up the steps and into the tractor cab. She sat there gaping at the various levers and gauges on the dashboard. Good grief! Did Hunter expect her to get the hang of this heavy equipment in one easy lesson?

He gestured toward the lever closest to her hip. "This is the power take-off. And this lever engages the baler. And this one is for the throttle."

Elyssa flung up her hand. "I don't even know how to put the damned tractor in gear yet and you already have me gobbling up windrows and spitting out bales!"

Nathan pointed toward the knob on the stick shift that indicated the position of the eight gears. "Put the tractor in third and ease off the clutch," he instructed. "This will be a piece of cake."

"Some piece of cake," Elyssa muttered. "I feel like I'm sitting in the cockpit of a jet. What are all these gauges for anyway?"

"Nothing for you to worry about. All you have to do is straddle the windrow so you can feed alfalfa through the baler. Just don't turn too tight on corners or you'll pop the hydraulic hoses attached to the machinery and we'll be out here the whole blessed night trying to clean up the mess and keep this rig running."

Elyssa listened intently as Nathan took her through the procedure, step by step. She had been up and down the field twice before she began to relax. When she realized how expensive the equipment was that she was controlling, she tensed again. One careless mistake and it would cost a fortune to replace broken gears, belts, and God only knew what-all. And she would be rushing off to the dealership again to pick up new parts.

"Calm down, Cutler. You're doing fine," Nathan reassured her. "When we circle back to the other baler, you can let me off and take over all by yourself."

"You trust me with this expensive machinery?" she questioned without taking her eyes off the windrow that stretched endlessly in front of her.

"I trust you, honey," he confirmed, his voice dropping to a husky pitch. "Too bad you can't say the same for me."

"I . . ." Elyssa cast him a hasty glance and then refocused on the business at hand.

Smiling ruefully, he trailed his forefinger over her high cheekbone, enjoying the satiny texture of her skin, even if he couldn't enjoy her trust. "You wanna tell me what Gavin had to say when he stopped you on the road? I hope he apologized for making an ass of himself last night."

"Are we talking about the same Gavin Spencer? He doesn't make apologies," Elyssa replied, eyes on the windrow. "It was nothing really."

"You're sure?"

She stamped on the clutch to bring the tractor to a halt, directly across from where Mo-Joe and Les were repairing the other baler. "I think I've got the hang of this now. Just don't step out in front of me, Hunter, unless you want to wind up rolled and baled."

"You can *roll* me over anytime, anywhere you please," Nathan murmured as he leaned over to plant a wispy kiss on her lips. "Just don't *roll* up any fences. You'll chew up the machine."

"Speaking of fences. There's a stretch of wire below the canyons that could use some work," Elyssa called after him, but he had already closed the cab door and hopped off the steps.

She eased out on the clutch and took off, wondering how her mother would react if she saw her citified daughter running a tractor and baling alfalfa alongside the hired hands. No doubt, it would be Jessica's worst nightmare come true.

Twenty-one

Distant lightning speared from blackening clouds and thunder rumbled toward the hay field. Elyssa had rolled up the last bale and had climbed from the tractor to watch the men frantically loading the remaining bales on the trailers. Gigantic tractors, equipped with hay forks that protruded like rhinoceros horns, stabbed at the twelve-hundred-pound bales. Machinery creaked and groaned as the bales were elevated and stacked three-high on the trailers. The headlights of pickups illuminated the darkness, casting shadows that turned the huge machines into lumbering monsters.

Elyssa glanced sideways when Hunter opened the cab door of the tractor he was using to load bales.

"Take your equipment back to the house!" he yelled over the roar of the machinery. "We'll be right behind you."

She clambered up the steps of the idling tractor and shifted gears, wondering which gear she should be using for road travel. Six hours of experience under her belt didn't exactly qualify her as a seasoned farm hand.

Easing the tractor into fifth gear, she bounced over the rough field and swung through the gate with more speed than she wanted. Hunter and the hired help could negotiate these monster machines with no sweat. Elyssa wasn't so confident of her own abilities.

When the rain swept across the field in sheets, she fumbled to locate the windshield wiper. The dust that had collected on the windshield turned to mud, making it impossible to see where she was going for a full minute. She mashed on the brake and waited for the wiper to clean the windshield. She definitely wasn't going to wind up in a ditch, damaging thousands of dollars worth of equipment. Hunter would have her head!

Thirty minutes later she turned into the driveway and aimed the tractor toward the gargantuan Morton building that housed the machinery. She decided to park her rig and leave the storing of the equipment to the men. No way was she going to try to maneuver into the building. She had had enough trouble handling the tractor in the field and on the open road.

Elyssa made a mad dash to the house, serenaded by drumrolls of thunder and soaked by pouring rain. She was drenched by the time she reached the back door and plunged into the kitchen.

Althea grinned at seeing her plastered hair and saturated clothes. "Your daddy would've been proud of you," she declared, while Elyssa stood there dripping on the floor. Althea then tossed her a towel from the stack that awaited the hay crew. "Go on upstairs and change while I put supper on the table. Nate just called on the CB to say they'd be here in fifteen minutes."

Elyssa glanced over to see Timmy in his high chair, munching on crackers. Claudia was nowhere to be seen.

"Are you sure you don't need help putting the finishing touches on supper?"

"I've been doing this for years," Althea assured her, shooing her on her way. "But you can set the table after you change."

Elyssa hurried off, looking like a drowned rat yet filled with a sense of pride and accomplishment. She had never felt quite this satisfied after her jaunts to D.C. to work the political machinery that had almost ground the country to a halt. Washington was gridlock country, but Rawlins Ranch was jumping with activity. She relished being a part of that.

Or she had until she strode down the hall to find Claudia leaning against the door to Hunter's room.

Claudia raked Elyssa with a mocking glance. "I'm surprised, I thought you wouldn't be caught dead helping with the haying. Isn't common labor beneath you?"

Elyssa towel-dried her hair, assessing Claudia's clinging clothes and caked makeup. "I don't consider myself too good to lend an extra hand when help is needed, do *you?*"

Claudia tossed her copper-blond head and looked down her nose at Elyssa. "I want more from life than scrubbing, cleaning, and cooking for farm hands."

"And you've taken great strides to improve yourself, I see." Elyssa clamped her mouth shut, scolding herself for dropping to Claudia's level.

"I know what I want," Claudia snapped. "I also know I had a chance of getting it until you showed up. Nate and I were getting along fine until you decided you wanted him, but you won't get him. He has obligations to me."

Elyssa had no desire to have her good mood spoiled by Claudia's baiting. She dismissed her by veering into her own room and closing the door. Claudia, however, invited herself inside.

"There's something you need to know," Claudia insisted, her chin tilting to an aloof angle. "I'm pregnant with Nate's child. I planned to tell him the other night when you interrupted us."

Elyssa felt as if she had been kicked in the stomach.

"I'm sure you prefer to believe nothing is going on between the two of us. And Nate probably refuses to admit it to you because he thinks he can do better with you. But fact is fact. And I'm not going to get rid of this baby just to make it easy for both of you. Just remember that while you're trying to beat my time with him."

And with that, Claudia left, shattering Elyssa's sense of contentment. She had just begun to trust Hunter, then along came Claudia to dispel her faith in the man.

Of course, there was always the possibility that Claudia was lying.

There was also the possibility she wasn't . . .

Elyssa wondered if the other men on the ranch were receiving sexual privileges from Claudia. The girl often flaunted herself. It was difficult to tell whether she was promiscuous or simply trying to grab Hunter's attention.

Sighing, Elyssa stripped off her wet clothes and donned dry ones. She wasn't sure how to deal with the information Claudia had delighted in giving her. What a shame this woman was Althea's daughter. Evicting Claudia would necessitate dismissing Althea who was indispensable. But having Claudia underfoot was like living with a coiled rattlesnake. You couldn't forget she was there, not with her hissing and rattling all the time.

Elyssa descended the steps, her spirits deflated. Even the laughter wafting from the kitchen didn't improve her glum mood. The sight of Claudia strutting her stuff and hovering around Hunter didn't help much, either.

Maybe when all the arrangements had been finalized, she would be better off returning to the Cutler Corporation. At least then she wouldn't be faced with Claudia's constant harassment. Hunter would just have to deal with the Tammy Faye Bakker clone. Elyssa could certainly understand why Claudia didn't dare get caught in the rain. She'd look like a clown with mascara streaming down her powdered cheeks in black rivers.

While the men washed up and dried off in the utility room, Elyssa set the table and helped Althea set out the food. Claudia was still in the utility room, kissing up, ignoring her two-year-old son who was launching plastic cows and horses onto the floor and babbling.

Luckily Timmy had Althea, Elyssa mused as she scooped up the toys and set them back on the tray, and if there was a way to oust Claudia, that would mean sentencing Timmy to a life with an uncaring and incompetent mother. More and more Elyssa realized that she herself was disrupting life on the ranch. She would always be the outsider here, never really fitting, causing resentment and creating new problems.

She reflected on what Althea had told her about Virgil feeling the bite of jealousy each time she had returned for a visit. She had been looked upon as a pampered child who lived in luxury in the citified social circles her mother had chosen for herself. To Cousin Virgil and Patricia, Elyssa symbolized what they thought they wanted.

The succulent meal Althea had prepared tasted like sour grapes to Elyssa. While the men talked and joked, she ate in silence, then excused herself from the table and ambled into her father's study, closing the door behind her. Rain drummed against the windows as she sank down into the chair to stare at Ely's portrait.

The room seemed so alive with Ely's presence that goose flesh rippled across Elyssa's skin. This should have been her lifelong home. Her father had wanted that, but Jessica had whisked her away. It seemed someone was always trying to whisk her away from where she wanted to be, from the life she wanted to lead.

She rested her head on the chair back and closed her eyes, absorbing the dynamic presence that engulfed the room. Must life be a never-ending battle? Elyssa supposed so. Her father had fought to make this sprawling ranch prosper while Gil and Virgil had taken unnecessary risks, counting on Ely to cover their losses. Now Elyssa was battling her own family, as well as Claudia Gilbert. What was the use? Why not give in and walk away?

Because we Rawlinses are survivors, tenants of this land. We've battled all the odds for decades. We come from pioneer stock and native American heritage. We may give out, but, by God, we don't give up!

Elyssa jerked upright when the insistent voice echoed through her mind, and that strange tingle skittered down her spine. She stared up at the painting, watching those piercing black eyes focus on her.

That was what was so unnerving about her father's portrait, Elyssa decided. Those eyes. They followed her around the room, constantly assuring her that her mission here wasn't complete. She had walked into the middle of a feud, had inherited difficulties. Turning her back on it all would be a grave disappointment to Ely. He expected more from her.

As for Claudia, Elyssa decided she wasn't going to let the younger woman manipulate her again. Jessica had used that tactic. Virgil had also employed it. Even Robert had tried his hand at it. And Elyssa had let herself be used, telling herself she didn't care, that it didn't matter. But she was sick and tired of it.

The creak of the door disrupted her thoughts, and she glanced up to see Hunter staring curiously at her.

"Got a problem, Cutler?" he asked.

Elyssa smiled dryly. Claudia undoubtedly expected her to keep silent and slink off to lick her wounds. That was why she had dropped the bomb, hoping to clear her path to Hunter.

"I don't have a problem," Elyssa informed him. "You do. Or so Claudia claims."

"Her again," Nathan muttered sourly. "Now what has that little troublemaker done?"

"She claims it's what *you*'ve done."

Nathan frowned. "I'm not in the mood for elusive answers."

To Elyssa's surprise, he wheeled around and stalked off. A minute later, he towed the reluctant Claudia into the office and shut the door.

"I think it's time we had a talk," he growled at Claudia. "I've been putting up with your nonsense for months. That little scene you staged the other night was a deliberate attempt to upset Elyssa and we all know it."

"It was nothing of the kind," Claudia protested.

"Wasn't it?" Nathan challenged. "I wonder."

Claudia glanced venomously at Elyssa. "What did you tell him?"

"I haven't told him anything," Elyssa replied. "You didn't expect me to, did you? Wasn't that the whole point, to provoke me into leaving, or at the very least backing away?"

"I don't know what you're talking about."

A calm settled over Elyssa as her gaze drifted back to Ely's portrait. If nothing else, she knew her father would always be on her side. That thought gave her the security and strength she needed to deal with Claudia.

"I'm sure you do." Elyssa rose from the chair and faced Claudia. "I think you should break the news to Hunter, rather than to me. He has a right to know."

"The right to know what?" Nathan demanded impatiently.

"Damn you!" Claudia hissed at Elyssa. "You're nothing but trouble. He said—"

When Elyssa's gaze narrowed warily, Claudia shut her mouth with a snap.

"Who said?" Elyssa persisted.

"What the hell is going on?" Nathan stalked toward Claudia, giving her the full benefit of his annoyance.

Claudia wrung her hands nervously when he bore down on her like a fire-breathing dragon.

"Tell me what you told Elyssa," he demanded. *"Now,* Claudia."

Claudia tilted her chin to a defiant angle.

Elyssa wondered if her declaration had been a ruse. She also wondered if the *he* Claudia mentioned had put her up to that stunt, whether the information was false or factual. The situation had a familiar ring to it. Virgil had employed such manipulative tactics twelve years ago to instigate what had turned out to be disaster for Elyssa in her dealings with Gavin. This might very well be more of Cousin Virgil's spiteful handi-work.

"According to Claudia, she is carrying your child," Elyssa announced.

"What!"

Claudia shrank away from the booming baritone voice that exploded inches away from her face.

"That's a goddamn lie and you know it." Nathan was out-raged. "I've never touched you, much less slept with you. And

I sure as hell don't appreciate your saying I did something you and I both know I didn't do."

He was positively livid, Elyssa noted. Claudia obviously had come to the same conclusion, for she backed away from him. Nathan braced an arm on either side of her, however, and when she found she'd backed herself into a corner, she stared wide-eyed at him like the frightened quarry of a deadly predator.

"Whose child is it, Claudia? Or is there a child?" Nathan demanded through clenched teeth.

Tears welled up in Claudia's eyes and trailed down her flushed cheeks. "Leave me alone," she blubbered.

"Not until I get some straight answers. You may be screwing around while your mother works hard around here *and* baby-sits Timmy, but you haven't been screwing around with *me*. Now who are you—?"

"Maybe I should leave," Elyssa said uncomfortably.

"No, you'd better stay," Nathan advised. "You may be the only reason I haven't strangled this lying little bitch." His blue eyes, like laser beams, bore down on the sobbing Claudia. "Now, tell me the truth or you're going to lose the good deal you've got going here. If I have to dismiss Althea to get you off this ranch, then I'll do it, much as I'd hate to lose someone as efficient and competent as your mother. Then you'll be scrambling for a place to live. And, God forbid, you might even have to go to work instead of lying around while your mother provides for you and your son."

"I was working and getting paid for it!" Claudia spat back at him.

"Call-girl wages, Claudia?" He sneered insultingly.

"Getting paid for what?" Elyssa interrupted.

"For causing trouble," Claudia burst out.

Elyssa wondered if she hadn't hit on the truth a few minutes earlier. "Was the whole point of this scheme to provoke me into leaving?" she wanted to know.

When Claudia didn't answer immediately, Nathan grabbed

her arm, giving her a jarring shake. "Answer the question, damn it."

"Partly," Claudia muttered. "And partly to keep you and Nate from getting too close."

"Who put you up to this?" Elyssa demanded while the younger woman shed tears.

Claudia looked frantic, her eyes became wide with apprehension. "If I tell you, he'll get even with me. Don't make me!"

"You don't have to," Elyssa reassured her. "Just tell us what you were getting paid to do. This conversation will go no farther than this room."

"You promise?" Claudia whimpered.

"Promise," Nathan reluctantly agreed. "But I'm not sure I still won't strangle you for letting yourself get dragged into such a spiteful stunt."

"Calm down, Hunter." Elyssa laid a hand on his taut arm, urging him to back off and give the sobbing Claudia some space.

Claudia inhaled in great gulps and then wiped her face, smearing her mascara so that it looked like war paint. "He paid me to convince Elyssa that you and I had something going so she wouldn't trust you. He said if I could get her to turn tail and run, things would be better at the ranch."

"And is this child you're supposedly carrying really his?" Elyssa queried softly.

Claudia sniffed and drew in a ragged breath. "There's no child. We're protected."

Elyssa surveyed Claudia's smudged face, absorbing the information the younger woman had begrudgingly given. "As far as I'm concerned, we didn't have this conversation, Claudia. You can tell your friend I refused to believe you. I also have a piece of advice for you. Don't allow yourself to be used again. If you want more from life than what you've gotten, then you're going to have to make a positive effort to change the way of things. You have a young son who desperately needs his mother. And you owe it to *your* mother to make something of yourself. She works hard to support you."

"And you sure as hell don't need a man who only uses you," Nathan growled at her. "Just look at Elyssa. She pursued a career and made a life for herself without thinking she had to have a man to support her. I can tell you, speaking from a man's point of view, I have more respect for an assertive woman than one who sees me as a meal ticket or a stepping stone."

"Well, what am I supposed to do?" Claudia wailed. "I have a baby, a high-school education, and a deadbeat ex-husband who won't pay child support!"

"Whining about it won't resolve anything. Using your misfortune as an excuse won't cut it, either," Nathan told her sharply. "Find a job or go back to school. But chasing men and hoping Prince Charming will come along will just waste valuable time. Are you going to settle for what you've got?"

Claudia sniffed loudly and blinked back her tears. "No."

"Then get off your butt and do something about it!" he snapped. "Nobody said life was easy. And if you don't mind a little constructive criticism, get rid of all that makeup and those skin-tight clothes. Subtle allure is far more appealing to responsible men than blatant invitation. Have a little respect for yourself, Claudia. You've been selling yourself short since your ex left you. But all men aren't like him. Try being yourself for once."

Claudia was bawling like a baby by the time Nathan finally backed off. She scurried out of the office and headed for the bathroom to wash her face.

"A little hard on her, weren't you, Hunter?"

"Hard?" Nathan echoed incredulously. "Hell, I went easy on her. She caused problems between us, and I don't like being accused of making a baby when I haven't even been tempted! When I find out who the hell put her up to that infuriating stunt, I'll—"

"Strangle him?" Elyssa chortled, watching Hunter fume.

"Well, I suppose that's one way to ensure Claudia doesn't catch the heat from whoever used her to get to me."

"And we both have a pretty good idea who it was, don't we?" Nathan growled.

"Do we?" Elyssa's primary suspect was Cousin Virgil, but after the hints Gavin Spencer had dropped, she was hesitant to leap to conclusions.

"Well, don't we?" Nathan challenged. "I can't see Gil doing the horizontal hokeypokey with Claudia. That only leaves Virgil."

"Or Dennis Humphrey, Cousin Patricia's husband."

Nathan laughed, his mood mellowing. "Yeah, I can see where Dennis might stray and be scheming enough to cause you trouble, to rack up Brownie points with his in-laws. I doubt Patricia is very accommodating in bed. Fooling around would mess up her fashionable hairstyles."

Nathan moved closer to Elyssa, pausing inches away to peer down into those twinkling, black diamond eyes and that impish smile that could melt bone. "Thanks for what you did," he said, his voice dropping to a husky pitch. His hand lifted, sliding into her silky hair, turning her bewitching face up to his.

"You mean for baling hay? You're welcome. I enjoyed it, even though I was afraid I was going to botch up and you'd chew me up and spit me out for damaging that high-priced tractor."

"I did appreciate the help, but that wasn't what I meant." His thumb grazed her lips while his gaze devoured her. "Thanks for believing the best instead of the worst, Elyssa. I've been battling your family's spiteful manipulation for years. Ely was the only one who gave me a chance to prove myself. In the beginning, he was as hard on me as I was on Claudia, even harder at times. Although he felt guilty about what had happened to my dad, he stayed on my case until I was dependable and responsible. I worked hard to gain his respect while Gil and Virgil waited like vultures for me to make the slightest mistake. It means a helluva lot to know you believe in me, even when everybody around here is trying to sabotage what's between us."

"What *is* between us, Hunter?" Elyssa peered up into those crystal blue eyes and her heart skipped several beats. She felt drawn into his electrically-charged aura.

His head dipped toward hers. He was tempting her and yet denying her by keeping breathless inches away from her.

"Why don't we go upstairs and find out?"

"We've already been upstairs a few times."

His kiss was as delicate as the dab of a honeybee courting nectar. Just enough to instill a craving for more than this light seduction. "And what did you find out?"

"I forget. Maybe you should refresh my memory . . ."

Elyssa looped her arms around his broad shoulders and leaned into his masculine contours. His body responded as instantaneously as hers, and his mouth came down on her lips—hard and hungry, insistent and possessive, driving all thought from her but instilling a need that fed itself. A sensual fog engulfed Elyssa as desire coiled in her very core.

A rough sound rumbled in Nathan's chest as he tucked her hips deeper into the cradle of his legs, pressing her to him as tightly as if there was nothing between them but naked flesh. The obsessive urge to sink into her pliant body any way he could struck him like a physical blow.

"God, woman, how can you forget the only thing I seem to remember?"

The rap at the door flung them apart as effectively as a bucket of cold water. Elyssa braced an arm against the wall and sank down onto the nearest chair.

Nathan, panting for breath, wheeled away, refusing to let whoever interrupted them see the condition he was in. Damn, he felt like doubling over and howling in pain! The fire Elyssa had sparked in him was about to burn him alive. He couldn't control himself when he got within two feet of her, couldn't even *try.* And it was getting worse with each passing day. Right now, he ached so bad he couldn't see straight, much less stand up straight!

"Elyssa?"

She sucked in a steadying breath. "Come in."

Mo-Joe Denson poked his ruffled head around the door and smiled apologetically. "Sorry to bother you, but I was wondering if you knew where Nate . . . ?"

Elyssa hitched a thumb over her shoulder toward the shadowy corner where Nathan was leaning into the wall, rigid as a fence post.

"Oh, there you are." Mo-Joe sauntered inside, assessed the situation, and grinned scampishly. "Checking for termites, Nate?"

Nathan still didn't dare turn around, so he swiveled his head to glare thunderclouds on Mo-Joe's sunny smile. "Did you come in here to annoy me or did you actually want something?"

Mo-Joe spared a glance at Elyssa's kiss-swollen mouth. He knew exactly why Nate wouldn't face him. It was damned amusing to see a man who usually retained absolute control in the agonizing condition Nate was in.

"I wondered if you remembered that I asked to take a couple of days off after we finished haying. I thought I might shove off tonight."

"Fine, whatever," Nathan said to the wall.

"I . . . um . . . also wanted to know if you might be able to float me a loan until I get back. I won't be here on payday. You can keep my check as collateral."

Well shit, thought Nathan. He was going to have to face Mo-Joe, but if that ornery scamp said one damned word in front of Elyssa . . .

"If you two will excuse me, I'd like to take a shower. Enjoy your weekend, Mo-Joe," she said.

When Elyssa had exited, Nathan pivoted to confront Mo-Joe.

"Having a *hard* time?" he asked.

Nathan glared him down. "You want a loan or not?"

Mo-Joe chuckled, undaunted. *"Not,* if it means I don't get to razz you. But hey, boss, don't worry about it. I'd be up against a wall myself. I like the little lady a lot. She jumps right in and helps out, as if she's no better than the rest of us. And with that gorgeous body she's got, and that angel's face, who could resist?"

"How much money do you want?" Nathan muttered.

"A couple of hundred if you can spare it."

"My, my, big weekend plans, I gather," Nathan retrieved his wallet.

Mo-Joe smiled and winked. "Bigger than yours, boss. I don't intend to spend all my time staring at walls."

"Get out and don't come back," Nathan snapped.

"Hey, I was just kidding around." His silver-gray eyes twinkled devilishly. "Damn, but you're getting sensitive. Carrying around a concealed weapon really affects your disposition, doesn't it?"

Nathan scowled. "Don't you ever shut up, Denson?"

He smiled brightly. "You could try bribing me."

Nathan slapped another hundred dollars in his outstretched hand. "Now get the hell out."

"I'll be back."

"Just my luck."

Twenty-two

Elyssa stood beneath the shower mist, soaking up the warm water that pulsated over her. She was concentrating on relaxing, trying to forget that exploding desire she'd experienced a few minutes earlier. God, she really had it bad! And she had condemned Claudia for crawling all over men? If it weren't for Mo-Joe's interruption, she could just imagine what might have happened in the office.

Elyssa heard the shower door slide open, and saw Hunter standing before her, sleek, muscular, and completely naked. As intimate as they had been, she had never seen his powerfully-constructed body in the light, had never dreamed the sight of him could have such an astounding effect on her. But even while her wide-eyed gaze ran over his sinewy planes and contours, coming to rest on the place where he was most a man, Elyssa found herself automatically turning away to shield the ugly scars that formed a patchwork of flesh on her hip. Hunter was perfection, an impressive work of art carved in steel-hard muscle. The thought of him seeing her in full light left her feeling awkward and terribly self-conscious.

His dark brow arched in amusement when Elyssa blushed and shrank back against the wall, both hands covering her left hip. "Do you really think that matters to me?" he questioned as he slid the door shut and stepped behind her.

"It will when you see it," she muttered.

"I already have." Nathan's arms glided around her and he

pulled her back against him as he trailed a row of kisses along the curve of her neck.

"When?"

"The morning I got up early to gather the rodeo stock," he said against her dewy skin. "I wanted to see what you were making such a fuss about without you waking up to create a ruckus about it."

"It . . . doesn't bother you?" she asked hesitantly.

"What bothers me is that it bothers you." His hands swept up to cup her breasts and tease the rigid peaks. "And in case you're wondering, I didn't come in here just to shower."

"No?" Her voice became almost harsh as his hands and lips began to work their delicious magic.

"Definitely not," he assured her huskily.

And when his lips skimmed down the column of her neck and his hands flooded over her breasts, surging, receding, teasing until she arched upward to him in breathless abandon Elyssa forgot about being self-conscious. When his fingertips folded over the hand which was still clamped to her hip, Elyssa tensed, uncertain of his intent.

"Relax, honey," he whispered in her ear.

"How can I when you cause my pulse to leap?" she choked out on a broken breath.

Nathan smiled against her wet skin. "I do that to you?"

"As if you didn't know."

"What else do I do to you?" he questioned as he drew her hand along with his over the flat plane of her stomach.

She gasped as he continued to guide her hand over her own naked body. "Hunter?"

"What, Elyssa?"

The shower massage hummed; so did her sensitive body. "What are you doing?"

"Showing you how good you feel to me."

His hand led hers downward to drift over the silky texture of her inner thighs. His finger glided between hers to tease the nub of passion. He could feel the liquid heat of her response burning around him as his fingertips delved deeper, stroking, arousing her until the breath tore out of her in a shuddering sigh.

"Hot silk, sultry fire," he whispered. "I can't seem to get enough of the feel of you, the taste of you. I want to savor you, feel you shimmering around me. I want to devour you and have you come apart in my arms. I want you in every way a man can have a woman—and then I'll want you all over again . . ."

Elyssa's body was responding to his intimate caresses, becoming entangled in the web of sensuality he was weaving. Desire pulsated in her, and when she trembled with the need he summoned from her, his hands receded, migrating over her skin in a languid sweep that ended by swirling around the tips of her breasts. Heated sensations expanded inside her, filling her with immeasurable pleasure.

Nathan gloried in the feel of her responding to his touch. He couldn't remember being so lost in a woman, so obsessed with pleasuring her in every way imaginable.

Since his short-lived marriage, he had gone sour on women, giving the ones who came and went from his arms only as much as they needed for him to satisfy himself. He wanted no emotional ties, no lasting relationships. He had made the ranch his life, guided by another man whose marriage had ended in a disappointing divorce. But along came this beguiling woman with eyes as dark as obsidian, carrying her own emotional baggage, hurts that had kept her passionate, giving nature locked and sealed for a decade. Now she was discovering her sexuality, the startling impact of her own needs.

For Nathan, being with Elyssa and watching her come alive in ways she'd never realized existed put him back in touch with a more innocent time in his own life, before his openness had been spoiled by a woman's humiliating betrayal. Elyssa smoothed the wrinkles from his soul and made him believe in new beginnings.

When he turned her in his arms to see the sparkle of desire he had ignited in those luminous eyes, another wave of awareness buffeted him. Her slick skin meshed against his in sweet promise, eager anticipation, and selfless abandon. As his mouth claimed hers, he was reminded once again that their pleasure could be so intense it bordered on pain. Wanting her was sweet agony, holding her so close that he could feel her pulse leaping in accelerated rhythm was pure bliss.

Elyssa shuddered in the sinewy arms that held her so tenderly, yet securely. At times like these she cursed her lack of experience. She longed to return the pleasure Hunter gave her. And when she touched him, when she mapped the whipcord muscles and powerful planes of his body, she cast all inhibition aside. Perhaps what they shared couldn't last forever, but she wanted to leave a loving memory burning in his mind.

A smile of satisfaction pursed her lips when her hand slid across the corrugated muscles of his belly to trace the throbbing length of his arousal and he trembled at her touch. Her fingers closed around him, brushing the satin tip against her thigh.

"Elyssa . . ." His breath trailed into a hoarse whisper. "Oh, God . . ."

Nathan's jaw clenched as her lips drifted across his chest to his abdomen. For him, the world tilted on its axis when she knelt before him to nibble playfully at him with her teeth, her tongue then flicking out to trace the length of him while she held him in the palm of her hand. Nathan nearly died as the slow sweep of her fingertips and lips dissolved everything around him except the vivid awareness of her touch, and he was held suspended in a dimension of time that, like the fog of the shower, blocked out past and future.

A low sound echoed in his throat when she took him into her mouth and gently suckled; he braced an arm against the wall to prevent collapsing with overwhelming need. She was driving him out of his mind, dragging him steadily toward that dangerous brink where control crumbled and desire sent him toppling into oblivion. But the instant before her inventive caresses sent him over the edge, she eased away, holding him without torturing him, letting him regain some measure of control. It was as if she had learned just how much stimulation he could endure before savage need consumed him.

When he could draw breath without his lungs collapsing, her tender assault began again. She kissed him until she drew a beaded response and then she tasted his fervent need for her. Her hands skimmed over the hair-roughened flesh of his thighs and swirled over his hips, bringing him closer to that sweet mouth that teased and satisfied.

As long as he lived, Nathan swore he would never step into the shower without remembering the delicious sight of her body sparkling with water droplets, without recalling the feel of her hands and lips pleasuring him . . .

If he lived, Nathan thought shakily. He wasn't sure he'd survive to remember these wild, sweet moments. Elyssa had taken him to the shuddering edge again, but this time she wouldn't allow him to pull back, to marshal his willpower. She was challenging him, testing everything masculine in him.

Nathan reached for her with shaky hands, setting her on her feet as shock waves of need riveted him. "I didn't want it to be like this," he groaned as his body arched helplessly into hers. "Too fast . . . too . . . desperate . . ."

Elyssa guided him to her, reveling in the knowledge that she had absolute control over him. "*I* did," she whispered as she lifted parted lips in invitation. "I wanted it to be exactly like this. Fast and desperate . . ."

Nathan clamped hold of her hips, lifting her to him until he was buried so deeply in the moist fire of her body that he couldn't remember what it was like not to be the pulsating flame inside her. As the spraying shower engulfed them, he drowned in the cloudy pleasure of ultimate possession and of being possessed. Elyssa didn't just accept his ardent passion as they moved in the ageless rhythm of love, she matched him thrust for frantic thrust, wrapping herself around him until they shared the same ragged breath, the same wild heartbeat—they were one.

Elyssa marveled at the tumultuous sensations that burgeoned inside her, giving herself wholeheartedly to each feeling that assailed her. She clung to Hunter as if he were her lifeline in a careening world where pleasure knew no bounds. They explored the ultimate depths of intimacy, and when the ungovernable spasms of release engulfed him, great tremors shook her.

"Some shower," Nathan murmured when he regained his powers of speech.

Elyssa rested her cheek on his palpitating chest and smiled. "The best I ever had," she assured him.

"The *only* one you ever had," he murmured, remembering with a great sense of pride and satisfaction that he alone had discovered her sweetest mysteries.

"Only the best," she said, tilting her lips to await his kiss. "Why begin anywhere else?"

Nathan grinned roguishly and offered her the tenderest of all kisses. "With that kind of talk, you'll have me thinking I'm the best thing that ever happened to you."

He wasn't far from wrong, but Elyssa was afraid to admit it for fear the words would come back to haunt her. She smiled into those glistening blue eyes that were surrounded by a fan of thick, wet lashes. "Could be that I'm kissing up, Hunter."

He chuckled as he eased away to grab the bar of soap. "What for? So you can keep me at your beck and call to steam up your showers?"

"Maybe," she said enigmatically.

There it was again, that hint of evasiveness, the indication that she was hesitant to tell him what she was really thinking for fear he would somehow betray her. But he refused to let her emotionally withdraw from him, distracting her with the one thing she *did* trust and understand, her attraction to him. At least there was that, he consoled himself.

He lathered his hands and took immense pleasure in soaping her breasts, her rib cage, her hips. "Before long, everyone on this ranch will know we're sharing more than the same house.

Mo-Joe is reasonably convinced of it already. Can you deal with that?"

"Does it mean I can have my way with you any time I please without shocking the hired help?" Her pupils dilated in response to his soapy caresses and Elyssa wondered if she would ever reach the point where Hunter could touch her without her coming completely unwound. She actually doubted she would ever become immune to this man. She had always been impossibly aware of him.

Nathan laughed softly as he handed her the soap. "Lady, I already told you that you could have your way with me anytime—anywhere."

His voice disintegrated when her fingers slid over him, headed for the most intimate of places again. He caught her hand, causing her to arch a delicate brow in teasing challenge.

"You did say anytime and anywhere, Hunter," she reminded him as her thumb caressed the blunt tip of his manhood and she felt his throbbing response.

"I did, didn't I?" he said hoarsely. "But maybe we should adjourn to the bedroom. We're running out of hot water."

The smile he kissed off her petal-soft lips indicated she seconded the suggestion. And this time when he took her with him into ecstasy, the lamplight illuminated the room. Elyssa didn't shy away, no longer self-conscious of her scars or tormented by the memory of how she had come to have them. Nathan had found dozens of ways to reassure her that even if her hip looked a bit deformed and the flesh was nowhere near creamy perfection, he didn't mind.

Elyssa adored him all the more for that. He made her feel beautiful, desirable. And when the loving was over, he cradled her against him in sleep, holding her possessively in his arms.

This, Elyssa realized, before she drifted away, was what rejuvenated her each time the outside world bombarded her. Nathan Hunter had become her source of energy and vitality. No matter what blows sent her reeling during the course of a day, he was there to restore her inner strength and provide unrivaled contentment. She realized that she needed him in ways she had never believed possible. She only wished she could trust him completely. By letting herself care so much, she was taking life's greatest risk . . .

Elyssa was astounded by Claudia's transformation. In fact, it was so overwhelming she wondered if this was yet another charade staged for her benefit. She remembered that Hunter had refused to let her leave when he lit into Claudia, and so suspected if the scene had been planned, it would not have been effective if she hadn't been there to witness it. Elyssa dared not let her guard down completely for fear of stumbling into yet another carefully arranged trap.

Claudia's choice of clothing now leaned more toward the subtly alluring than the borderline obscene. The heavy makeup had been modified to accentuate her appealing features. And even more impressive was Claudia's willingness to help her mother with daily tasks.

It did make one wonder whether the young woman was incredibly sincere or cunningly deceptive.

The men who showed up at the breakfast table made mention of how nice Claudia looked. She had gained their respect. And now, instead of come-hither glances, Hunter received smiles full of hero-worship. If Elyssa didn't know better she would swear Claudia *was* in love with Hunter. Why else had Claudia made this spectacular effort?

"I don't know what's come over that girl, but I'm relieved to see she's beginning to grow up," Althea said while she and Elyssa cleared the table. "You aren't going to believe this, but she mentioned taking night classes at the vo-tech this summer, and I nearly fell off my feet when she volunteered to tend the laundry and clean house so I could take the afternoon off. She must have been struck by a lightning bolt last night."

Elyssa said nothing, unsure how far to trust Claudia's new appearance and grand declarations.

The housekeeper worked silently for a few minutes and then frowned pensively. "Did you notice how quiet Dennis Humphrey was this morning at breakfast? Frankly, I'm surprised he keeps coming around after Virgil and Gil made themselves scarce. I'm sure Gil still intends to have Dennis draw his usual salary, even if he doesn't lift a finger until the property is divided."

"Maybe Uncle Gil sends Dennis to keep tabs on what's going on," Elyssa offered as she set the stack of plates by the sink.

"Or to find out the best time to make trouble," Althea predicted. "After that incident with the broken fences and scattered cattle, I kept expecting the farm machinery to be sabotaged. Luckily, the alfalfa was swathed and baled without disaster."

"You think Dennis has been planted here, too?" Elyssa queried.

"It wouldn't surprise me. He's a better follower than a leader. He always let Gil and Virgil tell him what to do. But at least he isn't what I'd call a freeloader. He's not above doing a day's work." Althea shrugged a cotton-clad shoulder. "Still, I'm always amazed when he shows up to pitch in. Of course, I watch what I say in front of him."

"Was Dennis around the day Dad died?" Elyssa inquired.

"Around somewhere, I suppose. But then, most of the men were helping move herds and checking fences. Dennis was on a horse most of the day, as I recall. Gil wanted to move a herd of steers to a new pasture before the livestock ate the grass down so far it wouldn't recover without being set aside until summer."

Elyssa was reminded of the comment her father had made the day he'd called. He'd said he was on his way to check some grass. She wondered if he was going to the same pasture Dennis was supposed to be working in. Elyssa cautioned herself against jumping to conclusions. After all, this ranch was enormous. There was pasture all over the place.

Althea paused to study Elyssa. "You asked me a similar question the other day. Is something bothering you?"

Elyssa shrugged. "I keep getting the feeling Dad's death and his decision to revoke the partnership might have been linked together."

Althea's eyes widened in shock. "You think his death wasn't an accident?" she chirped. "Good Lord!"

"I'm only saying it bears consideration. And if you remember anything about that day that might suggest the possibility, I'd appreciate it if you would confide in me."

Althea nodded agreeably. "I'll mull it over and see what I come up with. But there's always so much going on around here, with men driving in and out, I can't always keep up with things while I'm working."

"You didn't happen to see an accounting file on my dresser while you were cleaning, did you?" Elyssa dried her hands and closed the dishwasher.

"No, not that I recall. Are you sure you didn't put it back up?"

Elyssa strode off to double check. Sure enough, the file had been replaced, but the information she had pored over was gone. She was reasonably certain the only ones around here who might benefit from the loss of the financial statements were Gil and Virgil. That did not mean, however, that Dennis hadn't been sent to swipe the documents. Elyssa doubted Dennis was hanging around for nothing.

One hour later, while Elyssa was standing on the terrace that granted a bird's-eye view of the ranch, she spied Dennis slinking around the corner of Claudia and Althea's cottage. She wondered if Claudia had volunteered to work in her mother's stead to avoid dear ole Dennis. She also hoped Claudia had the gumption to end her affair with the married man. If Dennis's wife found out, she'd be furious. Patricia might not be totally satisfied with Dennis, but she wouldn't want anyone else to have him.

Elyssa caught her breath when Hunter strode out of the cottage door a few minutes later. She turned away, frowning. Damn it, when was she ever going to be sure just how far she could trust him? She had let him take possession of her body. She wondered what else he wanted . . . and why.

Elyssa dressed carefully for her scheduled meeting with Gavin Spencer. Since she didn't have a coat of armor at her disposal, she decided on a three-layered business suit. That in itself should indicate that she wanted no romantic tryst.

When she opened the front door to leave, Valerie was standing on the porch, suitcase in hand. "What are you doing here?"

"Ray called from Wichita, Kansas, and asked me to meet him here." She glanced down at the suitcase. "I decided to take you up on your standing invitation to come out whenever I liked." Val appraised Elyssa's fashionable bright green ensemble. "Are you leaving?"

"I have an appointment, but I shouldn't be gone long." Elyssa stepped aside, gesturing for Valerie to make herself at home. "How are things at the office?"

"Now that Robert has gotten the grand bounce, they're wonderful. But I miss you," Valerie insisted. "Robert's been having a hard time finding work." She grinned wickedly. "Now ain't that a cryin' shame? He may have to sell his sports car since he can't make the payments without his plush job. I've lost a lot of sleep worrying about him, of course. You, too, I'll bet."

Elyssa grinned impishly. "Robert who?"

Odd, she hadn't spared the man more than an occasional thought since the confrontation in her stepfather's office. And to think she had been engaged to that creep.

"Hi, Valerie. It's nice to see you again."

Elyssa pivoted to see Claudia standing behind her, smiling cordially at their guest.

"Here, let me have your suitcase," Claudia offered. "I'll take it upstairs and make sure your room is presentable."

"Thanks." Valerie cast Elyssa a what's-with-her glance when Claudia strode off.

"She's been converted, or so it would seem," Elyssa said.

"Somebody knocked the chip off her shoulder, did they?"

"Hunter," Elyssa reported.

"Figures. The man appears to work miracles," Valerie declared teasingly. "Look what he's done for you."

"Yes, well, I have to leave, Val. I'm sorry to abandon you, but I'm sure Twig will keep you entertained when he gets back."

"Um . . . Ellie?"

Elyssa swung back around to peer questioningly at Val.

"Would you mind if Ray . . . um . . ." Valerie blushed and cleared her throat.

"No, I don't mind." Elyssa grinned in amusement. "I doubt there would be much privacy in the bunkhouse. Mo-Joe left for a few days, but Les and Skeeter are still around."

"Thanks, I appreciate your generosity."

Elyssa chortled at her dreamy-eyed friend. "Well, we can't have Twig rolling in from a long haul to unload stock and then hightailing it back to the City, now can we? That would be a waste of two or three good hours when the two of you could be seeing each other. And after what? Three whole days? However did you two tolerate being apart so long?"

"I thought there was some place you had to be," Valerie muttered.

"There is."

With a wave and a smile, Elyssa sailed off. She would have preferred to visit with Valerie until Twig showed up, but she was on a fact-finding mission that involved a blond-haired barracuda fresh from divorce court. Valerie would spend her evening inviting amorous assaults while Elyssa fended them off.

This is one night I'll be glad to see end, Elyssa thought, even if Valerie won't.

Twenty-three

Nathan breezed in the back door with Ricky at his heels and made a beeline for the refrigerator. He had wolfed down lunch and missed supper, thanks to another clipped fence and more scattered cattle. Virgil was sure making life hell around here because his red carpet was about to be pulled out from under him.

Although Elyssa was hesitant to point an accusing finger at her cousin, Nathan pegged that weasel as the culprit. He was sure that Virgil had clipped the fences and had put Claudia up to her pranks. The sooner the private auction was over and Virgil was out of Nathan's hair for good, the better he'd like it.

"Here, let me warm that up for you."

Nathan turned with bowl in hand to find Claudia swooping down on him. "Thanks, Claudia. And you look terrific. Or did I already tell you that?"

She fairly beamed in satisfaction. "Yes, you did, but I enjoy hearing it." She laughed softly. "All this time I've thrown myself at you and worn sexy clothing and you've backed off. Now I've toned down my image and you're dishing out compliments."

Nathan sank tiredly into his chair, absently patting Ricky's broad head. "I know you think I was hell on wheels the other night, but—"

"I had it coming," Claudia finished for him as she punched the microwave timer. "I'm sorry I made trouble for you." She ducked her head and stared at the toes of her tennis shoes. "I'm sorry I was such an ass."

"We're all entitled to a few mistakes. But now that you have your head on straight, I hope you won't be influenced by the person who was using you to get back at me and Elyssa." As if he didn't know who that was!

"Yeah, well, I'm trying to make myself unavailable from now on." Claudia reached over to grab a plate and silverware before the oven timer shrilled. "And in case it doesn't work out with you two, maybe you'll come to appreciate the new me."

"Claudia . . ." he said warningly.

She set his supper in front of him and smiled ruefully. "I know. Not as much class and style. I just wanted you to know you were always my first choice."

"I'm flattered."

Claudia eased a hip onto the edge of the table and stared at Nathan while his dark head was bowed over his plate. "Someday I'm going to be just like her," she vowed. "I might not have Elyssa's connections and money, but I'll have her elegant style."

Nathan studied the resolute expression on Claudia's attractive features. "I don't doubt it."

"And I'll find a man who'll be a good father to Timmy, not one like his worthless daddy. Omigosh!" Claudia bounded to her feet. "I forgot to tell you Valerie is back. That's what I came in here to do."

"Back for what?" Nathan asked between bites.

Claudia grinned wryly. "Back for Twig, I presume. Apparently he lit out of Kansas City like a house afire and called her, asking her to meet him here."

Nathan smiled over his taco casserole. Talk about having it bad! Twig would be lucky he didn't have his driver's license revoked for speeding back to the ranch. The man hadn't wasted any time contacting Valerie, that was sure.

"Well, I'd better go relieve Mother. She's baby-sitting for

me," Claudia said on her way to the back door. "Thanks for stopping by after lunch to unclog the toilet after Timmy tossed in his rubber duck."

"No problem," Nathan replied. "Would you mind if I took Timmy with me in the morning to feed cattle?"

Claudia swiveled her head around, her jaw sagging, tears misting her eyes. "He'd love that. Thanks, Nate. I don't deserve your kindness after what I did, but I swear it won't happen again, no matter what the consequences I have to face."

"You could tell me who paid you," Nathan said quietly. "Then I could ensure there would be no consequences."

Claudia shook her head. "No, I'll handle it. Like you said, modern women are assertive. I've decided to take charge of my life."

When she left, Nathan dived into his meal like a starved tiger. Althea made taco casserole that was out of this world—with her own secret recipe of herbs and spices. Good thing Claudia had turned over a new leaf. He would have hated to dismiss her mother.

During the long, exhausting days of farm work, all a man had to look forward to was one of Althea's mouthwatering meals. Whoever said the way to a man's heart was through his stomach wasn't far from wrong. In fact, thirty minutes earlier, Nathan would have sold his soul for one of Althea's homemade meals. The only thing that would have made the evening better was sharing supper with a certain bewitching onyx-eyed woman . . .

Nathan curbed that lusty thought. He had made a pact with himself to be patient with Elyssa. Passion was still new to her, and she had rebounded from a broken engagement with a real fool. No matter what was between himself and Elyssa, he knew that, in the back of her mind, she still harbored doubts. Nathan supposed she always would, given her situation and her enormous wealth. She probably didn't think she could ever be sure whether a man cared about her or her money.

Nathan and Elyssa had come together at a moment when they had both been vulnerable, reaching out for compassion and overwhelmed by grief. Nathan did not doubt that Elyssa would not have surrendered to him if it were not for her vulnerability, the reckless sense of desperation that claimed her when her father died. He and Elyssa both needed to back away and examine their feelings. But that would be hell, Nathan decided. Elyssa was a fascinating habit he didn't want to unlearn.

One step at a time, he told himself sensibly. He and Elyssa had to get through this auction and deal with the bitter feelings that would inevitably explode because of it. They were simply going to have to enjoy each other while they could, without looking too far into the future.

On that logical advice, Nathan rinsed his plate and crammed it in the dishwasher. He could use a hot shower . . . The thought made him smile ruefully and wonder if he would ever bathe again without remembering how stimulating a shower could be.

Probably not . . .

Elyssa cut the engine and shut off the headlights. The remote area where the old Foster place was located was surrounded by thickets of cottonwoods and cedars. Nestled on the side of a hill, the house was protected from the icy blasts of the north wind. In the darkness, the partially modernized farmhouse had a haunted look about it, which contributed to Elyssa's unease. She didn't want to be here, but she was curious to know whether Gavin really did have information or he had baited her into thinking he had some.

Resigned to what would probably be an unpleasant encounter, she climbed from the truck and strode up the uneven walk. Dim light glowed through the curtains, and soft music wafted toward her before she reached the door. This little scene had trap written all over it. Elyssa wondered if she could artfully dodge Gavin's advances. After their last fiasco, she knew she would have to be on her guard.

The instant she knocked, the door opened to reveal a Gavin

recently showered and dressed in fashionable Western clothes that fit his athletic physique like a glove. His fair skin was squeaky clean, and the strong aroma of cologne suggested he had dipped himself in the seductive fragrance for her benefit.

With flamboyance, Gavin made a sweeping bow. "Come on in, sugar."

Said the spider to the fly. Elyssa peered cautiously around the room before entering. The lights were so low that the room was clouded with shadows. Sultry music added to the romantic atmosphere. Gavin probably was an expert at setting the mood for trysts. Too bad he hadn't spent more time wooing his former wives. But then, Elyssa supposed the hunt and challenge had always been more appealing to this one-time high-school heartthrob. He measured his worth as a man by the number of women he seduced.

This was a blond-haired wolf who was constantly on the prowl. Unlike the wolf, however, Gavin never settled into life with one chosen mate. Elyssa almost pitied the man; he thought he had everything going for him and yet had nothing at all. She was surprised Gavin had acquired as much material wealth as he had, considering his ex-wives took him—and very deservedly—to the cleaners.

Her assessing gaze scanned the room, noting the reasonably new furniture and the well-aged wine on the coffee table. Gavin might have suffered financial setbacks because of his divorces, but he wasn't penniless. Either that or his loan shark was generous, probably to ensure continued favors from this corrupt cop.

Elyssa tensed involuntarily when Gavin's arm glided around her waist to usher her deeper into his lair. A faint smile pursed her lips as she wondered if this was how the sultan's women felt when they were carted into the harem.

"Something amusing, sugar?" Gavin murmured close to her ear.

"You've certainly gone to a lot of effort," she observed.

"I'm trying to compensate for past mistakes."

Wasn't he just!

Elyssa sank down on the leather couch, disgruntled that Gavin dropped down so close beside her his arm brushed hers. It was a long, sectional couch with plenty of space, but she was sandwiched between him and the armrest.

"Would you like a drink, sugar?" he offered, reaching for the wine.

"I would like you to explain your enigmatic remarks that night on the road," she replied.

"Can't we relax a little first?"

"I'm as relaxed as I'm going to get."

Gavin sighed audibly. "Look, sugar, I realize you resent me, but I'm trying to make amends. Now we're both mature adults."

One of us is, Elyssa amended. She had her doubts about him.

"You implied there were problems on the ranch I didn't know about," she said, cutting to the heart of the matter as quickly as possible. "I'd like to have details before the auction."

One blond brow elevated. "Why? So you can use the information against Gil and Virgil?" He chuckled, but he laughed alone. Elyssa failed to see the humor.

"I believe in being prepared," she insisted.

"So do I, sugar. So do I." He tossed her a sly smile and poured himself a glass of wine. "Sure you don't want a drink?"

She nodded hesitantly. "Maybe just a glass." She could definitely use something to take the edge off her nerves. One glass would do that. Two would be disaster.

While Gavin poured her wine, Elyssa studied him in the soft light, hoping to catch him off guard. "Just how does Dennis Humphrey fit into all this?" she asked abruptly.

Gavin jerked up his head and glanced at her. "My, my, you really have been trying to scare up facts, haven't you? I guess I can't blame you. Dealing with Gil's clan must be maddening.

You're still very much the outsider in their eyes, the one who's holding a gun to their heads. I imagine that's infuriating for them."

"I'm sure," Elyssa agreed, accepting the drink and eying him shrewdly. "I wonder if it infuriated them to the point of desperation where my father was concerned. I also wonder if you know the answer to that and are waiting for the revelation to pad your pocket."

Gavin chortled and sipped his drink. "I've got to hand it to you, sugar, you're smart. Gorgeous and smart. Nice combination. Too bad I didn't see all that potential when I was in high school. Things might have worked out differently."

He rested his arm on the back of the sofa, letting his fingertips comb through her silky auburn hair. "But it isn't too late, sugar. With your brains and my connections, we could go places."

"And *my* money?" Elyssa smiled bitterly. "Let's don't forget that, *sugar.* No one else has been able to."

"And I can't forget that you're the one who got away . . ."

Elyssa tensed when his hand shifted to her shoulder, turning her into his waiting kiss. There was no gentleness, no sincerity, only possession. Kissing Gavin was like kissing a frog that would never become a prince. All this man had going for him was good looks and athletic prowess. He was as empty as a cavern. Even his embrace was uninspiring, unlike that of the cowboy who had taught Elyssa the true meaning of tenderness.

"God, what a fool I was," Gavin whispered as he lifted his head.

Elyssa didn't think he had outgrown his stupidity. He reeked with it. "I have been plagued with the feeling that my father's death was no accident, and I think you can tell me if I'm right. Make no mistake, Gavin. That is the only reason I'm here."

He half collapsed against the sofa. "Damn, but you're a tough case. What technique did Hunter use to get to you?"

"Who said he did?"

Gavin flung her a withering glance. "You and I both know

he's after the ranch. You're the key to it. What's he giving you in exchange for what he wants? Hot sex?"

Her fingers itched to claw the smirk off his face. "What is it you want in exchange for information? I'm offering cash. I'm sure you could use it. Supporting two wives and your children must be a strain on your wallet. How much, Gavin?"

"I'd rather have you," he said, leaning closer.

Elyssa leaned back as far as the sofa would allow. "I'm offering cash, nothing more."

"You're bribing a public official?" he asked in mock indignation. "I ought to haul you in, sugar."

There it was—the threat of using his position to his advantage. Elyssa glanced around the well-furnished room before staring into those bedroom eyes that had, long ago, intrigued her. Now they disgusted her with their lack of depth and sincerity.

"From the look of things, you've found other means to support you besides patrolling the county byways. I can pay better than my cousin. He's on his way out, after all. Siding with him will no longer be to your benefit."

Gavin chuckled heartily. "God, you really have learned to play the game, haven't you?" His hand lifted to trace the delicate curve of her chin and the lush texture of her lips. "I'll have to think about that one, sugar. Of course, I could use some incentive . . ."

When his mouth fastened on hers, Elyssa tipped up the glass of wine and dumped it on his head. Gavin lurched back, cursing.

"You little bitch! I ought to—"

She bolted off the couch before Gavin could latch onto her. "Call me when you're ready to discuss the price for your information." She stormed toward the door, only to find herself whipped around and slammed against the wall. Gavin's elbow collided with the lamp, sending it crashing to the floor. He let out another foul oath, his mouth twisting in an angry snarl.

"You want facts? Fine, I'll give them to you. Ely didn't have an accident, and I know exactly what happened and why.

But if you want me to name names I guaran-damn-tee that I want cash and more. I want *you*, whenever I decide to have you. I also want your promise that my name will never enter into this. You got that, *sugar*? And don't think you can go running to the county sheriff's office with claims of my with-holding evidence. I'll deny ever having this conversation or any knowledge of the incident.

"I learned a long time ago that the only way to get what you want is to take it and to make goddamn sure you hold a few strings that can be pulled when you need to. You mess with me and you'll regret it. I can play the game a helluva lot better than you. I've been practicing for years. I know things about people in this area that could cut a few throats. If I decide to call in favors, even you and your money might not be enough to satisfy me."

Flashbacks from the past assailed Elyssa while Gavin's hands pressed into her ribs as if he meant to crack them. She could almost see him looming on the canyon rim while she lay broken and bleeding. He had learned to employ threats to ensure the results he wanted. The technique had worked on her twelve years ago . . . and it was effective now.

It had been a crucial mistake to try to bargain with this corrupt cop. Now she knew for a fact that he had valuable information, but she could only acquire it if she played by his rules.

His hands slid upward until they fastened on her breasts, painfully crushing them while his torso mashed into the cradle of her legs. "When you finish cutting Virgil and Ely to ribbons with your auction and turn them over to the wolves, then come see me. Ten thousand dollars will make a nice down payment for the services I'll render and the satisfaction you'll get from me. *Then* you'll get your information."

Elyssa panted for breath when Gavin finally released her and stepped back. He was a card-carrying bastard, and she was a fool for trying to deal with him! She reached for the door knob, but Gavin's brusque voice halted her in her tracks.

"If you breathe one word of this conversation to Hunter,

you might not live long enough to find out what happened to
your father."

Elyssa stared at the menacing expression on his face, trying
to decipher what he meant by the remark. A cold chill slithered
down her spine, and old suspicions hounded her. Gavin hadn't
said Hunter was involved, but he hadn't said Hunter *wasn't*.
Good Lord! Had she let herself be deceived again? She had
begun to trust Hunter, and she wondered if that was going to
turn out to be a dangerous mistake.

She was so shaken that she didn't know what to believe or
who to trust. Certainly not Gavin. But what if . . . ?

"Don't tell Hunter," Gavin repeated threateningly.

Elyssa whipped open the door and rushed out to inhale a
breath of fresh air. She felt she had just dealt with the devil
and had come away singed to the bone. Gavin had confirmed
her suspicions about her father's death. But he was withholding
his information until she met his price.

Plunking into the pickup, Elyssa fought for hard-won composure. Gavin's threat rang in her ears and his last words echoed through her tormented mind.

Don't tell Hunter.

Elyssa cranked the engine and sped off. Her heart rebelled
against suspecting Hunter. Why would he dispose of her father
when Ely had willed him half the estate? It was Gil's family
who would profit most by continuing the partnership . . . according to Hunter.

It always came back to that, didn't it? *According to Hunter.*
Damn it, why did Hunter have to be the one who'd found Ely's
body, as if he had known exactly where to look? Why couldn't
it have been one of the other men? And why didn't Gavin want
her to mention their conversation to him?

And that dramatic scene in the office with Claudia—had
that been staged? Was that why she had refused to name
names? Had Hunter put her up to that entire performance, and
was the *new* Claudia part of the convincing act? God, she could

have been set up for the biggest con since Redford and Newman's in *The Sting!*

Elyssa reminded herself that Gavin could have been the one who disposed of Ely. There were unnerving similarities about the fall into the canyon and her father's fatal accident.

Maybe Gavin didn't want Hunter to know about his attempt to extort money because Hunter couldn't be easily threatened.

Maybe he had seen Dennis, Cousin Virgil, or Uncle Gil in the pasture that fateful day and had been accepting hush money until Elyssa had come along to make a better offer. Or maybe Gavin was feeding her suspicions for any money and sexual favors he thought he could get . . .

Elyssa muttered a curse. Every explanation sounded as logical as the others. She was going to drive herself nuts by trying to second-guess everyone and determine who was actually guilty.

She wanted nothing more than to rush back to the ranch, fling herself into Hunter's arms, and confide all her doubts and suspicions in him. But sometimes friends turned out to be our worst enemies. She was going to have to keep her distance from Hunter until she knew the truth.

Dear Lord! This had been an unbelievable month! She couldn't walk away and leave her troubles behind, but she was going to take a few days off and hibernate in her apartment.

Come Monday, she would write Gavin a check for the amount he requested and she would follow through with the auction to divide the ranch property. When she had the name Gavin was withholding, she would demand an investigation of Ely's death. Then she was going to set sail to the South Pacific, or some equally remote area of the globe. And she might never come back!

Twenty-four

In response to the insistent knock at the front door, Nathan stepped out of the kitchen to see Valerie, decked out in all her Western finery, making a mad dash out of the living room. He propped himself leisurely against the wall, an amused smile quirking his lips as Valerie swung open the door to find Ray Twigger on the porch, looking exhausted but exceptionally eager, if Nathan was any judge of a man's mood.

Nathan almost burst out laughing when Twig scooped the petite blonde up in his arms and kissed her. Valerie didn't resist, and the two of them seemed stuck together by Super Glue.

"God, I missed you like crazy," Twig rasped when he finally came up for air.

"Me, too." Valerie wound her arms around his neck and hugged him tight.

"I could use a quick shower and a whole night of—" Twig slammed his mouth shut when he noticed movement in the hall. He swore under his breath and reluctantly set Val to her feet. "Hello, *Mother*. I'm home."

Nathan ambled forward, Ricky at his heels. "Fast trip to Kansas City," he noted.

"I didn't take time out for eating or resting," Twig muttered.

Nathan accepted the expense voucher Twig handed to him. "I guess you'll want the rest of the weekend off to recuperate."

"I'm *taking* the rest of the weekend off," Twig declared. "I haven't had time off in two weeks."

Nathan glanced curiously around him. "Where's Elyssa?"

"I don't know for sure," Val offered. "She was on her way out when I arrived. She didn't tell me where she was going, but she was dressed in a bright green business suit, if that means anything."

It didn't, not to Nathan at least. "Did she say when she'd be back?"

"Later was all she said." Valerie's attention shifted to Twig when he slid an arm around her waist and pulled her close.

Nathan intercepted the look that passed between the pair and took the cue. "Well, if you'll excuse me, I think I'll catch the ten o'clock news and call it a night. Glad you're back, Twig."

"Not half as glad as I am," Twig murmured just loud enough for Valerie to hear him.

Nathan felt like an unnoticed stick of furniture when Val and Twig headed for the stairs, casting sheep's eyes at each other every step of the way. "C'mon, Ricky. Looks like it's you and me tonight," he said.

Ricky plunked down in front of the sofa and rested his chin on his paws while Nathan plopped on the couch to flick through the TV channels with the remote control. Fifteen minutes later the phone jingled and Nathan grabbed the receiver.

"Hunter?"

"Elyssa. Where are you?"

"At my apartment."

Nathan frowned at the information and the unnatural catch in her voice. "Are you all right?"

"I'm fine." Not really. Frustrated, confused, and suspicious, thanks to her encounter with Gavin.

"I thought you were coming back to the ranch. What are you doing in the City?" Nathan inquired.

"I wanted to take a Jacuzzi bath. Did I need your permission?"

Nathan grinned. She was in a belligerent mood. It was glaringly apparent in her voice and her flippant remarks. So much for their pleasurable truce. Fire and ice, thought Nathan. That perfectly described his relationship with Elyssa Rawlins Cutler.

"You dressed up in a business suit and left the ranch hours ago, just to drive to the City to use your Jacuzzi?"

"That's my story and I'm sticking with it."

Nathan leaned forward, his forearms braced on his knees, frowning in frustration. "Something has upset you. I know you well enough to know that. Where did you go tonight and what happened?"

"Back off, Hunter. I don't have to answer to you," she muttered irritably. "Just because we are . . . involved—"

"Passionately involved," he clarified.

Her caustic sniff came over the line. "It's not as if I've had the chance to make comparisons. Just how am I supposed to know that?"

"Because I said so."

"Ah yes, the gospel according to Hunter. I'm supposed to trust you explicitly. How could I forget?"

Nathan expelled a rough sigh and forcibly restrained his temper. "What's wrong, Elyssa?"

"Nothing," she snapped out more harshly than she'd intended. "It's late and I'm ready for bed."

"Need some company?"

"No. I want what I haven't had in more than two weeks—to be left alone!"

"Something is definitely wrong. I can hear it in your voice. I'm coming over."

"Absolutely not!" Elyssa practiced deep breathing to get herself under control. "It's late, Hunter. And I don't think you and I should . . ." She inhaled a shaky breath. "That is to say, I think it would be best if—"

"If what?" Nathan demanded when she hemmed and hawed. He had the feeling Elyssa wanted to call it quits. Oh, he knew it was for the best, knew he should never have gotten involved in this impossible situation. The cards had been stacked against him and Elyssa since the beginning, but he had never been able to stop himself from wanting her. She had become his greatest weakness.

The best mistake he had ever made . . .

"I—I don't think we should . . . see each other except in a business capacity," Elyssa stammered.

A muscle clenched in his jaw and he battled the anger and hurt her words instilled in him. "Anything else?" His voice was as hard as granite; Elyssa would have had to be deaf not to notice.

"No."

"Are you coming back tomorrow?" he questioned with all the indifference he could muster.

"No. I need to tend to some business, and it will take a while. I'll be back for the auction. I just wanted to let you know where I was."

When the line went dead, Nathan scowled. What the devil had happened? Where had Elyssa gone, all spruced up in a business suit, and why had she suddenly decided to call it quits and to spend the weekend in the City—as far away from him as she could get?

He couldn't help but wonder if someone had bent Elyssa's ear with more propaganda against him. There was an anxious note in her voice and an elusive quality to her answers. Whatever she had done tonight, and whoever she had done it with, she didn't want Nathan to know of her activities or to come near him.

Frustration burned his insides like dry ice. He had lost Elyssa's trust again. Her faith in him had been going up and down like a damned yo-yo for so long it was driving him nuts!

Swearing colorfully, Nathan stalked upstairs and tried not to hear the musical laughter and soft voices that wafted toward him from the guest bedroom. He envied the carefree pleasure Valerie and Twig shared.

Too many times in his life Nathan had felt unloved and unwanted. All through his childhood, he had been ignored and shuffled aside. Reckless Sid Hunter had been too busy playing the footloose cowboy, trying to convince himself that he hadn't cared one damned bit when his wife ran off and left him.

Nathan hadn't been raised during his formative years; he had simply grown up like a weed. At age twenty, he hadn't known what he wanted, except to escape his hard-drinking, fast-living, spendthrift father. But one year of marriage to the Texas barrel-racing queen who ran circles around him had been a year too many. Nathan had learned that wives were as undependable and unpredictable as parents, and he had found himself adrift, back on the rodeo circuit with his father who had finally eased off the whiskey because Ely Rawlins had cared enough to get them both pointed in the right direction.

Now, years later, Nathan was trying to repay a debt to a man who had been more of a father to him than Sid. He was battling impossible odds to see that Ely's wishes were carried out, and now even Elyssa had turned her back on him. That hurt the worst. It hurt like hell. Nathan hoped she was enjoying herself in her Jacuzzi because he wanted her like crazy and knew she was slipping from his grasp.

The spring winds were blowing gale force when Elyssa and Bernard Gresham arrived at the ranch for the private auction. Gresham, Cutler Corporation's legal advisor, had followed Elyssa to the ranch in his own vehicle, certain he'd get lost without a guide. Now the gray-haired attorney scurried along beside Elyssa toward the front door, his tie and coattails flapping in the wind.

As for Elyssa, she looked as if her hair had been styled by a cyclone by the time she plunged into the hall. She clawed her windblown locks away from her face to see Hunter awaiting her, his carefully schooled expression revealing none of his thoughts. She braced herself when her heart twisted painfully in her chest and then made the necessary introductions

"Nathan Hunter, this is Cutler Corporation's lawyer, Bernard Gresham. Bernard, Nathan is my business partner."

Nathan thrust out a hand, and Bernard greeted him with a cordial smile. "We appreciate your help, sir."

"For Elyssa, it's always a pleasure," Bernard replied.

Nathan wondered how sincere Bernard was. Folks had a tendency to kiss up to Elyssa because she was the goose who sat on two nests of golden eggs, and some of her mistrust and cynicism had rubbed off on him. He was becoming as suspicious of others' motives as she was. Now he could understand why she was never certain whether her associates were vying for position or manipulating her for favors. Nathan decided to reserve judgment on the grandfatherly-looking lawyer until he knew him better.

"I expect this will be an emotionally charged conference," Bernard said as he combed his gray hair back into place with his fingers. "These things usually are. Sometimes tempers fly. It's often more of a matter of *not* wanting your ex-partner to have a piece of property than it is of wanting it yourself." He regarded Nathan and Elyssa through experienced eyes. "I hope both of you have discussed what you want and why. When conflicts arise, and they will, you must present your arguments rationally. Although I represent your interests here, I intend to be fair."

Nathan was beginning to appreciate the plump attorney more by the minute. "Elyssa and I have only had the chance to discuss the property values briefly," he admitted, staring pensively at her. "I had hoped to go into more detail this weekend, but she was detained in the City."

Elyssa shifted awkwardly beneath Nathan's probing glance, but she managed a smile nonetheless. "Since Hunter has been closely associated with my father, and with the management of his half of the ranch operation, I will leave most of the decisions to him."

Why shouldn't she? Hunter knew exactly what he wanted and the value of the various sections of land, whether it was pasture or cultivated ground. No matter what his true motive, he had been Ely's protégé, groomed and trained to develop an eye for prime property and the productivity which could be expected from it.

Nathan cocked a black brow at Elyssa's comment. After the mood she had been in when on the phone, he'd expected belligerence. He would have given his eyeteeth to know where she had been Saturday night—and with whom and why. Could she have met with Bernard to discuss the conference?

"Elyssa and I haven't had much chance to discuss this meeting, either," Bernard admitted.

Well, that answered that question. So where the hell had she been, and who had put her in this suspicious, defensive mood?

The sound of an approaching vehicle caused the threesome to glance toward the door. In silence, they watched Virgil and Gil stride toward the house, holding their hats on their heads and looking grim.

The room temperature dropped ten degrees when Virgil and Gil stepped inside and waited for Elyssa to make the introductions.

"I placed extra chairs in the office," Nathan announced. "Althea filled the coffeepot. "Why don't we get started?"

Elyssa filed into the study behind Nathan, striving to keep her emotions carefully in check. When the group had seated themselves, Elyssa in her father's chair, Nathan handed Bernard the listings of the properties along with their legal descriptions before presenting copies to the Rawlins clan to peruse.

"I have designated each land section and its purpose in the partnership," he declared as he handed duplicate copies to Gil and Virgil. "The value of each quarter section is listed, according to the county assessor's documentations and property-tax returns. Naturally, some parts of the land are more valuable than others."

"I suggest we begin by calculating the total value of the

property and dividing it by half," Bernard said as he studied the list Nathan had assembled. "Both parties will have an equal amount of funds in our imaginary bank for bidding on the quarter sections they would like to purchase." He smiled faintly as he surveyed each somber face. "I would also like to remind you that this is no time for pettiness or revenge. Each piece of property must be objectively considered for its productive value, as it pertains to your future expectations. Do all of you understand and agree that this partnership is to be fairly divided for the benefits of all concerned?"

"Yes," Gil ground out. "I just wish I'd retained a lawyer as my niece thought to do."

Gil's look branded Elyssa a traitor for dissolving the family business in the first place, but she didn't wince, not when her father's protective presence lurked in the room to almost a tangible degree. Hunter couldn't have selected a better site for the auction. Ely's portrait hung behind her, as if he were overseeing the entire affair. Gil must have experienced the same feeling because he was staring over her head.

"I requested Bernard's presence only to ensure that we follow legal procedure. He is here as a moderator. This is still a private auction, among family," Elyssa contended. "The deeds to the undivided property will be handled by your own attorney, Uncle Gil. But initially we have to decide on the divisions."

"Fine," Gil muttered. "I want to keep possession of all the land where I run my steers and where Virgil's horse barns are."

"The east pastures, you mean," Nathan interrupted.

"And the cultivation ground where we raise wheat," Gil demanded.

Even Elyssa knew what Gil wanted. Hunter had explained the USDA wheat program to her in detail so that she could understand her uncle's motives.

"I agree that keeping the property east of the ranch house, where you have erected sheds and replaced fences, is reasonable," she replied. "But because the cultivation ground is part of the government subsidy program, its worth is not adequately assessed through the courthouse. USDA deficiency payments have to be taken into consideration."

Nathan stifled a grin when Gil and Virgil did double takes. Both men then glared daggers at him for seeing to it that Elyssa was well informed. Nathan simply stared at father and son with an emotionless expression.

"Hunter, do you have any objection to deeding the eastern sections of pasture to Uncle Gil and Cousin Virgil for the value indicated by the county assessor?" Elyssa inquired.

"None whatsoever. The western sections of the ranch are of comparable value and they are stocked with Ely's cows and calves. If we inherit the cow herd and are allowed to sell the calves, then Gil should be able to sell the steers or to run them on the pastures he was using while he and Ely managed the partnership."

"Do you wish to purchase the pastures your livestock is grazing?" Bernard asked Gil.

"Yes," Gil agreed.

Gil then rattled off the legal description of the quarter sections of pasture and their assessed values. Bernard's fingers flew over the calculator, tallying the prices to offer Gil the total he had spent on land.

"Do you object to letting Nathan and Elyssa purchase the western pastures listed at their assessed values?" Bernard inquired of Gil.

"No, but if the wheat ground is going to be divided, the alfalfa fields will be, too. We can't run steers without access to winter wheat pasture and supplemental hay."

"Nor can we raise cows," Nathan put in.

Gil's mouth thinned and he bared his teeth. "How do you expect us to put weight on our steers without enough winter wheat forage? I'll have to feed them hay if I keep them on dry grass and there will be no profit, come market time. I can't manage on *half* the wheat pasture and you damned well know it!"

"Then I suggest you either decrease the size of your herd to accommodate the amount of wheat ground you own, or rent some from us or one of your neighbors," Nathan blandly advised. "This is to be a fair division of property. We both know you had a great advantage during the partnership because Ely allowed you to use all the wheat pasture, even though it cut into his profits with the cow-calf operation. Besides that, the weaning calves he raised were at your disposal for your steer herd. You never had to pay handling fees and transportation as you would have done if you purchased young calves at the stockyards. The benefits you took for granted are now nonexistent. Both parties will have to adjust to the division of property and machinery."

Gil settled back in his chair and scowled. Virgil gnashed his teeth and glared at Elyssa whom he held entirely responsible for his impending financial disaster.

"Would you prefer to bid on each quarter section of cultivation ground?" Bernard questioned, glancing at Gil and then at Nathan.

"No," Gil grumbled sourly. "We will geographically divide the land as best we can." He shot Elyssa a disgusted glance. *"If* that is agreeable to my *niece,* of course."

Elyssa looked to Hunter for confirmation, which didn't endear her to her uncle and cousin. But then, she was long past caring on that count. When Hunter nodded agreeably, she voiced her assent. Things were going better than she'd anticipated. Gil had put up a mild protest, but he was being reasonable . . . thus far.

After Bernard had tallied the assessed prices of the cultivated property, he slumped back in his chair. "It seems that the wheat pastures to the east of the ranch house have a higher appraised value than those to the west, Mr. Rawlins. You are obviously receiving quality property, but you also have less funds left with which to operate in the next round of auctions. You're aware of that fact, are you not?"

"Yes," Gil clipped off.

"Elyssa?" Bernard glanced in her direction.

"Yes, I understand."

"Now then." Bernard straightened in his chair. "If I geographically divide the alfalfa fields listed here, Mr. Rawlins will not have enough funds in his imaginary bank of purchasing power to pay for his half."

"And I'm supposed to give up part of my hay fields?" Gil growled.

Bernard smiled tolerantly. "You just agreed that you had gotten the better end of the deal in wheat pasture. I'm no rancher, Mr. Rawlins, but I assume better wheat pasture means increased productivity of the crop and the ability to run more steers with expectation of profitable weight gain for market than Elyssa and Nathan can expect from their half."

"Yes, but they'll receive the same target price in the government program," Gil argued.

"But we can't expect as many bushels of grain to the acre at harvest," Nathan put in. "We will receive the same target price but hardly the same yield."

Gil had known his argument wouldn't hold water, but he'd been resentful enough to give it a try. He was going to have to grit his teeth and sacrifice part of the alfalfa fields to retain the best wheat ground.

"Oh, all right, damn it! But I'm going to be short on hay if I lose part of the alfalfa fields."

"And what am I supposed to do about my horses?" Virgil piped up. "They have to have top-grade hay, lots of it. I need every hay field I can get."

Nathan glanced at him. "I guess you'll have to *purchase* the extra hay required for your mares and studs."

Virgil glowered at Nathan, knowing full well what he implied. For years, Virgil had taken the hay he needed without paying the partnership. Now he was going to have to pay through the nose and sell off some of his brood mares to meet his outstanding debts.

"How many alfalfa fields will have to be sacrificed to keep this even?" Gil asked.

"Two quarter sections, if you agree to give up the fields that lie closer to the western half of the house," Bernard replied.

Gil propped his elbows on the arms of the chair and mulled over what he would gain and lose. He stared meditatively at the list of property on his lap and nodded reluctantly. "I'll keep the good wheat ground and sacrifice two alfalfa fields."

"Dad!" Virgil wailed in dismay. "You're cutting my throat. I can't function without hay."

"You may not have any horses left to feed after you pay—" Gil snapped his mouth shut and cursed his wagging tongue. He hadn't intended to confirm Elyssa's suspicions that Virgil was up to his neck in debt.

Elyssa felt Virgil's resentment when her cousin focused on her. He was holding her personally responsible for his woes. Well, tough. He had dug his own hole, and he had lived off Ely's generosity for years while he'd wheeled and dealed. Maybe family was family, but business was business. Virgil had overextended himself, and it was time he paid for taking advantage of family to promote himself.

"Are we all agreeable to the divisions of the property then?" Bernard questioned.

Virgil sulked. Gil nodded his red head in bitter resignation.

"Very well then, the two quarter sections of alfalfa that are geographically situated beside the western half of the ranch will be deeded to Ely's heirs. It also follows that the mineral rights for each quarter section will go with the land, and the income received from oil leases will be divided according to the property." Bernard set the first page of property listings and diagrams aside and proceeded to the second. "How do you wish to handle the tractors, grain trucks, and implements? I assume both parties will require machinery to work and sow their fields. Do you wish to follow the same procedure, using the appraised values of your inventory?"

"I concede all decisions in this area to Hunter," Elyssa announced. "He is better prepared to appraise the worth of the inventory."

She had the feeling this was going to take a while. There were plows, field cultivators, combines, drills, and who knew what else to be sorted out, along with a fleet of tractors—some of which were in better operating condition than others.

She hadn't meant to fling Hunter into a heated argument, but that was exactly what ensued. Gil and Vigil behaved like starved dogs battling for bones. They had been reasonably civil during the land transactions, but the implement division was another matter entirely.

Whether time and resentment were wearing on them, or whether they were balking in an effort to prevent being cheated, Elyssa didn't know. Whatever the case, they squabbled over discs, balers, and swathers while Hunter managed to keep his temper under control. She was certain she would have retaliated to Virgil's and Gil's snide remarks, but Nathan did nothing of the kind. He battled for his fair share without resorting to the cheap shots Gil and Virgil employed.

It was an exhausting procedure.

Twenty-five

Three cups of coffee and an hour and a half later, the auction ended. Bernard had a list of all property and machinery that would become Elyssa's and Nathan's.

When Virgil and Gil trooped off, Bernard turned to Elyssa. "What do you and Nathan plan to do about the wording of property deeds? Do you wish to conduct your own auction to divide your inheritances or do you want your names jointly listed on the documents?"

Elyssa's thick lashes swept up to meet Hunter's unblinking gaze. She waited for him to voice his preference so she could determine what he might have to gain by the tactic. He waited, wondering what she expected him to say.

Bernard's gaze bounced back and forth between Nathan and Elyssa, who were appraising each other with meditative concentration. "Would you like my advice?"

"Yes." Nathan never took his eyes off Elyssa.

"Give yourselves a few days to decide what will suit your business arrangement. It's going to take me more than a week to study the deeds and have the abstracts updated. Before we type up the documents, I'll be in touch with both of you."

"Thank you, Bernard. I . . ." Elyssa's voice trailed off when sunlight reflected off the windshield of the car that had just pulled into the driveway. A bemused frown knitted her brow when she realized the county sheriff had arrived.

When Gil and Virgil ambled over to greet the stocky officer, the unaccountable tingle that pooled at the base of her neck—

more often than she preferred in recent weeks—assailed her. The awareness that something was very wrong settled into her bones.

"I'll find out what's going on," Nathan volunteered.

"Well, I'd better be on my way." Bernard flashed Elyssa a smile. "If you need further consultation, give me a call."

She nodded mutely before he turned and left. Her attention was fixed on the four men who stood in a tight circle outside. Elyssa found herself nervously wringing her hands until Hunter paced back to the house, a bleak expression on his face.

"What's wrong?" Elyssa asked.

Althea emerged from the kitchen before he could respond. "I've got lunch waiting in here," she announced. "Twig, Skeeter, Dennis, and Les are drooling all over themselves. If you want something to eat, you'd better pull up a chair and be quick about it."

"We'll discuss it later," Nathan said to Elyssa.

"I want to know now," she demanded.

He didn't turn around, just ambled toward the kitchen as if he hadn't heard her. She knew damned good and well he had, though.

Her appetite quickly waning, Elyssa sank down between Twig and Les Fykes who were passing bowls and shoveling food onto their plates as if they had just come off prison rations. The expression on Hunter's face suggested whatever news he had received wasn't good. He did manage an occasional smile for Timmy who was jabbering in his high chair and cramming food in his mouth with his fingers.

Claudia was paying more attention to her son than Elyssa ever remembered seeing her do. Elyssa appreciated the change in Claudia's appearance and behavior; she just wasn't sure she could trust the reason for it.

"I spent the morning rounding up a few more strays and patching fence," Les Fykes reported to Nathan. "I hope you don't mind that I took Ricky with me. He made short work of tracking down the scattered cows on the goat ranch."

Elyssa knew the "goat ranch," a pasture north and west of the house where her grandfather had once raised goats and sheep until trouble with coyotes had forced him to sell his flock. Coyotes had wiped out one fourth of the flock before the rest could be loaded up and hauled to the stockyards.

"The goat ranch?" Nathan queried. "I checked those fences yesterday afternoon."

"Well, they'd been cut when I was there this morning," Les reported. "Luckily, only a few head of cattle had found the opening, and they were grazing in the ditches along the road."

"I hope you patched the fence there better than the one you did in the rock-canyon section," Elyssa spoke up.

Les swiveled his head around to gape at her. "Where?"

"The stretch of barbed wire at the base of the canyon by the low-water bridge," she replied.

"When were you there?" Les asked.

"Last week when I found the newborn calf in the canyon."

"I'll take care of it this afternoon," Les promised. "I got behind while we were haying." His attention shifted to Nathan and he grinned wryly. "When is Mo-Joe due back?"

Nathan didn't answer and his gaze dropped to his plate. He seemed disturbed by some thought he didn't bother sharing with his companions at the table.

Elyssa felt that apprehensive tingle again and wondered if Mo-Joe's absence had something to do with the sheriff's visit. Curiosity was eating her alive and spoiling her appetite.

"Does Mo-Joe really have a sister he visits in Elk City, or is that just his excuse to disappear for a few days every six weeks or so?" Claudia asked as she handed Timmy a slice of bread.

Twig grinned wryly. "I don't think Mo-Joe is visiting his sister."

"Probably sowing wild oats," Skeeter contributed.

Nathan said nothing. That only made Elyssa more apprehensive. She was ready to cram the rest of the food on Hunter's plate down his throat and drag him outside to explain what Mo-Joe's disappearance had to do with the sheriff's visit.

After what seemed a too-long meal accompanied by much idle yammering, Elyssa excused herself from the table. Although she tried to catch Nathan's attention and silently request that he follow her, he purposely ignored her.

Muttering, she sallied off to change clothes. In record time, she shucked her skirt and blouse and fastened herself into jeans and a flannel shirt. If Hunter planned to sneak off without discussing the sheriff's visit with her, she'd track him down. She wanted answers. Now!

By the time Elyssa ventured downstairs, all four men had disappeared. Claudia and Althea were cleaning off the table, and Timmy was toddling around the room, slapping his rubber hammer against cabinet doors and chattering like a magpie.

"Where's Hunter?" Elyssa questioned.

Wrist-deep in dishwater, Althea gestured her head toward the window. "He went out to get Twig and Skeeter started on spraying weed killer on the pastures. I think they're still in the barn or the workshop."

Elyssa made a beeline toward the door.

"Would you take Timmy with you," Claudia requested as she scooped up her son, rubbed off his milk mustache, and confiscated his rubber hammer.

Timmy loudly objected.

"Yesterday, Nate took Timmy with him to check cattle and Timmy was thrilled. Today, Twig volunteered to let Timmy ride with him in the rig," Claudia explained.

As the wriggling child was deposited in Elyssa's arms, she couldn't help but wonder why Twig and Hunter—especially Hunter—had taken a sudden interest in entertaining Timmy. Despite her suspicions, a smile tugged at her lips when she glanced down into Timmy's small face and huge eyes. She'd had little opportunity to be around children. She wondered how good a mother she would be. She also wondered if she would ever have the chance to find out.

"C'mon, Timmy, let's go for a walk," Elyssa murmured.

Timmy jabbered excitedly as she set him to his feet and clasped this hand. His little legs churned as he hurried out the back door, but Elyssa had to scoop him up into her arms again when he became sidetracked by a butterfly that floated past him.

By the time she reached the machine shop, Timmy propped on her hip, Twig was on his way out.

"There you are, shrimp." Twig winked at Elyssa before sauntering off with Timmy to climb into the oversize fertilizer rig with booms and hoses stretched out on either side of its fifteen-hundred-gallon tank. Timmy's laughter clamored in the wind, granting Elyssa a few more minutes' reprieve from the apprehension that hovered over her.

Les Fykes emerged from the barn, toting a saddle, blanket, and bridle. "I'm on my way to check that section of fence you mentioned," he informed her.

"Good, I had intended to tell you about it earlier, but things have been so hectic . . ." She lifted her hands in a helpless gesture.

"I know. It's been a regular circus around here lately," Les agreed before he ambled off to catch one of the horses penned in the west corral.

"Les! Take that cow and calf back to the pasture with you. There's no need to feed them cubes just for the fun of it," Nathan called out.

"Right, boss," Les hollered back.

Elyssa strode off to track down the source of Hunter's voice. She found him rearranging fallen square hay bales at the back of the barn. If the speed at which Hunter worked was any indication, he was burning off frustration. Elyssa knew the feeling. She was frustrated by wondering what the sheriff had said to frustrate Hunter.

"Well? Are you going to tell me what's going on, or do I have to tie you down and torture the information out of you, Hunter?" she demanded, hands on hips, feet askew, and temper roiling.

Nathan hoisted a square bale off the straw-covered floor and watched a nest of mice scurry for cover. After he had heaved the hay onto the stack, he took his sweet time about pulling off his leather gloves and pivoting to face the very impatient Elyssa.

"What did the sheriff want, Hunter?" she ground out.

Eyes, like chips of blue ice, zeroed in on her. "Why are you so anxious to know?"

"Damn it!"

Sprigs of alfalfa crunched beneath Nathan's boots as he approached, his mouth set in a grim line. "Sheriff Bently came by to tell us that Gavin Spencer didn't report for duty this morning. The dispatcher tried to get in touch with him around ten o'clock, but no one answered. She sent the deputy sheriff out to his house to check on him."

Wide brown eyes focused on Nathan's bleak expression. "And?"

"And Gavin was found dead. According to the medical examiner, he was probably killed Saturday evening. There were two glasses and a bottle of wine on the coffee table, and a lamp had been knocked to the floor. The homicide investigator has been called in, and the print people are taking samples. According to the sheriff, Gavin was killed by blows to the head."

Elyssa staggered back a step and struggled to take in air. Her lungs seemed clogged with dust, making it impossible to draw breath.

Nathan's gaze narrowed, monitoring her reaction to the news. "The sheriff wanted to know if we had seen Gavin in the area or if Virgil knew who Gavin might have been entertaining Saturday night."

Elyssa felt sick. "What did Virgil have to say?" she bleated.

"Not much—yet." Nathan scrutinized Elyssa closely. "But if I know Virgil, he'll add your name to the list of possible suspects when he thinks the time is right. He knows about your previous association with Gavin, and by the time he finishes relating what happened when you were a teenager, and tells about your scars and the bitterness you bear because of that fiasco, Sheriff Bently will be rapping on the door to ask questions and take a few fingerprints to see if they match the ones on the wine glasses."

Elyssa half collapsed against a stall. She knew exactly how a rabbit felt when trapped in a snare. Dear God! If she were indicted for murdering a cop her stepfather and mother would be humiliated. News like that would be splashed all over the newspapers and could cause considerable damage to Cutler Corporation's reputation. And heaven forbid Robert Grayson ever got hold of that tidbit! He would have camera crews out here in nothing flat. Of course, Cousin Virgil would delight in watching her be humiliated after she had left him high and dry when it came time to pay off his loan. There would be no positive character references forthcoming from the Rawlins family.

Elyssa's stomach churned. She should never have agreed to meet with Gavin. Whoever had disposed of him had taken advantage of a situation that left accusing fingerprints pointing in her direction. How could she prove her innocence when she'd look guilty as sin when the prints were matched and stories were verified?

"The sheriff is on his way to question Gavin's ex-wives to see if one of them might have been his companion for the evening," Nathan informed her, his blue eyes probing like scalpels. "Anything else you want to know?"

"No." The word was barely above a whisper.

Nathan strode closer, bracing his arms on either side of the stall where Elyssa had propped herself up on noodly legs. "Well, there's something *I* want to know," he growled into her peaked face. "Were *you* Gavin's Saturday night 'date'?"

Elyssa swallowed to keep her heart from jumping into her throat. "I . . ."

"Is that why you didn't want anyone to know where you were going? Is that why you sounded so rattled when you called? Did the instinct to escape the scene of the crime send you racing to the City? Was there too much blood on your clothes for you to risk coming back to the ranch and being seen?"

Elyssa blinked back the tears that pooled in her eyes. She was indignant and she was furious with Hunter for treating her as if he thought she had disposed of Gavin. Did he think so little of her that he actually believed she could take someone's life?

Nathan leaned closer, effectively pinning Elyssa in place with his powerful body and piercing gaze. "And what am I supposed to do when the sheriff starts asking *me* questions? Claim ignorance of the situation? I know goddamn well you and Gavin had a confrontation on the road last week because you came back with the buttons ripped off your blouse, and your friend Valerie told me you were dressed fit to kill when you went out Saturday night."

Elyssa grimaced, wishing Hunter would have selected another cliché besides that one. A sense of panic gripped her as he glared accusingly at her. She felt the walls were closing in, trapping her so she couldn't escape. She lashed out at Hunter, venting the frustration that was simmering inside her.

"You would love to see me convicted of the crime, wouldn't you?" she hissed at him. "Then you would have my half of the ranch under your control because I'd be locked away for a crime *you* probably committed. All you ever wanted was control of this ranch. You seduced me into siding with you. You convinced me to revoke the partnership and hold the private auction. Everything you've said and done has been to bend me to your own purposes—you and everyone else in my life!"

Elyssa inhaled quickly and then rushed on while Hunter

muttered several unprintable oaths. "My whole family has played right into your hands. My father's generosity worked to your advantage for years. And Gil and Virgil have made it easy for you by racking up debts so you could persuade me to divide the ranch."

She swiped at the betraying tears that trickled down her cheeks, then glowered at him. "And I've been the biggest patsy of all because I was a vulnerable, confused fool! I almost believed you had my best interests at heart, but you don't have a heart, Hunter. You even used Claudia to set me up with her little charades. And in return, you've taken an interest in her son to compensate for all the favors she's done for you!"

Nathan recoiled as if he had been slapped. If he hadn't known how little Elyssa trusted him before, he certainly did now. She had always believed the worst about him. She had always been suspicious of everything he said and did, had always looked for hidden motives and viewed his actions and reactions as deceitful ploys.

Elyssa ducked under his arm and stalked off. "You've got what you've always wanted," she hurled over her shoulder. "You can have the ranch. I don't want it, and I don't want *you!*"

When she veered into the tack room and emerged with a saddle and bridle, Nathan stormed after her. "Where the hell do you think you're going?"

"For a ride," she said between sniffles.

The bridle jangled like handcuffs and chains as she went to retrieve a horse, the sounds instilling a deeper sense of panic in Elyssa. She had to get away, to give herself time to gather her composure and collect her scattered wits!

"You think ducking the cops is going to help?" Nathan asked with chilling sarcasm. He watched Elyssa sling the saddle over the nearest horse. "It's a long ride to the Mexican border from here, Ms. Fugitive."

"Go to hell, Hunter," she retorted without doing him the courtesy of glancing in his direction.

"Where do you think I've been since I met up with you?" he tossed back at her.

Elyssa blinked back another round of tears and cursed all men everywhere—Hunter in particular. He had the ability to hurt her more than any man alive.

"You aren't planning a rendezvous this afternoon with some other man who is going to turn up dead, are you?"

Nathan leaped sideways when Elyssa kneed the black mare and nearly ran him down in her effort to escape him. Scowling, he stared after her, wishing he hadn't let his temper and frustration get the best of him.

When he'd heard about Gavin's death, he had suspected Elyssa had somehow been involved and he'd been furious with her for not confiding in him. He had tried to break down her stubborn defenses by firing the same kind of questions at her that she could expect from a homicide investigator. But the tactic had blown up in his face. His relentless badgering had ignited her temper and he had discovered how little trust and respect she had for him.

But he had known from the very beginning it would be a mistake to become involved with her; he just hadn't been able to resist her. He had yielded to a fierce attraction against his better judgment. Now he knew it would never work between them.

He also knew it wasn't his irresistibility that had first landed him in Elyssa's bed. If she hadn't been vulnerable, reaching out for consolation, he would never have become her first experience with passion. While she was being bombarded from all directions, trying to sort out Ely's estate, she had surrendered to him now and again, only as a distraction. But this off-again, on-again affair was over, once and for all. He would try to save her lovely neck from a murder rap, and then he was going to get the hell out of her life—and stay out of it.

* * *

Elyssa nudged the mare into a trot, riding west, wondering if she would indeed be better off if she just rode into the sunset, never to be seen or heard from again. As she rode, she reviewed her conversation with Gavin, trying to decide if he had said anything that might give her a clue as to who might have been responsible for his death—or for Ely's. Whoever had killed Gavin must have been lurking about, awaiting the opportunity to strike, but Elyssa didn't recall meeting other traffic on her way to or from Gavin's remote house.

Gripped by frantic restlessness, she sent the mare galloping across the meadow. As the wind whistled past her ears, blocking out all but her thoughts, she wondered how many people around Rawlins would be relieved that Gavin Spencer was gone. He had made no secret of the fact that he had information about more than one individual who wanted dealings concealed.

Elyssa began to think Gavin hadn't seemed desperate for cash after his divorces because he was accepting bribes. A man who found himself in financial straits didn't serve expensive wine to a guest, did he? And Gavin hadn't behaved as if he were desperate for money. He had been confident and self-assured.

That prompted questions for which Elyssa had no answers. Who had paid Gavin a call after she left? He was a police officer—a corrupt one, yes, but he should have been capable of protecting himself unless he wasn't expecting trouble from his companion. Could it have been another woman? Had jealousy turned to deadly violence?

Elyssa slowed the mare and paused on the rise that overlooked the rolling countryside. In the distance, she could see Gavin's rented house and she could barely make out the vehicles parked in the driveway. Investigators, she presumed, searching for clues. She shivered apprehensively. Even if Gavin Spencer had been an arrogant fool, cop-killing drew a great deal of publicity. She wondered how long it would be before the sheriff came calling, posing unnerving questions like the ones Hunter had hurled at her.

She scanned the pasture and the rock canyons that lay several miles to the south. Those canyons had always awed Elyssa, with their breathtaking beauty . . . and their danger.

She smiled bleakly, wondering how long she could hide out in those ravines and that thick underbrush before the sheriff hauled her away. She had the dispirited feeling she could look forward to nothing but barred windows and prison rations for years to come. But what hurt worse was knowing that in her fit of frustration, she had severed the fragile bond that held her to Nathan Hunter. It was over. She had angrily assured him that she wanted nothing more to do with him. Now it looked as if she would spend years in confinement.

Nathan poked his head in the back door of the house to see Claudia industriously cleaning the sink and counters. This was gratifying to behold after the months she'd spent loitering and pant-chasing. Claudia *had* inherited the ability to work hard from her mother.

"Could I talk to you for few minutes?" he asked. Claudia beamed in pleasure. "Sure, Nate. What's up?"

He motioned her outside and gestured for her to climb into his truck.

"What's going on?" she asked.

Once he had driven around the circle drive and headed down the gravel road, he met Claudia's curious frown. "I promised not to press you for answers, but something has come up. I need to know who paid you to stir up trouble between Elyssa and me."

Claudia stared out the window. "I'm afraid he'll take his frustration out on me." Her breath came out in a rush. "I'm trying to make a fresh start, Nate. I've got Timmy and myself to think about."

"Gavin Spencer was found dead this morning," Nathan said with shocking abruptness.

"What?" Claudia's hazel eyes rounded in disbelief. "Oh-migod!"

"I need to know exactly what you were paid to do and by whom." Nathan stared intently at Claudia's blanched face. "I have reason to believe Ely didn't meet with an accident—that both deaths might be linked."

That was stretching the truth, Nathan knew, but he needed the facts Claudia could provide, even if he had to frighten them out of her.

"Oh . . . my . . ." Claudia choked out. "Surely not . . ."

Nathan pulled through the gate that opened into one of the hay fields and turned to face Claudia. "Tell me exactly what you were ordered to do," he demanded.

She lifted a shaky hand to rake her fingers through her hair and swallowed audibly. "I was told to come on to you every chance I had, and to make certain Elyssa believed you and I had been having an affair before she arrived. I told Elyssa that we had been intimate and that all you wanted was her money, and that she shouldn't believe anything you said."

Nathan gnashed his teeth. Elyssa had been suspicious and mistrusting after what Grayson had done to her, and then Claudia had provided her with reasons to believe he had manipulated her. Just when Elyssa had dared to place a little faith in a man, someone came along to tear it down.

"What else, Claudia?" he asked grimly.

"I knew Elyssa would be back late the night I came to the house to seduce you," she reluctantly admitted. "And I was asked to take the accounting file that was in Elyssa's room. Dennis picked it up at the cottage after he got off work."

"Dennis?" Nathan echoed.

Claudia nodded. "He came by every night to see if I had turned up any information that might be beneficial."

"So Dennis paid you for your efforts, so he could keep the partnership in place?"

"Dennis only relayed information," Claudia explained. She peered at Nathan. "It was Virgil who paid me to be an informer. He and I—" She glanced away. "While we were seeing each other, he was slipping me a few dollars for spending money. But I broke off with him."

"How'd he take it?" Nathan persisted.

"He took it as well as he's taken everything else around here," Claudia muttered. "He's been cursing and growling like a rabid dog most of the time, swearing to get even with you and Elyssa for destroying him financially. He told me Gil ordered him to sell off his registered horses to pay his debts."

"I'll bet that went over well," Nathan said with a dry smile.

"You should have heard him ranting." Claudia shook her head in dismay. "I thought Virgil was going to pop his cork. He was mad enough to strangle anyone within arm's length. That's why I was afraid to tell you about him, and I'm probably cutting my own throat by doing it now."

Nathan put the truck in reverse and backed onto the road.

"What are you going to do?" Claudia asked anxiously. "If you tell him I told you any of this—"

"I won't," Nathan promised. "I have so many accusations to hurl at him he won't have time to consider where any of my information came from. Your name won't be mentioned."

Now Nathan had to pin weasley Virgil down and get some straight answers out of him. And he'd better be quick about it or Elyssa would find herself facing murder charges!

Twenty-six

Elyssa trotted the mare southward, oddly drawn to the canyons where she and Ely had both met with disaster. There was something hauntingly compelling about the labyrinth, especially with a brisk wind wailing through the trees. She swore she could hear her father calling to her from beyond the thicket.

Curse it, she had tried so hard to uncover the truth and look where it got her? She knew she was going to have to go to the sheriff and admit to her meeting with Gavin the night he died. She was going to have to face investigators who would probably have her believing that she had killed the corrupt cop!

Elyssa absently rubbed away the tingling sensation in her neck and reined down the slope to see if Les Fykes had located the portion of fence that needed repair. She found Les sprawled on the ground, taking a break and munching on a snack—some of Althea's homemade brownies. The string of fence Elyssa had requested to be replaced was now a wide gap between the mouth of the lower canyons and the low-water bridge.

Les glanced up when Elyssa's mare whinnied a greeting to the roan gelding that was tied to a fence post. "What are you doing out here?" he questioned in surprise.

Elyssa's shoulder lifted in a noncommittal shrug. "I see you're making progress."

Les popped the last bite of brownie in his mouth and nodded in agreement. "I took all the old barbed wire down, rolled it up, and hauled it into the wash in the canyon to prevent erosion. I'm afraid to leave for fear the cows will wander down here and take to the road again."

Elyssa dismounted and strolled down the steep incline to where eroded soil had gathered along the fence row. A frown clouded her brow when she noticed hoofprints and bootprints. She glanced back at Les's muddy boots.

"Did you and your horse get stuck in here?"

"Nearly," Les said as he leisurely climbed to his feet. "We're going to have to do something about this wash. We need to install a gate or metal panels that are more easily replaced when water rushes down the canyons, carrying debris that tears down a quarter mile of fence."

"It looks as if someone came close to getting stuck on the road." She gestured toward the tracks that fishtailed from one bar ditch to the other. "I'm surprised there's any traffic down here. There's nothing but Rawlins' property on three sides and one of the roads dead-ends at the river."

Elyssa frowned, remembering the night she had followed Gavin to this very spot and heard the rustling in the underbrush. The sound hadn't alarmed Gavin, but Elyssa had certainly wondered if a predatory animal had been lurking around. Or a flock of the wild turkeys known to roost in the trees in the canyons.

Les stuffed his hands into his work gloves and grabbed the roll of barbed wire. "Maybe this has become lover's lane for the high-school kids," he ventured. "Out of the way places like this make great locations for submarine races, or whatever they call it these days."

Elyssa wouldn't know about that. Her high-school adventures leaned more toward regaining the use of her leg and hours of reading on weekends at the private girls' school where her mother had sent her.

When she hiked up the slope to swing into the saddle, Les waved and grinned. "If I'm not back by dark, send somebody after me. I may be tangled up in this five-wire fence, up to my knees in mud."

Elyssa reined away, planning to return to the house to face the music. Then her gaze landed on the antiquated barn and the dilapidated cabin nestled by the thickets that lined the winding river. She had almost forgotten about the original homestead her great-grandparents had constructed after the land run of 1892.

It was there she and Virgil had played cowboys and Indians in their younger days. Elyssa vividly remembered the afternoon when Virgil had tied her wrists together and had left her hanging from the rafters of the barn. They'd had many a showdown around the wood-frame shack and barn. Elyssa always lost, of course.

The way things were going, she stood to lose everything . . . and very soon.

Nathan was relieved that his search for Virgil Rawlins took only a half-hour. Virgil's truck was parked beside the huge barn he had constructed for stabling his brood mares and studs—the ones that had cost him an arm and a leg. Nathan could imagine how desperate Virgil had become when faced with the prospect of losing his dream.

To sacrifice even one of his brood mares or studs was probably worse to him than tearing off both arms. The question was, to what extremes would Virgil go to protect his costly investment?

Nathan strode into the barn that was lined with stalls. Virgil was standing at the far end, stroking the muzzle of a mare and murmuring to her as if she were human. Typical, thought Nathan. The mare was offered more affection than Virgil had ever displayed toward his cousin. Elyssa had received nothing but abuse at Virgil's hands, while the horse was being treated like royalty. This testified to the distortion of Virgil's priorities. His selfish dreams were more important than family and friends.

The echo of footsteps brought Virgil's red head around, and

he scowled at the intruder. "Coming to gloat, Nate? Well, don't bother. Just get the hell off my property, since it still *is* mine, for the time being."

"I want to talk to you," Nathan demanded gruffly.

"Well, I don't want to talk to you. I've had enough of you for one lifetime."

"Did you have enough of Gavin Spencer, too?" Nathan baited.

Virgil jerked up his head and glowered mutinously.

Nathan propped himself against the adjacent stall and matched Virgil glare for glare. "I suppose Gavin knew you had given Ely a shove off the canyon rim and expected to be well paid for his silence. Too bad you were short of cash."

Virgil lurched around, teeth bared, eyes flashing. "Oh, no, you don't, you bastard, you're not pinning that on me! You and my bitch of a cousin have done enough already!"

"Come on, Virgil, I know you tried every trick in the book to get Elyssa to side with you and Gil so the ranch could pay your debts. When Elyssa made the mistake of voicing accusations, you ordered the bank to withhold information. And you're also the one who swiped the files of the ranch accounts so Elyssa couldn't use them against you. You've been flying around in desperation for two weeks."

Virgil scoffed at the accusation. "Because the bank company has me by the balls and my cousin decided to cut them off, you think I wasted Gavin?"

"He saw you clipping fences and scattering cattle," Nathan speculated.

"I did no such thing!"

"God, you're incredible," Nathan muttered. "You refuse to own up to your actions."

"I didn't cut the goddamn wire and I didn't kill Spencer!" Virgil all but yelled. "And I sure as hell didn't bump off my uncle, though I wanted to when you convinced him to break the partnership."

"That wasn't my doing."

"Yeah, right." Virgil smirked.

"I just thought you'd like to know I'm giving the information to the sheriff. He'll need the facts while he's investigating Gavin's murder."

When Nathan turned away, Virgil grabbed his arm. Nathan had expected an attack—a desperate attempt to ensure his silence. That wasn't the case, much to his disappointment. Virgil didn't give Nathan the excuse to lay him out.

"I swear to God I didn't have anything to do with Gavin's— or Ely's—death." Virgil's hand clenched on Nathan's forearm, giving him a fierce shake. "I'll admit I had the files swiped and I tried to turn Elyssa against you. And yes, I did cut the wires to buy myself some time and keep you occupied, but I didn't kill anybody. That's the truth!"

"Were you with Gavin Saturday night?" Nathan demanded to know.

"Hell, no. What do you think I am? Gay?"

"Are you saying Gavin was?" Nathan choked incredulously. What the hell was Virgil trying to do here? Throw Nathan off the track?

"Shit, no. You know what a ladies' man Gavin was. When there was a woman within ten feet of him, he couldn't keep his dick in his pants on a bet."

That comment left Nathan wondering if Elyssa had been too embarrassed to tell him the truth about what had happened Saturday night.

Grimly, he stared at Virgil. "I think you're guilty as hell. Do you have an alibi for Saturday night?"

Virgil clamped his lips together and glared daggers.

"Fine, you can answer to Sheriff Bently." Nathan jerked loose and stalked away, ever mindful of the man behind him, prepared for anything. Still, an attack didn't come, much to his surprise. He wanted proof of Virgil's guilt, and the bastard was giving him no satisfaction.

* * *

Elyssa nudged the mare southwest for almost two miles. A wry smile pursed her lips as she wondered if the old homestead wouldn't make a perfect hideout for a fugitive like herself. The only way to get to her was by horseback. There were so many steep hills and meandering creeks in the pasture that cross-country travel was hell on pickups, even harder on squad cars. The river formed a barrier on two sides, protected by dense brush and towering trees, not to mention the quicksand Virgil had threatened to toss Elyssa into if she didn't agree to participate in the war games he dreamed up.

For as long as Elyssa could remember, Cousin Virgil had been her tormentor, a thorn in her side. It left her to wonder if he still was. Maybe he had driven wedges between her and Hunter and had set her up to take the blame for Gavin's death.

Or was someone else involved? she asked herself as she blazed a path through the tall grass and underbrush that had overtaken this portion of the pasture. Although she was reasonably certain Virgil or Dennis Humphrey had schemed with Claudia to cause trouble, it disturbed her that Mo-Joe Denson had been conveniently absent the weekend Gavin died. Could there possibly be some connection? Mo-Joe was curiously secretive about his destination and his weekend activities.

Although Elyssa had nothing against Mo-Joe and she liked him well enough, she had become suspicious by habit. Too much was happening around the ranch to overlook details or possible suspects.

She urged the mare through the gate that separated the old homestead from the pasture. The horse hesitated and glanced around.

"C'mon, girl, it's just the spirits of the Cheyenne whispering through the trees." Elyssa clucked her tongue and forced the mare to go on when she was reluctant to proceed.

If Great-grandmother Rawlins were still alive, Mae would have been filling Elyssa's head with folklore about the Wise One Above who possessed more power than the sun and the Wise One Below. Thunder, Mae had told Elyssa, commanded the summer rain and battled the water monsters that lurked in lakes and rivers. Mae had spoken of the Hanging Road that led to the land of the Wiser One Above where The People made camps and hunted in the afterlife.

Great-grandmother Rawlins claimed to hear the voices of the spirits of the parallel world. Elyssa wished she were so closely attuned to The Beyond. She would dearly love to know who was responsible for sending her father—and Gavin Spencer—to an early grave . . . and who was waiting with wicked glee to see her put on trial for murder.

"Good Lord, Nate! What's with you?" Twig questioned when Nathan wheeled into the driveway and stamped on the brake, fishtailing in the gravel.

"Plenty," Nathan muttered, climbing from the truck. "Where do you want me to start?"

"I don't suppose this is a good time to ask you if it's okay for Valerie to come out tonight."

Nathan didn't have time to bother with Twig's love life when a murderer was running around loose and Elyssa could find herself public enemy number one.

"You and Val can do whatever the hell you like, whenever the hell you want to do it, as many times as you want to do it."

Twig grinned. "Thanks, *Mother,* but I really wasn't asking your permission. I only wondered if Val could stay the night at the house. I'd prefer that she drive back early in the morning rather than late tonight."

Nathan was certain having the bubbly blonde underfoot would take Elyssa's mind off her woes. In case bad came to worse, Val could provide moral support. "That's fine, just don't keep *me* awake all night because you plan to be."

When Twig turned to leave, Nathan frowned. "Where are you going?"

"To saddle a horse to take Timmy for a ride before Val arrives."

"What the hell are we running around here? A ranch or a nursery?" Nathan asked irritably.

"Hey, this was your idea, as I recall. You said since Timmy had a father who didn't give a damn about him, we should all pitch in and give the kid some attention and let Claudia know we're willing to offer support because she turned over a new leaf," Twig reminded him. "Besides, I like kids. I was one myself, you know."

The teasing smile slid off his lips when his attempt at humor failed to amuse Nate. "What's wrong? You look strung out, Nate."

Nathan heaved a frustrated sigh. "Gavin Spencer was killed this weekend. They found his body this morning."

"Holy shit!" Twig staggered back as if he'd suffered a body blow. "We've got a cop killer running loose?"

"He was found in his house, not on the side of a road beside his black and white," Nathan reported.

"A jealous ex-wife then?" Twig presumed.

Nathan wondered how much he should confide in Twig. Nothing, he decided. Since Elyssa had stubbornly refused to explain her involvement with Gavin, Nathan was going on nothing but assumptions. "The police are investigating," he said.

"God, that blows my mind. First it was Ely and now Gavin. People are dropping dead all around Rawlins." Twig shook off the grim thought and headed for the house to round up Timmy.

Nathan then propelled himself toward the bunkhouse, to find Mo-Joe towering over the suitcase that lay open on his bed. "Are you coming in or going out again?"

"Coming in," Mo-Joe replied. "I suppose you want the cash I borrowed for the weekend. I stopped by the bank while I was in town." He reached for his wallet, only to have Nathan fling up his hand in a deterring gesture.

"You can keep the money if you tell me where you were all weekend and with whom."

The good-natured smile slid off Mo-Joe's lips. "I thought

my private business was my own, unless it interfered with my work—which it never does."

"I suppose you heard Gavin was killed this weekend."

"Yeah, I heard it at the grain elevator," Mo-Joe confirmed. "So what has that got to do with my weekend activities?"

"I don't know. Suppose you tell me," Nathan shot back.

Mo-Joe gaped at him in disbelief. "What are you suggesting? That I bumped Spencer off?" When Nathan continued to stare bleakly at him, Mo-Joe scowled. "For God's sake, I wasn't anywhere near Spencer's place. The rumor in town is, Spencer was entertaining some sleazy female and she had enough of him."

"And you know nothing else about it?"

"Why should I? I wasn't here," Mo-Joe insisted.

"I know. That's what bothers me. I'd feel a lot better if I knew where you were and who can verify your alibi, in case it turns out you need one."

Mo-Joe muttered under his breath. "I was in the City."

"It's a big place," Nathan said. "Where were you and with whom?"

"God, I can't believe you're grilling me."

"And I can't believe you're so secretive," Nathan countered.

Mo-Joe snatched up his clothes and slung them into the dresser drawer. "I picked up my kid this weekend, if you have to know."

Nathan did a double take. "What kid?"

"*My* kid. Anything wrong with that?"

"I didn't know you had one."

"Well, I do. She's nine months old, and I only get to see her every six weeks, if I'm lucky."

Nathan was getting the feeling there was a lot he didn't know about Mo-Joe Denson. "Why haven't you mentioned this before?"

Mo-Joe hurled a pair of jeans across the room and watched them drop to the floor. His eyes flashed with resentment. "Because I don't like to talk about it. Nosy people start asking all sorts of questions—like you are now!"

"I wouldn't be nosing into your business if it wasn't important," Nathan assured him.

"And if I tell you, I want it to go no farther than this room . . ." When Nathan nodded agreeably, Mo-Joe continued. "Jillian's mother and I aren't married and never will be. I wasn't good enough for her. Her family threw a ring-tail fit when they found out Melanie was pregnant and I planned to marry her. They offered me a bribe to get rid of me. Before I knew it, they had Melanie believing I took the money.

"Melanie's father shipped her off to live with his sister in Arizona until the baby came. She's only been back in the City for three months, and I can't even talk to her alone because her father is always hovering around, ready to refute anything I say. She's been seeing some upstart executive her father hand-picked for her, and I only get to see my daughter if I don't fuck up dear daddy's plans."

"You were with your daughter all weekend?" Nathan prodded.

"No." Mo-Joe scowled sourly. "I was allowed to keep Jillian Saturday before taking her back to her grandfather. I spent Saturday night in my motel room with a couple of six-packs, cursing the fact that Jillian changes so much from one short visit to the next that it drives me nuts!"

Mo-Joe picked up his suitcase and hurled it toward the closet. "Anything else you want to know about the shit I put up with because I want Melanie and Jillian in my life and Melanie's son-of-a-bitch of a father makes sure I only get the scraps he lets me have?"

"No, and I'm sorry I had to ask," Nathan apologized.

"If you think I want to see someone taken out, you're right," Mo-Joe muttered. "But not Spencer. It's that snobbish bastard who feeds Melanie so many lies about me I don't stand a chance in hell of having her with me!"

Inhaling a deep breath, Mo-Joe struggled for control of his

temper. "Now, if you don't mind, I'd like to do the rest of my brooding in private so I'll be ready to saunter into the house for supper and look as if I don't have a goddamn care in the world!"

Nathan exited the bunkhouse, wishing he'd never entered.

Elyssa tied her mare to a tree and stood staring up at the dilapidated wooden cabin that dated back to the beginnings of a cattle empire. She smiled ruefully, envisioning the shriveled old woman she remembered from childhood, trying to imagine what Mae might have looked like at the turn of the century.

Great-grandmother Rawlins, so the story went, could take to the warpath when her temper was provoked. The Cheyenne might have been herded onto a reservation and forced to adopt the white man's ways, but Elyssa knew of one Cheyenne wife who had ruled the roost. But Mae had needed no bow, arrows, or hunting knives, not when Great-grandfather Rawlins worshipped the ground she walked on.

Ely had told Elyssa that his grandfather had been obsessed with buying up plenty of land to ensure Mae never had to feel hemmed in. Mae had wanted a home that breathed, and the old homestead breathed, all right. At one time, wide windows had graced all sides of the house, except to the north. Peter Rawlins had put his foot down when it came to blocking out the Blue Norther winds in winter. But every new wing that had been added to the original home contained spacious windows set in to pacify Mae. Great-grandmother Rawlins could stand in any room and view the towering trees that sheltered the winding river.

And Peter Rawlins had made certain his Cheyenne wife was content with him as well as their home. He and Mae had shared that special kind of love that doesn't come around very often. They had experienced that sense of rightness and satisfaction in belonging to each other.

Elyssa wondered how it would feel to be loved so devotedly.

Pensively, she ambled toward the house. Rusty hinges creaked as she opened the door to step inside. The abandoned homestead ached with emptiness, echoed with long-forgotten memories of other times, other ways of life, the merging of an Indian and a white heritage that had created a dynasty—a dynasty Elyssa had severed for all time.

The thought struck her, sharp as an arrow. She wondered what her great-grandparents would say about splitting the ranch in half. They had worked and toiled, had purchased land from disgruntled pioneers who didn't have the fortitude to battle the floods and droughts and to make the land prosper.

Still, one had to weigh tradition against present-day problems and adapt, Elyssa reminded herself. She had salvaged what she could of the ranch. She hoped her ancestors would understand . . .

She frowned when she wandered into what had once been the master bedroom at seeing hoes, shovels, and fertilizer applicators strewn on the floor. It looked as if someone had gathered tools for cultivating a garden. Elyssa wandered into the other rooms, finding nothing else unusual before she ventured back outside. She glanced toward the river, noting the clumps of dried grass encircling flowering weeds beneath the canopy of overhanging trees along the river.

When her gaze landed on the barn, where she had spent many an hour climbing in the loft and swinging on the ropes that had once been used to hoist bundles of hay for storage, Elyssa strode off. The barn wasn't as large as she remembered, but it was still a gargantuan structure. State-of-the art at the turn of the century, no doubt. Now it was too outdated and too far removed from the modernized ranch house to be useful. The homestead had been fenced off from the pasture and abandoned, to remain as it had been in the pioneer days.

Elyssa glanced at her watch. She really should head back to the house before she missed supper. But she wasn't all that anxious to return and find Sheriff Bently standing on the porch. She much preferred to investigate the barn, for old time's sake. It could very well be the last time she had the chance to walk in her great-grandparents' footsteps.

The minute she strode inside, memories came flooding back in full force. How she had anticipated her yearly visits to the ranch, and especially to this antiquated homestead. There was a compelling peacefulness about this isolated place that put Elyssa closely in touch with herself and restored her inner spirit.

She inhaled a deep, purifying breath and smiled in satisfaction. When she was within the confines of the old barn, the problems of the outside world seemed a million miles away. It was as if she were the only resident on the planet.

Smiling in remembrance, she reached out to touch the frayed rope that was tied to a towering wooden beam. This was where Cousin Virgil had left her hanging like a carcass of beef, the same place where he had locked her in the wooden granary as if it were a jail cell. At other times, they had climbed into the loft to fashion straw houses out of loose hay, and Elyssa had returned home only to have her mother fuss at her for looking like a filthy scarecrow.

Lost to nostalgia, she strolled past the broken stalls that had once housed her great-grandfather's milk cows, mules, and horses. The names of the animals had been etched in the wood and her own name was chiseled in the cedar supporting beam that stood in the center of the barn. Elyssa came to a halt and chortled at the whimsical memories that floated through her mind.

ELYSSA LOVES?

She remembered scratching that phrase in the wood with Virgil's pocketknife. Of course, at age ten, she hadn't known who she loved or what love really was. She wondered if love would always be a big question mark to her, wondered if anyone would ever really love her just for herself. She doubted it.

Shaking herself loose from that dismal thought, she strode toward the ladder that led to the loft.

"Elyssa?"

Startled, Elyssa glanced around to see Les Fykes silhouetted by the shafts of sunlight that poured through the barn door.

"Are you all right? What are you doing in here?" he questioned anxiously.

"I was just wading through old memories."

"In the hay loft?" Les asked, staring at the planks above him.

"I haven't made it up there yet," she said with a smile.

"It's getting late and we're both going to miss supper. I think you'd better ride back with me."

Elyssa wondered if he had received word that the sheriff was looking for her. He might have been sent out to round her up without alarming her. "Is something wrong, Les?"

"I didn't want you to get hurt out here," he replied.

"As you can see, I'm perfectly fine."

Les glanced apprehensively around him. "I wouldn't hang around this dilapidated barn and cabin if I were you," he advised. "It's liable to collapse on top of you."

"It looks sturdy enough to me," Elyssa said. "The wood has to be petrified by now. If an Oklahoma wind storm hasn't blown it down yet, I doubt it ever will."

"All the same, I'd keep my distance."

"Well, someone's been wandering around the place," Elyssa replied. "I found gardening tools stashed in the cabin."

"Oh?" His gaze leaped back to the house and then shifted to Elyssa who was leaning against the ladder that led to the loft. "I'll check on it tomorrow and gather up what's laying around."

Les seemed very ill at ease, she noted. God, he *had* ridden out to tell her the sheriff was looking for her, and he was trying to gather the nerve to give her the bad news!

"We'd better go back to the house," he insisted. "It's getting late."

"You go on ahead," Elyssa said. "I'll be fine. I just want to explore the loft." Without ado, she started up the ladder while Les stalked off, muttering to himself.

Twenty-seven

Twig ambled out the back door of the ranch house, toting Timmy on his shoulders. "Nate, do you know where Elyssa is? I want to tell her Val is coming."

"You mean she isn't in the house?" Nathan questioned in surprise.

"Althea and Claudia haven't seen her all afternoon."

Nathan scowled. Surely Elyssa hadn't taken his snide remark about hiding out like a fugitive seriously! "She must still be out in the pasture. Take a rain check on giving Timmy a horseback ride," he ordered. "We better go find Elyssa before dark."

Twig glanced up at the toddler whose fingers were clenched in his hair for support and then peered at Nathan's concerned expression. "What's wrong?"

An odd chill trickled down Nathan's spine. Three weeks ago, at about the same time of day, he had gone searching for Ely who hadn't returned from his ride. He grimaced at the unpleasant vision that came to mind. He kept seeing himself standing on the cliff, staring down at the tangled body half-hidden in the brush, feeling sick all over. That same feeling assailed him again.

You're letting your imagination run away with itself, Nathan thought. Elyssa is just fine. She's simply reluctant to return to the house because she expects a visit from the sheriff.

Before Nathan could reply, the crunch of gravel heralded

the sheriff's arrival. "Shit," Nathan grumbled. "If Virgil sicced Bently on Elyssa—"

"Elyssa?" Twig's thick brows jackknifed. "What the hell are you talking about?"

Muttering, Nathan stomped around the house to see Bently unfolding his bulky body from beneath the steering wheel.

"I'm looking for Elyssa Rawlins Cutler," the sheriff said in a businesslike voice. "Is she here?"

"Not exactly," Nathan answered.

Bently's eyes narrowed suspiciously. "Meaning?"

"She's out riding."

"I have a few questions to ask her. When do you expect her back? I plan to wait."

Nathan was afraid of that. "I'll ride out and see if I can locate her," he volunteered.

Twig deposited the wriggling Timmy in Bently's chunky arms. "I'll go help Nate. You can take Timmy back to the house. His mother is in there."

Bently stared at the child who was playing with the buttons on his uniform and then at the two men who jogged around the side of the house. Resigned to waiting for only God knew how long, Bently tramped toward the front door to return Timmy to his mother.

"Nate, are you going to tell me what the hell's going on or not?" Twig questioned as he scooped up a saddle from the tack room.

"I can't. The less you know, the better. You won't have to answer questions because you weren't around, and it doesn't matter anyway." He stalked toward the corral, laden down with equipment and a nagging apprehension that was heavier than the saddle.

"I hope you realize you're talking in circles," Twig grumbled. "And how long is this thing I'm not supposed to know anything about, and am better off not getting involved in, going to take? Valerie should be here any minute."

"Just shut up and saddle a horse," Nathan snapped. "Ricky!"

Twig flinched when Nathan's booming voice blasted holes in his eardrums. The horses bolted and scattered, turning their rumps to the two men who tried to grab their halters.

"Well done," Twig mocked sarcastically. "Now you've got the horses spooked."

"They aren't the only ones."

Twig eased up beside an Appaloosa gelding, sparing Nathan a quick glance before patting the horse's tense neck. He had always considered Nathan a stable individual who didn't allow his emotions to run rampant, but the man was behaving very strangely and he was talking in riddles. Twig decided to keep his mouth shut and follow along, asking no more questions since Nathan wasn't in the mood to provide answers.

With Ricky trotting alongside the horses, Nathan and Twig let themselves through the pasture gate. Nathan spurred his gelding, feeling the same frantic sense of urgency he had experienced the day Ely hadn't returned on time, reliving the sickening grief of finding his mentor and friend lying at the base of the canyon. He suddenly wished he could sprout wings, soar like a hawk across the ranch to locate Elyssa. Damn it, she could be any where and he didn't know which section to search first. He wished he could divide himself into equal pieces and ride off in all directions at once.

The fact that Sheriff Bently was waiting at the house filled Nathan with a sense of foreboding. He knew the incident was going to cause Elyssa embarrassment. Reporters would love to get hold of this story and milk it for all it was worth, dramatizing and sensationalizing it until the truth became fiction. Goddamn it! He didn't want her to have to endure that kind of humiliation or to be stuffed under an investigative microscope and picked apart with tweezers!

That was why she hadn't returned to the house, Nathan tried to convince himself. She didn't want to face the inevitable questions and news flashes. She was trying to delay the con-

frontations, granting herself time to rehearse her explanation
and get her emotions under control. She was probably delib-
erating whether to disclose what really happened on her fifteen
birthday and the bitter resentment she'd harbored for Gavin all
these years. Nathan had assured her that if she didn't mention
the incident, Virgil would come forward to reveal the damning
facts.

Good ole Virgil, Nathan thought with disgust. He'd bet the
farm that Virgil had tipped Sheriff Bently off, but Nathan knew
he had probably provoked that weasel into doing it.

Guilt sank its teeth into him. He had only wanted to force
a confession out of Virgil, and he had made things worse.
Damn, why hadn't he given Bently a call and pointed the sheriff in Virgil's direction, as he had threatened to do? If Virgil
admitted to the crimes Nathan was sure he'd committed, maybe
Elyssa wouldn't have to be questioned.

Nathan had admitted he handled Elyssa poorly and he had
screwed up royally by confronting Virgil. Who the hell did he
think he was anyway? Some hotshot detective? Some silver-
tongued lawyer . . . ?

That thought made Nathan flinch. He had the unshakable
feeling Elyssa was going to need a good lawyer real soon, and
there wasn't going to be a damned thing he could do to protect
her.

Elyssa climbed up the ladder into the loft and smiled fondly
in remembrance. Prickly tingles skated down her spine as she
stared up at the rafters, noting that pinpoints of sunlight twinkled like stars through the holes of the wood-shingled roof.
When she was a child, she had ascended into this loft, feeling
as if she were walking into a planetarium. The dome of darkness, embedded with sparkles of light, gave her the feeling of
being an entity in the universe.

Inching along the wall, Elyssa unlatched the door to let a
flood of sunlight pour into the darkened loft. Her breath caught

in her throat when she gazed at the river from her bird's-eye view. For a few glorious moments, she forgot the turmoil brewing around her, the aching emptiness that had hounded her since she had tried to write Hunter out of her life and hadn't quite convinced her foolish heart that was for the best.

Elyssa knew why Great-grandmother Mae had come to love this obscure homestead and had put up a fuss when her two grandsons had insisted she move to the cottage on the hill after Peter Rawlins died. Of all the places Elyssa had ever been, this old homestead felt like the one where she belonged . . .

Suddenly Elyssa understood Nathan Hunter's fond attachment to Rawlins Ranch. *Home . . . the place where he belonged.* For years, Hunter had been a vagabond, following in his restless father's footsteps, searching for that part of him that had been missing. He had found peace and contentment here, even though Gil and Virgil had tried their best to rout him from Ely's life. He didn't want to leave the place where his heart was any more than Elyssa wanted to rout him out of her heart.

The painful truth was, she was in love with Hunter, despite all her suspicions, despite her family's attempt to turn her against him. The awareness had come too late; she hadn't had the chance to enjoy being in love. But she couldn't deny her deepest feelings while she stood gazing out at the breathtaking beauty of a home that had been in her family for generations. Here, she was in complete touch with herself, with her thoughts, with the most private feelings in her heart.

Wearing a melancholy smile, Elyssa glanced down at the makeshift ladder, two-by-fours nailed to the outside of the barn up to the loft. How many times had she made that climb from the outside to reach the straw houses she had fashioned from hay?

Elyssa turned away from the loft door and received the jolt of her life. Although she wasn't an expert on the subject, she had the inescapable feeling that the dried plants strewn across the barn loft were marijuana! She suddenly remembered the well-mulched weeds she had seen growing beneath the canopy of trees along the river. She had made no connection between the plants and the gardening tools in the old cabin until she noticed the harvested crop in the loft . . .

I need to go check on some grass . . .

Her father's words exploded in her mind, and Elyssa staggered backward, bracing herself against the wall. She remembered hearing the click on the phone line the day she spoke to her father. Someone had been listening to their conversation. That same someone must have felt threatened.

Elyssa lurched around and headed for the ladder. She didn't have a clue as to what connection Gavin Spencer's death might have had—if any—to her father's not-so-accidental accident, but she had a pretty good idea why Ely had died. It wasn't because of his argument with Gil about splitting the ranch; it was because of the covert cultivation of marijuana on a secluded section of the ranch.

With fiendish haste, Elyssa descended the ladder and scampered out of the barn. A shriek burst from her lips when an arm shot out to snare her. She struggled to escape until a pocketknife stabbed at her throat.

"I really wish you would've come back to the house with me," Les Fykes muttered. "I placed an anonymous call to the sheriff's office after lunch and Bently should be there waiting to question you about Gavin's death. It would have been simpler for you to take the rap without knowing what was going on."

Suddenly everything fell neatly into place in Elyssa's mind, like a jigsaw puzzle. Les Fykes was the man who disposed of Gavin after she left him on Saturday night. No wonder Gavin didn't appear to be hurting for cash. He was probably on the take. He might even have been transporting the illegal crop. Who would have suspected a cop who made late-night rounds and stopped on abandoned roads to make connections with his partner?

Elyssa well remembered the sagging fence by the low-water bridge and the tracks beside the road. Les was obviously hauling his crop out by horseback to meet Gavin who distributed the goods. Gavin was certainly in a position to make connections with known drug dealers.

What an ingenious racket those two men had organized, using the irrigation from the river for the crop and an abandoned barn for storing their stash of illegal drugs. It would be difficult for DEA agents to track down the sheltered crop with aerial surveillance. And at the estimated street value of eight hundred dollars per plant, Gavin and Les had been doing a thriving business.

"I didn't want to get rid of your father," Les grumbled as he propelled Elyssa away from the barn. "But he stumbled onto our stash and I had to drive him off the rim of the canyon to silence him before he contacted the OSBN and they started asking a lot of questions."

In dismay, Elyssa watched Les give her mare a hard kick in the rump, sending the horse thundering away from the homestead so it would be difficult to trace Elyssa to this location.

"You're kidding yourself if you think people won't start asking questions," she said as Les shepherded her through the thick grass.

He chuckled heartily. "And you're kidding yourself if you don't think the sheriff is going to conclude that you're trying to elude the authorities because you're guilty of disposing of Gavin. While they're trying to hunt you down, you'll be stashed in the old root cellar, waiting for my return. No one will be surprised to learn you hid out and then sneaked back to the house during the night to get a pickup and make your getaway."

His hand thrust into her pocket to grab the keys and he smiled devilishly as he dangled them in front of her. "When you and your dad's truck wind up taking a wrong turn off the bridge into the river, Gavin's murderer will have met her fitting end."

Les used the toe of his boot to kick open the door to the root cellar. She stared into the gloomy dungeon where Great-grandmother Rawlins had once stored the labors from her garden. A musty smell rose up from the antiquated cellar like fog, clogging Elyssa's senses.

A horrified yelp burst from her lips when Les gave her an unexpected shove that sent her tumbling down the rotted steps into the black abyss. Before she could untangle herself from the broken canning jars, and whatever else she had landed on, Les slammed the door shut. With sickening dread, she listened to him drop the two-by-four latch into the metal bracket, sealing her in pitch-black darkness.

She groped around the cellar, trying to get her bearings, hoping beyond hope that she could locate an object that would serve as a makeshift club to beat down the door. She sincerely hoped Great-grandmother Mae had left something behind that would facilitate her escape. If not, she was going to be taking a midnight swim in the river.

She wondered how cold quicksand was this time of year . . .

Nathan swore foully when he spied the riderless black mare grazing with the herd of Limousin cattle that were silhouetted against the fiery crimson sunset. Even though he was worried as hell, he breathed a sigh of relief that he hadn't found the mare wandering near the rim of the red rock canyons. There was a chance that Elyssa's mount had bolted away from its tether when she'd dismounted to take a stroll. Nathan refused to think the worst, not yet, not until he was left with no other choice. He was not going to let his imagination run away with him, forcing him to leap to ill-founded conclusions . . .

A distant whistle caught Nathan's attention. He and Twig swiveled in their saddles to see Les Fykes waving his hat over his head. Nathan nudged his mount and thundered off with Twig and Ricky following at his heels.

Les smiled nonchalantly in greeting. "I just finished up that stretch of weak fence Elyssa mentioned at lunch," he calmly reported. "I hope I'm not late for supper. I'm starved."

"Have you seen Elyssa?" Nathan questioned without preamble.

"Not since lunch," Les lied, still smiling. "Why? Is she missing?"

Nathan gestured toward the riderless horse in the distance. "She went riding hours ago. We thought maybe her mount broke loose and left her afoot."

Les leisurely scratched his head and glanced across the pasture. "I haven't seen anything of her. Wherever she was riding, it wasn't on the canyon or river section or I would have seen her go by. Did you try the north ranges?"

"Not yet." Nathan shifted uneasily in the saddle. Before long, it was going to be too dark to search for her.

"I'd help you track her down, but I've got my horse loaded down with wire and tools," Les said, gesturing to the bulging bags behind his saddle. "But I'll keep my eyes open and take the long way back to the house to see if I can locate her. Should I saddle a fresh mount and bring Skeeter and Mo-Joe back with me to search for her?"

"No, Twig and I will take care of it," Nathan grumbled.

"Well, if you're sure."

"Les?" Nathan frowned curiously. "Why didn't you take a truck around to the low-water bridge to patch the fence? It would have been easier than packing wire and tools with you."

Les shrugged nonchalantly. "I never gave it a thought since I'm use to working off the back of a horse." He wasn't about to tell Nate he had gone by horseback to tend his secluded cash crop before repairing the fence.

Les reined toward the ranch house. A wry smile twitched his lips as he rode off. This was going to be as simple as silencing Gavin after he'd demanded hush money and a larger cut of the profits for transporting drugs. Elyssa had provided Les with the perfect setup for the crime by arriving at Gavin's house ahead of him. After eavesdropping on Gavin's thwarted tryst, Fykes had made quick work of the double-crossing cop who had begun to make a pest of himself.

Disposing of Elyssa would provide the sheriff with a simple explanation of Gavin's death. The sheriff would naturally come to the conclusion that she had gotten frantic and had attempted to escape before the she could be questioned. In her haste to outrun the law, she had met with an accident. It was perfect. No one would go snooping around the old homestead because the missing truck would lead the sheriff to the river bridge to find Elyssa's water-logged body.

All Les had to do was play it cool for a few more days. The furor would die down and things would be back to normal. In another year, he could pack up and leave Rawlins Ranch with a tidy profit from his marijuana cultivation. No one would be the wiser.

Long after dark, Nathan and Twig returned to the house, leading the riderless mare. Nathan blamed himself for Elyssa's disappearance. He kept remembering how hard he had come down on her early that afternoon in his attempt to wring a confession out of her. What he had done, instead, was alarm her into doing something rash and desperate.

He believed he had put the fear of God into her, and she had gone off on foot to escape the damning questions the sheriff intended to ask about Gavin's death. Not that Nathan thought for one minute Elyssa was responsible, of course. Too bad he hadn't reassured her of that instead of jumping down her throat, furious that she wouldn't confide in him.

Nathan hadn't said any of the things he had wanted to say to her. He had stood upon his injured pride and let Elyssa think he didn't give a damn if she called it quits, or that he wasn't going to lift a finger to help her when she was in trouble. He had been hurting, and he had taken it out on Elyssa. Now only God knew where she was!

"Ray? Is Elyssa all right?" Valerie questioned as the two men swung from their saddles. Her gaze landed on the riderless horse, and her breath caught in her throat. "Oh, my God! Where is she? What happened?"

Twig wrapped a comforting arm around Valerie. "We don't know exactly. We found Elyssa's horse, but not her. We'll have to wait until morning to search for her."

"Elyssa?" An unfamiliar voice caught Nathan's attention. He wheeled toward the back porch to see a tall, elegantly dressed middle-aged woman poised beneath the porch light, looking like an older version of a model straight out of *Vogue*.

"Who the hell is that?" Nathan grumbled in question.

"It's Ellie's mother," Valerie informed him. "When I got here, Althea told me the sheriff was waiting to question Ellie about that cop's death. I thought I should call Jessica and Daniel. They brought Bernard Gresham with them, in case Elyssa needed legal counsel."

"Well, shit." Nathan scowled at the news. "I hope the hell you didn't notify the TV stations while you were at it."

"I was just trying to help," Valerie murmured.

"Do me a favor and leave well enough alone next time," Nathan muttered. "I would have preferred to keep this quiet. If Virgil and Gil get wind of this, Elyssa's picture will be splattered all over the damned papers and on every TV in the state."

"Hey, take it easy, Nate," Twig snapped. "Val was worried."

"So am I, but you don't see me calling everybody I know, do you?"

"I'm sorry," Valerie whispered apologetically.

"Yeah, you're sorry and I get to face Jessica. I'm sure that's going to be fun and games." Nathan wheeled around and stalked off, leaving Twig to unsaddle the horses.

"Where is my daughter?" Jessica demanded sharply.

Nathan peered up to the porch to survey the regal woman

who had dealt Ely Rawlins such misery and had prevented him from sharing his life with his only daughter. Strikingly attractive though Jessica still was, there was an iciness about her refined features that repelled Nathan. She possessed none of Elyssa's warmth and wholesome vitality. No, Jessica seemed fascinating but cold.

"Nathan Hunter, I presume." Jessica looked down her nose at the dusty cowboy who loomed on the step below her. *"Where* is my daughter?"

"I don't have the slightest idea," Nathan replied as he stepped onto the porch. "My guess is, she's avoiding questioning."

"And you are incapable of tracking her down," Jessica said with a disdainful sniff. "I knew it was a mistake for her to come back here and get involved with a cowboy."

Nathan was *not* in a good mood. Jessica was spoiling what was left of his disposition, and she didn't seem to care how close she came to having her elegant features rearranged. Nathan couldn't remember wanting to slap a woman as much as he wanted to take a shot at this haughty snob.

"At least *I* care what becomes of her," he said stonily. "I'm not sure *you* do."

Jessica recoiled. "Your insolence will cost you dearly, Mr. Hunter. I will see to it that you don't get your hands on *my* daughter or *her* money."

Nathan smiled nastily as he reached around Jessica to open the door. When she made a display of removing herself from his proximity, as if he were too filthy to touch her, Nathan bit back a laugh. Althea had described Jessica accurately. The woman was a bitch.

"Excuse me, ma'am," he drawled in a mocking parody of courtesy. "I don't have time to stand here exchanging threats and insults with you. Is the sheriff still here?"

"Yes," she gritted out, glaring contemptuously at him.

Without another word, Nathan strode inside to find that his home had been invaded by several uninvited guests. Daniel

Cutler came as a pleasant surprise. The man actually seemed overwrought because his stepdaughter was missing, and he was outraged that anyone could possibly believe Elyssa had been involved in a murder. While Jessica did nothing but issue challenges and cast aspersions, Daniel was eager to help in any way he could. The sheriff, however, was another matter. Bently had had his knees whacked often enough by Timmy's rubber hammer to be in a foul, impatient mood.

"Well? Where is she?" he demanded.

"I don't know."

Bently's fuzzy brows furrowed on his broad forehead. "You don't know or you won't say?"

"I don't know," Nathan clarified. "We found her horse in the pasture but she was nowhere to be seen."

"So we can presume we have a fugitive on our hands."

"Come on, Sheriff, what could Elyssa possibly have done to warrant all this suspicion?" Nathan questioned as he dropped down on the sofa beside Bently.

"I received a tip this afternoon that she was seen at Spencer's home Saturday night. That makes her a suspect."

The news had Nathan scowling. Who the hell had set Elyssa up with that shrewd tactic? he wondered.

Bently levered his bulky body off the couch and adjusted the waistband of his trousers around his rotund belly. "I'm putting out an APB. Right now, she's our prime suspect." His narrowed gaze focused on Nathan. "If she turns up later, you *will* let me know, won't you?"

Nathan reluctantly nodded, then watched the sheriff lumber toward the hall. "Damn it to hell!"

Before Nathan could compose himself, questions started flying, everyone demanding to know what was going on. Nathan explained why the sheriff had come, and he described his own futile attempt to locate Elyssa. He also made the abrupt announcement that he wanted his home to himself and that he would be in touch the minute he had any new developments to report.

"If I can be of any help, just give me a call," Bernard Gresham insisted. "If worse comes to worst, I'll see to it that Elyssa has the best defense attorney in the state. This whole mess is ridiculous!"

Nathan smiled appreciatively at the gray-haired lawyer. The man did seem to have a sincere interest in Elyssa.

When Bernard had filed past, Daniel placed a business card in Nathan's hand. "Please contact me the second you know anything," he requested. "I don't want Elyssa to have to go through this humiliating ordeal alone. Her mother and I want to be there for her."

Nathan grumbled under his breath when Jessica sauntered toward him with her nose in the air, refusing to leave.

"I would like a private word with you before I go, Mr. Hunter," she demanded.

Nathan smiled wickedly as he led Jessica into the office and closed the door behind him. Jessica stepped back apace when she spied the lifelike portrait above the mantel, with gratification, Nathan watched the color drain from her face. He made a point of seating himself in Ely's chair, forcing Jessica to confront him and the portrait of her ex-husband.

"What can I do for you?" he inquired as he leaned back to prop his boots on the edge of the desk.

With visible distaste, Jessica appraised his nonchalant pose. "Elyssa tells me that she has become involved with you, obviously at a time of extreme vulnerability—and against good judgment."

Nathan ignored the insult. "Did she?"

Despite his irritation with Jessica, he was pleased to hear that Elyssa had mentioned him. She obviously wasn't as ashamed of their relationship as Jessica thought she should be.

"Yes, much to my dismay." Jessica primly folded her arms over her chest and ambled across the room, turning her back on Ely's portrait. "I'm sure you're flattered by her attention, but I am also certain you realize that nothing is ever going to come of this"—Jessica glanced briefly at Nathan—"this reckless fling. Elyssa is part of the social and corporate world. The two of you have very little in common."

"And I would never fit in, being just a dumb cowboy," Nathan finished for her.

Jessica smiled in that aloof way of hers that got on Nathan's nerves. "No, Mr. Hunter, you definitely would not belong in Elyssa's world." Retrieving her checkbook from her purse, Jessica made a dramatic display of writing out a sum to Nathan. "I think twenty-five thousand dollars will be enough to convince you to call an end to this ludicrous affair. I will see to it that Elyssa leaves you in complete control of her agricultural investments while she is jet-hopping for her father's corporate world."

"*Step*father," Nathan corrected through gritted teeth.

Jessica ignored that. She simply tore off the check and presented it to Nathan. "I *will* be able to count on you to let Elyssa down easy, won't I?"

Nathan returned her frigid smile and accepted the check. "I'll let Elyssa down nice and easy," he assured her.

"Good. I thought I could count on you to be reasonable."

Nathan watched Jessica abruptly leave the office, silently wishing her in perdition. He had just stashed the check in his shirt pocket when Althea materialized at the office door.

"What did the Queen Bitch want?" she demanded to know.

Nathan chuckled at the disgruntled expression on Althea's plain features. "My cooperation."

"She wants you out of Elyssa's life, doesn't she?" Althea muttered under her breath. "Don't listen to that woman. She is trouble. Always was, always will be. She no more cares what is best for Elyssa than she can fly to Mars. Elyssa belongs here. When she was a child, she came to life the minute she stepped through the front door, and she shriveled up inside each time Ely took her back to her mother in the City. Jessica is nothing but a snob who demands to have her way and tries to make life miserable for anyone who crosses her. I think—"

Althea snapped her mouth shut when she noticed the

amused grin teasing the corners of Nathan's mouth. "Okay, so I was eavesdropping," she admitted unrepentantly. "I've known all along that you and Elyssa had something going. And I, for one, think it would work out dandy if the Queen Bitch would crawl back under her twenty-four-karat gold rock and leave you two alone. Without Gil and Virgil around here, this ranch could be a real home for the first time since I can remember. And I'll tell you something else, Nate, if you give in to that uppity snob, you're a damned fool!"

Nathan chuckled at Althea's loud outburst. "Thank you for the compliment."

"You're welcome." Althea whirled about and then halted in her tracks. "By the way, thanks for whatever you said to get Claudia back on track. Now if I can just get *you* on track, things will be just fine around here!"

Smiling at Althea's uncharacteristic outburst, Nathan climbed to his feet. Late though it was, he knew he wasn't going to be able to sleep. He didn't expect the hired hands to scour the countryside in search of Elyssa, but he was going to saddle a fresh mount and do what he could to locate her.

He was just on his way out the back door when Twig and Valerie stepped onto the porch, wrapped arm in arm.

Nathan handed Twig a walkie-talkie. "I'll be in touch if I find any clues."

Twig nodded agreeably. "I'll keep it with me at all times."

The porch light revealed Twig's blush, and Nathan bit back a chuckle, knowing full well what Twig was thinking. It might prove inconvenient to have a walkie-talkie beside the bed if Nathan's timing was bad.

"I'll keep in touch," Nathan murmured before he walked off the porch.

Equipped with a battery-operated spotlight, a horse that wasn't easily spooked during night riding, and faithful Ricky at his heels, Nathan headed west. Funny, the twenty-five-thou-sand-dollar check in his pocket didn't even begin to compensate for the frustration of wondering where the hell Elyssa was. All the money in the world wouldn't be enough to console him if she met with disaster. He had the uneasy feeling her disappearance didn't have as much to do with the sheriff's visit as he preferred to think. He hadn't shared this concern with anyone else, but deep down, he was worried as hell.

Twenty-eight

Elyssa had been floundering around the root cellar, tripping over broken jars and groping for an object with which to break down the door. She was certain the weathered, rotted wood could be smashed to smithereens with enough determined blows. Thus far, her own head was the hardest object she knew of in the root cellar.

She finally located two three-gallon crocks that Great-grandmother Mae had used to distill the wine she made from grapes. She hoisted one heavy crock up in her arms and stumbled toward the door. Swinging the crock in an arc, she clanked it against the door until her arms gave out. After panting for breath for several minutes, she began the process all over again. Though it was impossible to measure time, she swore she had spent hours pounding on the door, yet all she'd received for her efforts were screaming muscles and burning lungs.

After the first porcelain crock shattered from abuse, Elyssa stumbled across the cellar to retrieve the second. Much time passed while she hammered on the door, wondering if she would ever make any headway. But finally the aged bolts that held the metal bracket in place shook loose from the rotted wood. Elyssa stepped up on the crock and, balanced on one foot, snaked her arm through the narrowing opening to nudge the two-by-four latch off the sagging bracket.

Free at last! Now, if only she could reach the ranch house without encountering Les Fykes. She knew what he planned to do; she just didn't know when he intended to do it. Without her watch she didn't know how much time had elapsed or whether she would have a chance to notify the sheriff so he could catch Les Fykes in the act of attempting to commit his third murder.

Bracing her hands on either side of the crumbling stone hatchway, Elyssa hauled herself out of her dungeon to inhale a long-awaited breath of fresh air. The Oklahoma moon hung like a gigantic silver globe in the night sky as she glanced toward the distant road that dead-ended at the river. There was no sign of approaching headlights. She figured Les planned to drive as far as the road would allow before hiking off cross-country to retrieve her. Hopefully, she would be long gone when he arrived.

After dusting the cobwebs off her, Elyssa closed and secured the door and then limped off, thankful she was still alive. She was sure Les would have disposed of her already if he hadn't wanted her death to look like an accident. People who drowned after nose-diving their pickups into rivers weren't bearing other wounds when retrieved from the water. She was grateful that Les had been so meticulous in plotting his crime; otherwise, she would already be a goner.

She had walked two miles, taking a wide berth around the red rock canyons, when she noticed the floating spotlight in the distance. Either a UFO was about to land or someone was searching for her. She had no idea who was holding the light, and she wasn't taking any chances, not with Les running around loose. For all she knew he could have altered his plan or purposely misled her. You couldn't trust a murderer, especially one as nonchalant and deadly as Les Fykes.

The man had totally deceived Elyssa with his laid-back manner, his seeming interest in the ranch, and his respectful attitude toward her. Of course, she did admit she had been far more attuned to everything Hunter said and did, wondering if he was the one who was deceiving her, to pay much attention to Les Fykes.

God, when she recalled all the suspicion she had directed toward Hunter she was filled with regret. Hunter had told her at the onset of this three-week ordeal that he was going to be the best friend she had. She had refused to trust him, but time had proved he had never lied to her and he was innocent of every accusation heaped on him. She had been afraid to trust the one man who *had* been honest with her because she knew he was the one who had the power to hurt her most. That made sense to Elyssa, but she doubted Hunter could understand her tangled reasoning.

If she survived being framed for murder, she was definitely going to beg Hunter's forgiveness. After all the anguish she had put him through, he deserved her trust and plenty of compensation. Elyssa promised to see that he got it.

When the spotlight swerved toward her, she dived to the ground and lay there like a slug, afraid to move for fear of meeting up with Les Fykes again.

"Damn it, Elyssa, where are you!"

She had never been so glad to hear Hunter's booming baritone! On her feet in a single bound, she dashed toward the spotlight.

Ricky barked his head off when an incongruous shadow bounded toward him, and Nathan's usually reliable horse bolted sideways.

"Elyssa? Is that you?" Nathan hollered, swinging to the ground.

She made no pretense whatsoever about being overjoyed to see him, but dashed straight into his arms, curling her arms around his waist, and practically squeezing him in two.

"Where the hell have you been?" Nathan murmured as he gathered her to his chest, reveling at the uninhibited reception. "You smell like mildew."

God! He hadn't realized how empty his arms had been until he held her again. The last few days without her had seemed like years. No way could twenty-five thousand dollars even come close to compensating for the pleasure that streamed through him while he cuddled her protectively against him. He wondered if Jessica, with all her wealth, could really afford his price.

Elyssa saw the headlights topping the distant hill and cursed in frustration. She bolted out of Hunter's arms to switch off the spotlight.

Nathan frowned at her curious behavior. "Damn it, woman, what is the matter with you?"

"Les Fykes is planning to kill me very shortly and—"

"What?" Nathan croaked.

"I'll explain on the way," Elyssa said hurriedly. "We have to get back to the old homestead before he gets there. He thinks I'm still locked in the root cellar where he stashed me and he's—"

"Les?" Nathan repeated, dumbfounded.

"Yes, Les. Now hurry up, Hunter. He killed Dad and Gavin, and I don't want him to get away!"

Nathan swung into the saddle and pulled Elyssa up behind him. He then reined his mount toward the old homestead. "Hand me the walkie-talkie in the saddlebag," he requested. "I'll have Twig notify the sheriff. If Les gives us the slip, we'll make sure this place is surrounded."

"Les took my keys so he could drive Dad's truck to the river," Elyssa informed him, handing over the walkie-talkie. "I'm supposed to be in such a rush to outrun the murder rap that I drive off the bridge."

"That son of a bitch!" Nathan scowled and turned his attention to the walkie-talkie. "Twig, call Bently. Tell him to get down to the river section PDQ and bring a backup. Les Fykes was holding Elyssa captive and planning to dispose of her."

"Les?" Twig trumpeted. "He told us he hadn't seen Elyssa all afternoon."

"He's obviously a liar as well as a murderer," Nathan growled. "Just get hold of Bently and tell him to haul ass. You round up Skeeter and Mo-Joe and get down here. I don't want that bastard to escape. In case the sheriff doesn't show up in time, the rest of us will be on hand to greet Fykes. And don't come empty-handed, either."

"Got it, Nate."

Nathan handed the walkie-talkie to Elyssa and nudged the horse into a trot. "I still can't figure Les's angle. What the hell did he have against Ely and Gavin? I can understand why he decided to let you take the blame, since you made the mistake of going to Gavin's house." He shot a quick glance over his shoulder. "You *were* there, weren't you?"

Elyssa looped her arms around his waist and rested her cheek on his back. "Yes," she replied. "He promised me the name of Dad's killer, but it was seduction Gavin had in mind. I dumped my glass of wine on his head when he went too far. Then he got furious and knocked the lamp off the end table in his haste to grab me before I could get through the door. He warned me not to tell you I'd seen him. If I did, he said I might not live long enough to discover who killed Dad."

"Shit," Nathan muttered. "Is there anyone in thirty square miles who doesn't warn you away from me? And you always believe *them* over *me*."

Elyssa smiled against the corded tendons of his back, relishing every second of close contact. "I guess Gavin thought he could threaten me and make it stick, but he must not have wanted to deal with you. Nobody seems to want to deal with you, Hunter. I guess that makes you a force to be reckoned with."

He chuckled at her comments. "So what does that make me? The bad guy?"

Elyssa squeezed him affectionately. "No, you feel pretty damned *good* to me."

Nathan had never received many compliments from this cautious and reserved woman. He guessed her life-threatening ordeal made her so appreciative.

"For a while there, I never thought I was going to see you again. I thought I'd never hammer my way out of that root cellar. Of course, that probably would have come as a relief to you since I have never been what you call—"

"Elyssa?"

His lips twitched in amusement. She was on an emotional roller coaster and as nervous as a caged cat, holding on to him as if he were a security blanket or a life jacket. He wondered if she even realized she had cast off all her inhibitions in dealing with him. Usually, she was only this unreserved while they were in bed. Nathan told himself not to think about that right now. He was about to track down the man who intended to kill Elyssa. He'd better keep his mind on that.

"What is it, Hunter?" she questioned as she snuggled closer to his muscular strength.

"Do you have any idea what sent Les on this killing spree?"

"The grass."

"The what?" Nathan twisted his head around, but he couldn't see Elyssa's face. It was buried in his backbone. She was pressed against him like a cuddly kitten, and it was making him crazy. "Would you please stop doing that?"

"Doing what?" she asked, bemused.

"Rubbing all over me. Damn it, how much willpower do you think I have?"

Elyssa jerked back when she realized she was clamped onto Hunter like a limpet to a ship. "Sorry, I guess I'm a little too glad to be alive. It was such a relief to climb out of that cellar that—"

"You're yammering again," Nathan pointed out, smiling to himself. "Now, about the grass?"

"The grass, right. Les was cultivating marijuana along the river—"

"Marijuana!" Nathan crowed in disbelief. "Good God!"

"I doubt God had anything to do with it. Les and Gavin were growing the stuff and transporting it to dealers."

"I didn't know anyone had been down to that old homestead in years. It's been fenced off. Ely wouldn't let anyone tear it down or disturb it."

"It was my favorite childhood haunt."

"That explains it," Nathan mused aloud.

"Anyway, I was wandering around the house and found gardening tools in the bedroom and dried plants in the barn loft. I was on my way to tell you when Les grabbed me and stuffed me in the cellar."

Elyssa glanced toward the moving headlights. "We'd better step on it. If Les gets there before we do, we might wind up . . ."

Her voice trailed off when Hunter urged his horse forward. Leather creaked and hooves pounded the ground as they trotted across the pasture with Elyssa holding onto Hunter for dear life.

Elyssa led the way into the barn to tether the horse to the center beam.

"Take this," Nathan whispered, folding his pocketknife into her hand. "And keep hold of Ricky's collar. I don't want him bounding out to greet a man he considers a friend."

"What are you going to use for a weapon, if you need one?" she whispered back.

"I'll find something," he assured her.

Nathan hunkered over to grab a two-by-four from the broken stall beside him. With the silence of a jungle cat, he crept toward the door to monitor Les's approach. Just as Elyssa predicted, Fykes thrashed through the underbrush. He made enough racket to raise the dead, so Nathan had no trouble tracking him by sound.

When Les strode past, moonlight reflected off the gun in his hand, and Nathan eased into the shadows of the barn, his body taut, his teeth gritted. Every time he thought of how Les had nonchalantly gone from one murder to the next to protect his stash of illegal drugs, he wanted to kick the hell out of him. Fykes had no conscience whatsoever. There was no telling how long that heartless bastard had been cultivating his crop on this obscure section of the ranch before Ely had stumbled onto the plants . . .

Nathan's thoughts trailed off when Les made a beeline for the root cellar. In one swift move, Les flipped the latch and flung open the door.

Nathan waited until he'd eased onto the first step and called out to Elyssa before he stepped outside. Things were going smoothly until the rotten step broke beneath Les's weight. When he yelped in surprise, Ricky barked his damned head off!

Ricky was one helluva cow dog; he wasn't worth much as a police dog, though.

Les came barreling out of the cellar and sailed around the corner of the barn, as if he were heading toward the river. Cursing, Nathan darted around the barn, keeping to the shadows. The bark of the pistol sent him diving to the ground, cursing into grass. He heard scuffling in the distance, and a sense of panic gripped him. He feared Les had discarded Plan A and had decided to hole up in the barn.

"Elyssa! Get out of there!" Nathan yelled as he rolled to his feet and charged back in the direction from which he had come.

A foul curse flew from his lips when headlights blared in the darkness and a siren shrilled. Good Lord, Bently and his backup were coming on like gangbusters—five minutes too late! The police were making such a production of their arrival, they were sure to send Fykes into panic!

A wild shriek erupted from the barn and Ricky barked. Nathan swore colorfully, certain now that Les had circled around to sneak in through the door of the granary on the south side of the old barn. Elyssa hadn't been able to escape in time.

"Nate!" Les boomed. "You call off the cops or Elyssa bites the bullet! I mean it. I'll take her out with me if I have to!"

Nathan didn't doubt it for a minute. Fykes had already proven he was only interested in protecting himself and his own interests. To him, Elyssa was dispensabl, unless if she could serve as a hostage to lead him to freedom.

"All right," Nathan called back to him. "I'll get Bently out of here, but it's going to take a few minutes."

"Well, hurry his fat ass along," Les growled impatiently.

Grimly, Nathan walked into the blaring spotlight of the two squad cars, shouting Bently's name. The sheriff thrashed through the brush like an elephant.

"What have we got here?" he asked, hiking up breeches that had sunk beneath his belly.

"What we've got is you tripping yourself up," Nathan hissed. *"Your* blaring sirens caused Fykes to panic. He took Elyssa hostage."

"Well, how the hell was I supposed to know what was going on?" Bently muttered in self-defense. "Twig just said to get down here PDQ."

"Bently, you here?" Les bellowed.

"Yeah."

"Good. Tell your men to kill the lights. I'm coming out with a gun to Elyssa's head. Any surprises and she's finished. You got that?"

"Damn you, Bently," Nathan snarled. "Don't expect my vote in the next election." He wheeled around and stalked off. "See if you can talk Les out of it."

Bently frowned at Nathan's departing back. "What are you going to do?"

Nathan didn't answer. He simply removed his boots, then flitted off like a shadow.

Meanwhile, inside the barn, Elyssa was wondering if she was going into cardiac arrest. Les had pounced on her from behind before she could react, the pocketknife Nathan had given her had gone flying, and she'd been sent sprawling in the dirt. After that, she had been afraid to blink for fear she'd miss seeing her life pass before her eyes for the final time.

Ricky was no help. He was wagging his tail at the man who planned to dispose of Elyssa.

"Les? Why don't you come on out before somebody gets hurt," Bently insisted. "We have the place surrounded. If you cooperate with us, things will go a lot easier for you."

Les shifted restlessly behind Elyssa, and his arms tightened around her ribs as if he were cracking pecans. She could barely breathe.

"If you don't ease your grasp," she panted, "I'm going to throw up all over you or faint."

"Just shut up," he snapped. "I'm trying to think."

But Elyssa couldn't. She was too nervous. When she was apprehensive she had a tendency to rattle nonstop.

"If I were you, I'd go out of here on horseback," she suggested. "They can't follow you over this rough terrain in squad cars."

"Les?" Bently called. "Come on out here and let's talk this over."

Fykes swore under his breath and bustled Elyssa toward the horse that was tethered in the middle of the barn.

"I'm coming out with Elyssa!" he yelled. "Back off, Bently."

"Come on, Les. Just stay calm and use your head."

Elyssa heard a swish behind her, but she had no time to react. Les slammed into her, causing her to buckle beneath his weight. Her breath came out in a whoosh when an elbow rammed into her, and then oppressive weight pinned her down, her face smashed into the dirt. She knew without glancing around who had come swooping out of the loft.

The weight that held her down suddenly rolled away, and a soft thud near her head indicated Les had lost his grasp on the gun. Elyssa snaked out her hand to retrieve the weapon, then scrambled onto hands and knees, searching for the spotlight she had set beside one of the stalls.

Ricky was barking to beat the band while the wild-eyed horse bolted back, alarmed by the curses, growls, and thrashing in the darkness. Elyssa located the spotlight and flicked it on to see Hunter in his stocking feet, beating the tar out of Les. It was clear Hunter had been in his share of bar fights during his rodeo days, for Les had his hands full just trying to deflect the punishing blows that hammered relentlessly at him.

Elyssa glanced up at the moonlight that filtered through the loft door she had neglected to close earlier in the afternoon in her haste to report the stash of marijuana. She was eternally thankful she hadn't shut that door; otherwise, Hunter couldn't have sneaked in to launch himself at Les's blind side.

The minute the spotlight flicked on, Bently's voice boomed. "What's going on in there?"

"Get in here, sheriff!" Elyssa bugled.

With one hand clasped around the pistol and the other on the spotlight, she monitored the lopsided battle. She was reminded of her first impression of Nathan Hunter. Hard as nails. A mass of potential energy waiting to explode. He was that and more, Elyssa thought with a great sense of pride and admiration. Hunter was the man she loved. But despite the tenderness and gentleness he could display when he touched her, he was hell on Les Fykes. The man didn't stand a chance when he'd aroused Hunter's wrath.

When Bently came waddling in with pistol drawn, he had to order Hunter off. Even then it took two brusque commands to get through. Elyssa had the feeling Hunter was letting out all his frustration on Fykes. At any rate Fykes had been beaten down before Bently rattled off his rights.

"I'll leave it to you to contact OSBN," Nathan said. "Fykes has been growing marijuana. Elyssa discovered it this afternoon."

As bodies came pouring through the door to shepherd Les off, Elyssa found herself gathered up in Twig's brawny arms and hugged zealously.

"Are you okay?" he questioned. "Val has been going nuts worrying about you."

"I'm fine," Elyssa assured him shakily.

"Elyssa, you ride back with Twig," Nathan ordered. "I'll bring the horse through the pasture."

"But—"

"Just go," Nathan commanded in a no-nonsense tone. "Your mother and stepfather were here earlier. You'd better call them. They're probably very upset, wondering if you're okay."

"But—"

"And Bently will probably want a statement. The sooner all this is behind you, the better."

Despite Elyssa's protests, Twig propelled her out of the barn.

Nathan slumped back against the stall and massaged his aching knuckles. His entire body was trembling like an idling motor, now that the worst was over. He needed time to get himself together. He had taken an awful chance by climbing up the makeshift ladder into the loft and pouncing on Les. But then, he hadn't figured Elyssa had any chance at all if Les tried to take her with him. He'd had to strike hard and fast to catch Les unaware. And now that Elyssa was safe, he allowed himself the luxury of falling apart. Lord, Ely would never have forgiven him if Elyssa had met with disaster. He wouldn't have forgiven himself!

Nathan scooped up the spotlight and walked over to untie his horse. The light beamed on the cedar post. A wry smile replaced the strained lines that bracketed his mouth as he stared at the phrase that had been carved in wood.

He swung the light to the dirt floor to retrieve his pocket-knife and breathed an enormous sigh of relief that this day was almost over.

Twenty-nine

"Ellie! Thank God!" Valerie gave Elyssa a fierce hug and then stepped back, frowning curiously. "Where have you been? You smell like mildew."

Elyssa decided she needed a shower, and quickly. She obviously stunk to high heaven. Everybody said so.

"Les stuffed her in an old root cellar," Twig said. "And we damned near lost her in a shoot-out."

Before Elyssa could excuse herself to take a shower, Althea and Claudia appeared in the hall, bearing food and drink.

"You'd better eat," Althea advised. "I know you barely bothered with lunch. Bently is coming by to take a statement, and you might as well deal with him on a full stomach."

Elyssa wondered if she would ever be allowed to bathe. She found herself herded into the living room, shoved down onto the sofa, and handed a heaping plate.

"Now eat," Althea commanded. "And tell us what happened. We've been worried about you."

Between bites of Althea's delicious beef Stroganoff, Elyssa related the incidents leading up to her captivity, her escape, and her confrontation with Les. She had just finished this account of her bad day when Bently lumbered into the room, hiking up his droopy trousers as he came. The sheriff took one look at Timmy and his rubber hammer and headed away from him.

"I would like to speak to Elyssa in private," Bently requested. When the congregation of concerned friends trooped out, the sheriff parked himself in a chair across from her. "First off, I want to know what you were doing at Spencer's home the night he was killed."

Elyssa took a swallow of coffee to lubricate her vocal chords, and then she presented the sheriff with a brief explanation of why and when she had gone to see Gavin. When Bently seemed satisfied with her story, Elyssa was greatly relieved that she didn't have to reveal her teenage encounter with Spencer.

"To tell the truth," Bently said as he settled his bulky body more comfortably into the chair, "I'm not surprised by this incident. We've heard reports from DEA agents that we have drug trafficking in the county. We just hadn't been able to pick up any leads. Which is no wonder since Spencer was part of the problem.

"There's a bigger problem with marijuana cultivation in the southeastern part of the state, however. Some of the old 'moonshine' families are now growing marijuana. I had my office run an MO on Les Fykes. Turns out his name is Fitzgerald and he got his start in southeastern Oklahoma where marijuana has been intercropped between rows of corn, soybeans, and wheat."

"So you think Les had experience in cultivating fields in remote locations," Elyssa said consideringly. "I must admit I didn't even realize what I was seeing until I found the dried plants in the barn loft. The plants beside the river were well concealed among the brush."

"You're lucky you didn't inspect that field real close," Bently told her. "Les had it booby-trapped."

When Elyssa frowned curiously, Bently nodded his balding head in grim confirmation. "It's not uncommon for growers to be a little paranoid about someone disturbing their valuable crop. We found fish hooks hanging at eye level around the plants. Les even drilled a hole in the fence post and rigged a shotgun to a trip wire. One of my men almost set the damned thing off while snooping around."

Elyssa cringed at the thought of running headlong into the booby traps.

"Unsuspecting landowners are usually the ones who suffer when they stumble onto the plants. The OSBN is sure there are at least a half-dozen unsolved murders associated with this kind of drug activity in the state. We destroyed over a million 'ditch weed' plants last year and it's a full-time job searching areas for possible crops."

Elyssa sank back on the couch, wondering how many other men had wound up like her father, with no explanation for what really happened to them.

"Well, I won't take up any more of your time." Bently hauled himself out of the chair. "I'm sorry you had to get involved in this grisly business, but you did manage to solve two murders. We're grateful for your help."

"I'm glad I didn't become the third victim," Elyssa murmured in relief.

"You were damned lucky, young lady. I could have shot Nate for that daring rescue attempt in the barn, but at least it turned out all right. Too bad Les decided to make his move before we could arrive on the scene and set a trap for him."

As Bently waddled out, hiking his breeches as he went, Claudia appeared at the door, wringing her hands and chewing on her bottom lip. "Elyssa?" she said hesitantly. "I just want you to know how dreadfully sorry I am about all the trouble you've had. I'm ashamed that I let Virgil talk me into causing problems between you and Nate. You're lucky to have someone like him on your side." She smiled wistfully. "I hope someday I find someone who looks after me with as much concern."

"Thank you, Claudia," Elyssa murmured before the younger woman disappeared into the hall.

Plucking up the phone, she then called her family in the City to assure them she was all right.

"Elyssa, I want you to come home first thing tomorrow," Jessica demanded. "Every time you go to that cursed ranch out in the middle of nowhere something disastrous happens.

You've been lucky to get out alive twice! Ranch life just isn't for you. My God, if you stay out there, it'll be like living with the Clampetts! You'll lose your social connections!"

Elyssa smiled to herself. The only "social connection" she wanted was at the Rawlins Ranch.

"And Daniel needs you at the office," Jessica persisted. "You're an asset to the company. Isn't she, Daniel?"

"Very much so," Daniel said over the extension phone. "We really would like to have you back, honey. And I'd like you to give me a call tomorrow. I need to discuss a business matter with you."

Elyssa glanced up to see Hunter standing in the shadows of the doorway. His arms were crossed over his muscular chest. His raven hair was ruffled from riding in the wind, and the faintest hint of a smile pursed his lips. He looked like a throwback to the Wild West—rugged, half-civilized, utterly powerful. *Salt of the earth. A real man.*

That familiar tingle pooled at the base of Elyssa's neck as her gaze met twinkling sapphire eyes. "It's been a long day," she said to her parents. "If you don't mind, I think I'll go to bed. We'll discuss my future plans at another time."

"Now, Elyssa, you listen to me!" Jessica protested. "I met that Hunter character when I was out there this evening, and my first impression wasn't a good one. Plainly speaking, he isn't of your caliber."

A lot Jessica knew. She hadn't seen Hunter in action this evening. And besides that, Elyssa was damned sick and tired of everyone warning her away from Hunter for their own purposes.

"Now, Jessica," Daniel said gently. "I thought Hunter seemed like a competent, reliable individual."

"Daniel! How can you dispute me!"

"Good night," Elyssa interrupted, her gaze and thoughts focused on the brawny presence that filled the doorway to overflowing. "I'll be in touch later."

Jessica was still talking when Elyssa hung up the phone,

but Elyssa was long past listening. She watched Hunter push away from the doorjamb and saunter toward her. When he reached into his pocket to retrieve the folded check, she frowned inquiringly.

"Your mother paid me exceptionally well to break off our affair and let you down easy," he said, as he held the check up in front of her, watching her blink in astonishment. "I don't believe in going behind people's backs and making deals. And since you were the one who called it quits, I figured you ought to have this check."

Elyssa was still staring, nonplussed, when Hunter turned and walked off. She couldn't believe her mother had had the gall to . . . No, it did seem like something Jessica would do to get her way. Hadn't she manipulated Ely so as to remove him from her life and Elyssa's? Hadn't she seen to it that Elyssa was so busy flying around the country her daughter barely had time for anything except keeping up with the corporate world, as Jessica had wanted? And hadn't Jessica also ensured that Daniel had adopted Elyssa so that all the Cutler money would remain in the immediate family?

Elyssa almost felt sorry for her mother. Jessica was so obsessed with wealth and position and structuring the world to suit her tastes that she cared about nothing else. She was a woman driven by the desire to improve her connections with the affluent. She couldn't function without being on the boards of clubs and charities. Elyssa had been unknowingly influenced by her mother for so long that she had almost fallen into the trap of marrying a man because it seemed practical and expected. What a mistake that would have been!

If she had learned nothing else from her trials, she had realized that life was too short and unpredictable for one to go along like a robot, doing what others thought should be done. She was going to reach out and grab hold of what she wanted, or at least she was going to give it her best shot. And what she wanted more than anything was that salt-of-the-earth cowboy with the sparkling blue eyes and rakish grin. When she was with Hunter, she felt whole and alive. She didn't care what anyone else thought. This ranch felt like home. *Hunter* felt like *home!*

Elyssa bolted to her feet and marched toward the hall, a vague ache in her hip and determination etched on her smudged features. When it came to Nathan Hunter, she had been fed nothing but lies. From now on, there would be nothing but truth between them—for better or worse!

At hearing the decisive knock at his bedroom door, Nathan smiled to himself. Bare-chested, he detoured away from the shower and went to respond. Elyssa stood before him with her chin tilted to a determined angle, looking like a rumpled, wind-blown urchin, but still gorgeous in Nathan's opinion. Of course, a man like Robert Grayson might find faded jeans, boots, and tousled auburn hair distasteful, but to Nathan, Elyssa looked wild, vital, and wholesome. He liked her like that.

Elyssa peered up into a ruggedly handsome face and glittering blue eyes, and her heart beat on her ribs. She wanted to reach out and trail her fingertips over the broad expanse of his chest, trace the muscles of his belly. As Valerie would say, Hunter was a veritable hunk. Salt of the earth. The spice of life.

"Did you want something, Elyssa?" he questioned, immensely pleased with the rapt attention he was receiving from her.

"I'd like to talk to you, if you don't mind."

"It's two o'clock in the morning," he pointed out.

"This can't wait." Elyssa marshaled her courage and invited herself into his room.

"Then by all means, do come in," Nathan said, grinning as she breezed past him.

She pivoted, drew herself up in front of him, and inhaled a fortifying breath. "First of all, I want to apologize for doubting your sincerity about my father and your desire to do what was best for this ranch. I am sorry to say I've resented you in the past because you spent years with my father, while I was deprived of him. I made no attempt to be anything except distantly polite when you came to the City with Dad. I envied you. You were the son Dad always wanted, and I was the daughter who had been shuffled out of his life for so long I wasn't sure Dad really wanted or needed me. At any rate he sang your praises so long and so loud that I disliked you."

"You envied me?" Nathan parroted in disbelief.

Elyssa nodded positively. "You were leading the life I wanted, hearing all Dad's cowboy philosophies, sharing the good times and bad."

Nathan impulsively reached out to limn the lush curve of her mouth, smiling at the memory of his first impression of Elyssa. "When I first met you, I was prepared not to like you, either," he admitted. "I figured you for a spoiled, selfish, pampered rich girl who was so wrapped up in her sophisticated world she didn't bother to make time for her own father, a man who worshipped the ground she walked on. I thought you cared nothing about the ranch because you never came for visits."

"Believe me, Hunter, I would have preferred to grow up here, but I was given no choice. My mother has mapped out my life according to her specifications. And after you came along, I thought Dad preferred you to me."

Elyssa retrieved the check from her pocket and returned it to Hunter. "I'm not the one who is going to call it quits. You're the one who is being well paid to remove me—firmly but gently—from your life. So you can damn well earn the money my mother is paying you."

He took the check, glancing at Jessica's precise signature, and then he stared pensively at Elyssa. "Your mother is right, you know. It would be for the best. Essentially, all I will ever be is your hired man."

Elyssa scoffed at the absurdity of that remark. "You seem

to forget I studied the accounts from years past, Hunter. And don't think I didn't go over them with a magnifying glass, looking for clues of embezzlement after being warned away from you so often. What I discovered, instead, were rising profits in the cow-calf operation and in the grain yields after you began supplemental feeding programs, improving pastures, testing soil for mineral deficiency, and fertilizing crops. You have become the driving force behind this ranch. Financial statements don't lie."

Nathan was pleased to know his efforts to improve the place hadn't gone unnoticed by Elyssa. Her opinion was the only one that counted. "Thank you. I did what I could."

"And you did it exceedingly well. No wonder Dad heaped accolades on you." Elyssa tapped her index finger on the check he held in his hand. "Now, do you want to get on with this? As you said, it's getting late."

"Get on with what?" he asked with a wry smile.

"The splitting of the sheets, so to speak," she clarified. "This is where you get to tell me to divide our joint property right down the middle and go back to jet-hopping and corporate executives like Robert Grayson. You may also do yourself the favor of getting my mother off your back."

Nathan studied the check with pretended deliberation. "Twenty-five thousand dollars is a helluva lot of money."

"Especially when all you have to do is tell me to get lost," she agreed, her heart sinking.

She had marched upstairs to announce what *she* wanted for a change, even if she was humiliated by the time this little scene ended. This was the time of reckoning. If she didn't force out the words that waited on the tip of her tongue—and quickly—she was going to lose her nerve.

"But there is something you need to know, or at least something you deserve to know after all the hell I, and my family, have put you through."

Elyssa drew in a fortifying breath, braced herself for the worst, and said, "I love you, Hunter."

Nathan's lips quirked as those long, sultry lashes swept up so she could meet his gaze. "I know."

Elyssa wasn't certain what to make of the comment. "You do?" she asked awkwardly.

"Yes," he confirmed.

By now she was getting a little irritated at the ornery rascal. "And what brought you to that conclusion, I'd like to know?"

"Two things. First off, when I came out looking for you tonight, you ran toward me for a change instead of away as you've had a tendency to do. You reacted on pure instinct, whether you realized it or not. And secondly"—he grinned scampishly—"I saw my name carved on the cedar post in the barn, directly beneath ELYSSA LOVES? I gave you the pocketknife to protect yourself. You carved totem poles."

Elyssa blushed beneath his teasing smile. "I couldn't resist," she admitted. "I've waited all my life to answer that burning question." She shifted uneasily from one foot to the other. "Well, now that you know what I came in here to tell you, I have one request."

"What's that?"

Her gaze dropped to the toes of her scuffed boots. "I would like one last night with you before you send me on my way."

Nathan shook his tousled raven head. "I'm sorry. That's one favor I can't grant you, though I would have given you anything else you asked of me."

Her heart gave a painful lurch. She was certain she had doubted Hunter so often he had lost all respect and affection for her. "Why? I'm not asking for a commitment from you."

Nathan's hands framed her beguiling face, lifting her downcast gaze to his roguish smile. "Lady, I don't want one last night with you. I want the rest of my life, even if I have to listen to taunting remarks about being your hired man. After coming so close to losing you tonight, I knew I was never going to be able to walk away, no matter what compromises I have to make. As long as I have you . . ."

Joyous laughter bubbled from Elyssa's lips as she flung her

arms around Hunter's neck and lifted glistening ebony eyes. "Do you mean it, Hunter? Truly?"

"I've never wanted anything more in my whole life." His voice was like a husky caress. He lifted her to him, letting her feel his raging need. "I never felt I belonged anywhere, to anybody, until I came here, until I found you. You belong to me, Elyssa, and you have since that first night. I don't want you because of your money and your connections. I want you because everything about you pleases me. And I want to belong to you, to please you for all time . . ."

His lips came down on hers in the softest, tenderest kiss imaginable, but when Elyssa was prepared to surrender all, Nathan retreated, leading her toward the shower.

"Spoil sport," she chided teasingly.

"No, *soiled* sport," he corrected. "You smell like a root cellar, and I smell like a lathered horse. Besides, I've been having the wildest fantasies lately about showers."

"Does that mean we're progressing to Chapter Three of *Hunter's Love Manual?*" she asked, with great enthusiasm.

Nathan glanced over his shoulder and grinned broadly. "Tonight, we're going to finish researching the whole damned book."

"Too bad it has to be such a short night . . ." Her voice trailed off when Nathan swung around to unfasten her flannel shirt, taking his own sweet time undressing her. "Hunter?"

"What, honey?" he said, all eyes and devilish smile.

"Isn't there something you want to tell me?"

"Yes, you have a gorgeous body."

"No, I don't," she contradicted.

"You do and don't get hung up on that scar thing ever again. I don't even want to hear it."

Elyssa had hoped for a confession of love, but when Hunter drew her beneath the pulsating shower massage and set his hands upon her, she forgot everything except the exquisite pleasure of touching him and being touched with such remarkable gentleness. He smoothed every last wrinkle from her soul with each gliding caress, each cherishing kiss.

Nathan reveled in Elyssa's helpless responses. He could almost taste her reaction on her skin, could hear the soft moan he wrung from her. His blood hammered through his veins with such intensity he could barely draw breath. With a groan, he bent his head to taste the roseate bud of her breast, and his hands slid over her curvaceous body, memorizing every inch of her slick skin. When his hand glided between her thighs to tease her and tantalize her, a shuddering heat was her response. His fingertips moved with deliberate gentleness, dragging a ragged cry from her lips.

The rippling sensations that assailed her sent Nathan over the edge. He moved toward her, aching to feel her shimmering around him, to hold on to her until a wild, ardent ecstasy consumed him and he knew only his obsessive need for Elyssa.

When that now-familiar tingle sizzled down her spine, Elyssa knew without question that she was where she would always belong. She gave herself up to him in wild abandon, returning each intimate kiss and caress, wrapping her love around him just as surely as she had given him her heart and soul. She could only hope that one day he would come to love her as deeply as she loved him, that he would whisper back the words that now flowed so easily from her lips.

She reminded herself that it might take time for Hunter's love to blossom and grow. He had never known much love in his life. His mother had abandoned him, and his father had ignored him. Worse, his wife had betrayed him. Elyssa vowed to offer him the unswerving devotion he deserved, the unwavering trust he had earned, and the love he had won from her.

When he came to her, his sinewy body communicating his intense needs, she burned with the need for him. Never had any emotion struck her with the impact she experienced when she and Hunter were one, an essence that transcended all physical bounds. No one had ever mattered to her the way Hunter did. He was becoming her everything, her reason for being.

A long while later, when they were nestled in each other's arms in bed, Elyssa's cheek nuzzled against the thrumming pulse of his neck, Nathan pressed a kiss to her forehead.

"Still awake?" he whispered.

"Mmmm . . ." she responded drowsily.

He felt her slump against him in sheer exhaustion. "Never mind, honey. We'll talk about it some other time . . ."

Thirty

The following week flew by in a flurry of activity. Nathan and the hired hands—one short—had been occupied with rounding up cattle and separating weaning-age calves from their mothers. The calves had been inoculated and branded before Ricky herded them to distant pastures. If there was one thing Ely had taught Nathan it was that if cows weren't placed well out of hearing range of their bawling calves, the herds would stampede through fences to reclaim their young.

The DEA agents had come and gone from the old homestead, clearing out the "ditch weed" that had been cultivated beside the river and confiscating the dried plants in the loft.

Nathan had heard that Virgil Rawlins had held an auction to sell off as many horses as necessary to pay the overdue interest on his loan. He doubted Virgil would ever forgive him, but the way Nathan saw it, the man had had a lesson to learn and he'd learned it the hard way. As for Gil Rawlins, he wasn't speaking to them. He and his son-in-law Dennis Humphrey were reorganizing the eastern half of the ranch. Gil, however, had swallowed his pride and sent Dennis around to ask advice on seeding pastures to improve grasses. Nathan had been more than accommodating, in the hope of burying the hatchet.

Nathan had tended to business during the day. Unfortunately, he was spending his nights alone.

Daniel Cutler had persuaded Elyssa to fly to Washington, D.C., to complete the follow-up on a government project that had been put on hold for a month. She had insisted the trip would be her last official duty for Cutler Corporation, other than her obligations as a member of the board of directors of the firm.

Nathan had been missing Elyssa like crazy, and had been anxious because he knew Jessica would exert her influence to make trouble. He hoped Elyssa's affection for him was strong enough to overcome her mother's pressure.

While Nathan walked on pins and needles, waiting for Elyssa to return, Ray Twigger was floating around with his head in the clouds. He had asked Valerie to marry him, and she had readily agreed. The pair were making arrangements to buy the entire rodeo-stock company and had put a down payment on eighty acres of pasture and a partially modernized farmhouse in the northern part of the county.

Daniel Cutler had been shocked when Valerie had handed in her resignation. In an effort to keep his whiz of a computer expert on staff, he had offered to set up a computer link to his office in Valerie's new home, requesting only that she make the drive to the City once a week to consult with him. Valerie had agreed to the proposition, since Daniel had also generously allowed her to use his high-tech equipment to computerize the new rodeo-stock business.

It seemed, after a month of unbelievable turmoil, life was beginning to settle into place. Nathan was the only one who had grown restless and irritable, for he feared Jessica had found a way to take Elyssa away from him, he would go out of his mind. Elyssa had been due back hours ago, and he hadn't heard a word from her in four days. Althea had volunteered to call the office every hour on the hour, but Nathan had vetoed the idea.

The plans he had made for his first afternoon with Elyssa in almost a week looked as if they were about to fall through. He had worked like a madman to catch up on all the duties he'd neglected during the past weeks. And here he was, pacing the living room, glancing at his watch every five minutes, wondering if Elyssa was going to return at all.

When he heard a car pull into the driveway, he strode out-side, breathing a long-awaited sigh of relief. He didn't even allow Elyssa to get both feet beneath her and stand up, but scooped her up in his arms and carried her into the house.

Delightful laughter bubbled from her lips the moment Nathan lifted his head from their steamy kiss.

"Does that mean you missed me?" she questioned, eyes sparkling.

"I wasn't sure you'd be back." Nathan set her on her feet in the hall and practically dragged her upstairs. "I was afraid your mother was having you shipped out of the country to avoid me."

Elyssa didn't bother to deny there had been conflict with Jessica. She and her mother had had a long discussion about Elyssa's future before she'd flown to Washington. When Elyssa had returned the twenty-five-thousand-dollar check and had declared her independence and her intentions, Jessica had pro-claimed that involvement with a worthless cowboy like Nathan Hunter would never work to Elyssa's advantage. Elyssa planned to prove her wrong . . .

"What are you doing?" Elyssa squawked when Nathan yanked off her linen jacket and slung it aside.

"Getting you dressed for the picnic we're having," he said, as he made fast work of the buttons on her silk blouse.

"A picnic?" Elyssa monitored his nimble fingers, her breath catching when his knuckles brushed over sensitive nipples in his haste to rid her of the business suit.

"Your welcome-home picnic." He handed her a flannel shirt and jeans. "I have something to show you. While you finish dressing, I'll get the basket and saddle the horses."

"What is it you . . . ?"

He was gone in the blink of an eye. Elyssa sighed at Hunter's peculiar mood. She had never seen him quite so im-patient and restless. He must have had a hard week. Well, he wasn't the only one. She had been rubbing shoulders with the muckamucks in D.C., and that always made her crazy. Thank

God she didn't have to go back again! She had kissed gridlock and bureaucracy good-bye!

Elyssa wriggled into her jeans and grabbed her boots, anxious to spend the day with Hunter. She deserved it after her tour of duty in Loony-Tune Land.

When Elyssa sailed through the kitchen, Althea sighed in relief. "Lord, am I glad you're back! Nate has been pure hell to live with this week."

Elyssa paused at the door, frowning inquiringly at Althea. "Have there been problems on the ranch?"

Althea smiled wryly. "Nope. But for a man I've always considered to be extraordinarily self-reliant, Nate hasn't functioned well while you've been gone. You aren't going to make a habit of this, are you?"

"Actually, I was just wrapping up loose ends on a project for my stepfather." She studied Althea. "Was Hunter really annoyed that I was gone?"

"When he wasn't wandering around like he was lost, he was a basket case. Just ask Mo-Joe and Skeeter. Nobody wanted to get within snapping distance of him without drawing extra pay for combat duty."

Elyssa smiled in satisfaction. Perhaps Hunter hadn't yet come to love her, but at least he had missed having her around, perhaps almost as much as she had missed him—she hoped.

Feeling encouraged by the information Althea had imparted, Elyssa ambled toward the barn. As satisfied as she was with her new life, there was one thing that would make Rawlins Ranch a paradise—winning Hunter's love. She promised to dedicate herself to *that* project, from now on.

"Nate?"

He flicked a quick glance over his shoulder while he set the saddle on the gelding's back. "Yeah, Mo-Joe, what is it?"

Mo-Joe propped himself against the top plank of a stall in

the barn and smiled gratefully. "I . . . um . . . wanted to thank you for what you did."

"No problem." Nathan waited until the cantankerous gelding released the breath he had been holding and then hurriedly tightened the cinch.

"I mean it, Nate," Mo-Joe said emphatically. "I don't know what you told Melanie when you called her. Hell, I don't even know how you got her number—"

That was simple. Nathan had rummaged through Mo-Joe's belongings after sending the cowboy on an errand. Sneaky but effective.

"—but she called me last night, and we were able to work out a few things. Now maybe I'll at least have a chance with her. I can't thank you enough for speaking to her on my behalf."

"My pleasure." Nathan slid the bridle over the gelding's head and listened to him roll the bit, crunching on it as if he were eating potato chips. "Elyssa's family sabotaged her thinking and turned her against me, so I know what you were going through with your would-be father-in-law. I thought Melanie had a right to know the truth." He tossed Mo-Joe a smile. "I hope I get to meet her one day soon."

"If I ever get her to the altar, I'd liked you to be my best man."

"Done."

"Hunter?"

Elyssa's voice poured over Nathan like warm honey. He drowned in the delightful sound. "I'm in here!"

"Do you know where Mo-Joe is? There's someone out here who wants to see him."

Mo-Joe pivoted and strode off. He stopped dead in his tracks at the barn door, lost to the lovely vision holding his child in her arms.

Elyssa stood aside, watching Mo-Joe stare at the dainty brunette like an acolyte adoring a saint.

"Melanie . . . ?" he breathed in stunned disbelief.

"Morrey?" the brunette said tentatively.

Morrey Joseph, do you suppose? Elyssa thought to herself. Was that the man's real name? For certain it was the man's child in the brunette's arms. The delicate little girl had her daddy's coloring and hair color. No doubt about that.

Elyssa swallowed the sentimental lump in her throat when Mo-Joe's paralysis ended and he rushed forward to engulf mother and daughter in his arms, nuzzling his forehead against Melanie's. Quietly, Elyssa tiptoed around the reunited family and zipped into the barn.

"Who wanted to see Mo-Joe?" Nathan questioned as he bridled Elyssa's black mare.

"Someone named Melanie and the cutest little baby girl you ever did see," Elyssa replied. "I didn't know Mo-Joe was married."

"He isn't."

"Oh." Elyssa glanced toward the barn door, bemused.

"As it turns out, Melanie's father's been feeding her lies to keep her away from Mo-Joe." He glanced meaningfully at Elyssa. "There seems to be a lot of meddling going on in the world. Having battled my share, I decided to play Cupid."

"That was sweet of you."

Nathan chuckled as he handed Elyssa the reins to her mount. "I don't think I've ever been called sweet before. Don't spread it around. No one hereabouts would believe you."

"Why? Because you've been a bear all week?" Elyssa ventured teasingly.

The tension that had been building in Nathan during those endless days alone drained out of him when he met Elyssa's enchanting smile. Everything was going to be okay, he reassured himself as he gazed into those glittering obsidian eyes. She still loved him, needed him. He could see it in her smile. Whatever Jessica had said to warn her off—and Nathan had had no doubt the woman had had plenty to say about him—Elyssa still cared.

"Come on, honey. I've got something to show you."

Elyssa followed Nathan out of the barn, smiling in amusement when she heard Mo-Joe talking baby talk to the little girl he called Jillian. When Mo-Joe realized he had an attentive audience, he made the introduction with so much pride Elyssa swore he would pop the buttons on his shirt.

"I'm very grateful to you, Nate," Melanie murmured, her gaze glued to the sinewy hulk of a man beside her. "I hadn't realized that my father . . ." Her voice trailed off when Mo-Joe scowled at the mention of the man.

"You can ask Elyssa what it's like to be brainwashed until you don't know what to believe and who to trust." Nathan's gaze darted to Mo-Joe and then settled on the attractive brunette beside him. "But, Melanie, I can guarantee you can count on Mo-Joe, come hell, high water, or both."

While Melanie and Mo-Joe devoured each other with hungry eyes, Elyssa tugged on Hunter's sleeve. Clearly, the reunited couple wanted to be alone to resolve their problems. "I thought there was something you wanted to show me," she prompted.

Nathan grinned and headed toward the pasture gate. "Did you think I was so lavish with my matchmaking abilities?"

"Definitely," she affirmed. "But I believe your work is done, Cupid. Mo-Joe can take it from here."

After a thirty-minute ride across the wind-tossed pasture, Elyssa frowned at the mound of dirt and gravel that formed a primitive bridge across a narrow neck of the creek. "Are we building roads these days, Hunter?"

"I decided it was time to make the old homestead accessible by tractor, at least. I put in a culvert for a bridge so the water could still follow its natural course and we could reach the place by some other means besides horseback."

"Why?"

Nathan didn't respond. He simply led the way through the shallows of the creek and up the hill. A few minutes later Elyssa gasped in disbelief when she topped the rise that overlooked the old homestead from a distance. The cabin had been whitewashed, and the antiquated barn boasted a coat of red paint. The tall weeds had been mowed down with the Brush Hog attachment Nathan had hooked behind a small tractor.

"It looks wonderful!" Elyssa complimented with satisfaction. "But what possessed you to—?"

"Because it's your favorite haunt," he cut in. "I want to be able to check on the place since you enjoy spending time there."

"That's really sweet."

"So you keep saying, but I keep telling you that's a word that has never been used to describe me," Nathan declared as he trotted down the hill, the picnic basket resting on his horse.

"Then you have obviously been misjudged," Elyssa said with great conviction.

When he halted and lifted Elyssa from the saddle, she frowned at his impatience, and he half-dragged her into the barn. "Hunter, what is going on? You're behaving very strangely."

"I thought you said I was sweet."

"I changed my mind. You're strange . . ."

Elyssa's voice dried up when she saw the recently cleaned barn, the repaired stalls, and a new ladder leading to the loft. A rope swing was hanging from the rafters. A saw horse with a broom for a head and a frayed lariat for a tail sat in one corner. Another sawhorse, with a set of horns nailed to it, served as a wooden bull. The old granary, now swept clean, boasted a small table and chairs that had belonged to Elyssa in childhood.

"What is all this?" she asked.

"A country playground. The kind I always dreamed of and never had. The kind I want my children to enjoy." He turned toward her, his heart in his eyes, a small velvet case in his hand. "You've got to marry me, Elyssa."

"My gosh, Hunter, are you pregnant?" she asked in pretended shock.

"No, but I would like us to be if we aren't already." He

tossed her a teasing grin. "It's time I started a family, after all."

Elyssa assumed she had the tongue-wagging Valerie to thank for revealing her previous obsession with starting a family while young. Still, as thrilled as Elyssa was with the proposal, she knew that she couldn't accept it. She had yet to earn Hunter's love. She had seen what had happened to her father when Jessica had been unable to love him, and she knew it hurt Daniel Cutler that Jessica could never really care as much for him as he cared for her. If there wasn't mutual love between Elyssa and Hunter, to marry him would only invite heartache.

"Elyssa?" Nathan prodded, frowning apprehensively. "What's wrong?" He expelled a rough sigh. "Damn it, I knew it! Jessica has been working on you, hasn't she?"

"No, she's accepted the fact that I intend to do exactly as I please from now on."

"Well then, what the hell's wrong? Why won't you marry me?"

Elyssa smiled ruefully as she stared into that ruggedly handsome face capped with wavy raven hair. "Because you don't love me the way I love you."

He broke into a smile, and his shoulders sagged in relief. "Oh, is that all?"

Elyssa glared at him good and hard. "Damn it, Hunter. That is *everything!*"

He propelled her forward to see a heart carefully carved in the cedar post, etched within it the words: NATHAN LOVES ELYSSA. Her knees very nearly buckled beneath her, as her gaze locked with his.

"I carved my message in the wood the night I discovered my name etched beneath yours. Now will you marry me?"

"No."

"What in the hell is wrong now?" he asked with a scowl.

"I want to hear you say it," she demanded with that characteristic tilt of her Rawlins chin.

"I've been saying it for two weeks, but you weren't listening."

"Blast it, Hunter! You have not! I would certainly have remembered something as monumental as that!"

He moved closer, his hands framing her elegant face, tilting her petal-soft lips to his. "Then you obviously skipped Chapter Seven of my manual," he whispered as his body glided seductively toward hers. "In body language, this is *I love you* . . ." His lips slanted over hers in the slightest whisper of a kiss. His right hand skittered over her shoulder and settled familiarly on her hip, pressing her intimately against his throbbing manhood. "And this means *I want you* . . ." He engulfed her in his arms until her body was meshed to his, sharing the same rapid heartbeat. "And this means *I need you* with me always or I'll turn into such a snarling bear of a man that nobody wants to come near me."

He bent his head to kiss her with all the pent-up emotion that raged inside him. "I love you, Elyssa. I go crazy when you aren't here with me. Marry me. Don't ever leave me. I can't tolerate the thought."

She tipped her head back, her auburn hair tumbling around her glowing face like a dark, fiery cloud. Her coal-black eyes lit up within their fathomless depths as she laughed with immeasurable pleasure.

Nathan had always adored those big, luminous eyes of hers. If the darkness had eyes, they would be as black and spellbinding as hers were. Yes, those mysterious eyes had first led to his downfall—a fall that had taken him all the way to the bottom of his lonely heart.

"Cowboy," she said with a sultry drawl, "you've just made me an offer I can't refuse."

"And?" Nathan prompted, aching to hear those magical words that aroused mystical feelings deep inside him.

"And you already know how I feel," she insisted, smiling impishly.

He slipped the diamond ring on her finger and brought her

hand up to brush his lips over the sparkling jewel. "Say it again. Say it forever . . . I want you to mean it."

Elyssa stared into sapphire blue eyes fringed with long sooty lashes, knowing Nathan Hunter would be the man she loved for all time. And that feeling tingled at the back of her neck, manifesting itself as warm, compelling flames channeled through her. She knew she could vow to love him forever, and mean it, because the feeling didn't lie. Great-grandmother Mae had said so. And Elyssa knew so. At long last, the dedicated devotion that Mae and Peter had shared had been revitalized, promising new traditions and hopeful beginnings.

"I love you, Hunter. I always will . . ."

In the loft, where Nathan had spread a pallet that overlooked the river, Elyssa proved her everlasting love for him, and he conveyed his deepest emotions in murmured words and gentle passion. The whispering wind echoed out of the past, offering a sweet promise for the future, ensuring that generations of heart- and soul-deep feelings would be passed on.

Love was the special feeling that could endure forever . . .